Retribution

Also by Shana Figueroa

Spice of Love

Vengeance

Retribution

A Valentine Shepherd Novel

SHANA FIGUEROA

New York Boston

This book is a work of fiction. Names, characters, places, and incidents are the product of the author's imagination or are used fictitiously. Any resemblance to actual events, locales, or persons, living or dead, is coincidental.

Cover Illustration by Craig White
Cover design by Scott Silvestro

Forever
Hachette Book Group
1290 Avenue of the Americas, New York, NY 10104
forever-romance.com
twitter.com/foreverromance

First Trade Paperback and Ebook Edition: February 2017

Forever is an imprint of Grand Central Publishing. The Forever name and logo are trademarks of Hachette Book Group, Inc.

The publisher is not responsible for websites (or their content) that are not owned by the publisher.

The Hachette Speakers Bureau provides a wide range of authors for speaking events. To find out more, go to www.hachettespeakersbureau.com or call (866) 376-6591.

Library of Congress Cataloging-in-Publication Data has been applied for.

ISBNs: 978-1-4555-6750-8 (paperback, print on demand), 978-1-4555-4011-2 (ebook)

To Chris, my husband and love of my life,
who will only know this book is dedicated to
him if somebody else tells him,
because he will almost certainly never read
it.

Chapter One

Valentine Shepherd ran so fast she thought her heart might explode from the strain. Her suburban neighborhood was quiet in the late morning as she rounded a corner and sprinted down the street. With the mid-July sun hard on her back, she crossed the invisible finish line in front of her house and slowed to a halt, put her hands on her knees, and threw up into the bright green grass. She wiped her mouth with the back of her hand and took deep breaths until the nausea subsided. No workout felt good enough without a dollop of pain—sore knees, joint pain, pulled muscles, nausea. Going easy on herself meant letting weakness fester, giving her enemies the upper hand. She'd be damned if she let that happen again.

Val walked half a block away from her house to cool down. She stopped mid-stride and stared at a car she didn't recognize, parked on the corner in front of a fire hydrant.

"BFG three thousand fifteen. BFG three thousand fifteen," she said to herself, committing the car's license plate number to memory so she could track down who it belonged to, who Delilah Barrister had sent to watch her. She hadn't had any contact with Delilah since the now-mayor of Seattle sent a batch of e-mails mocking Val for falling for her scam to kill her husband, but it was only a matter of time. Then again, why would Delilah bother to have someone stake out Val's house? She was a goddamn prophet—like Val, but better. More devious at least. Norman Barrister's widow probably knew what Val was doing every second of every day.

Val shook her head at the mystery car. It was likely nothing, and she was being paranoid again. "Shit," she muttered, turning away from yet another shadow to obsess over.

She stalked back into her house and kicked aside one of Stacey's raincoats splayed on the floor next to the door. She'd need to have another talk with her friend about leaving crap lying around for clients to stumble upon. Very unprofessional for the recently popular Valentine Investigations. Business had been booming since she'd "solved" the mystery of who killed Seattle millionaire Lester Carressa and exonerated his son and heir, Maxwell, of the crime last October. They'd even had to turn some clients away. Val hated saying no; she was often their last resort for justice. But even with Stacey's help and her own ability to glimpse the future, she was only one person against a world where cruelty and injustice were the norm.

Val rubbed her sweaty face on a dishcloth and threw open her fridge, shoving aside bundles of kale Stacey bought, but would never eat, to grab a beer from the back. She touched the cold glass bottle to her hot cheek, rubbed the condensation on her skin, and let it trickle down her neck. Then she twisted off the top and took a long drink. The immediate buzz was comforting. Dwelling on things she couldn't change would drive her mad. She should accept it and move on, like Max had done—

A lump grew in her throat. *Don't even start*, she admonished herself as she chugged the rest of her beer. *Don't think about him. He went on with his life. You can, too.* She looked at herself in the gold-burnished decorative mirror—the one she'd put up in the hallway across from the kitchen a million years ago, when she'd lived there happily with Robby and gave a shit about home furnishings. Her strawberry-colored hair hung in a high ponytail glistening with sweat, flushed face dominated by gray eyes the color of steel. She sneered at the woman behind the glass.

"How's being mayor?" she said to her reflection. "Working your way up to governor, still milking your dead husband's glorious legacy?" She stepped closer to the glass, imagining Delilah's premonition of this moment, the good laugh the mayor would have about it. "You know I'll kill you, right? I never thought I was capable of cold-blooded murder, but you've made me reconsider."

Her heart began to race again as she ground her teeth. She *would* stop Delilah somehow, and make her pay for killing Robby and trying to destroy her and Max's lives. Justice delayed wasn't justice denied, she reminded herself...except when someone had an entire evil organization protecting them. Goddammit, she needed another beer.

After she grabbed a fresh bottle from the fridge, she walked to the spare room she used as an office. Setting her beer atop one of the jumbled stacks of papers on her desk, she pulled aside a curtain that covered half her wall. For the millionth time, she stared at the collage of pictures, newspaper clippings, articles, and handwritten notes she'd pinned up, all connected with little strings. On the bottom: photos of her and Max, along with reports on the Science Center fiasco last year. To the side, two items: a picture of Sten Ander, corrupt Seattle PD Vice Squad detective and, unfortunately, her ex-boyfriend. The other item was a Post-It Note with a big question mark on it, representing Kat, Stacey's shady ex-girlfriend. Both had strings leading up to Delilah, their puppet master. Above Delilah: the "woman in white," who was another question mark, along with a secret group of powerful people she either worked with or for.

Val had pinned pictures of Robby and his sister, Josephine, on the left. They connected to Max—he, Robby, and Jo shared a father, Dean Price, though Jo had no idea. She hadn't heard from Jo since Dean's funeral; maybe Jo blamed her for Dean's suicide. Hell, Val still blamed herself sometimes. The image of Dean eating a bullet on his son's grave still shocked her with a jolt of despair that only copious amounts of alcohol could fix.

One string made a big half circle down the center of the collage, from the group at the top to a single pin below her and Max—their future child. That's what the cabal really wanted, the one thing Val knew for sure about them. Another knot tightened in her throat, and she chugged her beer to loosen it up. If that pin didn't exist, those evil people would never get what they wanted. Of course, it also meant *she* would never get what she wanted, either. But Max seemed to have found happiness, so at least they both didn't have to suffer.

More pictures and notes dotted the periphery, people and events around the world she suspected were connected to the mysterious group at the top—airline crashes, assassinations, coups, etc. Locally, just last week a Seattle union leader who'd been at odds with Delilah over some ordinance she'd wanted to pass died in a hiking accident. How convenient for the mayor. Val had already investigated the incident and come up with nothing incriminating, again. But one day soon, very soon, Delilah would slip up. Val would find some tangible connection between the mayor and this group, or some other evidence of her wrongdoing, and bring her down—

"That's some crazy shit, Shepherd."

Val jumped at the man's voice behind her. She dropped her beer bottle and lunged to her desk, where she kept a gun taped underneath the pencil drawer—one of many she positioned around the house in case of emergency. She ripped the weapon free and pointed it at the voice. Her eyes narrowed when she recognized Sten Ander leaning against the room's door frame, legs crossed and hands in his pockets as if he'd just stopped by to say hi.

"You know, you don't need to make a crazy wall collage on your actual wall these days," he said. "A computer will do the same thing. Get an app for that."

Val stared down the man who'd tried to murder her and Max on three separate occasions. She hadn't seen Sten since he'd shot Max in the stomach at the Science Center. He'd shaved off his giant 1980s beat cop mustache; now he looked like a darker, crazier version of Jeremy Renner. "Come here to finally kill me?"

"Yes, I came to kill you. That's why I'm unarmed—to show off my head-exploding psychic powers." He stared at her and scrunched his face in mock concentration, then relaxed and sighed. "Damn. I was sure that would work."

Fucking Sten. She'd never met a person so full of shit, and she'd met *a lot* of shitbags in her line of work. Val kept her gun trained on him. "What do you want, Sten?"

"I came to deliver a message."

"So spit it out."

"See, here's the thing. It's kind of complicated. I think—"

"Oh, for God's sake." Val lowered her gun and yanked the curtain back into place, covering the collage so clients couldn't stumble upon it and think she was…well, crazy. She shoved past Sten on her way to the kitchen. It was a risky move; he could probably kill her with his bare hands if he wanted to. But hell, she was angry—and intoxicated. She'd like to see him try.

Val threw open the fridge and pulled out another beer. "If you're gonna start with the bullshitting, I'd rather you just kill me." She popped the top off the bottle and took a long swig.

He sauntered into the living room and propped himself up on the sofa's arm. Addressing her over the partition that separated the kitchen from the living room, he said, "*I think*, before I give you the message, we should talk about your drinking problem. You'll never score another rich boyfriend as a paranoid drunk."

Val slammed her bottle down on the countertop. *Fucking*

Sten and his mind games. "You wanna talk?" She stomped around the partition and shoved her gun in Sten's face. "Let's talk."

He looked down the barrel of her Glock and lifted an eyebrow, more surprised than scared. For as long as she'd known him—since serving in the Army together, where they'd had a brief, intense fling—he'd never been particularly concerned about his own safety. It made him an excellent soldier, and predator. Fear for life and limb didn't motivate Sten, unfortunately for her.

"Tell me why you're working for Delilah."

"'Working' is a strong word. 'Indentured' is more accurate."

"Why?"

Sten sighed, and for half a second his laidback-asshole demeanor betrayed a hint of sadness. "Because I owe a debt I can never pay back."

Val gritted her teeth. "What does that mean?" She grabbed the lapel of his cheap suit, yanked him to his feet, and yelled into his face, "*What the fuck does that mean?* Why does everyone have to talk in goddamn riddles?"

"That's the condensed version," he said. "The full story would take all day, maybe all week..." Sten trailed off as his eyes drifted down to her wet cleavage, bulging over the top of her sports bra.

Of course he'd be thinking about sex as she assaulted him. Or maybe he was just pretending. He'd throw up any distraction to avoid telling her the truth about whatever game he and his co-conspirators were playing. Screw his games.

Val slapped him hard across the face. He jerked back a couple of inches at the shock of it, then rebounded toe to toe with her, dangerous anger flashing across his face. Good. Now he could have a taste of what she felt every day.

"Who's the woman in white?" she demanded.

He took a slow, measured breath, as if trying to summon his previous calm. "Who?"

"The woman who wears the white suit. Long black hair, thick British accent. I saw her in a vision. Who is she?"

He pressed his lips together, as if considering every possible way he could answer. Finally, he said, "Cassandra, the Alpha."

"The what?"

"They call her the Alpha because she sees all possible futures, all the time, or something like that. Without the sexing. As far as I know, she's the only one in the world. The rest of you future-fuckers are chumps compared to her."

So the terrible images of death and destruction that Val only had glimpses of, Cassandra saw *every waking moment of her life?* Sounded awful.

"What does she want?" Val asked.

"Hell if I know. I'm pretty sure she's insane. It doesn't matter what she wants anyway. She's more like a consultant. Northwalk gives the marching orders."

"Who?"

"*Northwalk*—the people at the top of your crazy wall. That's what they call themselves. Some kind of ancient surname."

"They're people like me?"

He sighed. "No. Jesus, Shepherd, keep up. As far as I can tell, there are maybe fifty or so of you future-fuckers in the whole goddamn world. Northwalk is just one of the organizations of rich, control freak assholes that pull your strings."

Just one? There were other evil cabals? Oh, hell no. "Why are you telling me all this now?" He'd never been this forthcoming before.

He enunciated each word, the anger she'd sparked with her first slap beginning to simmer again as he seemed to tire of their conversation. "Because it's pertinent to my message."

She scoffed. "Fuck your stupid message. What's Northwalk's endgame?"

"How the hell should I know?"

She slapped him again, as hard as she could. "Make an educated guess!"

Damn, it felt good to hit something. He rebounded closer to her, the anger in his eyes deepening. Where she stood less than a foot away from him, she caught a whiff of his scent. He smelled hot and dirty—like a delicious man. Sten was also easy on the eyes, she had to admit—dark and fit, with a dangerous aura about him. Just the way she liked her men, before she met Robby and discovered the joys of nice guys, while Max had embodied the perfect combination of good and bad. Sten had also been great in bed, she suddenly remembered. Rough. She'd liked it, back then. She hadn't been with anybody in a long time; not since Max. Oh, Jesus, she must really be drunk and desperate if Sten was turning her on.

"Ow," was all he said.

Guess the time for disclosure was over. "Get out."

"I haven't delivered my message yet."

"I said get out!"

She tried to shove him, but all the damn beer made her

clumsy. He easily grabbed her arms and flipped her faceup onto the couch, pinning her down with his body. A moment of panic seized her as she lay helpless beneath him. If he decided to kill her after all, it would take him little effort now—oh God, and she felt the hardness of his erection pressing against her belly. Son of a bitch. For the last eight months, she'd been haunted by this goddamn Northwalk conspiracy, where the only measure of control she could exert over her life was to cut out her own heart by pushing Max away. And here was Sten, physically restraining her and getting off on it. She was so tired of being the one on the bottom. She couldn't take it anymore.

"Here's the message," he said, his face a couple of inches from hers as she struggled underneath him. "Northwalk would like to extend you an invitation to work for them."

"Why the hell would I work for them?"

"In exchange for your cooperation, they'll take care of Delilah for you."

She stopped struggling and stared at him. Were they offering to kill Delilah? When she was with Max, she'd had a vision of Delilah as president of the United States, initiating a nuclear war. Maybe Northwalk knew about this possible future, and didn't want to see it come to pass, either. But Northwalk was evil, and they wanted her child. She'd never help them do anything, no matter what they offered.

"Tell them thanks for the offer, but the answer is no," she said. "I'll never be a slave like you."

What was left of Sten's smarmy demeanor cracked, and the anger she'd stoked finally overtook him. "I am *not* their slave! You don't know anything about me, Shepherd."

"Oh yeah?" she said, relishing every second she got under *his* skin for once. "Poor lonely Private Ander, won't talk about his past but fucks like a beast and takes orders like a champ! Too used to pleasing his masters to even consider having any agency of his own. Just point him at whatever you need killed, no questions asked!"

His grip tightened around her wrists. As his hard body pressed down on hers and his hot scent filled her lungs, he glared at her with rage and frustration that matched her own. Sten didn't want to work for them any more than she did, she realized. He hated them, too. He felt what she felt. A burst of heat shot through her body. She hadn't connected with anyone on a raw emotional level since Max, and it felt...*good*. Holy shit, did it feel good.

"Sometimes," he said through gritted teeth, "you have to let people use you to get what you want."

"Keep telling yourself that. I'm nobody's *bitch* like you are. Nobody's!"

When she thought he was close to breaking her wrists, he let go. "Fine. Take it out on me if you want, see what happens," he growled. "Do it!"

With her hands free, she shoved him to the side, and together they fell to the ground. She scrambled on top of him and punched him in the face. *Finally*, she was in control. She punched him again, the need for release so potent her skin trembled like a live wire. Sten was right; she needed to take it out on someone, use somebody.

A frantic euphoria hijacked her brain. Two more times she hit him, and he didn't fight back. As she lifted her arm to hit him again, he sat up and yanked her sports bra off, stitches ripping as he forced it over her shoulders and head in one quick jerk. With a grunt like an animal, he grabbed her nipple with his mouth and sucked hard. She gasped—*sweet Jesus*, that felt good. A noise between a whimper and a groan escaped her chest as a wave of desperate lust wiped away all rational thought. She needed something, *anything*, to dull the pain—

Val pushed him back to the ground. She reached into his coat breast pocket, took out his wallet, and flipped it open. Of course he had a condom with him—he was on the Vice Squad, after all. She pulled his pants down to his thighs, ripped the package open, and slipped the latex over him while he watched, his chest heaving and black eyes burning. Then she threw off her running shoes, shorts, and panties.

What the hell are you doing, Val? Stop—

She sat back and let him enter her with a thrust so strong it sent shock waves through her entire body. A guttural moan surged from her throat as she rocked on top of him. She licked her lips, closed her eyes, and thought of Max. The smell of his mountain spring shower gel, the bay rum aftershave on his neck, the way he'd felt inside her. God, she missed him. She hadn't known she could long for another person so much until he wasn't there anymore. Even the pain she'd felt after Robby's murder paled to the hole Max's absence left in her soul. Now she was willing to take anyone who came along to fill the void, anyone who made her feel something good, even her enemy.

Sten grabbed her and pulled her deeper onto him, directing her hips with strong, rough hands. She grabbed his dress shirt in her fists and blinked back stars that popped into her vision. A wave of dizziness swept over her, from the run and the beer, and now the sex. Her mouth watered and muscles tensed while growing weaker at the same time. She needed release. *Needed it.*

She struggled to breathe as the heat in her belly grew, until the pain she'd been holding in for eight months finally exploded—

I'm standing on the balcony of Max's house, the balcony where he threw his father to his death. The sky is overcast, the water is black. All the glass is cracked and trash is strewn everywhere. At my feet I see a weathered newspaper with a headline that reads: "President Barrister Declares War." Before I can check the date or read the article, the brightest light I've ever seen bursts in the sky and mushrooms upward. I hear and feel a rumbling that grows louder, shattering the glass around me, until a shock wave hits and I'm engulfed in flames—

Blur.

A light rain falls on a choppy expanse of water I recognize as Elliot Bay. Across the water, the Space Needle pokes through the skyline, glinting where the sun strikes it in breaks between roiling clouds. A group gathers on the rocky beach, just off a two-lane road: police officers, medical personnel, random onlookers behind a cordon. A coroner. Splayed on the rocks at the center of the throng is a body—a woman in a cocktail dress that used to be white, now soiled brown. Her matted blond hair bobs in soft waves of water that lap at her bloated, pale face. Milky eyes that used to be brown bulge from their sockets. Black ligature marks streak across her wrists and ankles. Nearby, a woman wails—

Like cigarette smoke, the vision faded from Val's view, and she was back in her living room.

Underneath her, Sten blinked as if trying to snap out of his own trance. The desperate anger they'd shared faded from his face, replaced by his usual smarmy mask. "Got tomorrow's lottery numbers?" he asked. "If you did, I think it's only fair I get half."

Val sighed and closed her eyes, trying to push away the image of yet another dead person from the future, as well as her recurring vision of Delilah destroying the world. She'd never had a real orgasm before, only these terrible—and mostly useless—glimpses of the future. Max was the one who saw numbers—stock market data and other financial information that had made him his millions. Val saw dead people, either during or shortly after their often horrific and painful-looking demises—none of it financially lucrative. The visions were weak when she was alone, stronger with another person, even stronger with someone she was attracted to, and strongest with another person with the same ability—someone like Max or Delilah. If she concentrated right before orgasm, she could sometimes guide her visions to reveal useful information to help her solve cases, like manipulating a dream. Unfortunately, she wasn't very good at it.

She'd wanted a distraction from her miserable life. Instead, she saw a random dead woman. Goddamn this horrible ability.

Val felt something brush against her face. She flinched and

her eyes popped open. Sten's fingertips caressed her cheek.

"I thought you passed out again," he said, his voice soft with a tenderness she didn't know he was capable of. "I don't think you're cut out for day drinking, Val."

"Shut up." Light-headed, she slowly pushed herself off him and sat in a heap on the couch.

Sten stood, peeled the condom off, and dropped it on Val's coffee table. He picked up her gun off the floor and put it on the table, too, as if replacing a tchotchke he'd knocked over. As he pulled up his pants and tucked in his dress shirt, his eyes lingered on her. Val sat slack on the couch, tired, naked, more than a little drunk, and covered in sweat. Shame flushed her cheeks. What the hell had she been thinking? Sleeping with Sten had been stupid, reckless, and worst of all, pointless. It felt great for a few fleeting moments—to experience control, to feel pleasure—but now she was back down the hole she'd started in; deeper, even. She should have shot him instead.

After a few seconds of staring at her, Sten straightened out his jacket and fished a business card out of his wallet. "If you change your mind about Northwalk's offer, or ever need to talk again, give me a call. Anytime." He set the card down next to the used condom. "Carressa doesn't know what he's missing with that vanilla fiancée of his."

She flinched. Of course he'd bring that up. *Fucking Sten.*

He finally left, giving her a couple of hours alone to prepare for the arrival of a new client—after she took a long, cold shower.

Chapter Two

Val handed a tissue to the sobbing middle-aged woman seated at the dining room table. Nora Monroe dabbed at her eyes and sniffled until Stacey returned from the kitchen with a mug of hot water, a tea bag bleeding into it.

Nora accepted the mug with trembling hands. "Thank you."

Stacey nodded and sat next to Val, in front of a pen and notepad she'd prepped. They waited as Nora sipped her tea. In the pause, Val took a long drink of black coffee from her own mug, trying to ease the hangover headache thumping between her eyes. She ignored the disapproving glance Stacey shot at her. Another lecture about Val's self-destructive behavior was brewing. Fantastic.

The hiccups in Nora's breathing eased, and she was able to talk again. "Margaret's been missing for about two weeks," she said. Stacey took notes and Val listened. "I usually hear from her once every couple of days. She'll tell me about what she's been up to, how work is going, if she's found a boyfriend yet—typical mother-daughter stuff. She's never gone this long without calling me. I know something's wrong."

Nora choked back another sob. Stacey patted the older woman's hand while Val scrutinized Nora's words.

"The police won't do anything since she's twenty years old and there's no evidence she's been kidnapped, or…or that some other bad thing has happened to her." Nora cringed and shook her head. "They say she's technically an adult and can disappear if she wants. But I know my daughter. She wouldn't just walk away from her life."

"When did you last have contact with Margaret?" Val asked.

"Right before the holiday—July second, I think it was. I talked to her over the phone. She said she was going to some fancy bar in downtown Seattle with her friends. Pan-something, I think it was called."

"Did her friends tell you when they last saw her?"

"Yes. They said she wasn't feeling well and left early, alone. That's the last time anyone saw her, as far as I can tell. But I'm not a professional investigator so I don't know for sure."

"Any crazies in her life?" Stacey asked. "Psycho ex-boyfriends—or ex-girlfriends—that sort of thing?"

"No…Actually, there was a boy in her sophomore year of high school who came on pretty strong. He sent her flowers and chocolates, and love letters. Margaret's very pretty, so she gets a lot of attention from the boys. She told him she wasn't interested and he backed off. Margaret never mentioned him again, so I thought he'd moved on. But maybe he didn't?"

"It's worth checking out," Val said. "Do you remember his name?"

"Yes—Connor Reston."

Val saw Stacey jot down the name. "We need a list of all Margaret's friends that you know of, the places she frequents, and a time line of her activities throughout the last month—everything you can remember."

Nora nodded, and a tiny smile flickered across her tear-streaked face—someone was finally taking her daughter's disappearance seriously. Val lived for these moments, when she gave people hope.

"Do you have a picture of her that you can give us?"

"Oh, yes." Nora reached into a tote bag she'd brought with her and pulled out a stack of flyers. "I've been putting these up around her neighborhood." She handed Val a flyer with a black-and-white picture of a smiling young woman, "MISSING" emblazoned underneath. Nora also passed Val a color photo. "That's the original picture, if it helps."

Val forced her face to remain neutral as her breath caught and her stomach fell. Blond-haired, brown-eyed Margaret was the living version of the dead woman washed up on the rocky shore Val had seen in her vision with Sten. Either this poor girl was already dead, or would be soon.

"Can you find her?" Nora looked at Val with wide, pleading eyes, her desperation settling over Val like a thick fog. "Bring my baby back to me?"

Val studied the picture. If Margaret was still alive, she didn't have much time left. Val's visions of dead people rarely prophesized events farther than a few days out. She needed to act fast.

She looked Nora straight in the eyes. "I'll find her. I'll bring her back to you. You have my word."

***

Val stood in front of her closet and held up a long-sleeved black cocktail dress. "Think this one will work?" she asked Stacey.

"Too conservative," Stacey said from where she was splayed on Val's bed. "If you want a bunch of rich assholes to talk to you, you need to ho it up, big time. Wear the skimpiest thing you've got."

A quick Internet search had identified the "Pan-something" bar Nora had mentioned: the Pana Sea, a swanky place on Fifth Avenue frequented by traveling businessmen and Seattle's financial elite. She also searched for any reference to Northwalk; of course, nothing came up. Assuming Sten had told her the truth, she didn't expect a powerful and secretive organization to pop up on Google, but it was worth a shot. She'd start some serious digging after they found Nora's daughter.

With no time to lose, Val planned to poke around the bar and try to retrace Margaret's steps while Stacey tracked down Margaret's friends and the Connor creep. Showing up to the Pana Sea in Val's usual jeans-and-T-shirt combo was unlikely to get the wealthy clientele talking, though. She returned the black dress to the back of her closet.

"I can go if you want," Stacey said, "You can stay here and sleep off your party of one—"

"I'm fine."

"Really? 'Cuz you looked hungover as shit—"

"I ran too hard this morning, all right? *I'm fine.* And anyway, you'd set off everyone's gaydar."

Stacey sighed. "If you say so. At least consider passing on the booze while you're there. Stay sharp."

"Yeah, yeah."

She rooted through her slim collection of fancy dresses—dresses she hadn't worn in years—until she found a red one with spaghetti straps, a heart-shaped neckline, and a skirt hem that ended at her mid-thigh. She'd forgotten she even owned the dress, and couldn't recall why she'd bought it to begin with. She held it out to Stacey.

Stacey nodded. "That'll do."

Val tossed the dress on her bed and began taking off her clothes. "So...I had a vision this morning."

"Really?" Lifting her head, Stacey gave Val a purposefully neutral look. "Alone or with another person?"

Shit. Val didn't want to open old wounds, but there was no way she couldn't mention it to her best friend and business partner—and ex-girlfriend. Damn that last part. She'd manipulated Stacey's latent romantic feelings for her too many times, and now any talk about affairs of the heart was fraught with uncomfortable tension between them. It was Val's fault. If she could make it right, she would, but—true to form—she didn't know how. Cultivating healthy relationships wasn't a skill she excelled at.

"Alone," Val lied.

Stacey relaxed. "Oh. Good for you. A nice solo-fuck is healthy. It's the first step in moving on."

Val looked away and suppressed a cringe. Her friend had never warmed to Max, but she'd go ape-shit if she knew Val had slept with Sten while drunk. Stacey would hog-tie her and ship her off to rehab for sure. She'd never told her friend that Max had the same sometimes-useful/usually-terrible ability Val had; after she and Max had broken up, it didn't feel right to expose his biggest secret, even to her best friend. *Were* they best friends anymore? Hell, Stacey was her *only* friend at this point in her sad life, despite the strain sharing the same roof had put on them. Maybe it'd been a bad idea letting Stacey move in after Robby died. Having another person to split the mortgage with was helpful for sure, but the additional scrutiny into Val's admittedly poor life choices was beginning to chafe.

"I saw Margaret dead on a beach somewhere."

Stacey gasped and sat up. "Oh my God. Do you know when it'll happen?"

"No. It was raining, though. Can you check the weather forecast for the next two weeks and find out which days it's expected to rain?"

"I'm on it."

"She had marks on her wrists and ankles, like from ropes or straps."

Stacey bit her lip. "You know what this means?"

"Yes."

"She's probably been kidnapped."

"I know."

"And they're holding her. Or she's already dead and they haven't dumped her body yet."

"*I know.*" Val pulled the dress over her head and shimmied it into place.

"Do you know which beach she'll turn up on?"

"No," Val said as she walked into the bathroom, "but it was across the bay from Seattle." She penciled on some black eyeliner. "So maybe Bainbridge Island or Harbor Viewpoint, I don't know. I couldn't tell."

"I can research water currents in the bay," Val heard Stacey say from the bedroom. "It's a shot in the dark, but might give us a clue to where she came from, if they dump her in the water and she washes up on the beach. It might not be a bad idea to drop an anonymous tip to the police, too."

Val scoffed as she brushed blush on her cheeks. "Yeah, right. Might as well tell them I saw Margaret get abducted by Big Foot for all the shits they'll give. Even if they took the tip seriously, she'll be dead before they get their act together and launch a real search. If we don't save her, chances are no one will."

She slathered on some lipstick, gave her head a couple of pumps of hairspray, then posed for Stacey in the bathroom doorway. "Well?" She flipped her hair over her shoulder. "If you were a rich asshole, would you confess your possibly criminal activities to me?"

Stacey's eyes ran up and down Val's body. "I can only speak as a *lesbian* asshole," she said with fake bravado, "but I'd tell you anything you wanted to hear, baby."

Val smiled. "Excellent."

Chapter Three

Val sashayed past lacquered oak tables and plush chairs upholstered in aqua-colored velvet, on her way to the sprawling bar that was the heart of the Pana Sea. Despite it being Wednesday evening, traditionally slow for a bar, the place hummed with men and women in expensive business suits and high-end clothing that looked unassuming but probably cost more than Val's monthly mortgage. Light pop music played as she felt hungry eyes follow her to the counter, assessing all her curves. Good. Hopefully one of these horny bastards would make the first move, and she could pump him for information while he stared at her breasts. She eased onto a barstool opposite colorful bottles of liquor in rows vaulted almost to the ceiling. A single muted flat-screen TV showed the local news in progress.

Val flagged down the bartender, a pudgy guy in his early forties or so, with a spiked hairdo too young for his age.

"Sam Adams, please," she told him.

He nodded, poured beer from the tap, and set the glass down on a coaster in front of her.

"Thank you." As he turned away, Val said, "Hey—um, what's your name?"

He smiled. "Eric."

"Hi, Eric. I'm visiting from out of town, and I made plans to meet my cousin here tonight. I don't see her, though, which is strange because she's usually real prompt—like, to an anal degree." Val rolled her eyes and smiled. "I'm afraid I got the day or time wrong, and she's not answering her cell. Her name's Margaret—blond hair, brown eyes. Has she come through here?"

Eric's brow furrowed as he thought about it for a moment. "I don't think so, sorry."

"Let me show you a picture, maybe that'll help." Val pulled her cell phone from her purse and showed Eric the picture of Margaret that Nora had given her. She'd transferred the photo to her phone to make it look as if she'd taken it herself.

Eric eyed the picture. Recognition flashed across his face. "*Margaret*, huh?"

"Well, yeah," Val said, playing the innocent out-of-town-girl angle. She gave him a confused laugh. "What other name would she go by?"

Eric leaned toward her and lowered his voice. "People know her here as *Celine*...get it?"

"Uh, no," Val said, though she was pretty sure what he meant.

Eric rolled his eyes at Val's naiveté. "Celine is the name she uses when she's *working*." He whispered, "She works for *Le*

Belle Donne, an escort service, if you know what I mean."

Val gasped and scanned the modest crowd around her. She spotted a few other beautiful young women dressed to the nines—high-class hookers working the crowd for a wealthy John. Nora would not be happy to learn how Margaret really paid her bills.

"Oh, my," Val said to Eric, her eyes wide.

"I don't know what your cousin told you, but a good girl like you shouldn't get involved in this stuff. Find a nice man to marry." He winked like he might just be that man, and Val resisted the urge to laugh in his sexist face.

A customer at the opposite end of the bar waved for service. Eric nodded at Val, then left to fetch booze for someone else.

So Margaret, aka Celine, was a high-end prostitute. Made sense, unfortunately. Prostitutes were easy targets for rapists and murderers, no matter the price range. It also meant Margaret's friends were probably lying when they said they were with her the night of her disappearance; they were covering for their friend's illegal second career. They'd be no help. The creepy high school admirer was likely a dead end, too. Her next step was to track down whoever actually *was* the last person to see Margaret alive—Celine's last John. Eric might know, though it meant breaking her cover.

Val sipped her drink while she waited for Eric to finish filling a large order of drinks on the opposite side of the bar. She glanced around in the dim mood lighting for a moment, then let her gaze settle on the TV, still showing the local news. Val flinched when Max appeared on the screen, a shovel in one hand while he waved at a small crowd with the other.

Text underneath him read, "Earlier Today: Maxwell Carressa Breaks Ground for New Harborview Medical Center Children's Cancer Ward." Max used the shovel to dig up a big clomp of dirt and toss it to the side while the crowd clapped. An older woman—probably the hospital director—rushed forward to shake his hand.

The closed captioning explained that he'd donated forty million dollars to the hospital for the new addition, to be called the "Lydia Carressa Children's Cancer Ward," named after his mother. A small smile flickered across her lips. Forty million dollars also happened to be the amount of money Max's father had embezzled, to flee in case Max ever told anyone about the years of abuse he'd suffered. No doubt the irony was intentional, though only she and Max knew the whole truth—well, Max, Val, and now his fiancée, she guessed.

Max walked to the side and joined his bride-to-be, Abigail Westford, daughter of a shipping magnate and all-American beauty with curly blond hair and baby blue eyes. She smiled and gazed at him lovingly as he said something about his mother's legacy and how much Lydia cared about children. Then he put his arm around her and they posed for pictures. Abigail's good-girl looks paired with Max's bad-boy charm made them an eye-searingly beautiful couple. His black, wavy hair was shorter than Val remembered, though his chiseled cheekbones and rough lips had the same Hollywood leading-man quality she couldn't stop thinking about. And his eyes—warm hazel with starbursts of brilliant green at their centers that haunted her dreams. Their child would've had those eyes, if they'd stayed together—

"He is really milking his fifteen minutes of fame, eh?" a man beside Val said with a soft French accent.

She turned to see an attractive gentleman perched on the stool next to her, wearing a simple black suit with a gray T-shirt underneath. He looked a little older than her—late thirties or early forties, maybe. His close-cropped blond hair and angular face with a hawk nose made him seem like a long-lost member of the French monarchy. He leaned casually on the bar and sipped from a tumbler of clear liquor and ice.

"No kidding," Val replied. "He's delusional if he thinks that hideous face will launch an acting career."

The Frenchman laughed. "I never thought Max would warm up to the media. He always tried to avoid them. I'm shocked at his sudden public renaissance. Doesn't seem like him."

Val raised an eyebrow. "You know him personally?"

The Frenchman shrugged. "I wouldn't say we're friends, but we've had some business dealings. He and Abby are at pretty much every charity event these days. I almost wonder if she's drugging him." He smiled. "I'm sorry, I'm being rude. My name is Lucien."

"Jane," she said, glad he didn't recognize her. Since they'd parted ways, Max had jumped whole hog into philanthropy work, dominating the spotlight. Val had been content to let word-of-mouth keep up the momentum for her business while laying low herself. She'd faded from the popular consciousness, though not before the modest ego boost of receiving—and declining—an offer to pose for *Playboy*.

"Are you a local, Jane?"

"Yes—I mean, sort of. I'm a grad student at WSU, so not too far away. I was supposed to meet my cousin, Celine, here tonight." Val leaned toward him, flipped her hair over her shoulder, and touched his leg with the tip of her shoe. "Do you know Celine?"

Lucien gave her a sly smile. "I know *of* Celine. Never had the pleasure of spending time with her." He picked a piece of Val's hair off her shoulder. "I prefer redheads."

"That's funny, because I prefer blonds."

He let out a chuckle like smooth water sliding over rough rocks. Damn, this guy oozed charm. Val might've considered hooking up with him for real if he hadn't thought he was picking up a prostitute.

"Looks like Celine has stood you up. Would you consider spending some time with me instead?"

Val sipped her beer—an excuse to avoid answering him for a few seconds while she considered her options. Rich, attractive people had all sorts of secrets they excelled at hiding. Max was a prime example. Lucien could have killed Margaret for all she knew. However, Val had the advantage of knowing Lucien might be dangerous and definitely couldn't be trusted, plus the gun in her purse. If she got him alone, she might be able to tease out of him who Margaret's popular Johns were, maybe which one she was with on the night of her disappearance. It was worth a try. If things went south, she would shoot him. She'd already blown one man's head off not too long ago. She could do it again if she had to.

Val put the glass down and pursed her lips. "Okay. Show me a good time, Lucien."

Lucien held out his arm; she took it. He led her to the front entrance, where a valet grabbed his ticket and ran off to fetch his car.

"Beautiful night, eh?" He slipped his arms around her waist and pulled her flush to him. "Not as beautiful as you, but still pretty nice."

Val threw her head back and laughed. He leaned in and kissed her neck.

"Very smooth," she said. "You probably say that to all—"

Chapter Four

Val woke up in the front seat of her car. She blinked a couple of times, put a hand up to shade her eyes from the bright morning sun pouring in through the windshield.

"What the hell?" she muttered to herself.

She sat up from where she'd been slouched over in the driver's seat. How in the world did she end up in her car? What time was it? What *day* was it? She'd been standing at the curb in front of the Pana Sea with Lucien, then…nothing. Val ran a hand over her dress, felt underneath her skirt; nothing torn, underwear still on. She looked at herself in the rearview mirror and didn't see any makeup smears or bruises. Her purse sat in the passenger seat. She snatched it up and rummaged through it. Everything was still there, even her fully loaded gun. She checked her phone. It was almost nine o'clock in the morning, the day after she'd visited the Pana Sea. Nothing seemed amiss—except for her complete memory loss of the last twelve hours.

Val gripped the steering wheel and tried to stay calm. Had she been drugged? Seemed unlikely someone could have spiked her drink at the bar, since she'd seen Eric pour her drink and it'd been right in front of her the entire time. Maybe the Pana Sea had a rape ring going where they somehow spiked women's drinks before they served them, or laced the bottom of the glass with drugs before the pour? Val closed her eyes and swallowed hard. *Rape ring.*

God, please don't let this be a rape ring.

She opened her eyes and exhaled. She'd never heard of a coordinated rape ring operated by an upper-class business. Nor had she ever heard of a rape drug that completely wiped someone's memory, with no dizziness or disorientation beforehand. Something very, very strange had happened to her.

Cold sweat trickled down her neck. "Just get home," she told herself as she started the engine with a trembling hand. "Figure it out from there."

* * *

Val stripped off her clothes as fast as possible and threw them in a corner. She stood in front of the bathroom mirror and ran her fingers over her entire body, searching for any bruises, cuts, or other marks that might not have been there before. She breathed a modest sigh of relief when she found none. Maybe whatever happened to her wasn't as bad as she feared.

Then she saw it—a flash of red just behind her ear. She froze for a second, then pulled her hair back. Val gasped when she saw a raw scar the size of her thumbnail, shaped like a circle with another red dot in the center.

Val grabbed the sides of the sink with white knuckles. Tears clouded her vision. *I should go to the hospital and get a rape kit done.* Then she shook her head. *No, not yet.* Something strange had happened to her, she'd been "marked" for some reason, but that didn't mean she'd been raped. She didn't know what it meant. *One step at a time, Val.*

After she dressed, she fired up her computer and looked up *Le Belle Donne*, Margaret's escort service. She found Celine's profile among a roster of about two-dozen beautiful women. Val scrolled through the mundane and probably made-up "facts" about Celine's passions and hobbies, then scanned the comments section at the bottom. PG-rated testaments to Celine's particular set of skills made up the bulk of the section. She paused when she spotted one innocuous-seeming comment, posted a day ago: "Loved Celine in her Rayvit video."

Val recognized Rayvit as an anything-goes Internet forum where people gathered to share pictures and videos on a million different subjects. Rayvit's *laissez-faire* attitude made it especially popular with creeps who liked to share revenge porn—sexually explicit photos and home movies of ex-girlfriends or other women who'd spurned them. It was possible that Celine's video referred to something benign, but Val doubted it.

She went to Rayvit and searched for any reference made to "Celine" within the last week. A handful of links popped up, most on the subject of cats named Celine, or Celine Dion.

One linked to a video titled "Finding Celine's Sweet Spot."

"Oh God," Val muttered, and clicked on the link.

A red velvet settee appeared, surrounded by walls of dark mahogany with paintings of forest scenes hung around the periphery. Atop the couch lay Margaret, naked and apparently unconscious.

Shit.

After a well-lit establishing shot—the video had the sickening air of a professional videographer—two naked men in masquerade-style masks walked into the frame.

Val stopped the video. If she watched any more, she might throw up. She'd known chances were high that Margaret's trail would lead somewhere dark and disgusting, but it still made her sick to her stomach to confirm it. What would she tell Nora about her poor daughter? Nothing for now—no good would come of it. But Val's investigation was far from over. The video had been posted two days ago, and Margaret hadn't been tied up. The ligature marks Val saw in her vision must happen later. Margaret could still be alive, held captive somewhere. Finding her was Val's number one priority.

She cued up a program to make a copy of the video before someone pulled it down. Even on Rayvit, videos of sexual assaults were eventually flagged and deleted from the site. When Val brought the people responsible for Margaret's kidnapping and rape to justice, the video would be a critical piece of evidence in court.

As the file downloaded, she called Zach, a local hacker she kept on retainer.

"Hi Val—"

Someone yelled in the background, "*Zachary, I'm not gonna ask you again to mow the lawn!*"

"*In a minute, Mom, God!*" Lowering his voice, he said, "Sorry. What's up?"

She would've laughed at the image of the teenage Goth kid pushing a lawn mower around, his black trench coat flapping behind him in the July breeze, if she weren't in one of the worst moods of her life. "I'm sending you a link to a video on Rayvit. Don't watch it. It's not pretty. I need you to find out who posted it."

"Yeah, sure. Might take a few days if the dude knew what he was doing and covered his tracks well, just so you know. See, you can spoof an IP address by—"

"Just work as fast as you can."

She hung up before he could finish one of the IT lectures he loved giving to anyone who'd listen.

After e-mailing Zach the link, she backtracked to the top of the thread where the "Celine's Sweet Spot" video had been uploaded. She read the title of the latest post, dropped just a couple of hours ago: "Red Delicious." Her breathing stopped.

Oh God no.

Her hand trembled on the mouse. She should wait for Stacey to come home and ask her friend to look at the video. That was the best thing to do, for her mental health. Maybe it wasn't her. Nah, it wasn't her. Val clicked on the video.

This time, a beige wall decorated with framed movie posters provided the backdrop for a white leather sofa. A naked redhead lay on the couch, also unconscious.

It was Val.

A naked man in a mask entered the frame and propped her legs up on his shoulders—

Val closed her browser. She put a hand over her mouth and stared at the floor while the world spun. For a moment she couldn't move, every muscle in her body paralyzed like the woman in the video. Then the despair that threatened to overtake her transformed in an instant to pure, hot rage.

Someone would pay for this. Someone would *die* for this. They had her word.

Chapter Five

The nurse handed Val a small stack of papers and brochures with pictures of sad-looking women on the front.

"We'll let you know the results of the STD and pregnancy tests within forty-eight hours," the nurse told Val in the hospital room. "We'll also store the biological evidence we've gathered from you and your clothes, if you decide you'd like to make a police report."

Val gave her a single, weak nod. A police report—what a joke. She knew from other rape cases she'd worked that the police would be no help. Even if she made a report, the backlog was so large it would be months—maybe even years—before they got around to running the DNA through their criminal database. She'd only come to the hospital for STD tests and emergency contraception.

"In the meantime, there are a lot of places you can go for support—group meetings, one-on-one counselors, anonymous chat rooms, and other resources. It's all in there." The nurse pointed to Val's papers.

Val supposed it'd be rude to throw the papers away right in front of the nurse. "Can I go now?"

The nurse nodded, then touched Val's shoulder. "It gets better, honey."

"Yes, it will," Val said with a dark edge that made the older woman frown.

Val brushed past the well-meaning nurse and stalked through the maze of sterile hospital hallways until she found the exit. Stacey stood from where she'd been waiting in the lobby. They walked in silence to Stacey's car.

From the driver's seat, Stacey asked in a tiny voice, "What now?"

Val took a deep breath. The next thing to do was to watch the video in detail and record every clue she could find about where her and Margaret's attacks had taken place and who the perpetrators might be, then go back to the Pana Sea with the gloves off and start fucking shit up. Val opened her mouth to explain the plan to Stacey, but her voice choked before she could get a word out. A sob ripped from her chest instead. She put her head in her hands and cried as Stacey leaned over and hugged her tight.

Those evil bastards. Fucking Lucien. She would make them pay in the worst way possible.

After what felt like an eternity, Val pushed her despair away and regained control of her emotions. She let go of Stacey and wiped the tears from her eyes. "Will you watch the video and take notes, please? I don't want to do it myself."

Stacey nodded while pushing away her own tears. "I know they don't have a great track record with you, but you should really go to the police—"

"So they can shame me?" Val snapped. "Quiz me on why I was there? What I was wearing? What I was drinking? How slutty I was on a scale from one to ten?"

"We have the video—"

"The video doesn't prove anything! It can be explained away as an amateur sex tape that I consented to and now regret. Especially when they find out I was pretending to be a hooker."

"Val, please—they're not all like Sten. You can't do this alone."

"I've got you."

"We don't have the same resources as the police."

"No, but we're not bound by their rules, either."

"Let me go to the police, then. I'll make an anonymous complaint—"

"Don't bother." Val checked her watch, then pulled her gun from her purse and racked the slide back. "When my sister was raped, she was shamed and humiliated so badly she killed herself to make it stop. All the women who show up at our office come to us because no one else will help or believe them. You know what the police will say to me? That I learned a hard lesson: don't go home with strangers. Well, I have a lesson of my own to give." She snapped the slide back in place. "If you rape a woman, she might come back and kill you."

* * *

Val drummed her fingers on her car's steering wheel as she watched the Pana Sea's back entrance from a street perpendicular to the entrance's alleyway. It'd been quiet until a delivery truck pulled up a few minutes ago. Now a team of two men unloaded boxes of liquor, swizzle sticks, and other supplies from the back and carried them into the building. One of the men was Eric, the bartender from the night before. After a few minutes of ferrying boxes, the other man motioned to Eric, communicating something while pointing to the street at the opposite end of the alley. Eric nodded, and the other man walked around the corner and out of sight, probably to run some errand. The coast was clear for Val to have a few minutes of quality alone-time with the bartender.

She hopped out of her car and hurried across the street at a quick trot, careful to stay out of Eric's line of sight as she approached. Val watched him from the corner until he went inside again, then she ran to the far end of the van and waited for him to wander back out. When his back faced her, she stepped out of cover and tapped him on the shoulder. As he turned toward her, she kicked him hard in the shin. Eric yelped and fell to his knees.

Val unholstered her gun and knelt beside him. "Hi, Eric. Remember me?"

Eric clutched his leg and glared at her. "You bitch—"

Val cracked him in the face with the butt of her Glock. He tumbled onto his side, cheek to the pavement.

"Every time you call me that, I'll pistol-whip you. Consider it sensitivity training."

He rubbed his cheek and cringed. "What the fuck do you want?"

"The guy who approached me at the bar last night—he called himself Lucien. Who is he?"

"I don't know."

She pistol-whipped him again. "That's for lying."

"I don't fucking know!" Eric spit blood onto the ground. "He shows up every other month or so. One of the rich assholes who like throwing money around and bringing whores back to their little clubhouse. That's all I know."

"Clubhouse? You mean he's part of a club?"

"Yeah—I think so. I don't know exactly what it is. I hear them talking about it sometimes when they're too drunk to keep their mouths shut. They call it the Blue Serpent. Only rich fucks and their playthings allowed."

Val touched the mysterious scar behind her ear. The Blue Serpent—goddammit, it *was* a high-end rape ring. What was it about having a lot of money that turned people into depraved scumbags?

"Was Celine with Lucien the last time you saw her?"

"No. She left with some redheaded guy I've only seen a couple of times. They call him Ginger. Real original."

Val tapped her gun against her knee. "What did you put in my drink?"

"Nothing."

She whacked him in the face again. It felt good to make *somebody* pay, even a small fish. Eric writhed on the ground for a few seconds before pushing himself up, leaning heavily on one arm.

"What did you put in my drink, Eric?"

"Nothing! I didn't do anything to your goddamn drink, bitc—" He scowled at the pavement and wiped his mouth.

Val stood and pointed the gun at his head. If he was lying, he'd die. She didn't think she could stop herself.

Staring down the barrel of her gun, and maybe also sensing how willing she was to kill him, Eric's face crumpled and he burst into tears. "I didn't do anything to your drink, I swear! I just work here. I have nothing to do with those rich assholes. *Please.* I have a girlfriend, and she's got a kid and I'm like his father figure..." He sobbed, soiling the pavement with his tears and snot.

If Eric faked his pathetic pleading, he deserved an Oscar. Val rolled her eyes at the blubbering man, then sighed and lowered her gun. "Find another job, Eric. This place is about to go out of business."

She stepped around him and left the way she came.

Chapter Six

Val bit her lip as she sat in her car, parked a safe distance from where she'd roughed up Eric a few minutes earlier. She stared at Max's face and phone number cued up on her cell. They hadn't talked in months, not since they'd broken up—not since *she* broke up with *him*, specifically. She'd tried to explain to Max how Delilah was always watching her, how they'd only been pushed together so they would have a child—a child that would be stolen from them. How they couldn't trust anyone. He swore they could work it out, pleaded with her to fight for their future, but she'd cracked. Throughout their time on the lam together, when Max had been wanted for murder, she'd accused him of running from his problems. But in the end, she was the one who ran. She was the weak one.

Per Eric, the Blue Serpent was a rich-dicks-only club. Max was the only rich dick Val knew personally. If she was going to infiltrate the club, it was either through him or not at all. No way would she try seducing another anonymous wealthy guy again. She swallowed hard, gave herself a figurative kick in the butt, hoped he hadn't changed his number, then dialed him up.

The phone rang several times, then went to voice mail. "*This is Max, leave a message.*"

"Uh, hi. It's…it's me, Val. I know you can probably tell it's me from your caller ID, but, you know, in case you deleted my number or whatever…" *God, I sound like a loser.* "Anyway, um, I need to talk to you—"

Her phone vibrated against her ear. She held it out to see someone trying to call her at the same time she left a message—Max. She switched over to him.

"Hello?" she said like an idiot who didn't understand how technology worked.

"Are you trying to call me? Or did you just butt-dial me?"

The sound of his voice in her ear made her smile. She was glad he couldn't see her grinning like a crazy ex-girlfriend. Val wiped her smile away and tried to stay focused. "Yeah, I tried to call you. I wanted to talk—I mean, I need to talk to you."

"Is something wrong?" he asked. Val heard chattering in the background, fading as he seemed to move away from a crowd.

"Yes. Something's wrong."

"Like what?" he asked, a hint of concern in his voice.

Val smiled again—he still cared, at least a little. Whether he cared about her or protecting his many secrets, she wasn't sure…no, it was her…she wished. She closed her eyes and shook her head. *You dumped him, Val. It's over between you two. Just get on with it.*

"I can't explain over the phone," she said, even though she

could totally explain over the phone if she'd wanted to. "Can we meet somewhere?"

"What, *now?*"

"Yes."

"I'm kind of busy right now."

"Please?" She cringed at the unintended desperation in her voice.

For a moment he said nothing. Val heard a woman's high-pitched laugh in the background, followed by a dog bark. Did he have a dog now, or was it Abigail's dog? It would be *their dog*, really. Or was he at someone else's house—Abigail's family, or a friend's place? She bit her lip as the silence between her and Max stretched into the better part of a minute.

"Fine," he said. "Meet me at Wicked Brew, on the corner of Queen Anne and Valley, in thirty minutes."

"Okay," she said with some difficulty, unaware she'd been holding her breath until that moment. "Thank you, Max."

"Bye." He hung up.

Well, it was better than nothing.

***

Val fiddled with her coffee mug and watched passersby amble past the Wicked Brew's window. She eyed her hazy reflection and noted that, once again, Max would see her looking like shit. No makeup, hair a mess, a bit pale from the stress of the last couple of days, and now a brown stain on her tank top from where coffee had dribbled down the mug's side when she'd taken a sip. Not that it mattered, but it'd be nice if she could get herself together for him just once. What did they say about breakups—looking good is the best revenge?

As she used her fingers to smooth out her hair in the window's reflection, a figure appeared behind her. She turned and saw him standing there, the first time she'd seen him in the flesh in almost eight months. He wore jeans and a T-shirt that looked loose enough to be comfortable but tight enough to show off his toned muscles and browned skin from an abundance of outdoor exercise. Running and boxing were his sports, she remembered. His tan made the gorgeous blue and green fractal tattoos snaking across both his inner forearms stand out even more. A day's worth of stubble shadowed his sharp cheekbones. The wavy black hair cropped short along the sides and longer on top caught the afternoon sunlight in a way the cameras couldn't relay.

Val's mouth watered against her will. Looking good *was* the best revenge—against her. Dammit.

She sat up straight and pushed away the image of what she knew he looked like underneath his clothes. "Hi," she said with a polite smile.

"Hi." Max didn't return her smile. He regarded her with a neutral expression—the mask he often wore to hide his feelings. Despite his passive face, his beautiful hazel eyes with their emerald green centers—the ones that could melt her from the inside—had a cold veneer. He sat in a chair across from her, leaned back, and crossed his arms over his chest like a shield.

Val pushed back a lump in her throat. He clearly didn't want to be there, with her. She wouldn't keep him long.

"How are you?" she asked, though if the press reports were accurate, she knew the answer was "fabulous."

"Fine," he said. "You?"

"Uh, I'm—" *Terrible.* She pulled at her hair, making sure it covered her scar. "You look good."

His voice was flat. "You, too."

"I heard about your engagement. I'm happy for you. You deserve to be happy, I mean."

He squirmed a little in his chair, the first sign of emotion he'd shown so far. "What do you want, Val?"

What she wanted was him. No matter how much she tried to convince herself otherwise, she still loved him. She loved him so much it filled her entire being and poured out of her in waves of desperate longing so strong she was surprised Max hadn't drowned in it yet. But she'd broken his heart. She loved him, and he hated her. He was better off without her.

She sipped her coffee, taking a moment to get her emotions under control, then asked, "Have you ever been to the Pana Sea?"

"A few times."

"Are you a regular?"

"No. Too many people for my taste. I only go if Abby wants to go."

"Oh." She hoped he hadn't noticed her flinch at his fiancée's name. Val drummed her fingers on the side of her mug. "Does she…know what you can do?" she couldn't help asking.

"Yes."

"And about your father?"

"Yes."

"And—"

"She knows everything, Val."

"Oh."

Val swallowed hard and put her trembling hands in her lap so he couldn't see them. Of course he'd told his fiancée everything. He trusted her. He loved her. Max began fidgeting with the hem of his shirt, his cool resolve waning as his eyes cast about, looking at everything besides Val. Questions about his current love life were irrelevant—and causing him pain, she realized. What they'd been through—what *she'd* put him through—had been a roller coaster ride of emotions most people wouldn't experience over their entire lifetime, let alone a few months. She'd hurt him deeply when she left; she knew that. The quicker she left him alone now, the better.

"Have you ever met a man named Lucien at the Pana Sea?"

Max's gaze cut back to hers, and he raised an eyebrow. "Lucien Christophe?"

"Maybe. Frenchman, blond hair, late thirties or early forties?"

"Yeah, that's him."

"What do you know about him?"

Max shrugged. "Nothing, really. He's in pharmaceuticals. When I was on the board of Carressa Industries, we sold him a small company that manufactured lab equipment. Now I see him sometimes at charity fund-raisers. Why do you ask?"

"I think he might be involved in a woman's disappearance."

His brow furrowed. "Who?"

"Her name is Margaret, but she goes by Celine at the Pana Sea. She works as an escort. She's going to die soon, if she's not dead already."

Max sat up in his chair, a deep frown etched on his face. "You saw it in a vision?"

Val nodded.

"And you think you can stop it?"

"I'm going to try. I have to try."

His face darkened.

"Lucien's part of a club called the Blue Serpent. Have you heard of them?"

"Yes." He started tapping his toe, his outer cool continuing to disintegrate.

"Are you a member?"

"No. I've only heard other people talking about it. Sounds more like a cult than a club."

"Can you get me access?"

Max scoffed. "That's why you asked me to come here? You want me to *join a cult* for you?"

"Only rich people can get in. You're my only rich…friend."

He glared at her. They would never be just *friends*. Either they'd be lovers or nothing at all.

"I'm not joining a cult," he said.

"Then introduce me to someone who's already in it."

"No," he snapped. "I'm not setting you up on a blind date with a cult member, either. I don't want any part of this." He stood to leave.

"Max, please." She grabbed his arm before he could walk away. A pulse like static electricity shot through her at the feel of his flesh. He glanced at her hand, then at her, and for half a second Val saw *her* Max looking into her eyes, the one that set her insides on fire, that wanted her as much as she wanted him. Just as quickly he disappeared, replaced by Abigail's Max. After she'd caught her breath, Val said, "Margaret will die if we don't do something."

"That's great you're willing to bend over backward to change the future for someone you don't even know. Congratulations on finding something *important* enough in your life to fight for. Good luck with that."

He didn't jerk his arm out of her hand, but he walked away with such purpose that he left her arm dangling in the air, grasping at his receding back, blurry through her tears.

Chapter Seven

Max still smelled grilled steak in the air when he returned to his condo after meeting with Val. Abby's soft laughter echoed through the entrance hallway from the enclosed patio on the other side of the sprawling living room, along with at least three other voices of lingering guests. Toby, their Jack Russell terrier, jumped up from where he'd been waiting next to the door for Max to return. He barked a greeting and wagged his tail. Max dropped his keys on a narrow table by the door, then cut to the left of the living room and climbed the stairs before anyone could notice he'd returned, Toby trotting after.

In the master bathroom, he dug a pill bottle out of the back of the medicine cabinet, tapped two capsules into his hand, and threw them in his mouth. He shot-gunned a glass of water and flinched at his depressing reflection, a deep frown etched across his face. The pills would help. The label on the bottle said Amerge, a migraine medication; it was actually OxyContin. He'd been prescribed the pain meds after that asshole Sten shot him in the stomach nine months ago. The pills had helped him through the worst of the healing process, then they helped him through his breakup with Val. Now they helped him get through the day. With multiple prescriptions and unlimited money, he effectively had an infinite supply of the stuff. At least it was safer than heroin, and easier to hide.

Max splashed water on his face and practiced smiling. Why did Val have to show up *now*, two months before his wedding, still driven, still fierce, still beautiful? He'd committed to this new life he built for himself, started thinking he didn't need the pills anymore. Then he saw her again, the only woman he'd ever loved—*first woman*, he reminded himself—playing with her gorgeous red hair. She'd turned and looked at him with steel eyes exactly as he remembered. All his feelings for her, the ones he'd painstakingly walled off brick by brick, came flooding back, and he knew he'd never wean himself off the goddamn pills—

"There you are."

He jumped at Abby's voice. From the bathroom doorway, she cocked her head to the side and gave him a warm smile, golden hair framing an angelic face. "Everything all right?"

"Yeah. Fine. Just a headache." Max wiped his face off on the bottom of his T-shirt, then shoved the bottle back into the cabinet. His hands shook, the emotional sucker-punch of his meeting with Val still reverberating through him. He braced them against the sink as nonchalantly as possible, hoping Abby wouldn't notice. *Calm down, Max.* He took a deep breath. "Valentine Shepherd asked me to meet her for coffee."

"Oh?" Abby's smile faded. "What did she want?"

"Help with a case she's working on. I told her...I'd think about it."

"What kind of help?"

"Eh, you know. The money kind." He shrugged. "Your brother didn't ask to spend the night again, did he?" he asked as he walked past her, on his way to the patio. Toby followed, like he always did.

"Not yet," she said behind him. He could hear the frown in her voice at another conversation about Val shut down. "But he probably will. You don't have a problem with that, do you?"

Max bounced down the stairs in an approximation of a happy person. "Nope," he said over his shoulder. Ginger's drunken hyena cackle blasted from the patio through the living room, and Max knew they might as well prep one of the spare rooms for him now.

"Dude, if you get a tattoo on the lower part of your back, it's a fuckin' tramp stamp, no matter what your girlfriend tells you," Ginger was saying to two other guys and a woman lounging beside the indoor pool when Max joined them. Abby's brother took a drag off his cigarette and let out a long exhale. The smoke curled up to the glass ceiling and disappeared between the window panes, tilted open to let the barbeque smoke out and fresh air in. Then he poked at the guy across from him with the same hand he held a beer bottle with. "You've been *pussified*."

Max grabbed a beer from the stainless steel cooler that came with the place, built into the wall. He sat back in a lounge chair next to Ginger, popped the cap off his bottle, and took a modest swig. He had to be careful; he could feel the pills working their magic, loosening him up. If he drank too much or too fast, he'd get lethargic, and the questions about his health would start.

Toby jumped into his lap and lay down. Max considered pushing him off, but he'd probably sulk off and pee on something out of spite. He didn't understand why the dog had taken such a shine to him. Abby had adopted him from a shelter shortly before their engagement. It was supposed to be her dog, really. She was the one who tried to cuddle and cooed at him, while Max treated him with respectful indifference. Instead, Toby imprinted onto Max; a poor choice, in Max's opinion. Abby said Toby's devotion meant Max was marriage material. Max thought it meant Toby was deeply disturbed. Maybe he and the dog were kindred spirits after all.

The woman, Carrie, rolled her eyes. "Roger's not *pussified.* It's a tattoo that says 'scholar master' in Chinese, above a *fleur-de-lis* symbol. It represents his Chinese and French heritage."

Ginger laughed. "That is even more gay!"

Carrie nudged the guy next to her. "Roger, show him."

"But, baby, it's personal," Roger said.

"Come *on*, Roger." Carrie shoved him hard enough to nearly knock him out of his chair.

Roger sighed, then stood, turned around, and pulled the back of his jeans down a few inches to reveal a black *fleur-de-lis* symbol underneath Chinese characters, tattooed just above his tailbone.

"*Booyah!*" Carrie slapped Roger's ass as everyone laughed. Hearing his cue, Max joined in with a fake chuckle. "All. Man. So fuck you, Ginger."

Ginger guffawed and punched Max's arm. Toby growled at the intrusion into his master's space. "You know, like, every language," Ginger said, "What does that tattoo *really* say?"

Max didn't know every language, but he did know Chinese; obviously, Roger didn't. The tattoo said "stupid boy." Roger would be crushed.

"It says 'scholar master,'" Max said. Roger wasn't close with his Chinese relatives. Chances were they'd never see his unfortunate tattoo. He'd better not go skinny-dipping in Shanghai, though.

Ginger shook his head. "I can't believe you let her talk you into that." He pointed at Max's arms. "Now *those* are some badass tattoos. I bet you get laid all the time with that shit—I mean, before you met my sister."

Mason, the man next to Roger, shook his head. "Jesus, Ginger, you're disgusting."

Max rolled his eyes at the redheaded idiot. He was tempted to blurt out the truth of how the tattoos were something he'd gotten after having sex with another man, just to see Ginger's reaction.

Even without the excessive alcohol, Abby's older brother had a severe charisma deficit. A man-child who lived off his rich parents, he bounced around Seattle, crashing parties and pissing people off. Nobody liked Ginger, real name Eugene. The only reason anyone tolerated him was for Abby's sake, and he stuck to her like a sucker fish in a dirty aquarium.

The glass door slid open, and Abby stuck her head into the patio. "Carrie, think you can help me with some goodie bags for the children's art show tomorrow?"

"Hell yes." Carrie finished her beer and stood. "Too much testosterone out here anyway."

"Go do your woman's work, woman," Ginger called after her.

Carrie flipped him off, then disappeared into the condo with Abby.

"Fucking chicks, man." Ginger dropped his cigarette into his empty bottle, then staggered over to the cooler and grabbed another beer. "I love it when they just shut up."

Max gritted his teeth and checked his watch. Maybe if he called a cab now, he could get Ginger to leave before the misogynist asshole decided to stay overnight.

Ginger looked at Roger. "You going on Saturday?" he almost whispered.

Roger frowned. "I don't know… I've got Carrie now."

Ginger scoffed. "Pussy." He looked at Mason. "You?"

Mason shrugged. "Nah. I went last time. Need a cool-down."

"You guys are fucking lame." Ginger collapsed back into his lounge chair. "Going alone sucks."

Max knew what it meant when they talked in vagaries. He usually ignored them until the conversation drifted to something else. But since Val had asked him… "You need a wingman for a Blue Serpent thing?" Max asked Ginger.

The other three men froze and stared at Max. He'd broken the first rule of the Blue Serpent club.

"Well, do you?"

Ginger gave Max a sheepish grin. "Uh, yeah, I guess, but, you know—my sister."

"Why does that matter? What do you do there?"

The three club members exchanged looks, then leaned toward each other in a huddle. Max got the gist he was supposed to lean in as well. He smothered an eye roll at their childish secret-club bullshit.

"There are two different levels," Mason said. "There's the low, entry tier, then the top one."

"We're in the entry tier," Roger added. "I'm hoping to get into the higher tier, but you have to be *invited*. I think I'm done with the low-tier shit."

"Because you're a *pussy* now," Ginger snickered.

"I am not—"

"But what do you actually *do* in this club?" Max cut in. "What's the point?"

"Parties," Roger said. "*Epic* parties."

Roger, Mason, and Ginger all nodded, in agreement for once.

Max arched an eyebrow. "That's it? Why not just go to a regular club?"

"Dude, you have *never* been to a party like this, trust me." Ginger punched Max in the arm. "Come with me on Saturday. I'll sponsor you, bro."

Roger frowned. "You sure that's a good idea? He's getting married to your sister in a couple of months..."

"This'll be his early bachelor party, one last time to let loose." Ginger looked at Max and smiled. "I won't tell if you don't."

All three men stared at Max, eager and nervous to bring him into the fold. Everything told Max this was a bad idea, that he should run as far away as possible from all things Blue Serpent related. Even Toby looked anxious. But Val had asked for his help. Even though he'd pretended to blow her off, the truth was he'd do anything for her. *Anything.*

"Okay," Max said. "Show me how awesome the Blue Serpent is."

Chapter Eight

After dragging Ginger into the guest room and turning him on his side so he wouldn't drown in his own vomit, Max switched off the lights of his finally empty condo. In the master bedroom, he kicked the dog out and shed his clothes, then sat at the edge of the bed, shoulders slumped, feeling unusually drained.

From the bathroom, Abby asked, "Do you want to come with me to the children's art show tomorrow?"

Max rubbed the bridge of his nose, a headache building between his eyes. Too bad he'd thrown out all his real migraine medication to hide the OxyContin. "Nah. I'm a bad influence."

"Come on, it'll be fun. There'll be arts and crafts, and a bouncy castle, and chocolate pudding, I think. You can't pass that up."

He smiled, but couldn't hold on to it and it faded away. Abby loved children—something he could never give her. He'd been up front about his vasectomy after they started getting serious. Though she said she'd be happy without having any of her own, he had his doubts. Toby made a poor substitute. Could be Abby faked it for him, told him what he wanted to hear so he'd let her get close to him. Maybe Val was right—the whole world really was out to get them. That thought made him smile again, bitterly.

He'd always been wary of trusting anyone, before Val. If he was being honest with himself, he'd admit he probably never would've dated Abby if Val hadn't made him realize he was capable of love—and desperate to experience it again. When he met Abby at a fund-raiser for impoverished schools, he remembered he used to like blondes. If he could love Val, why not someone else? The longer he dated Abby, the more he liked her—and the less he thought about Val. Until one day she mentioned marriage, and it occurred to him: Why not now? Why not embrace a good thing, try to have what other, normal people had? He didn't feel for her what he felt for Val, but love came in different forms. They made each other happy, and that was all he needed in his life now.

And the pills. But that was different.

Abby walked into the bedroom, running a brush through her hair and wearing only sheer panties and a camisole top. "What did Valentine Shepherd really want?"

Max sighed. *This* conversation again. He should've lied and said he'd gone to get ice cream. Anything Val-related sprung up a gauntlet of questions. In truth, Max had lied to Val when he said Abby knew everything. He'd told Abby *most* things. She knew about Max's ability—his curse—but she didn't know Val could do it, too. She knew about his father's abuse, but not that Max had killed him. She knew something had happened between Max and Val during their time on the run together, but he wouldn't elaborate. Val's secrets were her own and not for Max to disclose, not even to his fiancée.

"I already told you," he said, "She wanted money." That was true, in a way. He tried to stick as close to the truth as possible, and talk around the holes. But it was the holes that Abby always picked up on.

"But what did she want money for?"

"A missing person case she's working on. She didn't give me details."

"Are you going to give it to her?"

"I don't know yet."

Abby set her hairbrush on the dresser and walked to Max. She slid a leg over his lap, straddling him where he sat at the edge of the bed. "What's to decide?"

Max ran his hands up her back, underneath the flimsy camisole. He pulled her flush to him and kissed her soft neck. "I'm deciding if it's worth the investment," he mumbled into her skin.

"Just tell her no. Tell her you don't need the trouble."

"It's not that simple."

"Why not?"

Max lifted his head from her neck with a sigh, unable to hide his exasperation. "Because she saved my life. I owe her."

Abby frowned. "How long are you going to keep paying her back?"

Forever. Max rolled with her onto the bed until he lay on top of her. "I don't want to talk about Val anymore."

He kissed her deeply, dominating her mouth with his. When he felt her body arch into him, he pulled off her camisole and ran his lips down her torso, over supple breasts where he lingered on the hard outcrops of her nipples. She ran a hand through his hair and let out a soft moan.

"I wish you'd let me in," she whispered.

He didn't look up. "You are in." As far in as he could let her, anyway.

He slipped off her panties and made a trail of sloppy kisses over her stomach and across her hips, then into the wet middle. She whimpered as he made love to her with his mouth, caressing her sweet insides in the way he knew she couldn't get enough of. Her fine hair tickled his nose as she writhed around him, clawing at the bedspread, curling her toes. When her thighs quivered at the edge of climax, he stopped. He moved up until he was face-to-face with her as she panted underneath him. She wrapped her arms and legs around him and tried to pull him into her, pawing at his naked body in desperation for release only Max could give, but he wouldn't move.

"Please," she begged, in his sexual thrall. "*Please.*"

Max looked down at her for another moment, noted how completely she belonged to him. His own angel, who tasted like the color of her hair—honey, inside and out. And yet…He imagined himself getting up right then and walking away. What would she do? Keep lying there, waiting for him to return? What would *he* do? Go running to Val and beg her to take him back? Not again. *Never* again. She didn't want him. He needed to accept that.

Appreciate what you have, Max.

He entered Abby hard. She cried out, exploding like a popped water balloon in his arms. He surged through her as she clung to him, losing himself in her sweetness, pushing everything but Abby's warm wetness from his mind.

Her screams of ecstasy grew louder, and he willed himself closer to climax. He needed to be *here*, with *her*. Though he had stamina in spades, and making Abby come multiple times in one night had been fun in the past, his mind still reeled with thoughts of Val, and his plunge with eyes wide shut into the Blue Serpent. His attention itched to be somewhere else.

You have your angel. Don't think of the other one.

Abby's fingers dug into his back and she rasped, "Yes, yes, *yes!*" She threw her head back and he felt her insides tighten around him. He closed his eyes and thrust harder, deep into her as she bucked against him, consumed with an ecstasy he could only imagine. For him—and Val—this was the best part, right before.

Don't think of her.

"Abby," he moaned into her ear. "Abby—" His mind slipped away as he came—

9872649209010297192319831984784567189745279-
8761018439782742001902938151187892754298759-
8208475209348275876432736280391091092879155-
6367821232091841975678150928121810980419283-
7180975276185648921609854629680987654321—
The red raven flies above me in the moonlight, just out of my reach. She swoops down and cuts one sequence of numbers in half with her claw, swallows another section in her ebony beak. She beats her lustrous wings and flies away from me, fading until she's merely a ruby glinting in the light of an unseen moon. Come back, I call after her, come back—

Max blinked as the image faded, replaced by the pillow he'd collapsed into face-first. Abby still lay underneath him, though she'd pushed him to the side a bit so his deadweight didn't crush her. He turned his head to look at her and she smiled back, her cheeks flushed.

She stroked the back of his neck. "Do you feel it when I do this during your trances?"

"No." He rolled off her and rested his forearm across his eyes. "I don't feel anything."

Slick with sweat, she pressed her naked body against his and rested her head in the crux of his shoulder. "What did you see?"

"Nothing."

She gave him a playful nudge. "Does that mean the economy's going to collapse?"

He cracked a smile. "I mean nothing special—just numbers. Your dad's Southeast Asian Division will post a twelve percent loss next quarter, though. Drop him an anonymous tip if you want."

"I'll let him figure it out." She pushed his arm off his face and caressed his cheek, her eyes searching his. "I love you, Max. I really love you."

"I love you, too."

She smiled and her eyes grew moist. For a moment Max thought she might cry. Instead, she buried her head in his neck and lay with her arms around him. He rolled onto his side, away from her, closed his eyes, and pretended to sleep. With Abby pressed against his back, he thought of the red raven, of Val, and what his meeting with her might've changed of his future.

Chapter Nine

Val approached the McMansion of Michael Stevenson, one of three men she was pretty sure had raped her. Stacey had bitten the bullet and watched both Val's and Margaret's videos, writing down every detail she could about the attackers. Unfortunately, since each man had been nude and wearing a mask, "every detail" amounted to a rough estimate of height and weight, hair color, and a few birthmarks and scars that would normally be covered by clothing. In other words, it would be nearly impossible to make a visual ID without stripping a suspect down.

Except in the case of a dark-haired man in his late thirties with a patch of gray above his right ear. With the clues to her attackers' identities, Val had sat in her car in front of the Pana Sea for two days straight, from opening to closing, until she spotted him. While he was in the bar, she bribed the valet, broke into his car, and got his name and address off the registration. Could be Stevenson was innocent, and just happened to share a physical trait with her suspect. A cruise through his house might clear up the ambiguity.

A pickup with gardening tools in the cab hugged the curb out front while a man mowed the lawn. Val waved at the gardener to get his attention. When he saw her, he turned off the mower and removed his ear protection.

"Hi there," she called to him from the front walkway. "I'm looking for Mr. Stevenson. Is he here?"

"Yup." The gardener crooked his thumb at the house.

She thanked him, and he started up his mower again. This would be easier than she thought.

Val didn't knock. She opened the unlocked front door and walked inside like she lived there. Glancing around his foyer, she spotted a table filled with framed family photos. He had a wife and two preteen children. Wife was probably at work; kids at summer camp. A decorative wood carving like something sold at a farmer's market hung on the wall; it read "Mike + Vanessa." Footsteps creaked through the ceiling from the second floor. He worked from home; private law practice maybe.

Val walked into an immaculately clean kitchen with heavy mahogany furniture. On the counter sat a tidy pile of unopened mail. She riffled through it, picked out a thick envelope that looked promising. Val grabbed a knife from a butcher block and cut the envelope open; a monthly checking account summary. She noticed lots of checks made out to various charities, but nothing suspicious. Val sliced open another; a credit card statement. Scanning the charges, her eyes alit on one particularly huge purchase—five digits—to a company called Asclepius Inc. The charge was dated one day after her assault. She folded the paper and shoved it into her back pocket.

Val was about to slice open another envelope when footsteps on the stairs caught her attention. With a swipe of her arm, she dumped the pile of torn-up mail into a trash bin abutting the counter, then slipped the knife into her waistband, next to her gun in its concealed holster at the small of her back. A second later, Stevenson entered the kitchen.

He jumped when he saw her. "Jesus! Who the hell are you?"

"I'm from the Coalition of Concerned Parents of the Pacific Northwest. Are you aware there's an ongoing effort to cut after-school outdoor programs for disadvantaged children?"

"How did you get in here?" he stammered.

"Your door was unlocked. The quality of your children's education is at stake here, sir."

"My kids go to private school..."

"Of course they do, but cutting after-school outdoor activities for public school kids will result in a lower quality of life for everyone. What kind of world are we leaving for our children when we allow them to grow up without really understanding the joys of kayaking? Your wife, Vanessa, understood."

"You talked to Vanessa?"

"Yes, about a week ago. She didn't mention it?"

"No—"

"Well, we talked. She said she'd donate one hundred dollars to the Coalition. Told me to come by today and pick up the check..."

He shook his head and sighed. "Goddammit, Vanessa. I

wish she'd stop doing these things without telling me." He disappeared for a moment, then came back to the kitchen with a checkbook. Stevenson sat down at the kitchen table and flipped the book open. Val sat across from him and studied his face. He still didn't seem to recognize her. Maybe he was innocent after all.

"Who do I make this out to?"

"The Coalition of..."

He wrote, then glanced at her.

"Concerned Parents of..."

His pen scratched the check. He glanced at her again. Then his glance turned into a wide-eyed stare and the blood drained from his face.

"The Pacific Northwest."

Stevenson tore his gaze away from her and back to the check. He cleared his throat and started writing again. His hand shook.

"You recognize me, don't you?"

"No," he said without looking at her.

Val slipped the knife out of her waistband. In one smooth, strong motion, she jammed the blade through his hand and into the table's wooden surface underneath. Stevenson shrieked.

"How about now?"

He pawed frantically at the knife, but she'd embedded it nice and deep into the table. It stayed put, and him with it.

"What do you want?" Stevenson cried as he writhed in his chair, eyes wet and panicked. "I'll pay you! Anything you want!"

"I want to know why you thought you'd get away with raping a woman."

"I don't—I didn't know— He said you were a whore! That you'd been paid—"

"Who said that?"

"The butler guy— Jesus, I didn't know! I was fucked up that night, I swear! They gave us drugs. I didn't know—"

"Where is the Blue Serpent clubhouse?"

Breathing hard, he squeezed his eyes shut and tried to concentrate on something other than the huge knife speared through his hand. "It changes every time."

"Where was it last Wednesday night?"

"F—four-eighteen East Langdon Drive, I think."

"Was Lucien Christophe there?"

"I don't remember!"

Val unholstered her gun and imagined what his head would look like with a much-deserved hole in it. Stevenson started hyperventilating. He pulled uselessly on the knife. Every time he moved his trapped hand, he groaned in agony.

She pointed her gun at him. "Think hard, Michael."

"No—no, he wasn't there."

"Who were your partners in crime?"

"I dunno. I didn't recognize them. Everybody was high and wearing masks, for fuck's sake! I'm sorry, okay? I'm sorry! I didn't know!"

Val tapped her gun with her index finger and considered whether to believe him. The element of surprise plus extreme physical duress usually equaled not enough time to think of a plausible lie. And like Eric the Idiot Bartender before him,

Stevenson put on a convincing act. Val had a special way of keeping people honest. She believed he was sorry...that he'd been caught. Now, she needed to decide whether or not to kill him.

Val slipped her gun back into its holster. She walked to the counter and picked up a thick wooden cutting board. Gripping it like a paddle, she stalked toward Stevenson. The crush of his skull would be so satisfying...

"No," he begged when she raised the cutting board above her head. "*No!*" He threw up his free arm to protect himself.

Val brought the cutting board down on the hilt of the knife. Stevenson screamed as the blade embedded into the table another inch. There was no way he'd work it free now. She tossed the cutting board to the floor, then picked his checking account summary from the trash. Val turned the paper over and wrote on the blank side:

Dear Vanessa: I raped a woman. That is what I think of you.

Val lay the paper down on the far end of the table, three feet out of his reach. She looked down at him as he grasped for the note, tears running down his face. "Sucks to be helpless, doesn't it? You could always cut your hand free, if you really love your wife."

Val walked away as Stevenson screamed every curse word known to the English language. At the front door, the lawn mower drowned out his cries. She stepped outside into the hot summer day, clear blue sky in every direction. The gardener gave her a polite wave as he passed. Val waved back, and for a second imagined herself as a rich housewife, pampered and content with her privileged life, her only concern whether the lawn mower lines in the grass were crisp enough. Then she remembered why she was actually there, and felt sick.

***

Langdon Drive was actually a long driveway that led to a mansion hidden from the main road by evergreen foliage. The brown monstrosity loomed over the wooded area like an evil troll with glass eyes, waiting for a victim to wander by whom it could snatch and drag away. Rustic luxury. It made her nauseous.

With one swift kick the door popped open. Val figured she had about ten minutes before police responded to the silent alarm she'd surely set off. She did a quick scan of the first floor and found the place impeccably decorated with the bare minimum for furniture. There were no personal touches or mementos. It was a rental, she realized. Val made a quick sweep of the second and third floors; they had the same feel of a fancy hotel that the first floor did. Lastly, she went to the basement.

It was part of a sitting area next to a pool table and a wet bar—the white leather sofa. She'd only seen it for a few seconds in the video, but she would never forget it. This was where it happened. The fact that she couldn't remember anything was probably a gift. A part of her wished she'd never found out, the part that wished she was a normal person with a normal life. The part that told her she should let someone else deal with all the injustices in the world for once. The part that always argued for caution. The part that always lost.

Val swallowed hard and forced herself to rip the cushions

loose and look for anything left behind, like a condom. Her presence there now might contaminate the scene, but it was worth the risk. When she found nothing, she looked underneath the sofa, then combed the rest of the room; nothing. The house had been scrubbed clean. She considered burning it down. While she'd find it immensely satisfying to torch the place, the blaze might destroy any remaining evidence. Even a professional floor-to-ceiling scrub-down wouldn't remove every trace of hair, DNA, or something else that could be used in a trial if, in a best-case scenario, she ever got that far.

She glanced at her watch. Time to leave if she wanted to avoid a breaking-and-entering charge. Honestly, she was grateful for any excuse to get the hell out of that room.

Val rushed to her car and drove away in haste. A police cruiser passed traveling in the opposite direction, toward the house. The beat cop inside didn't pay her any notice. When it disappeared from her rearview mirror, she fetched her cell phone from her purse and called Zach.

"Tell me you have something," she said when he answered the phone.

"Oh, hey. I was gonna call you sooner, but my mom told me if I didn't plant some flowers for her, like *immediately*, she'd take my computers away. I swear she bought a hundred stupid pansies—"

"Spit it out, Zach!"

"All right, jeez. Like I was afraid of, the dude who posted the video knew what he was doing. He ping-ponged the trail all over the country, but I was able to trace the origin to a place in Lakewood, Washington."

Yes. Another lead. "Gimme the address."

"Six-four-three-zero Motor Avenue. But I'll tell you now, he's not there. I already Google Earth-ed it, and it's a closed-down car garage. Means he spoofed the IP address, like I'd do, if I were him. He could be anywhere in the country. Definitely in the US, though, if that helps."

"*Fuck,*" she hissed into the phone.

"Sorry. If I had access to PRISM, I could track him down no problem. You know, the NSA launched that program in 2007 and—"

Val hung up, then slapped the dashboard. *Goddammit!* Clutching the steering wheel with white knuckles, she took deep breaths and tried to calm her nerves. So tracing the video had led to a dead end. It wasn't her only lead. She called Stacey.

"I need you to find out who rented the mansion at four-eighteen East Langdon Drive last Wednesday night, and if that person rented any other properties within the last six months," Val said.

"Okay. Property managers for rich people have tight lips, though. I'll have to call in some favors. Might take a few days."

"As soon as possible, Stacey. You know what's at stake."

"Yeah, I know," Stacey snapped.

Val expected Stacey to follow up with a gripe about Val's rudeness, but she didn't. Stacey's pity must've tempered her response. Great, even her best friend was treating her like a wounded child.

"When are you coming home?" Stacey asked. "It's falafel night. We can sit and talk, catch up on the other cases, and maybe call a lawyer and get advice on what legal action we could take against the Pana Sea—"

"I'm not going to be home until late. I have to…go do something."

"You're not going to get drunk somewhere, are you?"

Val ground her teeth together. "Don't wait up for me." She hung up.

She tossed her phone into the passenger's seat. For a moment tears clouded her vision. She hated being reminded she was a fucking victim. The only thing that made it bearable was knowing that a victim could be reborn an avenging angel of the purest kind—one driven by a wrath that would not be quenched until the entire world paid restitution.

Chapter Ten

Stacey dropped her phone back into the tie-dyed tote nestled in her car's passenger seat. She took a long drag off the cigarette she'd been working on when Val had called. *As soon as possible, Stacey. You know what's at stake.* Stacey scoffed. *No shit, Val, I'm not a fucking idiot.* Of course Val meant the missing woman, not Val's own rape. Val would rather pretend like the latter never happened, with the aid of copious amounts of alcohol. And why shouldn't she? The drink-to-forget technique had worked well enough for her since the batshit craziness at the Pacific Science Center last year, and her breakup with *the perfect man*, Max Carressa. It all meant Stacey had to shoulder more of the burden of running Valentine Investigations, like actually following up on cases that weren't Margaret Monroe's, while the company's namesake slept off a hangover or fell off the grid for hours at a time. But what were friends for? Maybe she should fall off the grid for a little while, too, and give Val a taste of her own medicine.

Stacey shook her head at her petty thoughts. She wasn't being fair. Val was in serious pain and needed help—help she refused to accept from Stacey, for whatever reason. That's what chafed Stacey the most. Why wouldn't Val let Stacey help her? Was she holding out for her ex-boyfriend, like maybe he'd dump his hot fiancée and hook back up with her? That's not how men worked. Even super-gay Stacey knew that.

She jammed her spent cigarette butt into the ashtray. More petty thoughts. This case was getting to her. As soon as they found Margaret and brought Val's rapists to justice, they'd take a break and clear their heads, help each other heal, mend battered bridges. Val would hem and haw about how their work never ended and evil never slept and all that, but Stacey would insist. Maybe they'd go to Vancouver…No, Hawaii. She could already feel the sand between her toes and taste the Mai Tais—or maybe a virgin daiquiri, for Val's sake.

Stacey tapped another cigarette out of its pack and readied her lighter to fire it up, then stopped when she spotted what she'd been waiting for. Across the street, two gorgeous women carrying garment bags walked up to an apartment building and knocked on a first-floor door. Seconds later, a petite brunette answered, exchanged hugs with the other two, then ushered them inside.

Yup, this was definitely the place. After Stacey tracked one of Margaret's escort colleagues down, she admitted that a contingent of working girls had been solicited to work a costume party that night, and the friendlier women were meeting ahead of time to get ready together. The colleague didn't know Margaret personally or anything about the Blue Serpent, but one of these fine ladies might. In any case, it'd be fun to ask.

Stacey tossed her unlit cigarette back in her tote and walked to the apartment door the ladies had disappeared into a minute ago. The same gorgeous woman as before answered. She raised a penciled-in eyebrow at Stacey.

Stacey eyed the woman's breasts, barely contained in a bikini made of seashells. "Hi there!"

"Yeah?"

"I'm a friend of Margaret Monroe's mom—you might know Margaret as Celine? I'm looking for her. Can I come in?"

The brunette's skepticism softened into concern. "Oh my gosh, yeah." She opened the door for Stacey and beckoned her inside.

The apartment was a typical bachelorette pad, with pink tiger-print throw pillows and feather boas draped over bookcases. Seven or eight beautiful women in various stages of dress moved between the living room, a bathroom, and down a hallway Stacey assumed led to a bedroom. They regarded Stacey in passing with polite curiosity. Stacey smiled at them and nibbled on her bottom lip. In moments like these, she remembered why she loved her job, despite the unstable income.

"You said you're looking for Margaret?" the brunette asked.

"Oh—um, yes." Stacey worked to focus on only the one beautiful woman talking to her, though her eyes kept wandering.

"So she really is missing? I heard about it, but I wasn't sure. I haven't seen her in a while, but, you know, girls in this business come and go..."

"Her mom's concerned enough to hire us. I'm with a detective agency."

"Like, the cops?"

"No, we're private. Very discreet. We're looking for any clues that might help—people she knows, places she likes to go, any enemies she might have, that sort of thing. Did you know her well?"

"We did a few jobs together." Her eyes misted up. "She was really sweet."

"And you are…"

"Cindi."

"Nice to meet you. When's the last time you saw Margaret?"

"About a month ago. We worked a job in Bellevue together. Weird old guy, had us fuck each other while he watched from inside a closet and jerked off."

"Huh. I don't suppose it brought you closer together as friends?"

"No, but we went to an all-night diner afterward and got milk shakes. That was nice."

That *did* sound nice. "Have you ever been to a bar called the Pana Sea?"

"Yeah. I go about once a month, when I've got a gap in my schedule and want some extra cash."

"Anything weird ever happen there?"

Cindi shook her head. "Not to me…but Rachel said she thought somebody from that bar drugged her." She looked past Stacey. "Hey, Rachel, come out here!"

A bottle blonde came out a moment later, hopping on one foot as she pulled on a green sequined skirt with fringe at the bottom made to look like a mermaid's tail.

Cindi cocked her head to Stacey as she spoke to Rachel. "This lady's looking for Margaret. Tell her about that time you were drugged at the Pana Sea."

Rachel frowned. "There's nothing to tell, really. And it wasn't *at* the Pana Sea, it was sometime after. This guy Donald took me to a big house where he said a party was going on, but I don't remember the party, or even going inside. I don't remember anything until the next day. I woke up on a park bench."

A park bench. Jesus. Tossed out like a piece of litter. Sounded a lot like what happened to Val.

"Did you go to the police?" Stacey asked.

"No." Rachel's face fell. "Sometimes weird shit happens. You get used to it. I need to finish getting ready. Sorry I can't help more." She disappeared down the hallway, her steps quick to avoid being pulled back into another painful conversation.

You get used to sexual assault? That was not fucking right. No wonder Val didn't want to go to the police. Stacey turned her attention back to Cindi. "Has that happened to anyone else you know of?"

Cindi tapped her lips. "Something sort of like that happened to Becca, but she was at some other club, not the Pana Sea."

"Where can I find her?"

"I don't know where she lives. I haven't seen her in a while, since she...got sick."

Stacey shook off a moment of terror for Val. She knew Val's STD and pregnancy tests had come back negative. The illness and the memory loss were probably unrelated. Probably.

"Everybody's nervous to go solo these days, but the bills gotta get paid, you know? At least we can look out for each other at the parties." She glanced at a clock on the wall. "That's all I know. I have to finish getting ready, too. Will you tell me if you find her?"

Stacey's gaze flickered to Cindi's seashell bikini. "Of course. I'll come by as soon as I know. Hey, can I walk around and talk to the other ladies for a few minutes?"

"Sure."

Stacey didn't think she could learn anything more, but she *really* wanted to look around. In the bathroom, three women in thongs and the same mermaid bikinis as Cindi giggled with each other as they painted on makeup. Stacey eyed the perfect curves of their asses, imagined what it'd be like to run her fingers down that skin. They sent friendly waves her way. Stacey grinned back and moved on before they could sense her less-than-innocent motives.

She heard animated discussion among three or four women in a room at the end of the hall—probably the master bedroom—but she poked her head into a small guest bedroom first. A single woman inhabited this one, her back to Stacey as she sat in front of a vanity mirror and applied lotion to her completely nude body. Stacey did a double take; not because of the woman's flawless skin or exquisite form, but because Stacey recognized her.

"Kat?"

It couldn't be. Stacey's ex-girlfriend had disappeared right after the Pacific Science Center shoot-out, where her car had exploded—a car Kat had somehow rigged to explode, right before she lent it to Stacey. The official report said the car belonged to Norman Barrister's henchman, but Stacey knew differently. She had assumed Katrina fled the country after stomping on Stacey's heart in service of whatever crazy shit was going on with Val, but obviously she'd assumed wrong.

Kat looked in the mirror at Stacey, her icy blue eyes betraying a rare moment of surprise before melting into the alluring stare Stacey still imagined when she was with other women. "Hey, babe," she said in her familiar velvet voice.

"*Hey, babe?* Are you fucking serious?" Stacey crossed her arms. "I should turn you in to the goddamn police, you bitch."

"But that won't match the established narrative."

No, it wouldn't. A lot of anonymous, powerful people had worked hard to hide the truth of what actually happened at the Science Center that day—people Kat worked for, Stacey guessed.

"So you're a hooker now? Terrorism didn't have a nice enough retirement plan?"

Kat smirked, an elegant curve on her lips. "I like to keep my options open. Prevents being stovepiped."

"Sure, talk around me with your bullshit answers. There's no way it's a coincidence Val and I are looking for a missing woman she saw in a vision and you just happen to be here."

"That is strange." Kat squeezed lotion into her hand and rubbed it on her long legs, up and down her thighs. Heat blossomed in Stacey's belly. This bitch knew how to play her.

"Do you know where Margaret Monroe is?" Stacey asked with a sneer in her voice. Maybe Kat would surprise her and actually tell the truth for once.

"No."

"Do you know who raped Val?"

Another flash of surprise crossed Kat's face. "I didn't know she was raped."

Stacey lifted her chin, enjoying a moment of knowing something Kat didn't—unless Kat lied about that, too. "She was drugged by a guy named Lucien Christophe, then raped by three men while she was unconscious. You don't know anything about that?"

"No..." For a second Kat looked lost in thought, then her controlled demeanor took over again. She squeezed a glob of glittering goo from a tube, then rubbed it on her breasts, making circles around her nipples with her fingers. She met Stacey's eyes, and Stacey thought she might come right there. "I'm sorry about Val, if that's true."

"Of course it's true!" Anger stomped over her arousal. "Why the fuck would I lie?"

Kat shrugged. "You've always been protective of Val—too protective. Seems a little one-sided, don't you think?"

Stacey scoffed. "You sit there and talk like you *know* me, but you don't know shit." She turned to leave, then turned back. "And you have no right to psychoanalyze my life. I gave my heart to you based on a bunch of lies you told me. If you think I care for Val more than she cares for me, you should've given me something else to hold on to. I could've loved you like nobody else. Instead you fucking used me."

Kat's face fell into an emotion Stacey had never seen her express before; it looked like regret, or sadness, or both. No, it was Stacey's imagination. Wishful thinking. With tears in her eyes, Stacey left Kat and the apartment, to follow Val's lead and fall off the grid for a while.

Chapter Eleven

This is it!" Ginger said as he pulled up to a mansion in Blue Ridge isolated by a patch of evergreen forest.

"Whose house is this?" Max asked from the passenger seat of Ginger's Porsche. The modern glass walls brought back unpleasant memories of his father's mansion on Mercer Island, though with all the drapes drawn, it could look completely different on the inside.

"Dunno," Ginger said. "It's always different. I think the guy who runs these things just rents a place for the night."

"So you've met the guy in charge?"

"I've met the guy who takes my money. I'm pretty sure he's not the one in charge, though."

"And he throws one of these things every weekend?"

Ginger chuckled. "I wish. They come in clusters. Every three or four months or so, there'll be a bunch of parties. Then nothing. You got lucky, bro. Picked the right time to get on board."

Ginger stopped his Porsche behind a Ferrari—real subtle

for a secret-club party—and hopped out. A valet in plain clothes rushed forward and drove off with the car as Ginger strode toward the entrance, eager anticipation quickening his step. Max lingered at the curb for a minute to check his cell phone. He queued up a voice mail he'd been waiting for over a week to receive, and crossed his fingers it was what he wanted to hear.

"Hello, Mr. Carressa," a woman's no-nonsense voice said. "This is Josephine Price. I appreciate your offer to start a scholarship fund in my brother and father's names, but I don't think it's a good idea, since their deaths were so…controversial, and you are also…controversial." She sighed, and her tone turned angry. "Look, I don't know if you're trying to rehabilitate your image or add another notch to your philanthropy belt, but my family doesn't need your money. So stop offering." The message ended.

"Shit," Max muttered. He wished he had something other than money to give her, but he didn't. Maybe if he told her the truth, she'd finally stop hating him for the indirect role he'd played in Robby and Dean Price's deaths. *I'm your brother*, he'd practiced telling her hundreds of times in his head. *We have the same father, so…How 'bout them Mariners?* He'd never had a sibling, or any other family besides his horrible father, after his mother died. He thought he never wanted a family, but when he discovered he had a sister, he found himself irrationally curious about her. So far she'd rebuffed all his indirect attempts to meet with her. Telling her the truth seemed more and more like the only option. It made his palms sweat.

Max resolved to come up with another plan later and

slipped his phone back into his sport coat pocket, then caught up with Ginger as the man-child wrapped on the front door. A gorgeous black woman in a tight satin dress answered, all inviting smiles. Max repressed a frown in response. He had hoped the party would consist of lonely, rich men wearing black robes and exchanging secret handshakes while they drank highballs and chatted about sports, or something equally inane. Above all, he prayed this thing wasn't, in fact, an orgy, even though Ginger's enthusiasm argued to the contrary.

"Hi, Daneeka," Ginger said. He grabbed her ass and pulled her into a sloppy kiss.

She pushed him away and giggled. "Oh, *you*."

Max cringed and started planning his exit strategy. He'd owned a sex club not long ago—the Red Raven in Moonlight, now divested—though he wasn't himself a fan of public or anonymous sex, especially with his condition. Even if he had been, a quick roll in the hay was out of the question now that he had Abby. He'd scope the place out, get a read on the situation and anything suspicious for Val, then bolt. He didn't want to be at this party one second longer than necessary.

"Will you be having the usual?" Daneeka asked Ginger.

"Hell yeah," Ginger said. "Super-size it, baby."

She looked at Max. "And what drink can I have prepared for you, sir?"

"Vodka on the rocks will be fine, thanks."

She nodded, then motioned them into a dark foyer, where an older man in a crisp suit stepped forward and shook their hands. "Mr. Carressa, excellent you could join us."

Max gave the man a tight smile. So much for flying under

the radar. The man held out his hand expectantly, and Max wondered if he wanted a tip.

Ginger handed the man a credit card. He nudged Max to follow his lead. "It has to be black," he said, and winked.

Max hesitated for a moment, then fished his American Express Centurion card out of his wallet and handed it over. He could always cancel it and get another one if fraudulent charges popped up. The man pocketed the cards, then handed Max and Ginger a couple of masquerade ball-style masks off a table.

Max gritted his teeth. *Masks?* This whole thing kept getting worse.

Feeling like an idiot, Max slipped on the mask and followed Ginger and Daneeka through a hallway until they reached a large room lit in ethereal blues that shimmered off glass walls like an aquarium's interior. The whole scene looked like a mixer in an underwater grotto, with smooth electronic music humming in the background. About fifty men and women in masks loitered around the room, drinking and talking to each other. Beautiful women in bikini tops and long skirts made to look like mermaid tails, as well as a few men in merman outfits, worked the crowd. Max did a double take when he saw one man walk by swinging his arms as if he were swimming through the air.

Daneeka disappeared, and a mermaid walked up to them holding a tray with two drinks and two small paper cups perched atop. Max took the tumbler that was obviously his while Ginger snatched up a huge glass of brown liquid—probably a giant rum and Coke—as well as one of the paper cups.

"Aw, yeah," Ginger said before he tipped the contents of the cup into his mouth and chased it down with a long gulp of his drink.

The mermaid smiled at Max and nodded toward the remaining paper cup. With some reluctance he took the cup and peered inside. It held two pills, one red and one blue.

Ginger punched Max in the arm. "It's cool, bro. Just take them. It will *blow your fucking mind*, trust me." He leaned toward Max and whispered, "It's the whole point of these parties. Otherwise it's like a fucking junior prom in here."

Max didn't trust Ginger on anything, but if the pills were the main draw, then he had to see what they did. He threw the pills in his mouth and swallowed them with vodka. He wasn't too concerned with what the pills were; probably an Ecstasy derivative. He already popped OxyContin like candy. What was another illicit drug coursing through his veins? And if he overdosed... Well, Abby would be sad.

He wandered to the corner of the room while Ginger glommed on to a blond mermaid who bore a disturbing resemblance to Abby. Strangely, Max didn't recognize most people at the party. There weren't *that* many millionaires in the Seattle area, and they all ran in the same circles. Even with the masks, he'd still recognize Seattle's elite by their hair and clothing. This crowd must've contained of a lot of out-of-towners.

"I never thought I would see you here," a man with a slight French accent said behind him.

Max recognized Lucien Christophe's voice even before he turned to face the Frenchman. Lucien gave Max a cockeyed grin beneath a mask made of black feathers.

"I'm Ginger's wingman," Max said. He nodded toward Abby's brother, already making out with the blond mermaid on the far side of the room.

"Admirable of you. That can't be easy."

Max shrugged. "Depends what the pills do."

"The blue creates the dream. The red enhances pleasure."

Great—a dream orgy. "Did you make them?" Max asked as nonchalantly as possible. At least part of Lucien's financial portfolio included pharmaceuticals. He definitely had the means.

"Of course not," Lucien said with the easy confidence of a skilled liar.

"Do you know where the party host got all the mermaids? Are they hired escorts?"

Lucien smiled and cocked his head toward the crowd, growing more raucous as the drugs kicked in. "Look at them. What do you think?"

Max finished his vodka. A mermaid waitress appeared almost immediately with another one. He waved her off, then decided to push his luck. "You run these things, don't you?"

Lucien laughed and put his arm around Max's shoulders. "I have to tell you, I'm glad you came. Making conversation with rich idiots and women who only tell you what you want to hear becomes tedious after a while. You are so much more interesting." He slapped Max's chest. "I want to show you something."

He took a step away, one hand still on Max's shoulder. Max flinched when Lucien turned back to him. Blood leaked from beneath Lucien's feathered mask, crimson streaks dribbling down a pulpy face. Max blinked, and the blood was gone.

"I will be back shortly," Lucien said. "Don't go far, my friend." He clapped Max on the shoulder and disappeared down a side hallway.

Max stood frozen for a moment. What the hell had he seen on Lucien's face? He took a deep breath and tried to push the disturbing image out of his mind. A wave of dizziness hit him, and he put his head in his hands for a moment. When he opened his eyes again, he realized with a jolt that his whole body was immersed in water. He tried to swim to the surface shimmering above him, but no matter how much he flailed, he couldn't reach air. His lungs began to burn. With no other choice, he sucked in water…and felt fine. He could breathe underwater.

He could *breathe underwater!* Max didn't remember how he'd ended up submerged, but the blue pill must have allowed his body to convert water into breathable oxygen somehow. The underwater grotto he found himself in sparkled everywhere a sapphire blue. Neon fish swam past his head, scattering when he reached out to touch them. Other partygoers floated around him, penguins with human faces and naked mermaids whose tails transformed to bare legs and back again.

A smile grew on Max's face until he found himself giggling with childish delight. This *was* an amazing party—probably the best one he'd ever been to. He was *breathing under the goddamn water* in a tropical paradise! He'd never felt so giddy in his life. Max swam through the penguins and mermaids. The ladies smiled and winked as he floated by. Elation gripped him in a way he hadn't felt since…well, since he'd been in bed with

Val in the boathouse all those months ago. He flipped onto his back and watched the sun play on the surface above him, a moving mosaic of blues.

Then he blinked, and the water's surface became a dark ceiling with blue and white light splashed across it. The light faded and the plaster darkened with soot. Spiderweb cracks spread across the rotting surface, until the ceiling collapsed on top of him.

Max cried out and threw his hands above his head as he stumbled backward. He ran into someone, spun around to face a naked mermaid with lustrous blond hair, icy blue eyes, and a body he knew well, like a sculpted work of art.

"Kitty?" he stammered at his former personal assistant and casual sex partner. "You're a mermaid?"

A crooked grin played across her perfect lips. "It's something I do on the side."

"What're you doing here?"

"Reconnaissance and asset management. Mermaid things."

He'd been transported back to the underwater grotto. "The ceiling fell on me," he said as he swam in place. "Where did it go?"

Kitty took his arm. "Come with me."

She dragged him through the water until he forced her to stop. He stood in the mansion's main room again, silhouettes all around him, moving, multiplying, cutting into him and through him like millions of stenciled drawings laid on top of each other.

Max squeezed his eyes shut and put his head in his hands. "Oh God oh God oh God—"

"Come *on*, Max," he heard Kitty the Mermaid say.

Back in the wonderful water again. Kitty pulled him past penguins and other mermaids until she reached a quieter spot in the grotto. Then she pressed her bare torso to his chest and kissed him. She tasted the same as he remembered, sweet and sour like tart candy, though that might have been his imagination.

Max pushed her away. "I can't."

"I see you're busy," Max heard Lucien say behind Kitty. "Too bad. Next time."

Max nudged Kitty aside, but didn't see Lucien. She cupped his head in her hands and forced him to look at her. Her face had changed.

"*Val?*" he said to the redhead pressed against him. "Wh—what's happening?"

Val stroked the back of his neck, and his whole body responded like the first time he'd ever touched a woman. His hands trembled.

"You have to trust me," Val said with Kitty's voice.

She pulled him in for a kiss, and this time he couldn't resist. He kissed her back, drinking in her essence with a hunger that had gnawed at him for eight months. Every part of him wanted her, *needed* her, *ached* for her to fill the hole he'd been dumping drugs down and patching over with paper-thin promises to leave the past behind. He'd tried. He couldn't.

A guttural moan escaped from deep in his chest. "*Valentine.*" He kissed her neck, her shoulder; ran his hands along her soft breasts, silky back, plump behind. "Don't leave me again." He dropped to his knees and kissed her between her legs, savoring her taste, kissing away the pain her ability caused her, the wedge it drove between them.

"I see you're busy," Max heard Lucien say behind Val. "Too bad. Next time."

He stopped kissing Val and turned his head in time to see Lucien swimming away with three other penguins. Max squinted at his back. Hadn't Lucien already swum by and said those exact words?

He looked up at Val—and saw her pregnant belly. He gasped—How? When? Was it his? Of course it was his. A miracle child—the product they'd been pushed together to create, something neither of them wanted. But it made him smile. He put a hand on her belly and stood.

"Is it a boy or a gir—" The smile wiped off his face when he looked at her and saw Abby, face a mask of fury as tears flowed down her face. *You bastard. You said you loved me.*

"I'm sorry, Abby. I'm so sorry." His voice choked up. "I didn't mean to hurt you. I don't know what I'm doing."

She grabbed his wrist with a strength he didn't know she was capable of. "Max, snap out of it," she said with Kitty's voice.

"I love you. I'm sure I do. I promise. You're perfect. Any normal man would want you. I don't deserve you—"

"*Stop it.* We need to get out of here."

The walls around him burst into flames. Max cried out as tendrils of fire licked the ceiling and radiated a heat that seared his hair and burned his eyes. He spun in circles but couldn't find the exit. Penguins gawked at him as the inferno closed in.

"Swim away!" he yelled at the stupid birds, but they didn't move.

He tried to run, but everywhere he turned, there was only fire. He dropped to his knees as smoke filled his lungs and skin peeled off his face. His flesh cooked on his bones. He began to scream.

Max felt a sharp pain behind his head, then nothing.

Chapter Twelve

Facing the foot of Sten's bed, Val lay on her stomach as she drew what she'd seen in her notebook. Margaret in the water again, a newly paved two-lane road nearby, a yield sign. The Space Needle across a body of water. Same stuff as her first vision. She tapped her pencil on the paper and sighed. Even if she managed to figure out where Margaret's body would wash up, it would bring her no closer to discovering Margaret's present location, where she was hopefully still alive. She needed to see *where* Margaret would be murdered or, better yet, who would murder her.

As Val took a sip from a beer can—Sten only had the cheap stuff, but it would do—she heard him scoff from behind her. She craned her head to look at him, kitty-cornered on the bed from her, sitting naked with his back propped against the headboard. His skin, naturally a shade darker than hers from whatever heritage he refused to talk about, glistened with a fine sheen of sweat. The lean muscles cutting across his fit body made up the same soldier physique she'd wanted to fuck all night back in her Army days. At least she could take comfort in the fact that she could do a lot worse than Sten—physically anyway.

He frowned at an issue of *The Economist* in his lap. "What the hell, Netanyahu?" he said to the magazine's glossy pages. "Ben-Gurion would've never misread the political landscape that badly." Sten tossed the magazine on the floor, then pulled a cigarette from a pack on his nightstand. With the flick of a cheap lighter, he fired it up and took a long drag. "Cracked the case yet, Colombo?" Smoke curled out his mouth and vanished into the ceiling.

He liked to smoke after sex; Val remembered that from her Army days. Had he known what her "low blood sugar issue" really was back then, but never said anything? He knew a lot of things he pretended to be ignorant about, she now realized.

Val pushed a bead of sweat out of her eye. She touched the beer can to her cheek; the metal was already warm. Damn. Air-conditioning wasn't high on Sten's list of priorities, apparently. "Do you know a guy named Ginger?" she asked him.

"Negative."

"What about a club called the Blue Serpent?"

He paused for a moment, like he considered how to answer her question. He did that a lot. "No."

"Are you lying?"

He chuckled. "What's there to lie about?"

She shook her head and finished the beer in one long gulp, letting the can drop to the ground. The buzz, and the sex, were a nice relief from the horrible day. All her days were horrible lately. "How can you live with yourself, being such a shitty cop?"

"That's *your* baseless opinion. Last year I won Gruff the Crime Dog's Seattle Public Protector of the Month award twice in a row."

Val pointed at her notebook. "This girl's been kidnapped. She and... other women have been raped, and you just sit there and do nothing."

"I'm helping you now, aren't I?"

That was sort of true. He'd obliged her midnight booty call, knowing full well she only used him for a vision she hoped would give her another angle to pursue in her investigation. Better Sten than alone, or with Stacey—she'd never again risk their friendship that way. Val despised Sten as a person, but he offered sex she could control, and he got her off every time. She preferred not to think about the psychological implications.

"Why *are* you helping me? Did Delilah or Northwalk order you to?"

He snickered. "Hell no."

"Then why?"

Sten put an arm behind his head and leaned back. He puffed on his cigarette in quiet contemplation for a few seconds, staring at his useless ceiling fan as it pushed warm air around. "Say you know the future—hypothetically speaking, bear with me—and you want to prevent something from happening. But once you've *seen* it happen, you can't change it because now it's your past and the past has already happened. Schrödinger's cat and all that."

Max had talked about something like that before. The fact that Sten and Max shared similar deep thoughts about the universe shocked her. There really were a lot of things she didn't know about her enemy-with-benefits. "Okay…"

"But—hold the phone!—there happens to be one person on the entire planet who, through a fluke of biology and maybe some divine intervention, or maybe the opposite of divine intervention, *can* change the future after it's been seen. Now you can manipulate that person to change the past for you."

"So you're saying you want me to change something about the future."

"No."

"Then what the hell are you talking about?"

He sighed like he dealt with an idiot child. "What I want is for you to always be available when I call."

She laughed. Was he kidding? She could never tell with him. "You mean you want me to drop everything and come to you whenever you feel like it?"

"Yes." He snuffed out his cigarette in an ashtray. "Do you want my help or not?"

"Will you help me take down Delilah and Northwalk?"

"I'd love to, but the timing's not right. Trust me, I've been working on that little project for a long time. You'll have to accept my many other skills."

Val held his gaze for a long moment, his dark eyes as enigmatic as ever. She tried to get a read on his true intentions. Sten would be a valuable ally. He had access to Delilah, knew more about the strange conspiracy involving Max and Val than they did, and had police resources at his disposal. On the other hand, he'd brutally murdered at least one person she knew of, might have killed her fiancée, tried to kill Val, and almost killed Max twice. She had absolutely no reason to trust him—other than desperation.

Val scoffed at his offer. "Fuck you."

Sten smiled. "I'll take that as a yes." He pushed himself to his knees and crawled to where she still lay on her stomach at the opposite corner of his bed. He ran his hands up the backs of her bare thighs. "Let's start now."

Val tried to slap him away, but as usual he ignored her physical threats. "I didn't say yes."

He lay on top of her with his chest against her back, his weight pinning her down. She felt his hard cock rub against her backside as he gripped her forearms.

"So say no," he said.

Sten wedged an arm underneath her chest and inched his hand down her belly until he'd reached between her legs. He slipped a couple of fingers into her and stroked her insides.

"You're...crazy," Val said, her breath strained from his weight on her back and the fire he stoked with his hand. "I can't agree to that."

"Then say no."

"I—" A moan escaped her lips before she could finish. Why did he have to be so good at this?

Val closed her eyes as desire overwhelmed her senses. Sweat prickled across her arms and trickled down her back from where her and Sten's bare skin pressed together.

"You wanna find that girl?" he whispered into her ear.

"Yes," she breathed.

"What's her name?"

"Margaret."

"Where was she last seen?"

"A…bar, called…the Pana Sea."

One hand still stroking her, he reached down her back with the other and slipped a finger between her cheeks, into her opposite end. Val gasped at the sensation, a strange pleasure she hadn't experienced in a long time.

"Imagine you're in the bar, the Pana Sea," he said. "Imagine you're with Margaret, having a drink."

She choked out a dry laugh. "You're…my therapist now?"

"I'm helping you. That's our deal. So concentrate."

Before she could point out she hadn't agreed to anything, she felt his manhood ease into her backside. Val yelped at the pressure, uncomfortable at first until her body relaxed and took him in. He moved in and out of her in slow thrusts while his hand stayed inside her, stroking her front in time with his hips. Jolts of electricity shot through her with each movement. She clutched his bedsheets and tried to catch her breath, her whole body on fire with pleasure and pain.

"You're in the bar with Margaret," Sten said.

"Uhhn…all right."

"You finish your drinks and leave the bar together."

"No," Val said, panting. "She…left with a man named… Ginger."

"She leaves with Ginger. You follow them. Where do they go?"

"I don't know."

"Yes you do." His thrusts picked up speed and strength. "Believe that you do. Picture it. Be there with them, and then look ahead. Where do they go?"

Val whimpered, the incredible sensation he rammed through her pushing away all rational thought. "I—I don't know."

"*Yes you do.*" He wrapped his free hand around her throat and dug his fingers into her neck, not to choke her but to give himself a good grip so he could move into her as much as possible. The whole bed rocked along with his deep, powerful strokes, into her front and back. "Come on, Val. *Look.* Follow them. Hear the tires screech as they peel out of the parking lot. Smell the car exhaust in the air when they drive away. Feel the warm breeze in your hair while they cruise down the highway. Where do they go?"

How did he expect her to concentrate on his words while he turned her inside out? Val could barely hear him over screams of ecstasy she couldn't control, filling his tiny studio apartment.

"Where does Margaret go?"

Val let out a final throaty, desperate wail as lightning seized her whole body and she came—

Margaret wears a hospital gown and walks in circles around a laboratory. She holds her arms straight out at her sides and takes large, exaggerated steps. Her mouth is seized in a manic grin, dark circles under her wide eyes.

"I'm on the moon!" she says as she does laps around a metal table. "I'm weightless on the moon. On the moon. On the moon."

"Excellent," Lucien says from where he stands in the corner, a white lab coat over his dress shirt. He writes something on a piece of paper attached to a clipboard. "Let's try another one."

Blur.

Margaret is strapped to a metal table. She struggles against bonds around her ankles and wrists while tears pour down her frantic face. Lucien stands over her, holding a syringe of bright red liquid. She looks away and sobs as he injects it into her neck. He drops the empty syringe on a metal tray and retrieves a crowbar from a lab bench.

"No, please," she begs. "Not again."

He touches the crowbar to the middle of her forearm as way of aiming, then lifts the bar straight up.

She writhes harder against her bonds. "NO!"

With no emotion, he says, "Tell me what you feel."

He swings the crowbar down as Margaret screams.

Blur.

"You said you'd help me," a tall redheaded man in a tuxedo says to Lucien as the Frenchman emerges from a dark room.

Lucien takes a moment to shut the door behind him. A cypher lock clicks into place, securing the room. He straightens out the tie on his own tuxedo, then turns on the redhead. "I told you to wait. We can't talk here."

"I've been waiting." The redhead lifts his chin and folds his arms, but his fingers pick nervously at his sleeves. "I did what you asked. I want what you promised. Now."

The bonging of what sounds like a massive grandfather clock interrupts their argument.

"Soon," Lucien says. He nods toward wherever the bonging came from. "After."

Blur.

Margaret, strapped to the metal table again. Now she wears a white cocktail dress, the one she'll be wearing when she washes up dead on the beach. Lucien stands over her with a syringe of blue liquid.

"Please let me go," Margaret says, her words slurred like she's already under the influence of another drug. "I won't tell anyone."

Lucien cocks his head and smiles. "They always say that. I wonder if it's ever worked."

He taps the syringe, then eases the needle into Margaret's neck. "Our time has unfortunately been cut short. Thank you for your assistance. I will remember you as the most helpful one so far."

Val opened her eyes and the scene evaporated. Sten came into focus, lying on his back next to her, head hung halfway off the side of the bed. He smoked a cigarette and stared at the ceiling.

Finally, she'd seen something useful. What in the world had Sten done to knock that piece of information loose? It's not like she'd never had great sex before—Max still held the top spot—but she'd never been able to focus a vision that well.

"Jesus, Sten," she said, still short of breath. She felt weak and wet all over, like she'd just stepped out of a hot shower after a brutal workout.

He exhaled a long column of smoke. "You're welcome."

"How the hell did you do that—"

Val's cell phone rang from inside her tote bag on Sten's sad kitchenette table. A phone call at one thirty in the morning usually wasn't the kind she wanted to ignore. With muscles like jelly, she pushed herself off the bed and retrieved her cell. Her eyes widened when Max's face popped up on her caller ID.

He was calling *her?* After how their last meeting ended? And why would he call at this time of night? Did he know where she was? He'd never forgive her if he found out, though he already hated her so it really didn't matter. Nor was it any of his business, even if he did know.

She glanced at Sten, still lying on his back as he enjoyed his cigarette. He'd closed his eyes, crossed his legs, and appeared uninterested in Val's phone call—which probably meant he would listen to every word. Fucking Sten.

Val turned away from him. Keeping her voice low, she answered the call. "Max?"

"Val?" Max said. Club music thumped in the background.

"Yeah."

"Is this Val?" His voice trembled as if he were on the verge of tears.

"What's wrong?" She'd only heard him this upset once before, when he'd confessed to killing his father in a fit of rage after years of abuse.

For a few seconds she only heard his labored breathing. Then he spoke again, "Help me."

She immediately began gathering up her clothes, which she'd tossed at the foot of Sten's bed. "Where are you?"

"I don't know. I was at a party, and then I was underwater, and then there was a house fire, and now there's flashing lights, and…uh…I dunno…" His words slurred and he trailed off.

She heard a thump, then rustling, as if his phone had dropped to the floor and been picked up again.

A gruff voice replaced Max's. "Your boyfriend's fucked up, honey. He's at the Green Door Nightclub. Come get his ass outta here." He hung up.

"Shit," Val muttered. She rushed to throw on her clothes.

"Leaving already?" Sten asked. "The night's still young. So many possible futures to see."

"Lucien Christophe's torturing Margaret in a lab somewhere," Val said as she pulled her jeans on. "Find a reason to go to his house or business or wherever he's keeping her and stop him."

"Is this Lucien guy rich and white, like his name suggests?"

"Yes."

"Then no."

Val scowled at him. "You're disgusting."

"Your fuck visions aren't *quite* enough for a warrant, especially against a guy who can afford a fleet of lawyers, sorry."

Val slipped on her sneakers and threw her hair, still moist with sweat, into a ponytail. She felt incredibly dirty—in more ways than one—but there was no time for a shower. "Fine. Just lie there and be incompetent. Why stop now, right?" She grabbed her tote and walked toward the door.

"Hey," Sten said with a sharpness that made her pause. He

rolled onto his side toward her and nodded at his cell phone on the nightstand. "Give me your phone number. Your real number, not the burner you called me with."

Val stared him down. She hadn't agreed to any deal with him, though she sort of *had* agreed. If she needed to have sex with someone for the purpose of saving people's lives, and wallow in some dirty pleasure to escape her shitty existence, it might as well be him. He did have a…special touch. She had no idea what he planned to ask of her later, but she knew she'd come to regret it. Too late now. She programmed her name and number into his phone, then let it drop next to his ashtray.

"I am *not* your on-call whore."

He belly-laughed. "Last time I checked, *you* were the one using *me* for sex."

Val scowled at him, but couldn't argue. *What's he using* me *for, then?* She hurried out the door before he could proffer any more embarrassing truths.

Chapter Thirteen

The Green Door Nightclub thumped with life. Black silhouettes gyrated around Val while wild rainbows lit up the ceiling and bathed half-naked dancers in suspended cages. Though Val wasn't exactly dressed for the occasion, the bouncer let her through after she explained she was there to fetch her "fucked-up boyfriend." Val pushed through the crowd until she reached a bar in the opposite corner. She flagged down the bartender.

"My friend's passed out somewhere," she yelled over the music. "Is there something like a drunk tank in here?"

"A what?" the bartender said, distracted by trio of intoxicated women screaming drink orders at him.

"Fucked. Up. Boyfriend."

He pointed to a spot on the second floor, underneath a neon collage of foul words. Val nodded her thanks, then weaved through clubbers to where he'd motioned. A couple of bouncers blocked her path, standing guard over a set of VIP tables overlooking the dance floor.

"Fucked-up boyfriend?" she said. They nodded to each other. Apparently "fucked-up boyfriend" was the code phrase for exclusive access in this place.

One of the bodyguards led her to a sectioned-off area with a half-moon couch, sandwiched on both ends by cages holding a topless man and woman, respectively, covered in body paint and writhing to the music. Max slouched in the middle of the couch, eyes closed and arms and legs splayed like he'd passed out there. She rushed to him and knelt at his side.

"Max?"

He didn't respond.

"*Max.*" When he still didn't move, she looked at the bodyguard. "How long has he been like this?"

The bodyguard shrugged.

"How did he get here?"

He shrugged again, then walked away. Val couldn't tell if he didn't know or wouldn't say; probably the latter.

Val patted Max's cheek. "Max, wake up."

His eyelids fluttered, then opened. She breathed a sigh of relief.

"Val?" he said weakly.

She smiled. "Yeah, it's me."

He lifted his head off the couch. A slow grin spread across his face. "I thought you were a dream."

"No, I'm—"

He slipped one hand behind her neck, pulled her to him, and kissed her. All at once the rest of the world fell away and there was only him, rough lips joined with hers, tongue sliding against hers. Heart on fire, she sucked in his hot breath like water into the cracked desert. It filled her lungs and diffused into her veins until she thought she might explode from want of him. She remembered they were meant to be together.

No, we're meant to have a child together—a child that will be stolen.

With all the mental strength she had, Val pulled away. "I can't," she said, still breathless from his kiss. No matter what she wanted, he wasn't in his right mind.

"Don't...don't..." His hand slipped off her neck and his head fell backward. "Don't leave me again, red raven," he muttered.

Val took a deep breath and gave her head a little shake, trying to push his incredible taste out of her mind. "Come on, let's get out of here." She threw his arm around her shoulders and urged him to stand.

He pushed himself up on wobbly legs and walked with her, unsteady but able to support his own weight, thank God. Slowly they pushed their way through the crush of clubbers toward the exit until Max froze in the middle of the club. He pointed at the ceiling.

"Fire!" Max grabbed Val's arm and tried to run back the way they'd come, but the thick crowd blocked his egress. They stumbled to the ground together. He sat upright, then put his head between his legs. Val kneeled next to him, a canopy of writhing bodies above them.

"They're all on fire," he said, voice trembling.

She pulled on his arm. "Max, get up. There's no fire."

He wouldn't budge. What the hell kind of drug was he on? Val put her hand on his head, ran a finger along the outside of his ear. He lifted his head and met her gaze with terrified eyes.

Val pressed her cheek to his. "Come with me, please. I won't leave you again." She nuzzled his earlobe, relishing the whiff she caught of his mountain spring shower gel. An image popped into her head of him wet and naked in the shower, lathering it on his neck.

Reluctantly she pulled away, the corner of her mouth brushing against his. Staring hard at her lips in the way he had that melted her from the inside, he finally allowed her to help him stand. Val swallowed back a nervous lump. She didn't think she could resist again if he kissed her. Before he could test her resolve once more, she grabbed his arm and pulled him to the exit.

They stumbled through the parking lot and reached her car without another freak-out. Unsure where to take him, Val decided on her place. She didn't know where he lived, or if he'd want Abigail to see him in this state; her guess was no. If she took him to the hospital, there'd be media attention for sure, especially when they realized who she was in relation to him. Val knew he wouldn't want that, either. Her place was as good as any until whatever he was on wore off. Then he could decide on his own where to go next.

On the ride to her house, Max clenched his eyes shut and mumbled nonsense to himself, sometimes in different foreign languages. About halfway through the drive, he pointed to a state lottery sign and rattled off a string of digits. Val almost laughed; she was sure he'd just given her the winning numbers. Too bad she'd never remember what he'd said. But how could he see that now, while awake, and not in the trance of a vision? Maybe he wasn't as awake as he seemed.

When she got home, Stacey's car was gone and the house was dark. Val's roommate probably decided to stay the night at one of her girlfriends' houses. Good—Val didn't want to explain what the hell was going on. She eased Max through the door and up the dark staircase to her bedroom. If she left him on the couch, he might try to run away again, or get sick and have no one to help him. She eased Max onto her bed, then unthreaded his sport coat from his arms and popped off his shoes. He rolled onto his stomach, an arm and a leg hanging off the side, and seemed to pass out once more.

He looked in a safe configuration, at least for the moment, so she took a quick shower, glad to finally wash Sten off her body. Feeling clean again, she stood naked in her bathroom doorway and toweled her hair dry, watching Max sleep. She almost wished he'd open his eyes and look at her, take in every part of her like the first time they'd made love. No matter how her body responded to Sten or anybody else, her heart belonged to Max. It would always belong to him. Just like *they* wanted.

Pushing back tears, Val pulled on pajamas and slipped into bed next to Max. She only half slept through the rest of the night, hyperaware of him just a few inches away, the urge to touch him nearly overwhelming. She dreamt of holding his hand and jumping off a cliff into a pool of turquoise water. They broke the surface, surrounded by a tropical paradise, and kissed. "I love you," he whispered against her lips. "I love you—"

As the first rays of dawn peeked through her window curtains, Val jolted awake when Max sat straight up in bed, gasping as if he were about to scream. He froze for a moment, then swiveled his head around until his bloodshot eyes settled on her.

"Val?" he said with significantly more lucidity than the night before, though he still seemed uncertain if he could believe his eyes.

"It's me."

He pawed at his clothes as if to assure himself they were still on. "Did—did we..."

"No," she said, trying—and failing—not to sound disappointed. Was *he* disappointed? She couldn't tell; he looked confused more than anything else.

"How did I get here?"

"I picked you up from the Green Door."

"The what?"

"The Green Door—a nightclub downtown. Weren't you there for a... bachelor party or something?"

"No." He rubbed the back of his head and winced. "*Ah*, goddamn. She must have knocked me out and taken me there."

"Who?"

"Kitty—I think. I don't know." He rubbed his eyes with the palms of his hands. "Can I have a drink of water, please?"

"Yeah, of course."

She walked down to the kitchen and poured a glass from the tap. Before she could bring it up to him, he appeared at the foot of the stairs, disheveled clothes hanging off his perfect body, dark circles set in his handsome face—the very definition of a hot mess. He looked around for a moment—he'd never been in her house, she realized—then walked to a bookshelf and picked up a framed picture of Robby, the only one she still displayed. Max stared at the picture of his half brother for a long time. Then he put it back, shuffled to the dining room table, and collapsed into a chair. She spread peanut butter on a piece of bread—a simple breakfast she knew he ate often—and placed the food and drink in front of him.

"Thank you," he muttered, eyes downcast. He took a long drink of water and a small bite of the bread.

Val sat across from him and folded her arms. "So?" she asked, as proxy for a million questions.

He swallowed, then said, "I went to a Blue Serpent party."

A million completely different questions flooded her mind. "I thought you weren't going to help me with that."

"Well, I did," he snapped. "I did it for you—I mean, *because you* told me someone was going to die if I didn't."

"I didn't mean for you to go alone—"

"You don't mean for a lot of things to happen, Val, but they happen anyway!"

Flinching, she looked away. He was right; she didn't mean to hurt him, but she kept doing it anyway. She should've stayed away from him. But…she couldn't. She'd tried, she really did. The thought of never seeing him again made her nauseous. She wished she weren't so selfish, but there it was.

When she looked at him again, she found him staring at her, the anger on his face replaced by what looked like shame at his outburst, and something else—desire. He still wanted her, despite himself…or did he? She felt her cheeks heat up as the inferno he kept within himself, the one he struggled to control, crept out of him and into her.

We could make love right here, right now, on the kitchen table, she thought, but before the fire could engulf them both, he looked away. He crossed his arms over his chest—the shield again—and took a deep breath.

"There were pills at the party," he said after a moment, staring at the floor. "Probably made by Lucien, though he denied it. He said the blue one 'created the dream,' which I think means it's a hallucinogenic of some sort, and the red one was supposed to be an aphrodisiac—"

"Wait—you just took some random party pills? With no idea what they were?"

He looked at her and frowned. "Yeah."

"You could have died."

"So?"

Val knew he'd been heavy into drugs at one point in his life, but popping mystery pills at a party thrown by a cult seemed reckless, even for him. Maybe his new life wasn't as fabulous as it seemed.

He sighed and relaxed a bit, then fingered the rim of his glass. "The blue one was great. I thought I was swimming in a grotto, and I could breathe underwater. Then you were there, and Abby, and Kitty. All of it felt so real; I have to tell myself it *wasn't* real, that's how convincing the hallucination was. The red one didn't work right with me. At least, I don't see how Lucien could sustain a customer base if his clients normally had hallucinations of fire and destruction. It was almost like I was seeing the aftermath of the nuclear explosion you described when…when you were with me."

His gaze flicked to hers for half a second before he looked away again, awkward silence falling between them. He was likely recalling memories of their intimate time together—as she was. His touch, his kiss, his laugh, his sarcasm, his nerdy references, his whispers in her ear…She wanted it all back. Val traced the contours of his sharp cheekbones with her eyes, almost crying with the bone-deep need to use her fingers instead and feel his warm skin—to feel *all* of him again.

Max took a deep breath and squeezed his eyes shut. When he opened them again, he looked at her with a cool, controlled gaze and continued. "I also started seeing things before they happened, like people walking by and saying things to me in exactly the same way twice, and you were pr—" He cut himself off, swallowing words he didn't want to get out for whatever reason. Maybe he'd seen a future version of her, but why wouldn't he give her details? "The point is, I think it triggered whatever gives us our visions. Some of it was a hallucination caused by the blue pill, but the red pill brought on what looked like flashes of future events, all in a random jumble. Like before I learned to see numbers instead. It was…disturbing. The best and worst trip I've ever had. It's also possible the drugs interfered with the—um, a different medication I take."

What other medication? she almost asked, but it wasn't any of her business. When she'd first met him, he'd been on all sorts of pills for depression, anxiety, migraines, and insomnia, thanks to his nightmare childhood. It'd been naïve of her to assume all it took was the love of a good, stable woman like Abigail to make those things go away.

"Are you okay?" She balled her hand in a fist to keep it from reaching out for his.

"I feel normal now—as normal as it gets for us." He gave her a tiny smile that quickly faded.

"Was Lucien there?"

Max nodded. "Also a bunch of escorts dressed as mermaids. That might've been how he got access to the missing woman you're looking for, if escorts are a regular fixture of the parties."

"You didn't see a laboratory anywhere, did you?"

"No, but I was out of it most of the time. He wanted to take me somewhere, but I was…uh…distracted. The house was a rental anyway. I doubt he'd keep kidnap victims there."

"He's going to do awful experiments on Margaret. We need to get to her before it happens."

He eyed her with a roil of emotions—anger, uncertainty, frustration…hope? She'd said *we*. Oops. "You saw that in a new vision?" he asked.

She nodded, but didn't offer any more details. He didn't need to know where the visions came from. Hopefully, he never would.

Max looked away and frowned, but said nothing. He closed his eyes and rubbed the bridge of his nose. "That's all I know about Blue Serpent. You got what you wanted. Can you take me home now?"

No, she still didn't have what she really wanted—to be free of Northwalk and Delilah, and wrapped in his arms again. The best she could do was get through the day.

Val threw on some regular clothes and drove Max to the luxury condo he shared with Abby, in the Lower Queen Anne district of Seattle. He told her to stop at a curb in front of a wrought iron gate, an intercom and keypad affixed to a pedestrian entrance. They sat in silence for a moment, neither meeting the other's gaze.

Val spoke first. "Thank you for helping me. You didn't have to, but you did. After what I did to you…I owe you one." She smiled. "I'm one of those people who owes you a favor. Good to have, right?"

He met her gaze and smiled back, a real smile, his warm hazel eyes with their emerald starbursts looking into her, in the old way. "You don't owe me anything."

She wanted to kiss him so badly her lips burned.

He cleared his throat. "Well, uh, Abby's probably wondering where the hell I am, and if Ginger made it back in one piece—"

"Did you say Ginger?" Val sat up in her seat. "A redheaded man named Ginger?"

"He's Abby's brother. That's his nickname. He was with me last night, but I have no idea where he went after I lost touch with reality."

"He's working with Lucien! He's also the last person that people saw Margaret with before she disappeared."

Max let out a long, exasperated sigh. "Shit."

"Take me to him. Now."

"No!"

"He knows where Margaret is."

"Are you sure?"

"Sure enough."

He scoffed. "You cannot rough up Abby's brother on a circumstantial connection. He's going to be my brother-in-law, for God's sake. Holidays will be awkward."

"He's about to become an accessory to murder, so what would you prefer?"

"Do you know *what* he's doing for Lucien?" Max asked.

"I didn't see that."

"So try the nonviolent approach first. Follow him, see where he goes and what he does when he's not bugging the shit out of Abby and me."

Val considered an old-fashioned stakeout. "You know him, you can tell me if he does something unusual. Come with me?" She bit her lip, then forced herself to stop before he could see her anxiety. She'd probably be fine without him, but...hell, she just needed to be near him, to see him in the flesh, smell him, talk with him, listen to him, laugh with him. Maybe their hands could brush together sometimes. Nothing sexual had to happen between them. But being with him recently, if only for a few short hours, made her realize if she couldn't be a part of his life in some way, she'd die. She almost felt dead already. Maybe he could bring her back to life.

After a long moment when he stared out the window, Max said, "Fine." He opened the car door and stepped out.

"When?" she called after him. "It has to be soon."

"I'll call you," he said, and shut the door.

Val watched him walk away and smiled. He'd thrown her a bone, thank God. She could go on living one more day.

Chapter Fourteen

Which do you prefer for the fourth appetizer at our reception: sweet Maryland crab cakes, or crab and lobster Louise salad?" Abby called to Max from the kitchen.

In the living room, Max didn't look up from the tablet he'd propped on top of Toby, the dog planted in his lap. "Do I need to have an opinion? It's your big day."

"But it's *our* wedding." She sighed. "It'd be nice if you at least pretended to care."

"I do care. I want the second one, the crab cakes."

"That was the first one."

"Yeah, that one."

He heard her sigh again and say something about the importance of communication in a relationship, but he wasn't listening. He tried another search for Lucien Christophe, this time in his old Carressa Industries files. Max frowned when only two documents popped up, both related to the old lab equipment company acquisition. Neither contained any mention of Lucien's residence or office address.

After calling in a favor from an old business associate with real estate connections, Max had discovered Lucien not only patronized but owned the Pana Sea, though other people managed it for him. More publicly available information about Lucien proved difficult to find. For a rich jet-setter, he kept a suspiciously low profile. Other than the Pana Sea, his name wasn't connected to any property in the United States, either as a renter or an owner. He didn't want people to find him. Val probably knew all this already.

Abby's cell phone rang; she answered it. Max glanced up when he heard Ginger's name.

"Yeah, okay. Hope you're not stuck there too long. See you tomorrow. Love ya." She hung up.

"Who was that?" Max asked, knowing full well it had been her brother.

"Eugene," she said. "His flight out of L.A.'s been delayed. He won't be able to make dinner tonight."

"Oh." Max queued up an Internet search for every flight out of LAX to Sea-Tac that night. None were delayed. He turned off the tablet and chewed his thumb for a moment, deep in thought.

He should let it go. So Ginger had lied about his flight. Didn't mean he was up to something nefarious…though he probably was. Max could just give Val the information and let her follow him alone, but he promised he'd go with her. Worse, he *wanted* to go with her. Be alone with her. When he'd woken up in her bed, a part of him wanted to believe they'd made love. He would never cheat on Abby, but he couldn't deny a craving for Val that continued to grow in his heart, like a blooming crystal cutting up everything around it. But the feeling would pass if he kept his distance. It *had* to pass. He'd barely gotten over her the first time. He couldn't do it again.

Max pushed Toby out of his lap and stood. He strolled up the stairs to their bedroom, quietly shut the door behind him. Then he took out his cell phone and called Val.

She answered on the first ring. "Hi."

"Where are you?"

"Right outside your house, stalking you. I've been lax on my crazy ex-girlfriend duties. Making up for lost time."

He rolled his eyes. "You're staking out the Pana Sea, aren't you?" If she was low on leads, he guessed the best way to track Lucien down was to wait for him to return to a location she knew he frequented—like the Pana Sea.

"Margaret's been missing for *twenty days*," she said, a new edge to her voice. "Besides her mother, I'm the only person looking for her. When I find Lucien, I'm going to cut off all his fingers, one by one, until he tells me where she is."

Max cringed. He knew she wasn't exaggerating. She must've seen some horrible things in her vision. He hoped someone had been there to comfort her, even if it couldn't be him.

He glanced at the door, huddled over his phone, and spoke in a hushed voice. "Ginger's supposed to be flying in from Los Angeles tonight. He was going to meet us for dinner at our place, but he just called to say his flight's delayed. I checked every flight he could possibly be on. They're all on time."

"So where is he really going?"

"Exactly. He gets in at six thirty tonight. I'm sure he'll take a taxi from the airport. You should follow it and see where he goes."

"Okay. Where should I pick you up?"

Max hesitated. Nothing good could come of this. He should *really* say no. Pacing in a circle, he ran a hand through his hair and pressed his lips together. *Say no, Max.*

"Outside Wicked Brew," he spat out. Shit, he couldn't say no. He'd already promised he would help her. He couldn't back out now. He'd allow himself to see her one last time, get his fix of her, then go cold turkey and get her out of his system. After this, he was done. "But I need to be back by eight, at the latest. I mean it."

She laughed. "Don't worry, Cinderella. I'll get you back before the clock strikes eight."

"See you in twenty minutes." He hung up, sure he was making a mistake. At least if he was with Val, he could stop her from maiming Lucien or Ginger. Maybe.

***

Parked at the airport's departures curb in Val's car, they caught Ginger leaving the terminal of his on-time flight. With an unusually determined spring in his step, he hopped into a cab. Max and Val were quiet as she concentrated on following the taxi from a distance that wouldn't arouse suspicion, though Max doubted Ginger was aware of his surroundings enough to notice a tail in any circumstance.

When the cab pulled up to the Pana Sea, Val hissed, "*Motherfucker*," with a malice that made him wince. He'd never seen her with so much barely contained rage before, not even toward Norman and Delilah Barrister. For Ginger's sake, Max hoped Abby's brother was a mere patsy in Margaret's kidnapping. God help him if he wasn't.

Only three minutes later Ginger emerged from the bar holding a plain cardboard box about six inches square. He jumped back into the cab, and it pulled away.

Val gave the cab a ten-second head start, then followed. "He usually do courier work?" she asked Max.

"I don't think so. I've never known him to do *any* work, honestly."

"He and Lucien spend time together?"

"Not that I know of. But I'm not his keeper. I don't know what he does all the time."

"How about...Michael Stevenson?"

"Nah, Stevenson's too much of a snob to be seen with Ginger. Why're you asking about Michael?"

Val shrugged. She was quiet after that. He didn't press. If it was important, she'd tell him. For close to an hour they followed the cab through rush-hour traffic to a seedier part of town, where it stopped in front of a rundown redneck bar called Billy's Roadhouse. Ginger got out, cardboard box in hand. He took a few steps toward the entrance, then stopped when someone called out to him from the adjacent parking lot. A thin, balding man wearing a pair of blue coveralls hustled over to Ginger. The two shared a quick fist-bump.

"Know that guy?" Val asked.

"No."

The thin man admired Ginger's box, then they disappeared

into the bar together. Val opened her car door to follow them inside.

Max grabbed her arm, and something that felt like electricity passed between them at the touch of her skin, just like when she'd touched him during their first meeting at Wicked Brew. She looked at him with her storm cloud–colored eyes, face framed by her gorgeous red hair cascading down the shoulders of the leather jacket she wore, and he forgot what he was going to say. Then it came back to him.

"Don't," he said as he forced himself to let go of her arm, to stop touching her. "Ginger will recognize me."

"He won't recognize *me*."

"No, but you can't go in there alone. Wait until he comes out. Then we'll follow him again. The cab's still waiting for him. He won't be in there long."

Val huffed in protest but shut the door. She drummed her fingers on the steering wheel and stared at the bar's entrance, while he tried to stop thinking of excuses to touch her again. After a couple of minutes of silence passed between them, she asked, "Have you heard of a company called Asclepius Incorporated?"

"No. Why?"

Val grabbed her tote from the backseat, pulled a manila folder stuffed with papers out of it, then dropped the folder on his lap. "It's a company I think Lucien might have used to rent a house for a recent Blue Serpent party. I did some digging, and the only address listed for the company just happens to be where the Pana Sea is."

Max picked through Val's case file, filled with newspaper articles, website printouts, and handwritten notes. "Asclepius is the Greek god of medicine."

"Okay?"

"The Pana Sea…pretty close to *panacea*, now that I think about it. A remedy for all diseases."

"So they're obviously connected, then. They've got to be. Lucien owns the Pana Sea, you know."

"I know."

She frowned at him. "You knew before or after I asked you about it the first time?"

He returned her frown. "After. If I'd known, I would've told you. I only found out today, after making some phone calls."

Her frown turned into a smile. "You looked into it for me. You didn't have to. Thanks."

"I know I didn't have to," he said a little too defensively. Max looked away so she couldn't see the frustration in his eyes. Logically, he wasn't obligated to do anything for her, but he always did anyway. He had no goddamn willpower when it came to her. After he took a slow, measured breath, he said, "I figured you'd find out anyway. I was curious."

"Oh. Sure." Val resumed drumming her fingers on the steering wheel. A minute of awkward silence later, she seemed to remember something and began riffling through the folder in Max's lap. He froze while she dug so close to…well, between his legs. Oh God, he felt himself growing. Son of a bitch, she still did it to him, and with embarrassing ease.

She held a grainy printout of an old photograph up for him to see. "Who does the guy in the back look like to you?"

"Um…" Swallowing hard, he took the photo at the same

time he subtly pushed the papers closer to his stomach, hopefully hiding his erection. "Which one?"

"Him." She pointed at a figure in the third row of an old-timey black-and-white faculty photo. A placard on the bottom read, "*Université de Montpellier*, 1931." The man in question had an unmistakable hawk nose and the sharp cheekbones of an aristocrat. A Christophe.

"A distant relative of Lucien's?" Max asked.

"I found it while looking for any possible relatives he might still have in France. That guy is Gérald Gahariet. I figured if Lucien got a medical degree in his home country, like most people do, then maybe he went to a university his parents or grandparents attended, which isn't uncommon. When I saw this picture, I assumed that man was a distant relative of Lucien's. Thing is, Gérald didn't have any children, or siblings. He fell off the grid somewhere around 1953. No death certificate."

Max raised an eyebrow. "Are you saying you think this *is* Lucien?"

She threw up her hands. "Fuck, I don't know. He makes weird drugs that do weird things. Maybe he found one for immortality."

"That's a stretch..."

"He's also got a drug that can completely wipe a person's memory for at least twelve hours with no dizziness or side effects, something I know doesn't exist in modern medicine. And I saw him doing awful Nazi-type experiments on Margaret. If he's been at it for more than half a century, maybe he did stumble on something that extended his life." She gritted her teeth, then sighed. "It's crazy. I'm crazy. I don't know. Forget it."

Val grabbed the folder out of his lap and tossed it in the backseat. She fell silent and went back to staring at the bar.

He didn't think she was crazy, but definitely stressed. Max snuck a good look at her. She was still beautiful, but she also looked tired. Unnatural lines creased her face, her cheeks and lips a shade paler than normal. The aged jeans she wore looked looser than he remembered, as if she'd lost weight. Her eyes harbored a sadness that hadn't been there before.

"We'll find Margaret," he said to her. "If there's any chance she's alive, we'll find her."

We—he hadn't meant to use the plural. It'd been a Freudian slip. She'd done the same thing at her house, the morning after the Blue Serpent party: *We need to get to Margaret before Lucien kills her.* They were in this together now, whether he liked it or not. As long as Ginger remained somehow involved in the woman's disappearance, he couldn't back out. Max had to shield Abby from whatever her idiot brother was up to. And Val needed support. The case was obviously wearing on her. He knew her in a way no one else did. He wanted to be there for her—as much as he could, anyway, without crossing the line.

She met his gaze. A slow smile spread across her face as if she took in all the meanings of what he'd said. Her cheeks flushed, and she closed her eyes and leaned her head against the driver's side window. In a flash he saw her lying naked in his arms, felt the warm skin of her neck against his lips, her soft breast in one hand while he stroked her hair with the other—

Max forced himself to look away and push the image out of his mind. Sweat broke out all over his body. He rolled down the window to get some air flowing, yanked up the arms on his long-sleeved shirt, and wiped his wet hands on his jeans. Goddammit, this closeness was killing him. He'd accepted it was over and moved on from their relationship, even though doing so had nearly destroyed him. His plan to see her once more and get her out of his system was backfiring. With every second he spent in her presence, he felt the connection that bonded them together strengthening, his desire for her growing. And it would only get worse.

"Where's my invitation to the wedding?" she asked, a slight grin still on her face.

That's right—he was getting married to another woman in two months. Shit. Max wiped sweat from his brow that'd gathered underneath his baseball cap. "It's in the mail."

"Liars go to Hell, Max."

He let out a wry laugh. "You really wanna hang out with four hundred of Abby's closest friends and relatives?"

"No, but I want to eat free fancy food. Wow, four hundred on her side? For real?"

"A big chunk of that number are her father's business associates. Why pass up an opportunity to make more money just because it's your daughter's wedding?" Fucking greedy bastard. Patrick Westford reminded Max too much of his own father—Lester, not Dean. Luckily Max wasn't marrying Patrick, and didn't intend to spend any more time with the man than absolutely necessary, despite Abby's desire for the two to become besties.

A hint of a frown played across Val's lips as she seemed to consider his words, and what he actually meant by them. Val could accurately guess what he was thinking. She knew him better than anyone. "How many total?" she asked.

"Four hundred and three, plus or minus two."

"Come on." She gave his arm a playful slap. There was that electricity again. *Ignore it, Max.* "Who'd you invite?"

He puffed out a breath of air. "Let's see: Michael Beauford, the CFO of Carressa Industries—you've met him before—and Juanita, my father's longtime housekeeper, and...Yeah, that's it."

"What about all your new charity circuit pals?"

"They're Abby's friends, not mine. I can't stand most of them. Bunch of boring blowhards."

Val laughed. "Oh, Max. Still as antisocial as ever."

He cracked a smile. "I can't help that nobody likes me." His smile fell into a frown. "I thought about inviting Josephine, but decided that would be weird."

Val lifted her head off the glass. "Does she know?"

He shook his head. "I don't think she ever will. She won't talk to me."

"Do you want me to talk to her? I could—"

"*No*. It's...better this way." He wasn't sure it really was better, but it was what it was.

They were quiet once more, until Val slapped his arm again. "Tell her in code. Send her a series of puzzles of increasing difficulty that spell out 'I am your brother' in Latin. As your sister, she'll be helpless to resist trying to solve them."

He snickered. "Or I could rent a biplane and write it in the sky with smoke."

"Or hire a singing telegram lady."

"Announce it on the Jumbotron at a Mariners' game."

"Perfect solution—rent out time on a cable access channel,

hire a professional choreographer, and have dancers perform 'The Secret Connection between Maxwell Carressa and Josephine Price' in interpretive dance."

They belly-laughed together until they ran out of breath. "I think that's the worst idea I've ever heard, for anything," Max said, wiping tears from his eyes. Damn, it felt good to have a real laugh with someone. He could do this all day…they *could* do this all day, if Val wanted to…No. She didn't want to be with him. She'd made that clear. His usual frown settled back into place and he stared out the window, striving to look at anything that wasn't her.

"Max," she said, and he glanced at her again. She gazed at him with wide, wet eyes, her lips parted, breath shallow.

"Yeah?" His heart leapt into his throat. *She's going to tell me she loves me. She's going to ask me to not marry Abby. And I'm going to…I'm going to…Jesus, I'm going to say okay—*

A burst of cackling laughter broke the spell between them. Val sat up in her seat, her attention snapped back to the bar.

"*Son of a bitch,*" she said. Ginger had just emerged, alone and without the package. He waved at somebody still in the bar behind him, then got back in the cab. When it began to pull away, Val didn't start her car.

"Aren't you going to follow him?" Max asked, knowing he was about to get an answer he wouldn't like.

"I wanna know what's in that box." She opened her car door and stepped out.

"Wait. It's too dan—"

She slammed the door and stalked toward the bar.

"Shit," he muttered. Pulling down the sleeves of his shirt so no one would see his tattoos, he jumped out and hurried to catch up.

They walked into a moderately busy bar, air thick with the smell of stale cigarette smoke that permanently infused every surface despite a decade of smoking bans. It was dark enough that Max guessed at least half the overhead lights didn't work. County music twanged from a cracked jukebox in the corner. Most of the blue collar crowd turned to stare at them. Max lowered the bill of his baseball cap over his face as far as it would go and prayed no one recognized him, though the crowd seemed more interested in the beautiful redhead in front of him. Instinctively he moved closer to her, so his chest almost touched her back—a protective gesture he knew she didn't need, but he couldn't help himself.

Val, of course, didn't bother trying to keep a low profile. She marched through the bar and studied every face, looking for the thin man in coveralls, ignoring the angry or lascivious stares she got in return. When it became obvious the thin man wasn't in the main bar area, she headed for the men's bathroom.

"Val, let me—"

She shoved the bathroom door open. Max rolled his eyes and followed her in. A guy peeing at a urinal jumped when he saw her, jerked his pants up, and shoved past them in his haste to get away from whatever was about to go down. Val peeked under each stall in turn, then settled in front of one for handicapped people. With a swift kick she busted the stall door open.

"What the fuck?" the stall's occupant hollered.

Over Val's shoulder, Max saw Ginger's friend sitting backward on the toilet, fully clothed and hunched over the toilet tank lid. The man turned to face Val, white power and an angry snarl on his face. The name "Cal" was embroidered on the chest pocket of his coveralls. Ginger's mystery box sat opened on the toilet tank's lid, next to a palm-sized mirror with lines of the same white powder on it.

Val folded her arms and glared at Cal. "Why did Ginger bring you drugs?"

"Fuck off, bitch," Cal said as he used the back of his hand to wipe his runny nose.

"I can fuck off down to the police station if you'd like, and tell them you've got a shit-ton of coke on you right now. Want that instead?"

Cal rushed to pack up his box with unsteady hands. "You can't do shit."

"I can, actually. And I will. Unless you want to tell me why Ginger brought you drugs he got from the Pana Sea, which just happens to be owned by Lucien Christophe, narcotics-maker extraordinaire."

"Lucien who?" Cal narrowed his eyes at her for a moment as if he was trying to recall something, then recognition creeped onto his face. His mouth curled into a sneer. "Oh *yeah*, I remember you. *Red delicious*."

Max had no idea what Cal referred to, but mention of the apple seemed to flip a kill switch inside Val. She descended on him with the viciousness of a wild animal, punching him in the face until he tumbled onto the ground, then kicking him in the chest as he lay prone at the foot of the toilet, all before Max could even register what was happening.

"Fuck you, you piece of shit!" Val shrieked.

Jesus, she might actually kill him. "Stop!" Max tried to grab her arm, but she violently shrugged him off. As Cal writhed on the ground, she grabbed his box of drugs and spiked it into the toilet.

Cal cried, "No!" as what Max guessed was several thousand dollars' worth of coke sank into the toilet water. Energized with a new fury of his own, Cal jumped up and shoved Val against the side of the stall. As he brought his arm back to slug her, Max stepped between him and Val, grabbed Cal's fist with one hand, and punched him in the stomach with the other. Cal crumpled to the ground.

With a roar, Val tried to lunge past Max to get at Cal again. Max grabbed her in a bear hug and dragged her out of the stall as she fought against him.

"I'll show you what public humiliation feels like," she yelled at Cal as she struggled to free herself from Max's grasp. "You can tell your friends this bitch beat the shit out of you!"

"Let the lady go!" a gruff voice demanded behind Max.

Two meaty hands grabbed Max's shoulders and yanked him from behind. Val fell out of his arms as he stumbled backward until he hit the bathroom wall. A big redneck dressed like a lumberjack reared back his fist. Luckily for Max, boxing happened to be his sport of choice, and he easily dodged the redneck's punch; it slammed into the brick-and-mortar wall instead. Max followed up with his own punch to the man's nose, if only to incapacitate the guy for a short time. Blood poured from the lumberjack's nostrils. From the corner of his eye, Max saw Val reach behind her. She was going for her gun.

He wheeled around and seized her arm in an iron grip. "*No.*" A bar brawl was one thing; a shoot-out quite another. He knew what it was to fight a murder charge. Her life—and her conscience—didn't need the grief.

Moaning, Cal crawled out of the stall on his hands and knees. She glared at him like she might kick him to death anyway. Then her eyes met Max's, and he saw hatred in them, rimmed with tears of agony. The pain written on her face filled him with an almost physical torture to match, and he thought he might kill Cal himself for whatever the bastard had done to her.

An older man with a dishtowel thrown over his shoulder burst into the bathroom. "What the *hell* is going on in here?"

"He attacked me," Cal wheezed, nodding his bloodied head toward Max.

The older man—probably the owner—scoffed. "Y'all get the fuck outta here," he said to all four of them. "Now."

Max released his grip on Val. After a tense couple of seconds, she let her hand fall away from her gun and stomped out of the bathroom. Max followed close behind. When they walked back outside, he breathed a deep sigh of relief that things didn't go as badly as they'd come very, very close to going. Val leaned forward with her hands on her knees like she might throw up.

The redneck came out next, holding a wad of paper towels to his bloodied nose. He glanced at Max as if he might want to continue their fight, but after eyeing Val and apparently realizing they were together, he shrugged and sulked away instead. Finally, Cal came barreling out, spry again despite the beating he'd received, probably thanks to the drugs.

He pointed a grimy finger at Val. "You owe me—"

Max grabbed the lapels of his coveralls and shoved him hard to the ground. "Get out of here before I kill you."

Cal scrambled to his feet and stumbled away from them, toward the parking lot next to the bar. "Yeah, right. You wouldn't…"

"I would." Max stalked after Cal, ensuring a good distance separated him from Val.

"I know you," Cal said, shit-talking Max even as he retreated. "You're that rich asshole that got away with killing his father. *Carressa.* That's you, right? Well I'm gonna sue you for assault. And I'm gonna tell everyone that you threatened to kill me. Once a killer, always a killer."

Max gritted his teeth and balled his hands into fists. He really did want to kill this guy; in a consequence-free world, maybe he would have. After everything he'd done trying to become a functional member of society, this human stain would destroy it all, not to mention whatever he'd done to Val.

Cal fumbled for his keys and unlocked the door to some piece of crap sedan. He jumped into his car as Val appeared next to Max. Max glanced at her; she gave Cal a disgusted look but wasn't holding her gun, thank God. Cal pushed down the manual lock on his car door and sneered at them.

"I'm gonna sue you for every penny you have!" Cal said behind the driver's side window, "and your whore girlfriend, too!" He flipped them the bird.

Then he began to cough like he had something stuck in his throat. Within seconds his coughs became hacks, then desperate rasps as he struggled to breathe. He clawed at his throat, rasps turning to gurgles as blood leaked out his mouth and nose. His whole body convulsed, then his eyes rolled back in his head and he went still.

After a moment when neither of them moved, Max stepped forward and peered into the window, looking for any signs of life. He tapped his fingernail on the glass. Cal stayed motionless, his face covered in blood and mouth locked in a silent scream.

From behind Max, Val asked, "Is he dead?"

"I think so."

"How?" She walked next to him and scanned the inside of the car through the windows. "I don't see any gas. Maybe the drugs—"

"We gotta go."

For once she didn't argue, and they rushed back to her car and drove away before anyone could see them in the vicinity of Cal's body. They drove in silence for a while, until the initial shock of Cal's bizarre death wore off.

Finally, Max asked, "Are you going to tell me what that was about?"

Val let out a long sigh. "Margaret was raped when she was abducted. That asshole had something to do with it."

"How do you know?"

"I found a video of it online."

Max winced. Poor woman. "He was in the video?"

"No."

"So how did his mention of apples tip you off?"

"What?"

"Red delicious."

Her whole body tensed. "He...I...It's nothing."

"You almost killed him over it, so it obviously wasn't nothing."

Val shook her head and wouldn't say any more. Max folded his arms and quietly seethed for the rest of the ride back to where he'd parked his car at Wicked Brew. She was shutting him out. Again. He should've expected as much. She'd cut him out of her life once before. It'd been stupid of him to think she'd let him back in. He should've listened to the rational part of his brain and kept his distance. If Val wanted to suffer in silence, then that was her choice.

She pulled up to the sidewalk at Wicked Brew and put her car in Park. "I'm sorry I got you into this," she said without looking at him. "I shouldn't have asked you for help. I was"—she shook her head—"desperate and not thinking straight. I won't bother you again."

"You do not get to unilaterally decide if I'm involved," he said, gripped by a sudden fury. "It's too late. You want to keep secrets from me? Fine. I don't care. I'm not your boyfriend anymore. But I just saw a guy spontaneously choke to death on his own blood, right after we had a loud fight with him in a bar where at least one of those rednecks probably recognized me, and I'll likely get questioned by the police about it tomorrow morning and I don't know what the fuck I'm going to say. So *no*, I can't pretend this never happened, even if I wanted to. But thanks for considering the consequences, now that it's too late."

Max got out and slammed the door behind him. He marched to his car, the only one still in the lot, and drove home imagining all the things he should've added to his tirade: You *broke up with* me, *yet you expect me to do your bidding while you keep me in the dark? You know everything about me—things that could send me to jail for the rest of my life if you wanted—so why don't you trust me? Am I just a resource to you? A rich plaything you think you can manipulate anytime you want? You're willing to put your life on the line to find this woman you've never met before, but you wouldn't fight for us? Our relationship wasn't worth it? Did you ever feel anything more than lust for me? You were the* only *thing I cared about in my entire miserable life and you walked away. You just walked away…*

Max pulled into his carport, turned the car off, and rested his head on the steering wheel. He took deep breaths and tried to calm himself. He was overreacting, letting the whole bizarre situation dig up grievances he'd buried—and he hadn't taken his OxyContin pills in a while, further souring his mood. Max fished the bottle out of his pocket and tossed a couple in his mouth. He needed to get a grip on the present and let the past go. All he had was his future—with Abby. There was nothing else.

Suddenly exhausted, Max trudged up the back stairs and entered his dark condo from the door connecting to the kitchen hallway. Toby's collar jingled at his feet. Max knelt and scratched Toby behind the ears.

"You've hit your affection quota for the day." He winced when the dog licked his face.

Abby's voice reached him from the living room. "Finally back, huh?"

Max rose and walked through the kitchen. He found her curled up on the couch, reading a magazine under the soft glow of an end table lamp.

"Yeah, uh..." He took off his baseball cap and ran a hand through his hair. "I didn't miss dinner, did I?"

"It's ten o'clock, Max."

"Shit, I'm sorry."

He hoped this would be one of those times she'd laugh off his bad behavior, knowing he meant well, like she usually did. She didn't.

Abby put her magazine down and stood up. "Where were you?"

He hated lying to her, even though he knew she wouldn't like the truth. How was he any better than Val if he did? "I was helping Val with her case."

Abby's eyes narrowed a fraction. "I thought she needed money."

"She needed someone *with* money, to give her access to an exclusive club. A woman's missing, and...well, I can't just do nothing."

"Is that blood on your shirt?"

He looked down and saw crimson splotches from the redneck's nose on his chest. "We were in a fight with someone who might have had information on the missing woman. It's not as bad as it looks." *Except for the dead man in the car that'll be discovered any minute.*

"A *fight?* Why are you helping her if she's putting you in danger? Just file a missing persons report with the police and be done with it!"

"It's not that simple."

"Then explain it to me. Explain to me why you have to be the one to help her."

He didn't want to lie, but he couldn't tell her that her brother was likely involved in the rape and possible murder of a woman. Or that he'd just seen a man inexplicably drown in his own blood. Or that he and Val were connected like no other two people on earth. Or that he loved Abby, but…if Val died, he would die, too. Or that, in a moment of weakness, he'd been a heartbeat away from leaving her for Val. So instead of lying he said nothing, just gaped at her like an idiot and hoped she'd accept his silence—exactly what Val had done to him in the car.

Abby reacted as well as he had, though sadness overlaid her anger. With tears in her eyes, she walked away from him and up the stairs. He heard the door to their room shut, not with a slam but with a dull, definitive thud. Max walked to the kitchen and poured himself a glass of water in the dark. He took his migraine medication bottle out of his pocket and swallowed another dose of OxyContin. He chased it down with the water, then went back to the living room, clicked off the light, lay down on the couch. Toby tried to lie on his chest; Max pushed him off. The dog settled between his legs instead. It was still warm where Abby had sat up waiting for him, the perfect woman he was going to marry in two months. He was surrounded by everything he'd ever wanted, before he met Val, and he'd never felt so empty.

Chapter Fifteen

Val sat in her car behind a shuttered gas station, out of view of the main road. She sipped from a bottle of lemon-flavored vodka she'd bought right after dropping Max off at the coffee shop, and waited. She had washed Cal's blood off her hands in the liquor store bathroom, but her knuckles still throbbed.

God, she was losing her fucking mind.

She didn't even know what Cal had to do with her rape. Maybe he'd only watched the video online before Rayvit took it down three days ago. He didn't match Stacey's description of her attackers; none were bald. But when he'd slurred "red delicious" at her with no remorse or shame whatsoever, she'd lost it. She would have killed him if Max hadn't stopped her.

And now Max knew she wasn't telling him the whole story. But how would she explain it to him? She didn't want his pity; getting it from Stacey was bad enough. Nor did she want to mess up his nice life—any more than she already had anyway. He didn't deserve to be burdened with her personal problems, too. She didn't know how he'd react, but she did know he had killed someone in a fit of rage once before—assuming he still cared that much about her, which of course he didn't. He had Abby. And she had no one.

She'd almost told him she loved him. He probably would've laughed in her face. There was no way he'd leave someone as perfect as Abigail Westford for messed-up, self-destructive Val, no matter their connection. Especially not after the shit she kept putting him through. Even though he had a dark side, at his core Max was a kind and decent man, often pushed to extremes by people who took advantage of him—people like Val. She deserved every biting word he threw at her.

Inside Val's coat pocket, her phone pinged with a text message. Checking it, she saw it was from Stacey: *Where r u? Need to give status to clients*... Val turned her phone off and tossed it in the backseat. Her friend could handle the other clients on her own, and Margaret's was the only life-or-death case they had. Val needed to give it her full attention. And she wasn't in the mood for Stacey's judgment or pity. She didn't want to talk about her feelings; she wanted them to go the fuck away.

Headlights appeared in her rearview mirror. A sedan pulled up next to her. The engine died, then Sten got out of his car and slipped into Val's.

"You rang?" He glanced at the bottle of vodka in her hand. "Fun's already started, I see."

She took another swig of alcohol. "There's a dead man in a car outside of a bar called Billy's Roadhouse in Lakewood. He...drowned in his own blood, I think. Something like that. I'm not really sure."

"Huh," Sten replied with mild curiosity. "Another unfortunate friend of yours?"

"I don't know who he is. His coveralls said 'Cal.' He was snorting what looked like coke, and I think that might've killed him. You ever heard of a drug that makes your face and throat hemorrhage blood?"

"Nah, but you know kids these days—huffing paint and shoving horse tranquilizers up their asses. A little face melting wouldn't stand in the way of a good high."

"Yeah, well, I'm pretty sure the drugs originated from Lucien Christophe, the man you refuse to investigate because he's rich and white. So not only is he kidnapping women, he's distributing deadly drugs. That enough for you to care yet?"

"Getting warmer. Depends on what we find at the crime scene."

Val sighed. Of course he still didn't care. "Max and I got in a brawl with this guy a few minutes before he died. We didn't kill him, but when someone finds his body, I'm sure people from the bar will mention the fight. They might ID us. Can you throw the police off our trail?"

Sten lifted an eyebrow. "You want me to interfere with a murder investigation?" He leaned back in his seat and threaded his fingers behind his neck. "Can do. Anything else?"

"Yeah. I want to make a missing persons report."

"For who—Margaret Ann Monroe, also known as Celine for a good time?"

She hadn't told him Margaret's full name, or her escort pseudonym. "How did you know—"

"When I was shagging you last, you gave me enough details to follow up, so I did. You wanted my help, didn't you?"

Val scoffed. "So it only took me having sex with you for you to give a shit?"

"Missing prostitutes do fall into my job jar. I've added her name to the three dozen already in the queue."

"Do you know a guy named Ginger was the last person seen with her, at the Pana Sea, which Lucien Christophe happens to own?"

"Yes, and Mr. Eugene Westford swears he had sexual relations with her in his car before dropping her off at a party, which she later left by herself. Multiple people corroborate his story."

Val let her head fall back into the headrest. "Fuck." She took a long drink. Even with police resources, Margaret's trail had gone cold. And Sten had been unperturbed by her mention of Max. He already knew everything she did, probably more. Val was one step behind.

"Adults are allowed to disappear," he said. "That's the great thing about being an adult. That and voting."

She glared at him, clenching her teeth so hard she thought she might break her jaw.

He shrugged at her barely contained rage. "Without any clear evidence of foul play, there's nothing we can do. Sorry, that's how the justice system works. If you don't like it, take it up with your Congressman."

"I saw Lucien kill her! Her body's going to wash up on a beach any day now."

"Ah, but not everything you see comes true, correct?"

He was right; rational, even. A rarity for Sten. It was possible she'd seen a future that wouldn't come true. At this point, all she could do was hope for Margaret's safe return—and fight for justice.

"I also want to report a rape," Val said.

"Margaret again?"

"Yes." She took a deep breath and closed her eyes. "And mine."

She expected him to laugh at her, to roll his eyes and throw out some smart-ass quip about regretful sex or how prostitutes couldn't be raped. When he said nothing, she glanced at him. He studied her face, maybe trying to gauge her sincerity, though his own face remained unreadable.

"When?"

"Mine happened the night you came to my house." Val's voice trembled, but she forced herself to spit it out. She had nothing to lose. "I'm not sure when it happened to Margaret. Probably the night she left the Pana Sea with Ginger, after he supposedly dropped her off at a totally innocent party."

"Who?"

"Three for me; two for Margaret. I tracked one of my attackers down—Michael Stevenson. I don't know who the others were. I was drugged and don't remember. Another fucking weird drug, probably courtesy of Lucien. The same thing happened to Margaret. I only know the attacks happened because I found videos of them online. Probably got millions of fucking hits." She paused to take another long drink. The bottle shook in her hand. "The dead guy at the bar knew something about my video, and then he mysteriously died. Since there are no such things as coincidences for people like me, he must be involved.

So... So, I want to make a report, and have a police officer investigate, because I've been doing a shit job of it myself."

Sten stared at her, face still a passive mask. His eyes lacked their usual smarm, however. He almost looked serious. "Don't make a report."

"Are you fucking kidding me?" Val yelled at him. "I should keep my mouth shut so horrible people can keep doing horrible things? Roll over and accept that life is a soul-sucking death march from one trauma to the next? That we're all just *things* to be manipulated and coerced and used and—"

"I'll take care of it."

She gave him a mirthless laugh. "You? Really?"

"That's our deal."

"How?"

He picked up the metal cap from the center cup holder and screwed it back onto the liquor bottle she still clutched in her hand. "By doing what I do best."

"Being an asshole?"

He smiled. "Yes."

She didn't know what he meant to do; likely the usual—nothing. Val rubbed her eyes, swiping away tears that gathered as the world tried to crush her. "What do you want from me, Sten?"

"I already told you—be available when I call."

She scoffed and tossed the vodka bottle into the backseat. "Whatever you *really* want, just take it. Take it all. Take everything." He might as well. She was a shit PI and a shit girlfriend, with a shit ability to see shit futures.

Sten folded his arms and drummed his fingers on his biceps.

No smirk, no eye roll, no smart-ass reply. Not amused to be the audience to her meltdown. "Anything else?"

They were alone in the dark together, the only light from a streetlamp on the other side of the gas station. They might as well have been the last two people on earth. Val reached into his coat pocket and retrieved his wallet; he didn't stop her. She flipped it open and pulled out a fresh condom. He watched in silence as she shimmied off her jeans and underwear, then straddled him. She unzipped his pants. Already hard, she slipped the condom on. His hands cupped the flesh of her behind as she slid him into her.

"Show me something happy," she said, rolling her hips into his in a slow, deep rhythm. "I don't care if it won't happen. Just show me."

His gaze ran up her torso, tracing an outline from her naked waist to the nape of her neck until his dark eyes settled heavily on hers. "Do you prefer the ocean or the forest?"

Val closed her eyes. "The ocean."

"You're at the ocean with someone you love. The sky is clear." He slipped his hands underneath her shirt. Her skin tingled where he ran his thumbs across her nipples. "The water is warm."

He was quiet for a while as she moved against him, slow and deliberate, relishing the sensation, a moment of pleasure in a storm of misery. It still felt good, even after being violated, even without love. Her body wasn't broken; only her soul.

He pulled her deeper onto him, his chest heaving into hers as he eased her closer. "There are boats on the horizon," he said at almost a whisper, breath hot on her neck. "How many boats do you see?"

"How many am I supposed to see?"

"It's your future. See what will be. Picture them clearly."

Val imagined basking in the glow of love, jumping into an ocean of warm water, coming up for air and scanning the horizon. She looked for the boats, then gasped as tendrils of fire rushed up her spine—

I see two blips on the horizon—sailboats with white masts gliding over the water, far enough away that I can only tell they're moving if I hold out my arm and watch the patch of blue between the blips and my thumb slowly grow. I lie on a small yacht in the middle of an ocean of turquoise water dotted by far-off islands, and let the sun dry salt water off my bare skin. Max sits at the edge of the boat, naked and brown, throwing pieces of bread into the water. Birds circle and pluck bits from the sea.

"They could see you," I say to him, pointing at the boats.

He shrugs. "They're too far away." He doesn't care anyway. Nudity's never been a big deal to him.

"If they're paparazzi with telescopic lenses, you're in trouble."

"You're in trouble." He throws a piece of bread at me that bounces off my naked breasts.

"Nobody cares about me. A Carressa dick-pic would go viral, though."

He stands, walks over, and lies on his side next to me. He runs a finger from my collarbone to my belly button. "You're starting to show."

I laugh. "You're making me fat."

Blur.

A Frisbee flies overhead, caught by a teenage girl who throws it back to her partner. I'm surrounded by families in a public park, the Seattle skyline glinting in a clear, azure sky. A warm breeze tickles my skin. The grass around me is so green I think someone's littered the ground with emeralds. A little boy runs up to me with blond hair and gorgeous brown eyes with bursts of green at their centers.

"For you, Mommy," he says, and hands me a dandelion.

I reach for him as he runs away from me to gather more flowers. I feel kisses on the back of my neck, hands resting on my shoulders.

"Let him go," Max whispers into my ear. "He'll be back."

Blur.

I light a paper lantern over the ocean and let it go. Max stands next to me. Tears trickle down his face. We watch the lantern float away until it's only a speck in the evening sky. A tribute to our lost son—

In a bittersweet afterglow, Val opened her eyes. Sten breathed hard underneath her, sweat moistening the collar of his dress shirt.

"Do you need me to keep going?" she asked. It wasn't explicitly part of their deal, but if she was going to use him for sex, she could at least ensure he was satisfied. Maybe he'd count it toward her debt.

He laughed. "Val, the generous lover. I never would've figured. Thanks but no thanks. I come when you come. I'm efficient that way."

She slid off him and pulled her clothes back on as he did the same.

"Happy now?" he asked.

Her visions of Max were always the same. They were happy together, then they had a child—sometimes a boy, sometimes a girl—then the child went missing and they were miserable. Max couldn't understand. He hadn't *seen* it like she had, over and over again. Whatever happiness they found with each other wouldn't last.

"You did your job," she muttered.

"I aim to please."

"You can go."

"I have your permission to get back to my actual job now? Thanks." He opened the car door. "Until next time." Sten stepped out, then dropped his head back in. "And don't drink and drive." He shut the door, got back into his own car, and drove away.

Val closed her eyes and let her head fall backward. What the hell was she doing? Having sex with Sten so she could fantasize about a future with Max she was determined to prevent? She *was* losing her fucking mind. Val felt around behind her for the vodka bottle. She found it, unscrewed the cap, put the bottle to her mouth, then stopped. An unexpected but familiar taste lingered on her lips, like red meat with a hint of tobacco and mint chewing gum—Sten's mouth. He must have kissed her when she was in her trance. Why would he do that?

Maybe he cared. Fucking Sten. The thought made her laugh so hard she cried.

Chapter Sixteen

Max tried to focus on the last chapter of *Capital in the Twenty-first Century* in its original French, but his eyelids kept growing heavy and he'd have to shake himself awake. It wasn't the author's fault. He'd upped his dosage of OxyContin when the previous amount failed to keep thoughts of Val away. His father had begun making appearances in his nightmares, too, lecturing him about family and loyalty and sacrifices, before the touching began. Then he'd wake up in a cold sweat, furious with himself for putting up with the monster for so long, and needing to pop his meds to calm down. And so went his nightly routine.

In the day he'd catch himself thinking of Val, her crooked, sly smile, the smell of apple shampoo in her hair, the salty taste of her skin, the feel of her lips against his, when they'd first made love in the boathouse, their epic fights over a future she couldn't face. He'd wonder what she was doing at any given moment, who she was sleeping with, if she thought of him at all. He would turn his phone over and over in his hands, thinking up excuses to call her just to hear her voice, or maybe set up a meeting so he could see her, until he forced himself to drop the phone, get up, and take Toby for a walk or go for a run instead. The part of him that still loved her wouldn't die, and it wouldn't shut up. So he took extra meds to keep those voices silent. And so went his daily routine, until the days blurred into one another.

After a few more minutes of trying, Max gave up reading. He flipped to the last page and wrote a series of numbers at the top—the winning combination for next month's state lottery. He would leave the book at the library, or donate it to a used book store. If some lucky economist made it to the end, they'd be rewarded with a golden ticket into the world of one-percenters.

Max shut the book, then shook his head, opened it again, and tore the last page out. He'd tried the divine-charity trick before almost twenty years ago, when he was a stupid kid who thought he could use his ability for good. Make the torture of his own existence meaningful in some way other than to feed his father's greed. Lester found out, as he always did when Max tried to exercise some agency without his knowledge. As if someone told him. During the subsequent beating, Lester had "explained" to Max that a dead-on prediction of winning lottery numbers wouldn't go unnoticed by the media. A legion of treasure hunters would track him down. Max had to admit Lester was probably right. Maybe one of these days he'd do it anyway, and jump off a bridge before they could find him.

He crumpled the paper into a ball and tossed it at the kindling box next to the fireplace. It missed and bounced off the wall, rolling onto the carpet. Toby launched from Max's feet and chased the ball as Abby walked into the living room. She knelt to pet him; Toby eyed her hand and growled.

"*Toby*," Max snapped.

She gave up trying to make nice with the stupid dog and sat next to Max.

"So...I wanted to talk to you about something," she said.

Max forced himself not to cringe. "Okay." *Please don't ask about Val or the bar fight again.* Every time she did, and he refused to give details, the tension between them ratcheted up another notch. It was a small miracle the police hadn't shown up yet to question him about the dead guy in the parking lot.

"I want to go back to school for my graduate degree in art history, after our wedding."

Art history sounded like a pretty useless degree. Then again, he had a business degree he never used. Whatever floated her boat. "Okay."

"That's it? Just 'okay'?"

"What else do you want me to say? You don't need my permission."

"No, but I'd like your support."

"You've got my support."

"Do I?"

Great, this *was* another conversation about Val. He willed himself not to get angry. "You always have my support, Abby." He put his arm around her rigid shoulders. "You'll be my wife in less than two months. I'll always be here for you, no matter what you want to do."

He pulled her to him and kissed her. She relaxed in his arms and nestled her head in the crook of his neck.

"I want to go to couples counseling," she said.

Max felt his calm resolve wane. Another touchy, familiar topic. "You know I can't do that."

"We could at least try it."

"I've been to psychiatrists before. They can always tell I'm hiding something. Then they insist I come clean so the 'healing process' can begin, and I can't."

"So tell them the truth, like you told me."

He pushed her away so she faced him. "They won't believe me." Frustration he couldn't suppress crept into his voice. "I told you because I trusted you, and I could prove it. How am I supposed to convince a psychiatrist I'm not crazy? Jack off in front of him and then spout off tomorrow's NASDAQ numbers?"

"I could back you up—"

"No."

She looked at her feet, her mouth a tight line. "Does Val know what you can do?"

"*Stop* asking me about her." He stood and folded his arms, holding in the urge to yell. "No, she doesn't know. Only you know. Everyone else I've told is either dead now, or didn't believe me."

Her gaze met his, and he saw doubt in her eyes. Either she knew he was lying, or she didn't believe anything he said anymore.

Max knelt beside Abby and took her hands in his. "I'm only helping Val because an innocent woman is going to die if we don't do something. That's it, baby. I promise. There's only you." He meant every word. Val didn't trust him, and she didn't love him. Val was gone, no matter if his heart couldn't accept it. Abby was with him, and she loved him. Abby was all he had.

Through tear-rimmed eyes, his fiancée asked, "Then why haven't you made love to me since the day you met her for coffee?"

Max froze. Shit, was that true? It was. "I—" His mouth moved, trying to come up with an explanation, but nothing came out. He'd been busy searching for Margaret. He'd been taking too many pills. And his stupid preoccupation with Val was distracting him from the things in his life that mattered. Max felt the heat of shame flushing his cheeks. Goddammit, he could get Val out of his system. He could fix things with Abby. He could.

The bong of the front door intercom interrupted their painful conversation.

Abby's jaw clenched, and she let out a slow, controlled exhale. "I'll get it." She rose and disappeared down the hallway toward the intercom next to the door.

Max took a deep breath, forcing himself to think clearly and not panic at what an outside observer would think was the slow death of his engagement. He needed to get a hold of his life again. He'd get in Abby's good graces again, have sex with her and remember what she felt and tasted like, and all the other things he'd enjoyed up until a couple of weeks ago. He would remind himself why he loved her—because he *did* love her.

He went to the kitchen and poured himself a cup of coffee from the fresh pot Abby had brewed a few minutes ago. Maybe later he'd go for another jog to clear his head. From around the corner, he heard Abby invite somebody in over the intercom. He'd leave for a three-hour run right then and there if it turned out to be Ginger. While she remained out of sight, Max snuck to the liquor cabinet and dumped a couple of shots of whiskey into his black coffee. Toby trotted over and barked at him.

"You're not in a position to judge, rageaholic," he said to the dog's accusing eyes.

A minute later, Michael Beauford walked into the kitchen with a twelve-inch square box in his arms. His craggy face split into a genial grin. "Max! How are you, my boy?" He dropped the box on the kitchen counter, then embraced Max in a hug.

Max wasn't big on hugging, though he made exceptions for certain people. Michael was one of them. The CFO of Carressa Industries was the closest thing he'd had to a father figure, and had been Max's only supporter during his run from the law last year.

After Michael hugged Abby, she kissed him on the cheek. "I'd love to stay, but I said I'd go shopping with Carrie." She leveled Max with a cool half-second glare, then left. Dammit, he *would* make things right with her.

Michael crooked his thumb toward the box. "That was on your doorstep when I came in. Doesn't feel like a bomb."

"Thanks for potentially getting blown up for me. Coffee?"

"Nah. The wife's banned caffeine, thinks it'll cut my life short. Like living to eighty-six instead of eighty-seven is a real tragedy. I'll take a glass of water, though."

Max poured him a glass, and they sat down at the kitchen table.

"How's life treating you?" Michael asked. Though he leaned back and relaxed in his chair, he looked Max up and down with wise eyes that took in Max's every movement for clues to things unsaid. Max squirmed under the scrutiny. He had a lot to hide these days.

"Eh, you know." Max shrugged. "Abby's busy with wedding minutiae. We've been...okay." He sipped his coffee, wincing at the whiskey he forgot he put in there.

"Wow." Michael made a popping sound with his lips. "You really know how to spin a picture of premarital bliss."

"Every couple has their ups and downs. So I'm told." He'd had some casual relationships before, got good at faking orgasms for a sheen of normalcy, but none of them had come close to being marriage-worthy—not counting what he'd had with Val, which was in a class all its own.

"True enough." Michael drummed his fingers on the table. "I'll be honest—I'd like to say you look good, but you really don't."

Max frowned. One thing he'd always liked about Michael was his friend's ability to tell the truth to people's faces. Max usually appreciated the candor. Not today.

"I'm fine. Everything's fine," he said, but couldn't meet Michael's eyes. The CFO had seen Max messed up before, knew what he looked like when he was off the wagon, as he'd been right after his father's death. He didn't want Michael to worry about him.

"Well, good," Michael said. "I'm glad you moved on from

all that unfortunate business last year. I thought you'd take more time to settle into your independence and hard-won freedom, though. You look like a man suffering from whiplash, trying to change too much too fast."

Max brought his coffee cup down on the table with a hard clink. "Are you saying I shouldn't get married?" Who the hell was Michael to lecture him about how to get on with his life? No one knew the entirety of what he'd been through—no one but Val.

"I'm not saying that," Michael said in a softer tone, perhaps sensing he'd pushed too hard. "All I'm saying is that you look like shit. Maybe you need a break from…whatever it is you do all day. Knitting, I assume."

"You came over here to tell me to take a vacation from knitting?"

"No, actually." Michael straightened in his chair. "I came to talk business."

"Let me guess—the board's finally found a way to force me to sell my shares."

"No again." Michael chuckled. "I'll have to tell them you're not, in fact, a fortune-teller."

Max choked on his coffee.

"I know, I kill me, too. But seriously—they want you to come back to the company."

Max wiped his mouth with the back of his hand. "They want me back on the board?"

"Yes, in some capacity, though probably not CEO again, sorry. Carressa Industries has been turning a quarterly profit at about the market average since you left, which as you know is *worse* than average for us. We're used to performing ahead of the pack, because that's the way it's been for over a decade—right about when you joined the company. Lately our quarterly earnings have come in under expectations, and shareholders are panicking. End of the world, might have to sell their yachts, et cetera. They don't think it's a coincidence that the pinnacle of our prosperity just happened to coincide with your tenure. They don't know how you did it, but they know it was you."

Max remained silent. Only his father knew he used his ability to decide which companies to acquire and which to divest of at exactly the right times. There was no way anyone would guess he could literally see the future, even if that was the only explanation. And Max highly doubted his father would've told anyone else. He was a prized family secret, a golden calf to be bled dry.

"I am the board's emissary of goodwill. We want our financial genius back, and we're willing to make generous concessions—embarrassingly generous, even. Name your price. So...are you bored with knitting yet?"

Max chewed on his thumb for a moment. He honestly didn't know what he thought about the offer. He *was* tiring of the charity circuit. Raising money for worthy causes was definitely fulfilling, and he relished the opportunity to finally contribute to the world in a positive way. But all the expensive dinners and fancy galas with rich, boring people were beginning to wear on him. And when he wasn't doing charity stuff, he was doing...nothing, really. Puttering around the house. Reading. Exercising. Popping pills. Obsessing over Val. Fighting with Abby. A better way to occupy his brain did sound appealing, though going back to using his ability for the company's financial gain felt too much like old times.

"How long do I have to think it over?" Max asked.

"However long you need. Or until you get arrested again. Whichever comes first." Michael leaned toward Max, a new intensity in his eyes. "Listen, kid. Take it from me when I say the Devil makes work of idle minds, and you have one hell of a mind to get up to no good. No amount of drugs is gonna whip that sucker into submission if it doesn't want the life you're trying to live."

Max flinched. Before he could offer a rebuttal, Michael clapped him on the shoulder and stood.

"I'd say my emissary mission's complete. Come back to the company or don't, it doesn't matter to me, honestly. I'll probably drop dead any day now, so what do I care? Do what you wanna do, Max. Simple as that. I'll see you soon, I'm sure, one way or another." He gave Max a quick hug on his way out the door.

Max rubbed his temples and leaned against the kitchen counter, next to the mysterious box. Goddamn Michael, he knew Max too well. Of course he could tell Max was on drugs. Everyone could probably tell, except poor Abby. She wanted to believe the best in Max, and ignored most evidence to the contrary—until recently, that was. The truth would crush her.

It's cruel of me to keep her hanging on. I should let her go.

The thought hit him like a punch to the stomach. If he couldn't make it work with Abby, he couldn't make it work with anyone. He *would* make it work. The next time he'd see Michael would be at his damn wedding.

Max grabbed the box and ripped it open without concern for the frailty of its contents. He expected to find an early wedding gift, maybe a five-hundred-dollar gravy boat. Instead, buried beneath layers of tissue paper, he pulled out two masquerade-style masks; a wolf and a fox. Max turned them over in his hand. They looked handmade and high-quality, like the mask he'd worn at the Blue Serpent party last week. He set the masks down, picked up the box, and scanned its sides; no address label. Finally, he turned the box upside down and dumped everything out, tissue paper and all. An envelope fell onto the counter. Max ripped it open and pulled out a card made of smooth papyrus that read in cursive script:

Maxwell Carressa and Abigail Westford
You are cordially invited to the Northwest Mountain Lodge
on July Thirty-first at Ten O'clock in the Evening
Formal Attire, Masks Required
Bring Your Sorrows and Be Cleansed

A small coiled blue snake was embossed on the bottom of the card—the Blue Serpent. Max guessed he held in his hand an invitation to the coveted top-tier event, despite his bad behavior at the lower-tier party. Assuming Lucien ran these things, why would he want to bring Max into the inner fold? He couldn't imagine he had anything Lucien wanted. And the requirement of a tuxedo as well as the addition of a significant other probably meant something more substantial than a drug-fueled orgy.

He dropped the invitation on the counter and pulled his cell phone from his pocket. With a trembling hand, he dialed Val. Finally, he had an excuse. But this was the *last time*. It rang, and kept ringing.

"Come on, Val, please answer the fucking ph—"

"Hey," she said, sounding tired.

Max cleared his throat, stifling a relieved sigh. She hadn't shut him out completely after all. "Have you found Margaret yet?"

"No."

"Are you still convinced Lucien's got her?"

"Yes."

"Well, Abby and I just got an invitation to a Blue Serpent top-tier party. It's something fancier than the party I went to. The invitation says, 'Bring your sorrows and be cleansed.'"

"What the hell does that mean?"

"I don't know. I'm not versed in cult-speak."

"If you tell me where it is, I can stake it out, maybe sneak in and look for Margaret or clues to where Lucien's keeping her."

"Why would you sneak in when we can just walk in with my invitation?"

"Max…"

"There's no way I can bring Abby. I'm not dragging her into this mess."

"Who am I supposed to be then?"

"Be Abby. Everyone will be wearing masks. Just wear a wig, too, don't say anything, and you'll pass for her. From the head down, you look close enough. You're more athletic, and your breasts are fuller, and—"

Jesus, Max, shut up! Thank God Abby wasn't around to hear him drooling over his ex-girlfriend's body.

After a pause, Val said, "I don't know if we should—"

"Do you want to find Margaret or not?" he snapped. "Because I'm not giving you the address so you can run in there and get killed, or kill somebody yourself. We do this my way or not at all."

She let out a defeated sigh. "When?"

"Saturday, ten o'clock. Wear a formal dress. I'll pick you up at your house. And don't bring a gun this time, for Christ's sake."

He hung up before she could argue, then let his head drop into his hands. Another potentially disastrous plan kicked into motion. Why couldn't he just let it go? He groaned as he admitted the truth to himself—he couldn't pass up the opportunity to see her again. And it would probably get him killed.

Chapter Seventeen

Val fluffed her blond wig as she sat in the passenger seat of Max's car, adjusting one of the fake blond curls so it covered the circular scar behind her ear. She swiped on some lipstick and took a moment to check her makeup in the vanity mirror. Why she even bothered with makeup was a legitimate question, given she'd be wearing a fox mask all night. But it seemed odd to don a gorgeous black satin gown with no effort to make the rest of her body look just as nice. Thank God for the mask, though. Her facial features didn't resemble Abby's at all. There'd be no way she could pass for Max's fiancée without the fox muzzle covering most of her face.

He'd only told her their destination after he picked her up. Per the GPS in Max's car, they were about ten minutes out from the Northwest Mountain Lodge, where something strange was certain to happen—hopefully not another sex party. Pretending to be her ex-boyfriend's fiancée at an orgy would be beyond awkward. It was bad enough as it was. He looked impossibly handsome in his tuxedo and slicked-back hair, the textbook picture of a dark, smoking-hot millionaire. Though he finally got to see her looking good—by far the most put-together she'd ever been for him—he'd said nothing when he first saw her.

Instead, he stared at her for a long time, taking in every inch of her, the amber in his eyes popping like embers as the fire in him burned hotter and hotter, until she swore he was about to kiss her. She found herself leaning forward against her will, beckoning his lips to hers. But his gaze cut away, and he didn't look at her again or speak on their drive to the lodge. Maybe she'd read him wrong, projected her own wants and desires onto him. His whole body seemed tense, as if being in her presence caused him physical pain. Forcing herself to mentally and physically back off, she distracted herself with her phone as he drove. She wished she could keep him out of all this chaos, but there was no putting that horse back in the barn.

Max surprised Val by pulling into a gas station and parking his car away from the pumps. He reached into his breast pocket and pulled out a joint and a lighter. He lit the marijuana cigarette and took a long drag.

Val raised an eyebrow. "Seriously?"

"I'm nervous. If I don't chill out before I get there, it'll look suspicious."

He held the joint out, offering her a hit; she shook her head.

"You look nice," she said, resisting the urge to lick her lips at the same time. He looked better than nice, but admitting she wanted to rip his clothes off with her teeth might be a bit awkward.

He shrugged. Max went to swanky charity events all the time. A tuxedo was probably like a second skin to him, nothing special. They sat in silence as Max stared out the window, lost in thought. It reminded her of when they'd been on the lam, trapped in a fleabag motel room for days while Max healed from the severe beating Sten had delivered. He'd stared out the window thinking God knows what for hours. Always his mind churned, a puzzle forever trying to solve itself. It drove him nuts sometimes, he'd told her.

After a couple of minutes where she snuck glances at his gorgeous face without being too obvious about it, he said, "Carressa Industries wants to hire me back to the board."

"No kidding. What made them acknowledge your existence again after all this time?"

"They want me to lead the company back to better-than-average returns—using my knowledge of the future. They don't know that's how it works, but that's what would happen."

"You don't have to use your ability. You're still a whiz with numbers."

He shook his head. "There's too much randomness in the market. I'd need to *perform*." He spat the last word. All he'd done his whole life was perform for other people.

"If you don't want to perform, why are you considering it?"

He sighed as if he wasn't sure of the answer himself. "It's something to do. And charity work is worthwhile, but..."

"Boring?"

"Yeah."

"What does Abby think?"

His gaze flicked back out the window. "I haven't told her."

Val wasn't sure what to make of that. It couldn't be good that he'd failed to mention a critical life decision to his fiancée. Maybe it had nothing to do with Val. She wasn't a major part of his life anymore.

"If you're asking my opinion, I think you should take the job, but do it without using your ability. Give yourself a real challenge."

"Hmm," was all he said. He took a final drag of his joint, then carefully extinguished it with his fingers and put it back in his pocket. He looked at her. "Ready?"

"Whenever you are."

He started his car and drove the final few miles to the Northwest Mountain Lodge. They pulled up to the posh country club twenty minutes late, a ploy to avoid any forced socializing that might expose Val's true identity. She took a deep breath, slipped on her mask, and prayed these rich assholes weren't chatty. Then she nodded to Max, who looked sexy and ridiculous in his wolf mask, and they opened their doors together.

A man in a servant's tuxedo and a blank white-faced mask took Val's hand and helped her out of the car. Suppressing the urge to recoil from his touch, she smiled politely, her mouth and eyes the only visible parts of her face. A moment later Max was at her side. He took her arm as another creepy-faced valet drove away with his car.

"You look nice, too," he said to her, just above a whisper. Such simple words, yet they thrilled her to her core. Maybe he'd wanted to kiss her after all. She was glad he couldn't see her blushing.

Together they walked toward huge ornate oak doors. An army of servants in white masks wordlessly ushered them into the building and through a series of rooms that became darker as they went in, like descending into the bowels of a dungeon. Val walked with her head high and shoulders back, striking a pose of confidence for any potential observers. Secretly she clung to Max's arm for support, warm and strong beneath the expensive fabric of his suit. Finally, they came to their destination—a dimly lit function hall, opulent in burgundy and dark woods, a small and high stage in the center like something used for intimate concerts. About a hundred people surrounded the stage, all in tuxedoes and ball gowns, all sporting unique animal masks. They whispered with their partners but didn't mingle with anyone else. They were waiting, Val realized.

A waiter approached Max and Val and offered them a tray of crystal goblets filled with a clear liquid. They each took one out of politeness, then sniffed the contents after the waiter disappeared. Val dipped her finger in and touched it to the tip of her tongue before Max could stop her. He scolded her with his gaze, pissed she'd take the risk of sampling an unknown substance after what he went through at the last Blue Serpent party.

"Water," she told him.

He frowned and eyed his glass with suspicion anyway. Val looked around again; everyone who held a drink had water. No one had food. She would've made a joke to Max about this being the lamest party she'd ever been to, but a bong like an ancient grandfather clock interrupted her. She knew that sound.

Val grabbed Max's arm again. "That's it—the noise I heard in my vision, when Ginger talked to Lucien. He's coming—"

The lights dimmed even further until they stood in almost complete darkness. No one spoke as the bonging filled the room. Val found herself holding her breath, the tension as thick as the blackness that surrounded them. She flinched when an overhead light flooded the stage. A single man stood in the center, black robes flowing down his body, a long beak like a scythe and glass eyes covering his face—a plague mask.

"God is cruel," he said, his voice replacing the sound of the grandfather clock as the only thing Val could hear besides the pounding of her heart. His slight French accent confirmed what she already knew, based on her vision and his ancient medical costume—the man was Lucien. "You have *worked* for the finer things in life, you have *worked* for luxury. You have *earned* your status. But God has cursed you. God will rip from your grasp all the spoils you have worked for. You have everything, and yet you are helpless."

Val felt Max tense. This speech was meant for people like him—the rich, the entitled, the damned. His "curse" was what made him wealthy and ruined his life at the same time.

"But I am merciful. I will give back what God has taken from you." He held his hands out to the crowd. "Bring me your sorrows and be cleansed."

The crowd held up their hands to Lucien. Did they know it was Lucien? "Cleanse us, Blue Serpent," they said as one.

Like the picture of Death choosing a victim, Lucien pointed to a woman in the crowd. "Come to me and be cleansed."

Bodies parted and made a path for the woman up to the

base of the stage. She struggled up the steps, tubes trailing from beneath her panther mask to an oxygen tank a man carried behind her. One of her arms was crooked at an odd angle, a symptom of some crippling ailment. She reached Lucien and stood before him, rasping to catch her breath. The man with the oxygen tank—probably her husband—clutched her good arm to keep her steady. Her frail body trembled like she might collapse at any moment. Lucien took the woman's arm and motioned for her husband to back away; he did so, tentatively.

In one smooth motion, Lucien ripped the tubes from the woman's nose. She cried out. The crowd gasped, including Val. He spun her around, manipulating her like a rag doll, his robes nearly engulfing her entire body.

Then he seized her face in his white-knuckled hand. "Do you believe in me?"

"Yes," the woman choked out.

"Will you accept from me that which God has cruelly withheld?"

"Yes!"

"Then be cleansed."

She drew in a ragged breath and her body went rigid. Then she began to shake and writhe in his grasp. Her crippled arm flailed at her side. She shrieked when her forearm snapped away from her body, then her wrist popped into line with her forearm. The woman's whole twisted arm unfolded one sharp crack at a time until it fell at her side, a mirror image of her good arm. Her strained rasps became strong breaths, and she relaxed as whatever agony she'd experienced ebbed. Lucien let her go and stepped back. She stood at the foot of the stage, no longer struggling to support herself or nursing a crippled limb. Val heard sobs beneath the panther mask. Her husband dropped the oxygen tank and rushed to embrace her, sobbing along with his newly healthy wife.

"Oh my God," Val whispered. Shocked murmurs that echoed her own ran through the crowd. "That can't be real." She looked at Max. He still gaped at the couple. "It must have been staged, right?"

He blinked as if snapping out of a trance. "I have no idea. I think the man she's with is Marty Paul, a hedge funds manager. I heard through the grapevine his wife was seriously ill, but…I don't know what just happened."

"Blue Serpent, heal me!" a man in the crowd yelled.

"*Heal me!*" someone else's desperate voice echoed. Soon a cacophony of pleading filled the room. Val could only guess at the net worth of all these people, but they literally begged at Lucien's feet for a scrap of something money couldn't buy. He was right—they had everything, yet were helpless before him.

Lucien held up his arms and the lights dimmed again, though his grotesque outline remained visible, like a massive vulture. Val guessed he was warming up for his second act. Morbid curiosity urged her to stay, but her obligation to Margaret won out.

"Let's go," she whispered to Max. With the lights dim and room filled with frenzied voices, she guessed they wouldn't get a better chance to sneak away and search the bowels of the building for Margaret or some clue to where she could be.

With a slight nod he took her arm again, and they slipped back to the room's entrance.

"Bathroom?" Max asked a white-masked servant opening the door for them.

Without speaking, the servant pointed down a hallway to his left. Val assumed there was a man with a life behind the mask, despite the blank, foreboding figure he cut. She wouldn't be surprised if their contracts required them to be as creepy as possible. Fear and desperation were the major themes of Blue Serpent events, she realized. Sex, drugs, and promises of miracle cures were the ploys that got people in the door.

They walked in the direction the servant sent them until they were out of his sight. Then Val cut left and pulled Max down a hallway perpendicular to the bathroom.

"There's a stairwell down here that will take us to the basement," she whispered. "If Margaret's in the building, that's where she'll be."

"And you know this…how?"

"I looked up the floor plans on my phone while you drove."

"Oh."

"It's not like you were making great conversation."

"I had things on my mind."

"I know, Max. It's a permanent state you're in." She glanced at him and grinned.

He rolled his eyes. "One of us has to think before leaping into danger."

"I could've planned better if you'd told me where we were going beforehand."

"If I had, you'd have gone without me, guns blazing, and you know it."

"*No.* Okay yes, but—" A flash of movement caught her

eye. A man emerged from around the corner about fifty feet away—a security guard with a gun on his hip. She threw herself into Max and shoved them together into the recessed nook of another room's entrance a mere second before the man turned to look at the spot they'd just been in. Val squished her chest flat against Max's in the small nook, held her breath, and prayed the guard hadn't been close enough to hear them talking. After what felt like an eternity, she heard receding footfalls, then silence. She risked a peek down the hallway; empty.

"Shit, that was close," she whispered, and breathed a sigh of relief. She shouldn't have. Max's scent flooded her lungs: his natural musk, his cologne, his bay rum aftershave. Paired with the warmth and strength of his body pressed against hers, and his arms wrapped around her body, she felt dizzy, nearly overpowered by his essence. She lifted her head and met his white-hot gaze. His eyes searched hers, traced the outline of her lips. He was going to kiss her this time, she knew it. She wanted him to. She needed him to. Her mouth parted and she lifted her chin—

He pushed past her and stepped back into the hallway. "Can we hurry up and get the hell out of here, please?" he said, his voice breathless and strained.

"Uh…yeah." Val cleared her throat and forced herself back to reality. "Follow me."

With an increased sense of caution and no more chatter, she led Max to the stairwell. She slipped off her high heels and raced down the stairs, Max close behind. At the bottom they peeked through the door into the basement area, ensured the coast was clear, then skulked through a finished hallway with connecting rooms for storage and office space.

Val stopped in front of a room with a cypher lock. "In my vision, I saw Lucien come out of this room and talk to Ginger, right before the show."

She guessed Ginger lurked nearby, probably in the crowd with the other sick rich people. She couldn't wait to get her hands on him, as soon as Max gave the okay. She tried the door; locked, as expected. Val jiggled the handle, testing the strength of the lock, then shoved her shoulder into it. When the door didn't budge, she reared her leg back to try kicking it in, alarm be damned.

Max put a hand on her arm. "Don't." He stepped forward, stared hard at the cypher lock as he chewed his thumb, then punched in an eight-digit number. The lock clicked open.

"Someone did prep work of his own," she said. "Hopefully not on the drive over."

He snickered. "You'll never know for sure." His rare smile fell into a frown. "You know it's unlikely Margaret's in here, right? He wouldn't keep her in a semi-public place."

"I know that, Max. I'm not stupid."

Knowing the odds was one thing; hoping anyway was another. When he pushed the door open, Val barreled past him into the dark room, praying to a God she had little faith in that Margaret would be there, alive and still in one piece. She held her breath and flicked the light on.

Yet again, God did her no favors. She and Max stood alone in an upscale if generic office, a mahogany desk and executive leather chair set up for the use of guests. Val took a moment to push back a lump in her throat. She surveyed the room and shook off her disappointment. Margaret remained missing, but they'd found the next best thing—Lucien's temporary office space. A laptop sat on the desk. An odd silver suitcase leaned against the opposite wall, next to a rolling tote.

"You look through the computer," she told Max. "I'll take the suitcase." She would've preferred to just grab the computer and run, but they'd almost certainly be caught trying to sneak anything large out of the building if they intended to keep up their ruse and leave the way they came in.

Max pulled off his mask and dropped it on the desk as he concentrated on the laptop. Val pushed her own mask off her face but didn't remove it completely, fearing she wouldn't be able to get it back on without messing up her wig. As she knew he'd done with the cypher lock, Max used information he'd gleaned from earlier visions to crack open password-protected files while Val searched the suitcase. She unsnapped a couple of latches on the side and lifted the top. Black foam surrounded a collection of what looked like medical equipment. She recognized a jet injector, but not a palm-sized gadget next to the injector with three wires and a plastic tube sticking out of a triangle-shaped body.

Val held up the triangular gizmo for Max. "What is this?"

He glanced up from the laptop for half a second. "I don't know. I'm not a doctor."

She couldn't believe he hadn't at least read about how to be a doctor, with all the books he devoured. Val put the gizmo back and eyed another mysterious object, this one a series of seven tiny glass flasks connected with a strange red metallic tubing. None of the odd objects had serial numbers or brand names on them. She popped the lid off a thermos embedded in the foam. Vials of different colored liquids sat inside its cool interior; no labels.

"I think Lucien made a lot of this stuff himself," she said.

Max didn't take his eyes off the computer. "Could be. He's got hundreds of diagrams for strange devices in here, some of them scanned copies of very old plans, going back decades."

She remembered the almost one-hundred-year-old photograph of someone who looked suspiciously like Lucien. Maybe her initial speculation about Lucien's immortality wasn't so crazy after all. "Why would Lucien host wild, drug-fueled orgies and elaborate faith-healing performances, all under the same Blue Serpent moniker? What do those two things have in common?"

Max looked up, seemed to think about it for a moment, then frowned. "One to spread sexually transmitted diseases, the other to cure them."

"Stacey told me a few of the escorts she talked to reported missing time, then later some of them got sick. Maybe Lucien's using high-end prostitutes to spread illnesses through wealthy communities, then charging them for the cure."

Max cringed. "That's disgusting. If he really can cure previously incurable diseases, why doesn't he accept his Nobel Prize in medicine instead?"

"Because he's a greedy piece of shit." Val slammed the suitcase closed. "Still doesn't explain where he's getting the blueprints to make these magical cures."

Max stared at the wall next to Val's head for a long moment. "Maybe he's like us."

"What?"

"Arthur C. Clarke said, 'Technology sufficiently advanced is indistinguishable from magic.' What if he can see future medical technology?"

Val shook her head. "You've got to be fucking kidding me."

"It's one possibility."

"All the more reason for us to shut him down." She opened the rolling tote and pulled out a stack of documents, some printed and some handwritten, all in French. "Shit," she muttered. Max knew French, but he was busy with the laptop. She did her best to scan for Margaret's name. The grandfather clock began to bong again. They were out of time.

She picked out a couple of memos addressed to Asclepius Inc., hoping they'd be useful in some way, folded them up, and shoved them into her bra. "We gotta go."

Max stayed hunched over the laptop. "Wait. I found a couple dozen videos. If one features Margaret, that's a smoking gun he's involved in her disappearance. When did you say you saw her video online?"

Oh shit. "It was…uh…I don't remember. Max, let's go. Now. Come on."

He squinted at the computer. "This one's recent. It's—" He froze.

Val's heart raced. A cold sweat prickled up from her neck. "We should go. Please."

The blood drained from his face. He gaped at the screen as utter horror twisted his features. Then his gaze cut to hers, crushed by what he'd seen and how it would affect her. She swallowed hard, and felt her own blood leave her cheeks.

Then he realized what her lack of surprise at his reaction meant. His horror turned to numb shock. "You knew about this?"

"I'm handling it."

"You knew about this, and you didn't tell me?"

"It's not your problem."

He stared at her.

"I didn't want to bother you any more than I had to."

He kept staring.

"The whole world doesn't need to know, okay? I'm not ashamed, I just don't want to deal with people treating me differently. Like I'm damaged, or…or a freak. It's bad enough with our condition."

He said nothing. He didn't have to. The devastation in his withering glare told her everything.

Tears crept into her eyes. "It's not like you go around telling people what your father did—"

"I told you!"

She jumped. A sob rose in her throat. She put a hand over her mouth for a second to hold it back. "What would it have accomplished if I'd told you? It would've only made you upset, like you are now. It happened, and it can't be undone." Her voice grew small and weak. "I didn't want to mess up your perfect life. You're finally happy, and…and…"

She didn't know what else to say. He wasn't listening anyway. The blood had returned to his face in spades, and his whole body had stiffened like a spring pulled to its limit. In his eyes boiled a rage she'd never seen in him before—a pure, all-consuming anger he barely controlled. It was the rage that killed his father, she realized, so intense that just being in his presence sucked the air from her lungs.

With one lightning-fast movement, he picked up the laptop and slammed it into the ground. Val yelped as it exploded into a thousand pieces. Bits of electronics and hard plastic showered her feet. Then he stalked out of the room.

Val took a ragged breath, her whole body trembling. Why did he have to find out like this, in the worst possible way? She'd asked so much of him, and he'd done it all, despite the cost to himself. She should've told him. He'd trusted her with his most intimate secrets, but she hadn't trusted him with hers. She'd never seen him so furious before. He would never hurt her, but Lucien...Hopefully Max would just go home, and not storm the stage to kill the man who'd orchestrated her rape.

With Lucien's laptop shattered across the room's floor, there was no covering their tracks now. She picked up pieces of what looked like the hard drive and wedged them inside her nylons, so they stayed put against her inner thighs. It felt uncomfortable, but if she stepped carefully, she could make her stride look natural. All she could do now was beat feet out of there, pretend to be Abby and make up some excuse about a lover's spat, then ask for a cab. She wiped tears off her cheeks and slipped the mask back over her face. As seemed to always be the case, she would be finding her own way home.

Chapter Eighteen

Val gripped the edge of the lobby's granite countertop with white knuckles, as if she could dig her fingernails into its smooth surface. "I said Asclepius Incorporated. *Asclepius.*"

The receptionist held his empty, nonconfrontational smile in place. "I'm sorry, ma'am, there's no company by that name in the building."

"I know Asclepius rented space here in the past." Val showed the receptionist the crumpled paper she'd swiped from Lucien's office the night before. "Can you at least tell me what space they used when they were here?"

"I'm sorry, ma'am, I don't—"

Val slapped the paper on the countertop. "God, just let me talk to your manager already." She knew she should've been nicer—more flies with honey and all that—but she wasn't in the mood to play along. Not after last night.

The receptionist's steely smile slipped into a slight frown, and he made a call on the phone behind the front desk. "Julia, can you come to the front, please? I've got a *customer* here with some *questions*."

A moment later, a woman who might have been about Val's age emerged from the "Employees Only" door, though graying hair and a square build made her seem older. "Can I help you?" Julia asked.

"Asclepius Incorporated rented office space in this building at some point in time. I know because this memo lists this building in the return address. So can you tell me where they used to be?"

Julia glanced at Val's paper, then smiled. "Oh yes, I remember a man from Asclepius coming in here often, about six months ago. Christophe, I think his name was. I didn't see him again after their lease expired and they didn't renew. Too bad, he was a really nice guy. Very charming. *French*."

"He's under investigation for rape and kidnapping."

Julia's smile fell like a lead weight. "Oh."

"Where is the space he rented?"

"On the twelfth floor. There are doctor's offices there now."

A seed of hope sprang up in Val. Doctor's offices were perfect places to conduct experiments on people, though how Lucien could get unwilling participants up there and keep them imprisoned without attracting attention was an open question. "I need to go up to those offices and look around."

Julia's eyebrows furrowed. "Who did you say you were again?"

"Abigail Westlake, with the Seattle PD."

"Can I see your badge?"

"It's in the shop right now. Listen, all I want to do is look around. You can follow me if you want."

"I can't let you up there without some identification, or a warrant."

Great, someone was a *Law and Order* fan. "You're impeding a criminal investigation."

Julia set her jaw and put her hand on her hip like a stern mother. "I don't know what you're really doing here, but the only people allowed in this building are employees and people with appointments. Please leave."

Val gritted her teeth and shoved the Asclepius memo back into her pocket. "If you want to put innocent people's lives at risk for the sake of your draconian rules, then fine. I'll be back with my badge, and a warrant." She stalked to the exit, then cut right just before the revolving glass doors. In a quiet corridor, she took a pen from her pocket and flipped the fire alarm. Val tossed the ink-covered pen in the trash as she exited the building with the other evacuating occupants. She snaked through people loitering in the parking lot, got into her car, and waited.

Two minutes later, a couple of fire engines roared up. They'd have to sweep the building, even for a false alarm. If she couldn't search Asclepius's old offices, the fire department would do it for her. Val drummed her fingers on the steering wheel and watched the firemen enter the building. Twenty minutes later, they came out, got back in their trucks, and drove away.

"Fuck." Val pounded the dashboard with her fists. "*Fuck, fuck, fuck!*" Another dead end. Her last hope was the mangled hard drive.

She drove to Zach's house in the Kent suburbs. Usually she didn't go to his place, since his mother was around most of the time, and it made doing business with him face-to-face awkward. This time, it was just Zach at home—his mom had gone to the plant store—and he gleefully led her to his room.

"Uh, sorry about the mess," he said, pushing dirty clothes off the foot of his bed. "I don't normally, you know, get girls up here..." He blushed, a bright flame across his face when contrasted with his pale skin and black eyeliner.

"It's fine." Without sitting down, she handed him a baggie with the hard drive pieces inside. "I need you to see what information you can pull from this."

He emptied the baggie into his hand, the pieces clinking against the huge silver skull-and-crossbones ring he wore. "Damn. Someone throw this off a building or something?"

"Can you work with it or not?"

"Hmm...maybe. Probably."

"Good." She dropped five twenties on the desk in the corner he'd piled high with computer equipment. "The sooner the better."

"You always say that."

"Because it's always true."

As she left his room, he called after her, "Hey, you can come by anytime and I can show you how I do my magic, it's pretty cool—"

She stepped outside and shut the front door behind her.

Back in her car, she let out a long, exhausted sigh. At this point, she had no choice but to tell Nora that even though she knew who had her daughter, she still couldn't prove it. Nor had she been able to find Margaret, despite being only a few steps behind Lucien.

She should also apologize to Max, maybe in a couple of days, after he'd cooled off. What could she say that would make up for keeping such a big secret from him? He'd told her a lot of things about himself that weren't any of her business. Hell, she knew practically everything about him. And he knew almost everything about her. That intimate knowledge bound her to him in a way she would never experience with any other person. Her stupid, stubborn heart couldn't give him up, no matter how hard she tried to force it to.

Val took a deep breath and pulled out her phone. Might as well start the process of making uncomfortable calls, beginning with Nora. She paused when a new e-mail notification popped up, from an address she didn't recognize. An article was embedded in the message: "Mysterious Death Outside Local Bar Baffles Authorities." Val's blood pressure spiked as she read the story of Calvin Williams, a Lakewood mechanic who'd somehow choked to death on his own blood. The article speculated about possible viruses. Was someone trying to blackmail her?

Then she read text underneath the article:

Calvin Williams: cokehead and amateur hacker. Five arrests. One conviction for drug possession with intent to sell, two misdemeanor convictions for mail fraud and unlawful cybercrimes, sp. hacking into corporate servers and personal e-mail accounts. Restraining order in effect for stalking ex-girlfriend.

It was signed simply at the bottom:

Asshole.

Sten had sent this to her.

So Cal had worked in Lakewood as a mechanic…hadn't Zach told her the spoofed IP address where Margaret's video came from originated from a car garage in Lakewood? If Lucien was the source of the rape videos, maybe he hadn't intended for them to pop up on the Internet. Could Cal have hacked into Lucien's computer and stolen the videos? It was also possible Lucien sent the videos to certain sickos—people like Ginger—as a fucked-up "memories" keepsake for recruitment, and Cal hacked into their accounts and found the videos. The second scenario seemed more likely, given Lucien's gift for covering his tracks. Could be Cal targeted Ginger in particular because the two knew each other. The mechanic had a history of selling drugs—maybe he was Ginger's dealer? And when Lucien found out about the theft, he dispatched Ginger to take care of the problem, with poison in the form of a bribe.

It seemed a viable theory, taking into account everything she knew so far. How could Max be engaged to a woman whose brother was such a piece of shit? Val assumed Abigail and her brother grew up together. Was she really so much better than Ginger, or just better at hiding her depravity?

Val scoffed and shook her head at her spiteful thinking. Here she was, hoping her true love's fiancée was somehow a demented psycho—after *she* pushed *him* away. Pathetic. Val started her car. She'd call Nora after she was done being an emotional basket case.

On the way home, she rehearsed the conversation she knew she needed to have with Nora, though her mind kept wandering back to Max and what she should say to him. Jesus, a woman was being tortured somewhere, and she fretted over her ex-boyfriend. *Way to have your priorities straight, Val.*

Feeling like a complete piece of shit by the time she pulled up to her house, she saw an unfamiliar car parked in her driveway. Val put a hand on the gun at her hip, then relaxed as Josephine stepped out of the driver's side. She hadn't seen Robby's sister since Dean's funeral close to a year ago. She couldn't think of any pleasant reasons why Jo would make an impromptu visit.

As soon as Val got out of the car, Jo asked, "Why does Maxwell Carressa keep trying to give me money?"

"He's what?"

"He keeps offering me money, first as a scholarship fund in Robby and my dad's names, then as a charity donation. You…know him. Why is he harassing me?"

"Maybe you should ask him."

Jo scoffed. "I don't want anything to do with that asshole. He killed my father."

"He didn't kill your father. I was there when it happened."

"Well, Carressa somehow pushed him to do what he did. Dad never would've killed himself."

Except he did, right in front of Val and Max. In fact, Val was the one who'd pushed him. The familiar taste of bile rose in her throat. "It was Dean's choice to take his own life," Val said, repeating what her logical brain knew was the truth, though it didn't help her sleep at night. "It's not Max's fault."

"If it's not his fault, then why does he keep trying to pay me off? Tell him to leave me the hell alone."

Val sighed. Max would be furious with her for this. But he

was already furious with her, and sitting on the truth was making things worse. "Max is your brother, Jo."

Jo blinked as if Val had spoken a foreign language. "Excuse me?"

"He's your brother; half brother, specifically. Dean had an affair with Max's mother. Max was the result. He's probably trying to give you money as an excuse to have some contact with you."

Jo's mouth fell open. "That's a lie," she said, her words choked.

"Dean told us himself, right before he . . . passed away. I don't think he'd lie about something like that. You're Max's only immediate family member; vice versa for you now, I guess."

Jo pressed her lips together as if prepping for a yelling fit. Instead tears filled her eyes and her shoulders slumped. She let out a trembling breath, then turned away from Val, got in her car, and drove away.

Poor Jo. Poor Max. Val rubbed her eyes with the palms of her hands. A headache began to take root, born from too much pressure between her ears, from the weight of the entire goddamn, terrible world. She itched to call Sten, the perfect drug for relief with a side of self-loathing. No, she wouldn't do it again. He'd already done too much for her. Just thinking about what he might want in return made her shudder. She went inside, made a beeline for the fridge, cracked open a beer, and rubbed the condensation on her face. Three more beers and the last terrible twenty-four hours would only be a nattering in the back of her mind. At least Stacey wasn't around to give her shit about it. Where the hell was her roommate?

Val hadn't seen her in…days, it seemed. She didn't remember. Fuck it. Val couldn't take Stacey's pity anyway. It hurt too much.

She took a long, desperately needed drink of her beer. Of course that's when Sten called.

"Hey, beautiful," he said. "Didn't catch you at a bad time, did I?"

"I'd rather you call back when I'm drunk."

"I assumed you were always drunk."

"What do you want, Sten? Is this a booty call?"

"Please. Meet me at the corner of Second and Pine Street in an hour." He hung up.

"Shit," Val muttered, then chugged the rest of her beer. Time to pay her pound of flesh.

Chapter Nineteen

The corner of Second and Pine Street bustled with the tail end of rush hour traffic. Val parked on Second, then took a moment to bounce her head off the steering wheel a few times. If she knocked herself out, she'd have an excuse for not showing up…Nope, wasn't working. Shit. She took a deep breath and heaved herself out of the car. Squinting at the sun blaring in her eyes and wishing she could curl up in a ball and sleep for a week, she walked to the corner and scanned the area. No Sten. Maybe he wouldn't show. Hell, of course he'd show. She had to wait. Val was on his schedule now.

In the worst-case scenario, he'd order her to kill someone. She wouldn't commit murder, even if it meant reneging on their deal and suffering his wrath. She wouldn't seriously harm an innocent person, either. In fact, there were a lot of things she wouldn't do under any circumstance. He might have to kill her. She didn't doubt he was capable.

Val felt her cell phone vibrate; a text from Sten. Down the alley. She walked to the nearest alleyway on Pine, a dirty stretch of asphalt barely two car lengths wide and cast in shadow by the setting sun. In the center, Sten leaned against his unmarked police cruiser, casual in jeans and a plain dark blue T-shirt. Seeing him like that reminded Val why she'd been attracted to him in the first place, back in her early Army days. He struck an effortless, cocky pose, lazy expression hinting at a hidden intelligence. He made people come to him. Val set her jaw as she approached. She wanted to be free of him—and not. He made her body feel good, and he could hone her visions like no one else, despite the oily feeling he left on her soul afterward. And, God help her, he was the only person she could relate to anymore, now that her primary emotions were anger and frustration.

Sten opened the back door of his cruiser and motioned for her to get inside. She hesitated for a moment, wary of where he would take her, but decided her options were limited and got in the backseat. At least there was no one else already in there.

"Scoot over," he said.

She did so. He slipped in beside her and shut the door. Then he grabbed her legs and yanked them toward him. She yelped when her back bounced off the leather upholstery. He popped off her shoes, tossed them to the side, then pulled down her pants.

"I thought this wasn't a booty call," she said, letting him tear off her jeans and panties.

"It's not." He glanced at his watch, then ran his hands up her naked thighs. "But we've got a little time to kill, and you look like you're going to explode. You need your pressure valve released, baby." He spread her legs and dipped his head down.

"Don't call me that—" Her breath caught when she felt his tongue slide inside her. The car became a sauna as her body exploded with heat. She gasped for breath while Sten's mouth caressed her, played with her, sucked on her. God, he was good at this—too good, like a terrible drug she couldn't quit. She loved it as it killed her. He went on for a blur of time, soft and relentless. Her thighs trembled, body edging toward climax. Another terrible glimpse of the future was coming, either of someone dying, or the world ending, or a life with Max she couldn't have, or worse. Not again.

She mustered all her willpower. "Stop," she said, her voice breathless. "*Stop.*"

Sten lifted his head so his eyes met hers. "Why?"

"I can't." Her chest heaved with the effort to calm herself down. "I don't want to know the future. I can't take it anymore."

"Are you sure?" He slipped two fingers inside her while his thumb rubbed her clitoris in slow circles. A spike of pleasure shot through her. "I can make it a pleasant experience."

Val squeezed her eyes shut and shook her head. "No. Please."

Sten sighed and removed his hand from between her legs. "Have it your way."

He moved up beside her and wedged his chest between her prone body and the seat back. His head propped on one arm, he used his free hand to skim his fingers along her bare thigh. Val lay limp beside him, the pressure of her day replaced by the raw need for sexual release that she took deep breaths to suppress. She tipped her head to the side until Sten's moist shirt touched her nose. If anyone had seen them at that moment, she and Sten might've been mistaken for lovers.

He'd stopped when she asked him to. She hadn't expected that, not after being used and violated by so many other people. The sliver of power he'd given her meant a lot more than he probably realized. A tiny kernel of real affection for him popped inside her.

"You taste good," Sten said. "I don't say that to every woman, just so you know."

"You tried to kill me once." She said it as much to remind herself as to rebuff Sten. No matter the positive feelings she was beginning to have for him, she couldn't forget he was a killer.

"That was for show. I wouldn't have killed you. I can't anyway."

"Why not?"

"Politics."

Another vague clue. "But you would've killed Max."

"Nah...well, maybe. That one was kind of up in the air."

She scoffed. "If you're going to kill him, you might as well kill me."

Sten leaned over her. She opened her eyes and watched his lips come within an inch of hers, so close she could smell coffee and mint on his breath. Maybe she could settle for Sten. He wasn't so bad. Yeah, he'd done some terrible things, but so had she. They weren't that different. Hell, she needed somebody, anybody. His lips parted.

"Don't be so dramatic," he said. He slapped her thigh and she jumped. "Enough dillydallying. Get dressed and meet me at the corner. Don't take more than two minutes." He sat up and got out.

Val pushed herself into a sitting position and took a moment to reorient back to reality. *Of course* she'd never date Sten again. What the hell had she been thinking? He might not be willing or able to kill her, but if Max was fair game, then Sten was her enemy, no matter their shared interests. If he so much as looked at Max crossly, she'd beat him until his own squad mates couldn't identify his body.

Val threw her clothes back on and walked to where Sten stood on the corner. He didn't bother turning to face her, his concentration consumed by whatever lay ahead.

She folded her arms. "Now what?"

"Follow me."

They walked down Second Street, Sten's stride quick but not urgent, though she sensed an effort on his part to look casual so they wouldn't draw attention.

"About the mechanic, Cal Williams," Val said behind Sten. "Did you search his house?"

Sten glanced at her over his shoulder. "Yes."

"Did you confiscate his computer?"

"Indeed."

"Can I have the hard drive?"

"Negative."

"Can I at least look at it?"

"Nope."

Fucking Sten. "You know it'll take your super-competent police friends months before they get around to examining that hard drive. There could be evidence on his computer that he's the one who uploaded the videos of Margaret and me onto Rayvit. Just give me the goddamn drive so I can take care of it myself."

He snickered. "And what's your plan if you find your rapists?"

She cringed at the term. *Her rapists.* At least he believed her. "Something like Stevenson, maybe with more castration."

"That's hard to pull off on a dead person."

She stopped. "What?"

Sten walked a few more steps, then doubled back when he noticed she wasn't following him anymore. "Jeffrey Cartwright died in a tragic boating accident two days ago. Eliot Salier will soon perish in a freak house fire...or be mauled by a bear, I haven't decided yet."

Val gawked at him for a moment. He'd already searched Cal's computer and identified her attackers—and taken care of it, like he said he would. She should know better by now than to underestimate Sten. That dangerous kernel of affection for him grew a little larger. "Don't kill Salier. I have a better idea."

"I thought it didn't get any better than castration." He glanced at his watch again. "Hold up your end of the bargain, and you can tell me all about it." He resumed his march toward their destination.

After they walked another block, Sten took a right onto Pike, then a quick left onto First. He stopped a few steps from the corner of First and Union, checked his watch, and shoved his hands in his pockets. He turned toward her like they were a couple chatting about where to get dinner.

"That's the Four Seasons Hotel." He cocked his head an inch toward the building across the street. "See that black car parked out front?"

Val looked past him at a shiny service sedan waiting at the curb. The car's driver stood a foot away, ready to swoop forward and open the door for some wealthy bastard. "Yeah."

"In three minutes, a man in a blue Armani suit and orange silk tie will come out of the hotel and get into that car." His gaze held hers. "Don't let him get in the car."

Val raised an eyebrow. "That's it?"

"That's it."

"Why do you need me for this?"

"You have a special touch."

"You mean you want me to change something about the future, and this guy not getting into that car will do it."

Sten's face hardened with a seriousness she'd never seen in him before. "We shall see."

Val fought back a sick feeling. "Do I need to keep him out of this car indefinitely?"

"Yes."

"What if he gets into another car?"

"Doesn't matter. You now have two minutes."

"And what if I can't keep him out of the car?"

"Then you've failed to hold up your end of our bargain."

"Which means what? You'll *wish* you could kill me really badly?"

He cocked his head and smiled. "I don't have to kill you to punish you."

A crystal-clear statement. Val walked past him to get a better look at the car and the driver. There were a lot of ways she could keep this mystery man from getting into his car. She could take the driver hostage. She could set the car on fire. She could shoot out the tires. She could shoot the mystery man.

Unfortunately, those obvious options came with jail time. Subterfuge was her best bet.

"One minute," Sten said.

Val crossed the street and walked toward the car, careful to look casual despite feeling the opposite, as Sten had done. She stopped ten feet from the car and pretended to check her phone, twirling her hair like a ditz for effect. From the corner of her eye, she saw a heavy man in a blue suit exit the building. Val held up her phone and pretended to pose for a selfie, mugging for the camera. Her palm-sized screen confirmed he wore an orange tie—her mystery man. A posse of half a dozen business types barking into cell phones surrounded him, including one severe-looking guy in a black sport coat—a bodyguard. Mystery man seemed quite the player.

When they reached the sedan, Val sprang her trap. The bodyguard covered the mystery man's rear. His eyes rolled off her as he scanned for threats. The driver opened the car door while the business posse talked over each other about deadlines and meetings. Still pretending as if she were enraptured by her phone, Val walked briskly toward the bodyguard—so briskly that when she slammed into him, she could believably ricochet off him and into the car, and "accidentally" shove her elbow through the side window.

Val clutched her arm and wailed. "Oh my God!" Blood dripped onto the pavement. Damn, that hurt more than she thought it would.

A moment of shock gripped everyone around her. The bodyguard looked confused, suspicious, and concerned at the same time. The business posse gave second-by-second plays to whoever was on the other end of their phones. Hotel staff ran forward. Mystery man stared at her.

"My *arm!*" Val whined when a concierge rushed to her aid. She glared at the bodyguard. "He ran straight into me!"

The bodyguard still looked confused. Over the concierge's pleas for her to sit down, she heard the driver say into his cell, "We need a new car here *now.*"

Mission accomplished.

"Don't touch!" She slapped the concierge's hand away from her bleeding arm. "It super hurts! Owww—"

The mystery man spoke with a strong English accent. "*Valentine Shepherd?*"

Val froze.

He met her gaze with wide, fearful eyes. His voice trembled. "Are you Valentine Shepherd?"

Shit. How did he know her? Maybe he recognized her from the news last year? She didn't remember ever seeing him before.

As she looked at him, he took a step back. Panic gripped his face. In a blink he sprinted away from her, fleeing blindly into the busy street—right in front of a bus. It slammed into him and carried his body on its grill until it screeched to a halt amid horrified screams. Her jaw hanging open, Val stared stupidly at the twisted form of the mystery man as chaos reigned around her—a bloody chaos she'd created. She forced herself to look away, and her eyes wandered to Sten. As his eyes locked with hers, a wicked smile spread across his lips. He flashed her a subtle thumbs-up, then disappeared in the crowd.

Chapter Twenty

It took Max a moment to realize the wetness he felt on his cheek was Toby licking his face. He turned his head and saw the dog on his bed, sitting next to him. Toby wasn't supposed to be in there. He didn't remember letting the dog in, but he didn't remember much of anything besides throwing on one of his awful charity tuxedos, downing a generous handful of OxyContin pills, sitting at the edge of his bed, and staring at the walls for God knows how long. Max tried to push Toby away, but his arms felt weak and his hand slipped off the dog's head in a clumsy caress. Toby wagged his tail.

Abby walked out of the bathroom clad in a sapphire silk gown, gorgeous as usual. She smiled at him, her warmth for her fiancé recently renewed. After returning from the Mountain Lodge, he'd made love to her like he swore he would, but—God, he'd had to force himself to. He'd *performed*, feeling nothing for her, and he hated himself for it.

"Are you sure you're feeling all right for this?" Abby asked as she fiddled with an earring. "You don't have to go."

Of course he had to go. Abby's father was throwing this particular charity ball. Patrick disliked Max, thought he was a lazy playboy. Wasn't completely convinced Max didn't kill his father. Smart man. If Max didn't go tonight, he'd never hear the end of it. Abby wouldn't say anything to Max—not directly, she never did—but she'd hint at her disappointment, make sad faces his way, mention how she wished he'd get along better with her father. Her family's approval was important to her. For that reason, she shouldn't have dated Max to begin with, but he must have been too delectable an opportunity to pass up—wealthy, mysterious, good in bed, decent-looking, and all that other stuff women liked beyond reason. He guessed she thought she could make her family accept him, "reform the bad boy" or some shit.

As if one day, maybe after Max saved Abby from a dastardly kidnapping plot or a humiliating social faux pas, Patrick would put his hand on Max's shoulder and say with a proud grin, "Son, I was wrong about you. All this time I thought you murdered your father so you could burn through your inheritance with impunity, but now I see you're worthy of my daughter. I'm glad to have you in the family—"

"Max?"

He blinked, his eyes adjusting from the wall to Abby. "What?"

"I said are you sure you want to go tonight?"

"Yes. I'm fine. Just took too much migraine medication." He tapped his temple. "Medicine head. It'll go away. You look good, V—very good."

Jesus, he almost called her Val. Exactly the person he didn't want to think about. Nausea roiled in his stomach again as images of her naked, unconscious body being violated flashed through his mind. And she didn't trust Max enough to tell him. She preferred to manipulate him into helping her than give him the truth of what her crusade against Lucien was actually about. After everything they'd shared, he thought *some* part of her must still care for him, but he'd thought wrong.

He must really mean nothing to her.

And Lucien…that disgusting, bottom-dwelling, fucking piece of shit rat bastard. Max would kill Christophe if he ever saw him again. First, he'd cut off Lucien's balls, hands, and tongue, in that order, so the Frenchman could experience a *fraction* of the pain he'd caused Val and other women unlucky enough to cross his path. Then he'd burn Lucien alive—

"Max."

"What?"

"Did you hear what I said?"

"Huh?"

She frowned. "Are you sure you're all right?"

He looked down and saw his hands balled into tight fists. Forcing them to unclench, he said, "Yeah. Some…fresh air will clear my head, I think." He stood slowly, careful not to stumble in front of her.

Abby's furrowed brow betrayed her skepticism, but in the end, pleasing Daddy was more important. "Let's go then."

He swallowed a desperate sigh, then patted Toby's head. "Be good."

She drove on account of his medicine head.

Then he was standing in a dark room with translucent white porcelain on the walls. The Seattle Art Museum, Max remembered. Raising money to restore a public section of the waterfront damaged in a storm last year. Something like that.

"And he had such beautiful eyes," a middle-aged woman with chandeliers for earrings was saying to him. "Like he could see right into your soul." After a moment, he recognized her—Rhonda Gallagher. Widow of Nigel Gallagher, bank chairman. "Well, *you* would know a little something about beautiful eyes." She winked at him.

Why would Max know that? Was she talking about him?

"I loved that horse. I really wish he could've sired more foals before we had to put him down." Rhonda sighed and sipped from her champagne flute. "Oh well. They can't live forever, I suppose. Did your family own horses?"

"No." Max turned away before she could launch into another inane topic. He spotted Abby in the center of the room, talking to a tall, stocky man with a close-cropped donut of hair—her father. At least Ginger wasn't around. He'd jetted off to somewhere in East Asia, probably to partake of a little sex tourism. Yuck. Max grabbed a glass of wine off a tray as a waiter walked by. If he kept the glass to his lips, maybe he wouldn't be expected to talk.

"There you are," Abby said, taking Max's arm as he walked up and stood beside her. She smiled at him, radiating charisma for them both. "I was just telling Daddy about my plan to go back to school. Events at places like this make me remember why I got a degree in art history to begin with. So beautiful."

"Uh-huh." Max sipped his wine.

"I'm sure you'll be successful at whatever you do, cupcake," Patrick said. "Maxwell, what have you diversified into lately?"

"I don't diversify," he muttered.

"So you think your father's money will last forever?"

"*Dad*," Abby said, feigning embarrassment for Max but really hoping he'd throw her father a bone and pretend to care about the latest financial bullshit.

This was the part where Patrick offered Max a job—the better to exert control over his future son-in-law. "If you're going to come to me hat-in-hand one day when your inheritance runs dry, you might as well earn my money. My Northern Asia line still has a management position open and..."

Patrick's voice became a droning noise. Max stared at the porcelain to the right of Patrick's head, perfect discs of white suspended in black cases. These particular sets were Japanese, created during the Second World War. Written and baked into their glossy surfaces were names of noble family members who'd died in the conflict, and prayers for their souls—

A boisterous laugh caught his attention. A laugh he recognized. He heard a snippet of conversation. "Huge! You would not believe it," someone said. A Frenchman.

"If you're just sitting on your shares, you should—*Ah!*" Patrick jerked backward. Max realized he'd turned toward the conversation and let his wineglass tip sideways at the same time, spilling Merlot on Patrick's expensive shoes. "What the hell are you—"

Letting the wineglass fall, Max walked toward the voice, a smooth timbre with a slight French accent. A confident voice, a charming voice. A voice full of lies. With each step he took, his anger grew, bubbling up through the fog of opiates until all the white porcelain around him turned red. Max pushed through a crowd of bodies until he saw him.

"I would have thought he was lying, but I saw it with my own eyes," Lucien said to a captivated audience of almost a dozen people. "A baby Loch Ness monster, he called it, right on his wall." His gaze wandered to Max and stayed there. "Ah, Max! Good to see you. You're well traveled. You must have some interesting stories to tell of supposed magical beings, yes?"

Max slugged Lucien in the face. Lucien dropped to the ground as the crowd gasped. Max sprung on top of him and channeled every ounce of energy he had to pound into oblivion the man who'd raped the woman he loved. Lucien threw up his arms but his weak defense was no match for Max's fury. His fists found Lucien's head, chest, shoulders, arms. Every strike landed with the force of murderous rage.

"Max, stop!" Abby's voice floated to him over a cacophony of screaming and yelling. "*Stop!*"

He ignored her. Monsters deserved to die. If Max had to kill Lucien with his bare hands, so be it.

Then he was being dragged away. Lucien's pulpy face receded, blood pouring down his chin from a smashed nose and cut above the eye. *No!* He was so close, *so close* to exacting justice for Val. Max struggled to free himself, thrashing his arms and legs, gnashing his teeth, growling like an animal.

Rough hands flipped Max over and shoved his face into the floor. Security guards. They pried his arms behind his back. Handcuffs snapped around his wrists. Then they hauled him to his feet. Everyone was yelling at him, gawking at him, crying at him. Furious, shocked faces blurred past as the security guards dragged him away, his legs unsteady, lungs on fire, head spinning, unable to recall what he was even doing there before he saw the monster.

***

Max flinched when the camera's flash went off. He blinked back green spots.

"Turn to your right," a police officer ordered. "Hold the sign at shoulder level."

Max turned to his right and pressed the stenciled sign with his name on it against his shoulder.

"Hold it higher."

Max inched it up.

"Lower."

He lowered it.

"Too low."

Just take the fucking mugshot! he almost said, but gritted his teeth and did as he was told. He didn't have the energy to fight anymore. He wanted it to be over, no matter what they did to him. After a round of photographs, they took his fingerprints. Max stared dully at the walls, not arguing, not reacting, not caring. A ragdoll in the process. Drunk and disorderly, one policeman said. That rich guy got away with killing his father, another whispered. They stared at him, then looked away when he noticed. They asked him if he wanted to make a statement; he said nothing. They threw him in a cell.

Max counted the ceiling tiles until he drifted into a fitful sleep. Snakes slithered through his dreams, eating little birds by swallowing them whole. Then they crawled into his mouth and took the place of his intestines, until his gut writhed with snakes. The clang of his cell door woke him.

"Come on," a policeman said as he held the door open. "Your lady made bail."

Max staggered to his feet. He noticed for the first time his swollen knuckles, blood splotches on his dress shirt, bow tie hanging crooked off his collar, scuffed shoes. The fog over his brain was lifting, leaving behind a growing nausea in his stomach and an emptiness in his chest. He glanced at the ancient clock bolted to the wall; half past 1 a.m. Max followed the policeman through the station and felt the stares of curious onlookers more acutely than the night before. The cop led him somewhere other than the entrance; a back door of some kind. Abby waited there, still in her silk gown though her hair looked messed and makeup faded. Dark circles lurked under her eyes. She regarded Max with tight lips.

"We have to leave this way," she said, her voice hoarse. "There's media out front."

He walked past her, out the door, and to her car. She drove while he sat in the passenger seat and stared out the side window.

"Why did you do that?" Abby asked when they were halfway home.

Max continued to stare out the window.

"Max, why?"

He couldn't explain.

"Please tell me."

If he told her, it was over. Officially over.

By the time they reached his condo, Max's palms were sweaty and his stomach was gripped by nausea. His head was beginning to split open. He needed more pills. Rushing inside, he blew past Toby and ran up the stairs to the master bathroom. Max threw open the medicine cabinet's door, knocked a bunch of other bottles to the ground, and dug out his OxyContin. He pawed at the cap. The goddamn thing was stuck, and his sweaty hands weren't helping. He slammed the bottle against the sink basin, trying to loosen up the cap, harder each time, until blood from his bashed fingers stained the porcelain.

"Goddammit, talk to me!" Abby yelled from the bathroom's doorway.

He spiked the bottle in the sink. "What do you want me to say, Abby? You want me to confess my deep, dark secrets to you? I already fucking did that!"

She gasped at his sudden outburst, then lifted her chin, ready for a fight. "Tell me why you attacked Lucien."

"You really wanna know? Fine. I'll tell you fucking everything. Lucien runs the Blue Serpent cult and he rapes people. Sometimes he tortures and murders them, too. And Ginger helps him. *Your brother* rapes, tortures, and murders people. Because all those rich fucks at the charity events we keep attending think it's fun. It's their idea of a good time when they're not pretending to give a shit about poor people or the environment. Happy now? Are you happy you know?"

Abby gaped at him, her big blue eyes made wider with disbelief, and disgust. "That's what you've been investigating with Valentine Shepherd?"

"Yes, that's what we've been investigating." He snatched up the OxyContin bottle again. The cap finally gave and twisted off.

She eyed the pills he dumped in his hand. "What is that, really?"

"OxyContin," he said without looking at her. He threw pills in his mouth—he didn't know how many—and leaned his head under the faucet. Water poured straight into his mouth and sprayed his shirt.

Her eyes filled with tears. "I…I think you might be having a break from reality."

He choked out a mirthless laugh and ripped off his bow tie. "Yeah, sure."

"You need help. Anyone who endured what your father did to you would need—"

"I am not a fucking invalid! This has nothing to do with him! *Nothing!*"

"It has everything—"

"My father is *dead*. Lucien is still alive, and your brother's working with him." He narrowed his eyes at her. "Did you know this whole time?"

"Is that what Val told you?"

"No, I saw it for myself. With her…I saw her…" Max closed his eyes and leaned against the sink as a wave of nausea passed through him. The pills weren't working fast enough. He saw Val on Lucien's computer again, felt her pain…When Max opened his eyes, tears flowed down Abby's face.

"Do you love her?"

All at once the anger left him, replaced by cold despair. Whatever he felt for Abby, it wasn't enough. It never would be. He loved Val—only Val, and no one else. He'd love her until the day he died. And she didn't love him.

Though he didn't speak, the look he gave Abby must have told her everything. Her face crumpled. "Did you ever love me?"

The words stuck in his throat. He forced them out like one might induce vomiting after swallowing poison. "I tried." It was the meanest thing he'd ever said. But she wanted the truth, and he couldn't live a lie anymore.

A sob ripped from her throat. She fled from the bathroom and ran down the stairs. He heard the front door open and slam closed, then all was quiet.

Max's legs gave way and he sat in a heap on the edge of the bathtub. He let his head fall into his hands. What had he done? His cruelty toward poor Abby made him sick. He should've let her go before things got this far, but instead he'd lied to himself, pretended he could be a normal person and live a normal life. Tricked himself into thinking he could love anyone but Val. Not only had he murdered his own father and let everyone think it'd been a tragic accident, but he'd fallen desperately and completely in love with a woman who wouldn't have him. Then he'd ruined someone else's life because he couldn't face the truth. If he'd succeeded in ending it all years ago, the world would've been spared the wreckage of his continued existence.

Max eyed the pill bottle still in his hand, more than half full. He swallowed all the rest of its contents, then threw the empty container across the bathroom.

It never worked. He'd tried many times, and it never fucking worked. Those attempts were before the red raven, though. She'd *seen* him die, and then saved him. But she wasn't around now. Maybe she'd changed something in the order of the universe, and he could finally leave this hopeless world.

Max picked up a crystal seashell at the head of the tub, part of a set he'd bought before Abby moved in. He hadn't picked it out; an interior decorator did. *Make it look like a human being lives here*, he'd told her. He threw the shell across the room. It shattered against the wall. Toby whined from the bedroom, cowering out of sight. Max picked up another shell and threw it, then another, and another, until the bathroom tiles were littered with broken crystal.

Then he tore through his condo, smashing and tearing apart anything he'd bought specifically for the purpose of looking normal, which was almost everything. Commissioned portraits, tchotchkes from around the world, hand-crafted furniture, finely etched glassware. Useless junk, all of it. After an orgy of destruction, he stumbled back into the bathroom. He took a framed picture of a seascape off the wall and spiked it into the bathtub. Glass erupted, and he felt a sting on his palms. He thought he might've cut himself, but his eyes wouldn't focus on his hands when he looked for blood, and the bathroom spun, and cool floor tile touched his face. The last thing he sensed was the stupid dog barking furiously.

Chapter Twenty-one

Stacey's voice reached Val through a haze of sleep. "Get up!" She kicked the bed.

Val's eyes cracked open. The sun burned. She blinked and wiped away crust from the corners of her eyelids until the world focused. After a moment she realized she wasn't in her bed but on the living room couch, where she'd passed out the night before after drinking a few beers…More than a few.

"I said get up!" The couch rocked with another swift kick.

"Jesus, Stacey," Val muttered. "I'm tired. Leave me alone."

"Bitch, please. It's almost one o'clock in the afternoon."

Val moaned and forced herself to sit up. Her arm ached through the bandage wrapped around her elbow, dressing the stitches she'd had to get after shoving her arm through the car window. A headache pounded behind her eyes, and her mouth tasted like spoiled milk. Then she remembered why she'd done this to herself. She'd killed a man.

Stacey stalked to the coffee table. "I'm officially tired of this," she said as she snatched up empty beer bottles. "It's time for you to get your shit together."

Val rubbed her temples and let out a long sigh. "Can you lay off? You wouldn't believe the day I had—"

"*You* wouldn't believe the hoops I've had to jump through to convince our clients we're still working on their cases. You know, the clients that *aren't* Nora Monroe and her missing daughter? If we don't work on other cases, then we don't get our fee and the mortgage doesn't get paid and I can't believe *I'm* the one telling *you* this."

Val stood and shuffled to the kitchen. She found a bottle of Tylenol in a drawer, poured herself a glass of water, and downed a couple of pills, like they'd relieve her guilt somehow. "Monroe's the only life-or-death case we have. It takes priority."

Stacey dumped her armful of beer bottles in the recycling bin. "I understand that, but I think at this point we've done all we can. You said the police are finally looking for her, so let them take responsibility."

Val scoffed. "You mean let her die?"

"I mean this case is killing you. Look in the mirror, for Christ's sake. You're a mess—and not a *hot* mess, just a mess." She threw up her hands. "And where the hell have you been disappearing to lately?"

"Where the hell have *you* been? Every time I come home, you're not here. Why am I the bad one because I'm not around?"

"I've been juggling all our other cases, Val, while you've been getting blitzed. Where were you yesterday, before you stumbled home and drank yourself into a stupor? What happened to your arm? Just be honest with me, for fuck's sake!"

Val looked away. She took a deep breath, her shoulders slumped. Stacey was her best friend. She deserved the truth. Maybe her reaction wouldn't be as bad as Val feared. "I was with Sten."

Stacey's mouth fell open, her silence a substitute for a thousand questions.

"Sten agreed to help me with the investigation. In return, I agreed to do him a favor."

Stacey folded her arms and glared at Val. She nearly whispered the words, "So you trust a man who almost killed you, but not me."

"I had to. There was no one else—"

"You had me!"

"No I don't! I don't have you!" Tears welled in Val's eyes, and she grabbed her head as if it might explode. "You don't understand what it's like to be violated, to be used, to be alone, to be angry and sad all the time, or to love someone who doesn't love you! You have *no fucking idea!*"

Stacey folded her arms and took a long, trembling breath. "But *Sten* understands?"

Val rubbed her wet eyes with the palms of her hands. "Yes."

They stood in silence for what seemed an eternity. Stacey's arms stayed folded as she regarded Val with a new skepticism. The kitchen counter separated them, but it might as well have been a hundred-foot chasm.

Stacey's voice had a cold edge. "I'm sorry you can't deal with what happened to you in a healthy way. And I do, in fact, know what it's like to love someone who doesn't love you. I'm intimately familiar with that feeling, actually."

Val felt her cheeks heat up as a fresh lump grew in her throat. Was this the end for them? They'd been through a lot together, known each other almost their entire lives. But after the chaos last year with Delilah and Norman Barrister, after Robby's death, after Max entered Val's life, things had been different. They'd both changed in ways that were beginning to seem incompatible with the other.

A chime from Val's cell phone interrupted the painful standoff. The special double-chime. *Oh no.* Val rushed to her phone.

"What's that?" Stacey asked.

Val tapped her phone awake and maneuvered as quickly as possible through the menu. "I set my phone to double-chime if Margaret's name popped up on a Google Alert."

Their showdown temporarily suspended, Stacey unfolded her arms and bit her lip as Val pulled up the alert—a news article, just posted: "Local Woman's Body Found—"

"No," Val whispered. "*No. No. No.*" She dropped her phone and ran to the TV, flicked it on, and scrolled through the menu with shaking hands until she found a network airing the local news. Stacey and Val watched the screen together, both slack-jawed.

A blond woman in a clear rain slicker addressed the camera as police lights flashed behind her in the rain. "Sources confirm the body that washed ashore this morning as that of a local woman named Margaret Monroe, first reported missing two weeks ago. No word yet on the cause of death, though foul play has not been ruled out..."

They found Margaret on a rocky beach, just as it had been in Val's vision. Val had killed a man the day before by changing his future, but no matter what she did, she couldn't save Margaret. Everything she'd done had been for nothing. A sob exploded from Val's chest, so powerful her whole body spasmed. A tsunami of grief poured forth, out of her mouth in wails and into her cupped hands. She cried so hard she thought her body might turn itself inside out. Stacey's hand touched her shoulder, but instead of turning to her friend for comfort, Val ran up the stairs and shut herself into her room.

All she saw was death. Sometimes she caused it. Only twice had she been able to change it—she'd saved Stacey from drowning years ago, and Max from being beaten to death by Sten. She hated her ability. *Hated it.* It cursed her with the knowledge of terrible things to come, dangled the possibility of changing the future for the better, then crushed that hope. A vow of celibacy might not be so bad. At least then she could pretend she had a normal life, without knowledge of the future to torture her.

Val didn't know how long she lay on her bed, impotently crying. A voice of reason in the back of her mind told her to put on her big girl panties and get up, but the voice wasn't strong enough.

A soft knock sounded on the bedroom door. "Val?" Stacey opened the door a crack. She held their home phone, the one they used for business. "There's someone on the phone for you—Michael Beauford, I think he said his name was. I told him to call back later, but he says it's urgent."

Val sat up. If one of the only people Max trusted was calling her concerning an urgent matter, she'd better damn well answer. She'd be putting on her big girl panties sooner rather than later after all.

Working to steady her voice, Val took the phone. "Hello?"

"Valentine Shepherd?"

"Yeah?"

"You might not remember me, but we met last year when Max was shot and—"

"I remember you. What's urgent?"

He sighed. She heard a deep strain in his voice. "It's too much to explain over the phone. You need to come here."

"Where?"

"Harborview Medical Center—the psychiatric ward."

Chapter Twenty-two

The psychiatric ward of the Harborview Medical Center glowed with natural light. The sun's rays softened through frosted glass skylights that warmed the pale wood décor. As Val walked through the lobby, she sensed the façade was meant to be inviting and comfortable. It almost worked. From somewhere inside the ward, a woman screamed. Val jumped.

She ignored her unease and forged ahead, scanning the area for Michael Beauford. Val turned and saw him walking toward her, a man in his late fifties wearing an immaculately tailored suit, though his laidback demeanor made him seem approachable nonetheless. The genial expression she remembered from last time they met had been replaced with somberness. Knots of worry stiffened his shoulders.

"Hello again," he said in a friendlier tone than she would've had given the circumstances.

Val took in the ward's pretense of safety, its fake promise

that everything would be all right despite the screaming. She swallowed back a lump in her throat. "Max is here."

Michael nodded.

"What happened?"

"Well..." He seemed to consider how honest he should be. A slight shrug of his shoulders told Val he'd settled on the brutal truth. "He overdosed on pain pills. The docs aren't sure if it was an accident or an attempted suicide. Given how badly the paramedics say he trashed his condo, they're leaning toward the latter explanation."

Val rubbed her mouth in what she hoped looked like thoughtful contemplation, and not barely contained panic. She thought Max had finally achieved the perfect life—perfect house, perfect fiancée, freedom, respect—even though she'd seen and sensed the cracks in the mask he presented to the world. But *suicide?* Max had tried to kill himself before, when he'd been under the thumb of his brutal father. But whatever gave them their prophetic abilities also wanted him to live, and he'd somehow always survive to stay trapped in a life he had no control over.

Val looked past Michael at the far wall, a pleasant shade of yellow. "He's had a hard life," she said, her voice strained with tears she struggled to keep in.

"I know. I figured as much about a decade ago."

Val met his gaze and saw deep wisdom in his eyes. Did he know Max killed his father? She guessed he did, but also knew why, and stood by Max anyway.

"His fiancée found him?"

"Actually, his neighbor found him. Max's dog was raising

holy hell, so the neighbor went over to investigate, let herself in, then called an ambulance. Good thing the desire to shut up a yippy dog is more powerful than social decorum. Otherwise, Max would be"—he swallowed, and for a second fear dominated his friendly eyes—"he'd be dead."

So this time Max's dog served as the agent of fate. She didn't even know he had a dog. It occurred to Val that Michael still hadn't told her why he'd asked her to come. "Where's Abby?"

He knotted his brow, again considering how he should answer. "I don't think they're together anymore."

At this news Val's tears leaked out. She cupped her head in her hands and quietly cried. She *had* ruined his life. She wouldn't leave him alone, but wouldn't be with him, either, and those decisions ended with him in the psych ward. After a minute she took a deep breath, lifted her head, and wiped her tears away. "You want me to apologize?"

"No," he said as if she'd suggested something ridiculous. "I want you to get him to talk."

"Talk to who?"

"*Anybody.*" He stepped closer and lowered his voice. "Listen, I don't know if what he did was an accident or not. But now he's stuck here, and the doctors won't let him out until they're sure he's not a threat to himself or others. Problem is, he won't talk to anyone—not me, or the doctors, or Abby. The only reason I'm here is because I'm still listed as his emergency contact. In that capacity, I called you. I know you two have…something. Something he doesn't have with anybody else, not even Abby. Normally it wouldn't be any of my business, but"—he lifted his hands—"here we are."

Val pulled at her hair. She wanted to talk to Max, but she didn't know what to say. She feared she'd make things worse, though she wasn't sure how that was possible.

"Please," Michael added, sensing her hesitation. "He'll rot in here. You're my last chance to convince him to save himself."

After a long pause in which Val considered what she or Max had left to lose, she nodded. She had to try. Michael gave her a weary smile, then exchanged words with the front desk clerk. A couple of minutes later, a nurse emerged from a Staff Only door and led Val into the main section of the ward.

The part of the psychiatric hospital that actually housed all the patients looked similar to the lobby—soft light, pale wood with rounded edges, yellow walls. The only significant difference was the sea of blue hospital gowns and slumped shoulders that marked the patients. Most seemed lethargic, probably on sedatives. TVs dotted the periphery of the room. Val flinched when she spotted a photo of Margaret on one of the flat screens, a segment of a local news program in progress. She forced herself to look away, but the wound had already been salted.

The nurse stopped and pointed to a spot along the far wall, next to a window. Max's head poked up from a chair paired with an empty table, his black hair a sharp contrast with the pale blue gown that sagged off his body. He slouched in his seat, his back to her, unmoving. The nurse retreated to give them privacy.

Taking slow, measured steps, Val circled around him until she could see his face. She gasped at the man in front of her. It was Max, but in the most broken state she'd ever seen him.

The normal tan of his healthy skin had turned a sickly shade of white. His sharp cheekbones hollowed out his face, and dark rings circled his hazel eyes. He stared dully out the window, totally lost in his own thoughts.

"Max?" Val said quietly.

His gaze cut to hers and sharpened as his mind snapped back to the present. He sat up in his chair and hugged his chest. He didn't seem sedated, thankfully. Just lost.

"Hey," he said. His voice sounded hoarse, she guessed from the tube they'd shoved down his throat to pump his stomach.

"Hey," she replied.

Last time they'd exchanged greetings in a hospital, it'd been euphoric. After barely surviving a standoff with Norman, and then Sten, they'd been happy to be alive. Now, not so much. He squirmed under her gaze and looked away, as if he was embarrassed. Hell, Stacey had told Val she was a mess only a few hours ago, and she hadn't bothered to clean up since. Max wasn't alone in looking like shit warmed over.

Val took a chair adjacent to Max at the table. "Michael called me."

"Oh."

"He's really worried."

Max didn't respond. He glanced at her bandaged elbow but didn't ask about it. She searched for the right words while he ran his fingers along a scratch on the table's surface. Both his hands had bandages wrapped around his palms.

"What happened to your hands?" she asked.

"Cuts," he said flatly.

"How did that happen?"

"Glass."

On purpose, or accident? Were the cuts deep? Were they serious? So many questions she wanted to ask, things she wanted to say that clawed at her throat to get out. But he was the one who needed to talk, not her. "Will you have scars?"

He responded with a slight shrug. A minute of silence passed where she picked at her own bandage around her elbow. Her heartbeat steadily increased as a howl tried to work its way up from her chest. Maybe she could hug him, or hold his hand. Just touch him. God, she wanted to fold him into her arms with every fiber of her being. But she couldn't. He clearly didn't want her there, no matter what Michael thought.

Without lifting his eyes from the table's marred surface, he said, "I'm sorry about Margaret. I saw it on the news."

Val gave her head a tiny shake. "We…tried." She bit the inside of her cheek to keep from screaming.

"And I'm sorry about what happened at the Mountain Lodge. I"—he swallowed; it looked painful—"overreacted."

He still wouldn't look at her. His hands shook and his shoulders stiffened as if he nursed a secret ball of pain. She realized he must be going through serious withdrawal, feeling terrible nausea and aching. But he didn't mention it. She wanted to cry *for* him, to wail and gnash and scream at the world in his place, if it would lessen his own agony. She'd even make a scene in the middle of the ward if he asked her to, or if she thought it would do any good. But instead he sat there, saying nothing. Maybe the direct approach would work better.

"Why are you here?" Val asked, her light tone a contrast to the weight of her words.

"I like the chocolate pudding they serve."

She spat out a laugh, delighted for a fleeting moment by his small attempt at levity even if he'd only said it to dodge her question. He didn't return her smile. His mouth stayed locked in a frown.

Val rested her hand next to his on the table, the familiar desire to touch him nearly overwhelming, as always. She drummed her fingers instead. So far, she was doing a shit job of convincing him to save himself. "How long are you going to stay here?"

He looked at her hand, still avoiding her eyes. "I don't know."

He wasn't talking. Val had to talk. What was she going to say? Whatever it was inside her trying to get out, she couldn't delay it any longer.

"I'm sorry I didn't tell you about what happened to me." She took a labored breath, her heart thumping hard. "It wasn't fair of me to ask for your help and then keep you in the dark about all the...details."

Max finally met her eyes, though his face remained impassive.

"I didn't tell you because—"

Because it wasn't any of your business. Because I didn't want you to pity me. Because I didn't want you to freak out. Because I didn't want to ruin your perfect life.

"Because I love you." The words tumbled out, and the dam broke. "I love you and I can't stop loving you. I tried to move on like you had, but I couldn't. It's divine irony, I guess, since I'm the one who pushed you away. But I was weak and I couldn't deal with the knowledge that there would always be people watching us, waiting for us to have children that would be ripped from us." Val wiped away tears that had escaped down her cheeks. "And you seemed happy with your new life. I meant it when I said you deserve to be happy. I didn't want you to lose that, because of me. But I guess I'd misjudged how happy you actually were." She glanced around the mental ward, full of fake comfort. "So...so I can't help but think that if I hadn't pushed you away in the first place, none of the stuff with Lucien and the Blue Serpent and...this place would've happened. We might've saved Margaret together." She took a trembling breath. "I can't do this anymore. I'm tired of flailing through life. I feel lost, like I want to go home."

Val looked at him then. She'd told him everything, even the things she hadn't been able to admit to herself until that moment. His passive frown was gone, and though he wasn't smiling, his eyes had come alive with a dozen different emotions. He didn't just look at her; he looked *into* her as she bared her soul to him.

"Come home, Max." She touched the top of his hand with her fingertips. Goose bumps popped up around his hospital bracelet. "With me."

A savory warmth spread through her body at allowing herself this simple, honest contact. Finally, she offered him everything she had to give. She should've done it months ago, in his hospital room after Sten had shot him, when she'd laid her head down on his chest and realized she truly loved him.

Max looked into her for a long time, the new flood of emotions making his face unreadable. Desperation crept into her heart. She'd experienced a lot of terrible things in her life and come out the other side battered but still standing, even if just barely. But if he decided to stay in the psych ward, it would truly break her.

His arm moved, and for a frantic second she thought he might yank it away as he'd done at their first meeting in Wicked Brew. Instead he turned his hand over so his bandaged palm faced up and pressed against hers. His fingers slid across the inside of her wrist and gripped her tight; she gripped him back. Then he smiled, an upturn of his lips so slight it might've gone unnoticed to anyone else, but she saw it touch his eyes.

"Okay," he said.

Chapter Twenty-three

Max told the doctors whatever they wanted to hear. Most of it was a lie: *I accidentally overdosed. I've never had a drug problem before. I didn't like my father, but I was sad when he died. No, nothing else in my past is worth mentioning.* Some of it was the truth: *I became addicted to pain pills after I was shot last year. My fiancée and I had a fight. I was upset. I overreacted, but I'm better now.* Val visited him in the hospital every day for as long as they'd let her stay, and though they never talked about anything too serious—they were never really alone, after all—he felt his mood drastically improving, his will to live returning. After three more days of psychotherapy and observations, the doctors told him he could leave. They needed his bed for someone with real problems, not a rich guy piddling away his dad's inheritance on expensive drugs.

Michael brought him some regular clothes to change into so he didn't have to walk out the door wearing the tuxedo he'd been brought in with, now covered in blood, sweat, and vomit. Max tossed the suit in a trash can next to the vending machine, not at all sad he'd never wear it again. The hospital was nice enough to let him leave out a semi-secret exit, one they reserved for celebrities—usually rock stars—who needed to sneak out the back. Paparazzi stalked the front entrance, waiting for him to emerge so they could shove cameras in his face and scream questions at him. They knew about the fight at the museum, his arrest, the split with his fiancée (an anonymous source confirmed, of course), the emergency trip to the hospital, the extended stay at the psych ward. It was a story too salacious not to relentlessly pursue. And if they saw him leave with Val, the PI he'd hired last year when he'd been suspected of murder... The Internet explosion would reverberate for weeks.

Max waited inside by the window next to the secret exit. He clenched his eyes shut as a wave of nausea came and went. Though withdrawal symptoms still plagued him, they eased with each passing day. The achiness throughout his body subsided, nausea came less often, and the pill cravings ebbed. He'd kicked a serious heroin habit in his early twenties, so he knew he could get through it if he was motivated enough. And now he had a reason to face his demons once more instead of ignoring the problem.

Through the window, Max saw Michael's black sedan drive up to the curb. He pulled his baseball cap down over his face and hustled out the door, slipping into Michael's passenger seat without spotting any reporters.

Michael clapped Max on the shoulder and smiled. "Free at last."

Something like that. Max returned his smile with a weak grin. He was out, but not content, not until he went home. And home was wherever Val was.

He heard a familiar whining and looked in the backseat. A small suitcase sat on the driver's side, filled with what Max assumed were clothes and toiletries to tide him over until he bought new ones or went back to his condo on his own. Behind Max, Toby spun in circles inside a dog carrier. Through holes in the side, Toby's dark eyes met his, and the dog barked. The carrier began to vibrate with the strength of Toby's wagging tail.

"He tried to bite me when I picked him up," Michael said as he pulled away from the hospital. "Mean little bastard."

"Abby didn't want him?"

"She said he was *your dog*." Michael snickered. "I believe it."

Max looked at his hands, both palms covered with a large Band-Aid. He hadn't needed stitches, thankfully. Keeping his head down not so much out of fear of reporters as out of shame, he asked, "How was she?"

They turned onto the highway. "Not happy, but not terrible. She didn't lay into you as badly as she could have. She's strong, she'll move on. I don't think she'll bad-mouth you to the press."

Max didn't care about what she said to the press, but it did assuage his guilt a little to know he hadn't crushed her. Maybe she finally realized what a terrible boyfriend and fiancé he'd actually been.

"I'd be worried about her father, though, if I were you. You know how us moneyed types are—vindictive."

Max suppressed a laugh at the thought of Patrick trying to

ruin him. He imagined Abby's father shaking his fist and vowing to take every penny Max had in revenge for his daughter, not knowing it wasn't possible. Max was almost tempted to let him, just so Patrick could feel some kind of satisfaction and move on. Abby would know it was useless, though. Max's ability provided him with essentially infinite money. It was all he had—that, and Val.

And Val. Max lifted his head and let the sun warm his face. He closed his eyes and smiled. *I have Val.* Well, he also had Michael—and Toby, too, for whatever that was worth. At that moment the world didn't seem so bad, and he felt stupid for trying to leave it too soon.

Michael spoke again. "Also, remember when I said the job offer from the board was good for as long as you needed to think about it, or until you got arrested? I was joking about that second part, but then you actually got yourself arrested, so..."

Max's mouth twitched into a crooked smile. "That's all right. Walmart's always hiring."

"But here's the deal—they still want you, but they don't want you to be a public figure in the company again. On the books, you'd be a regular Joe Schmo financial analyst, but paid about ten times more than normal." Michael glanced at Max, saw his cocked eyebrow. "They still want your magic, just not the liability."

Michael hadn't asked him why he attacked Lucien, or about his drug addiction, or his time in the psych ward. But he'd helped Max anyway, and hadn't asked for anything in return. It didn't seem normal.

"What do you want me to do?" Max asked.

"I want you to get better."

"I mean about the job."

"*I mean* I don't give a rat's ass about the job, Max. You need to focus on fixing whatever is wrong inside of you."

For a moment Max wondered if Michael could be part of the cabal of people Val swore conspired to manipulate them. Lester had pulled Max's strings all his life, using his familial loyalty to trick him into accepting things no sane person would tolerate. He wouldn't fall for it again. "Why do you care what happens to me?"

Michael threw up a hand, palm up, exasperated by Max's stubbornness. "Because you need a father."

Max waited for him to elaborate, but he didn't, and then the words sank in. *You need a father*—one in the classical sense, *Leave It to Beaver* style. One that cared. The concept was so foreign to Max he wasn't sure how to react. But a key part of loving someone, he was beginning to realize, is that you told them the truth. So he started there.

"If the board thinks I'm some kind of financial prodigy, they're wrong," Max said. "I can see the future—literally."

Michael gave him the side-eye. He probably thought he misunderstood.

"Specifically, I can see pieces of the future, mostly financial information. That's why Carressa Industries did so well when I worked there."

Michael opened his mouth to say something, but his jaw hung instead. His eyes stayed glued to the road. He didn't know what to say, and Max didn't blame him. No one ever believed him at first.

"I know I just came from a mental hospital, ironically, but I'm not insane. I'd prove it to you, but the mechanics of it are, uh, complicated. I'm telling you because it's an important, if unfortunate, part of who I am." He choked out a mirthless laugh. "God, it's pretty much defined my entire fucking life."

Michael nodded slowly, his eyes still on the road. "Okay," he said like a man trying to placate a crazy person.

"You don't have to believe me now. Just promise that if something happens to me, you'll look after Val. She'll need your help, like you've helped me." He took a breath, and hoped to God he wasn't wrong to trust Michael. "Because she can do it, too."

Now he'd really spilled the beans. Michael looked at him, assessing, measuring, judging. A deep frown pulled his face down. "I promise I'll help Val if something happens to you."

If I get committed to the loony bin again, he meant. At least Michael didn't immediately turn around and take him back to the psych ward. It was the best reaction he could've hoped for under the circumstances. He flicked on the radio. "So...how about them Mariners?"

Michael's somber face broke and he laughed.

After a few more miles they left the highway and cut through a swath of suburbia until they reached a public park. Michael drove toward the back, to the head of a running trail dense with evergreen trees, out of sight of the main road. A jolt of anticipation shot through him when he recognized Val's blue Honda Civic parked at the end of the lot. This was it, finally.

Michael parked next to Val's car. A quick look around didn't reveal any obvious reporters or paparazzi who might've followed them. The dog howled in his crate. Max got out and retrieved Toby from the backseat. Holding the crate to his chest, he filled his lungs with sweet pine air. He'd only been in the hospital for four days, but it felt like he'd been trapped in a hole for years, only now reaching the surface.

"Sorry about the other night, Toby," he said. He wiggled his finger inside one of the crate's holes; Toby licked it.

Val and Michael emerged from their respective cars at the same time. She nodded at Michael, then looked at Max. Her hair fell in loose waves over her shoulders, framing a delicate face dominated by steel-blue eyes. Her lips parted, and already he felt them against his, tasted the coffee she drank for lunch, smelled the apple shampoo in her hair, heard the high-pitched, breathy moan she made when he touched her the way she liked—

Toby whined and thrashed in his crate, pulling Max out of his reverie. He'd been staring at her, and she at him, he realized. He felt himself blush, like they were awkward kids at a high school dance.

Michael turned to Max and opened his arms, and Max lowered the crate to his side so he could give his surrogate father a hug. "Get better, boy, I mean it," Michael said as he crushed Max against his chest.

"Thanks for everything," Max said. "I'll call you soon."

That made Michael smile; calling was something Max needed to be alive to do.

Michael grabbed Max's suitcase and dropped it into Val's trunk, then swept his hands from Max to Val. "Over to you," he said to Val. She gave him a hug, and Max saw them exchange hushed words, some of which probably had to do with Max's confession on the ride over. Val nodded, and Michael gave her a weary smile as they pulled away from each other.

Max walked forward and stood in front of Val. Every inch of his skin tingled with the need to embrace her, but he didn't trust himself not to cause a scene. He clutched the crate instead, an excuse to keep his distance. Michael clapped Max on the shoulder one more time, then stepped away as Max shoved the dog crate into Val's backseat. Max climbed into the passenger side and waved at Michael a final time as Val drove out of the parking lot.

When side streets blurred into the highway, Val asked, "Are you—"

Behind Max, Toby howled.

"Are you—"

Toby howled again. Rolling his eyes, Max leaned into the backseat and popped the crate open. Toby launched into Max's lap and ferociously licked his face. Val laughed as Max pushed the dog away.

"Are you hungry?" she asked. "I can stop and pick up something if you want."

"I'm fine." He forced Toby to sit still and used his shirt to wipe slobber off his face.

"How'd you end up with the dog?"

"Toby. He hates everyone else."

Val laughed and eyed the dog. "Is that so?" She lifted her arm to pet him.

Max grabbed her hand in the air. "Don't. He bites."

He held her hand for a moment, enjoying the feel of her skin against his, until Toby licked her fingers.

She jerked her hand away. "Ew," she said with a smile. "I guess he doesn't hate *everyone*. They say *you* can't get along with anyone, either. Shows how much they know."

"'They?'"

She frowned, looking uncomfortable she'd brought it up. "Oh, you know. The TV."

"So you've been following my latest humiliations in the news." Not like it was hard. Max's embarrassing escapades and the mysterious death of Margaret Monroe dominated the airwaves. At least she knew what she was getting herself into with him.

"No, not only that. I've been following you since…well, ever since I met you, pretty much."

He'd been on her mind this entire time? A slow grin spread across his face. All these months, she'd loved him and been thinking about him, just like he'd continued to love and think about her, despite the lies he'd told himself. Wow, what a couple of idiots they'd been to think they could have lived happily without each other.

He let his eyes linger on her, unabashed, in a way he hadn't been able to before, when he'd been trying to convince himself he loved Abby. She looked a lot better than the last time he'd seen her; healthier. Color had returned to her skin. A little mascara darkened her eyelashes and lip gloss moistened her mouth. She'd put on makeup for him. She didn't need it, but the effort touched him.

Though she kept her eyes on the road, he saw her cheeks heat up. "Stop that," she said.

"You're beautiful."

"I'm trying to drive."

"You know how badly I want to kiss you?"

A blush crept up her neck. "I said stop that."

"Right *there*." With the tip of his finger he touched the spot where her neck curved into her shoulder. He felt her shiver. "It's been too long."

She chuckled. "You kissed me just a couple of weeks ago, at the Green Door."

"Really? I thought that was a dream."

"It wasn't."

"So then I actually did swim around an underwater grotto with a bunch of mermaids and penguins?"

"I can't say, I wasn't there for that part. But it's probably safe to assume it happened just like you remember."

He hoped not; much of the night had been terrifying. The strange visions of the future, everything burning…blood running down Lucien's face, a future that came to pass the night of the museum fight. He expected a call from his lawyer any day now to tell him Lucien was pressing assault charges. The injustice of it sickened him. Too bad he hadn't managed to kill the bastard when he'd had the chance.

Thoughts of Lucien soured his mood, and he was quiet for the rest of the ride.

It didn't take long to reach Val's home, an unassuming two-story house on a suburban street lined with houses all built off variations of the same plan. Her place stood out for its sloppily mowed lawn and flowerbeds overgrown with weeds.

She parked the car and turned the engine off. "Well, here we are."

Max looked past her and frowned. "Damn."

Val scoffed. "I know it's not as nice as *your* place, but—"

"No, over there." He nodded toward where he looked, down the street at a nondescript car parked on the side of the road. "Reporters."

Her eyes widened. "Seriously?" She craned her head to get a better look.

"See the glints from their camera lenses? It's a dead giveaway."

"How'd they find out so quickly?"

He let out a dry chuckle. "Welcome to my life."

She puckered her lips in an angry pout, then threw open the car door, retrieved Max's suitcase from the trunk, and stomped up her front walkway as if daring the reporters to photograph her. Max followed, keeping his head down even though he knew it didn't matter; it was obvious who he was. After they went inside, she slammed the door behind them and snapped the blinds shut.

She looked at Toby, still cradled in Max's arms. "Does he need to go outside or something?"

"In a bit." Max put Toby down. "Don't pee in here," he told the dog.

"That's all it takes?"

"Yup."

She snickered. "He *is* your dog."

Max stepped farther into Val's house, walking to the photo

of Robby he'd looked at the last time he was there. Max's half brother posed on a tropical beach somewhere, a drink in his hand and a toothy grin on his face. He wondered what would've happened if Robby hadn't died, if Robby and Val had married, if Max somehow found out about their shared paternity and struck up a friendship with him. Would he still have fallen in love with Val, quietly pining for a woman he couldn't have? Would she have secretly loved him, too?

Did somebody really kill Robby so Max and Val would be together? He didn't want it to be true, but if he was being honest with himself, he preferred it to the alternative. *Something a terrible person would think.*

He ripped his eyes from the picture as another wave of nausea crept up from his stomach. His legs felt weak, and he lowered himself into a sitting position on Val's couch. He closed his eyes and concentrated on not throwing up.

He heard Val ask from the kitchen, "Do you want me to get you some Suboxone?"

Michael must've told her about the pills, not that it wasn't hard to guess. He wished she didn't have to see him like this, but Suboxone would only drag things out. Best to get the withdrawal over with as soon as possible. Max wiped sweat from his upper lip. "Nah, I'll be fine. But thanks for the offer."

"Do you want some water?"

"I'll take that."

With his eyes still closed, he heard water pour into a glass.

"I kept telling myself I'd kick it tomorrow," he said. The water turned off. "Always tomorrow. I did it once with heroin, years ago, and I thought I could do it again. But I'd always find some excuse not to: that I wasn't ready for Abby to know, that I had to prepare for the withdrawal, that everybody liked me better when I was high, and a bunch of other bullshit. The truth is, since you changed my future, I wondered if that meant I could die. Without the drugs, I worried I might find a gun, put the barrel in my mouth, and pull the trigger again, to see if it would finally work."

The nausea passed, and he opened his eyes. The room came into focus again, a collage of subdued blues and charcoals Max guessed were by Robby's design; the colors didn't seem Val's style. Toby laid with his head on Max's shoe. Max scratched him behind the ears, then stood. He walked around the couch to where Val waited with a glass of water. Her tear-rimmed eyes reminded him of rain about to fall from dark, roiling storm clouds.

"Some people might call me an alcoholic," she said. She held the glass out to him. "You're not alone. You never were."

She'd suffered more than he thought—a lot more. They both had. He took the water with one hand, but held her outstretched arm in place with the other. Setting the glass down on the kitchen counter, he brought her hand to his face and kissed the inside of her wrist. He thought he could feel her heartbeat with his lips, her pulse quickening underneath the delicate flesh. Her fingers brushed against his cheek, then threaded through the hair at the back of his neck. She pulled him to her.

They embraced, not only as lost lovers but as two halves of a whole who'd been desperate to return to each other. He kissed the spot on her neck he'd coveted in the car, even warmer and softer than he'd imagined. The smell of apples wafted from her hair, and he pictured them standing alone together in a huge, beautiful orchard, under a clear blue sky. He'd never felt more comfortable, more at home, than in that moment, holding her. He made a slow trail of kisses up her neck, stopping at her ear. He let out a long exhale, and with it went his worries, fears, and pain. His body slackened, and it was only with great effort he kept himself from collapsing into her arms.

"I love you," he whispered in her ear. He should have said it a long time ago. He'd told Abby he loved her because she said it first, and he'd responded in kind because it was what she wanted to hear, and what he wanted to believe. He told Val because he couldn't *not* say it anymore. "I've always loved you."

"I love you, too," she whispered back. Though she'd already told him, it still made him smile to hear it again, proof that he hadn't been dreaming or hallucinating. If he could've bottled that moment in time, he would've done so.

The sound of someone opening and closing the front door broke the spell. He looked up and saw Val's roommate at the threshold of the living room, glaring at them. Max had only met her once before; her reception of him on that occasion had been chilly, to say the least. He wasn't sure why she disliked him so much; probably thought he was a bad influence, which was basically true.

Val pulled away from him and turned to face her roommate. "Hey, Stacey. Um, you remember Max?"

He tried to smile warmly. She did not reciprocate.

"Yeah, I remember Max—from the news reports that say he beat the shit out of someone at the Seattle Art Museum a few days ago, then got committed to a mental hospital."

Val's lips tightened and she sighed. "He'll be staying with us for a little while."

"And you couldn't tell me this before now because..."

"You haven't been returning my phone calls."

"If you'd been home for more than three minutes in the last four days, you could've told me to my face."

Toby barked from where he'd made himself comfortable on the couch. He wanted this fight to end as much as Max did.

Stacey gave the dog the side-eye. "How long?"

"I don't know."

She scoffed. "Fantastic. Maybe we can use his rent money to pay some of the bills that're piling up." She marched into the kitchen, threw open the refrigerator door, and began pulling vegetables out.

"What are you doing?" Val asked.

She slammed an onion on the counter. "It's taco night. I'm making tacos."

Val took Max's hand. "I'm going to show Max the second floor. We'll be down in a minute to help."

Stacey waved them away. "Sure. Whatever."

Val pulled him out of the living room.

"Toby, stay here," Max said before they ascended the staircase. Toby whined, but stayed on the couch.

Max followed Val into her bedroom. He hadn't spared a moment to look around the last time he was there. He'd been too distracted by his bizarre Blue Serpent experience and the possibility he might've cheated on Abby, and his conflicted feelings when Val told him nothing had happened between them. Evening sunshine glinted off pictures of brightly colored birds mounted on the walls, gorgeous drawing that looked like they might at any moment erupt from the glass and flit about the room. Many hung crooked; jostled, then ignored. He wondered where she'd gotten them, then guessed they'd been Robby's, too. A couple of half-spent candles sat on a chest of drawers, next to a photo of a teenage girl with Val's hair but paler blue eyes—her sister. He recognized a bottle of over-the-counter sleeping aid pills on her nightstand.

Val picked up some stray clothes tossed on her bedspread and threw them in the corner. She crooked her thumb at an adjacent door. "That's the master bathroom. Stacey's bedroom is at the end of the hall, just so you know."

"I'm sorry if I'm imposing on her. I can stay in a hotel—"

"No." Val grabbed his arm as if she was afraid he might try to flee, which was exactly the last thing he'd do. "I like you here."

Max took her other hand in his and laced their fingers together. "If you say so." He kissed the back of her entwined hand, and she blushed.

"She said something about bills. Do you need money?" He would pay her entire mortgage and all her bills on the spot if she'd asked him to, yet she hadn't mentioned her finances at all.

Val rolled her eyes. "Stacey's just being a drama queen. We've hit kind of a rough patch recently, but we'll get through it. I hope. It's complicated. You know how lifelong friendships can be."

"No, actually, I don't know. I haven't had any of those."

Val rolled her eyes. "Oh my God, Max. You don't have to

admit to being such a sad sack, you know." He chuckled, and she bit her lip, looking suddenly anxious. "Can I—can I tell her what you can do? That you're like me? I think it would help her understand why we're together."

Max looked away for a moment in thought. He'd just told Michael about their ability because, he'd realized, if you loved someone, then you gave them the truth. If Val truly loved Stacey and trusted her friend to keep a secret, then he didn't have a problem bringing Stacey into the fold.

"I think that's what *brought* us together," Max said, "but I don't think that's *why* we're together. You understand me better than anyone else in the world, but I would have loved you whether or not we shared the same ability. Because what I love about you has nothing to do with that."

Val's lips parted and her eyes grew wet as she stared at him—*mooning*, it was called. He didn't normally like it when people did that to him, but he soaked it up when it came from Val. In fact, he felt himself doing the same to her.

"But yes," he finished, "you can tell her."

They stared at each other for a moment. His skin grew hot, and he felt himself hardening.

Val exhaled. "Thank you. Well, I'd better try to broker a peace and help with taco night."

She began to pull away from him, but he gently held her in place. "Wait."

He drew her flush to him. Where did he begin? He felt as if he'd been starving for months and was suddenly presented a cornucopia of everything he'd ever wanted. He needed one kiss. Just one. Max leaned into her, and she rose to meet him.

He kissed her lightly at first, only a brushing of his lips against hers, like touching the petals of a flower. Then he kissed her again, deeper, harder, caressing her tongue with his, feeling the arch of her back through her clothes. His flesh caught on fire, and he realized not only did he love her completely, but he also wanted to fuck her more than he wanted to breathe.

Her hands slipped underneath his T-shirt, explored his abs, and glided up to his pecs. He yanked the shirt over his head and flung it away. Her top came off just as quickly; the bra underneath unlatched and tossed to the side so their bare chests touched. She wove her fingers through his hair and pulled him closer, as close as they could get to each other. He ran his lips up and down her neck, licking the salt off her skin, drinking in the tiny pearls of sweat that bloomed with his touch.

She let out a breathy moan, the one that gained in pitch when she liked the way he touched her, the sound he'd been waiting for. "I missed you," she said.

He couldn't stand it any longer. Max swept her into his arms and dropped her on the bed. She laughed as she bounced against the mattress, her face flush, lips red and moist. He popped off her shoes, then slipped her pants and panties down her legs in one handful until she lay naked before him—a king's feast, just for him.

He kissed her ankles first. Smooth skin over hard bone turned to smooth skin over soft flesh as he ran his tongue up her leg, followed by his hands. He wanted to taste her everywhere, feel her everywhere. He'd done it before, in the boathouse all those months ago, but having experienced it once only made him want her more. When he reached her thighs, she breathed harder, and when he tasted her, she gasped. Every woman had a unique flavor, and he'd sampled many; it was an easy way to get them off while prolonging his own awkward or fake climax. But Val's taste was exquisite, a bouquet of everything he enjoyed about sex, everything that made the act good. It was her essence and he couldn't get enough. She writhed and moaned as he lapped it up with relish, losing himself in her, until she grabbed a fistful of his hair and yanked him up.

"God, stop," she said, nearly out of breath. "I can't have you like that."

She seized his bottom lip with her teeth while she pawed at the button on his jeans. Max helped her with the zipper, then kicked off his pants and underwear. Finally they lay skin to skin, her legs wrapped around him, his arms around her. Her hands explored every inch of his torso as if she'd never touched him before. Maybe she was getting herself reacquainted, or maybe she felt what he felt—a desperate need to know, to feel, the good and the bad.

Her hand slipped between his legs, fingers skimming down the hard length of him. He trembled and pulled back. He'd only wanted a kiss. After everything that'd happened to her in the last few weeks, he didn't want to rush things or pressure her into doing anything she wasn't ready for. And her visions could be terrible, traumatic. Yet he was the one who trembled, about to lose control.

His cock pressed against her wetness as she stroked him, each caress a pump of pressure to his system. With her other hand she ran a finger along the outside of his ear.

"Max," she whispered. "I love you so much."

Before he could stop himself, he entered her hard. He cried out with her, the feeling so divine it took all his willpower not to come immediately. Every thrust was ecstasy times a thousand, tiny explosions of heaven that resonated through him and passed into her. She moved with him, breathed with him, and looked into his eyes, his soul, as he gazed into hers. They were the only two people in the world.

The fire in him reached a fevered pitch. His whole body vibrated, inside and out. It seemed like they'd only just begun, yet already he felt the numbers coming. Usually he had stamina in spades, but they'd been apart too long. Max forced the mad rush of his hips to slow, then stop. He searched her eyes, wet and awash in raw emotion. A tear slipped from the corner of her lashes and leaked down her cheek. He wiped it away with his thumb.

"I don't want to hurt you," he said.

Val cradled his head in her hands. "You won't. You can't." She kissed him gently. "Come with me."

Max pulled her hips up until her chest arched into his and she threw her head back, her body a reed bending into his storm. He moved deeper into her, harder, faster as she clawed at his back, her moans louder, higher.

"I love you," he said between kisses. "I love you. I love you."

He possessed her body, consumed it with his own, but his soul belonged to her. When she screamed as she came, he let loose a roar of his own as the tentacles of the greatest pleasure he'd ever known seized his mind and pulled him away so they collapsed into each other's arms.

Chapter Twenty-four

I'm running down a corridor of concrete inlaid with metal doors. As I reach a corner, I slow and raise my gun. My heart pounds against my rib cage. I wheel around the corner and recognize Lucien's back in a white lab coat, scrambling away from me. I shoot him in the back. He drops. I close the distance between us, and only then do I realize there's someone else with him, a man he'd been forcing forward, now in a crumpled heap next to Lucien. That man is Max.

My bullet went through Lucien and hit Max. He's dead. I killed him. Oh God he's dead, he's dead, he's dead—

Blur.

I'm running down a corridor of concrete inlaid with metal doors. As I reach a corner, I slow and raise my gun. My heart pounds against my rib cage. I wheel around the corner and recognize Lucien's back in a white lab coat, scrambling away from me. I almost shoot him before I re-

alize he's dragging someone with him, and that person is Max.

"Stop!" I say.

Lucien spins to face me, holding Max in front of him as a human shield. Max thrashes and tries to fight back, but he's pale and sweaty, his movements weak. He looks like he can barely stand. Lucien holds a syringe of mysterious liquid to Max's throat.

"You're going to let me leave," he says.

From behind me the sound of police sirens wafts through the corridor, getting louder.

"Let him go." There's steel in my voice. I'm not negotiating.

"I let him go when I'm gone. Then you may claim him and make your babies."

I know he's lying. He won't let Max go. He takes a step back; I shoot him. I'm usually a good shot. But not today. The bullet strikes Max in the head, passes through his skull and hits Lucien. Both men crumple to the ground.

Max is dead. I killed him. Oh God he's dead, he's dead, he's dead—

Blur.

I'm running down a corridor of concrete inlaid with metal doors. As I reach a corner, I slow and raise my gun. My heart pounds against my rib cage. I wheel around the corner and recognize Lucien's back in a white lab coat, scrambling away from me. I almost shoot him before I realize he's dragging someone with him, and that person is Max.

"Stop!" I say.

Lucien spins to face me, holding Max in front of him as a human shield. Max thrashes and tries to fight back, but he's pale and sweaty, his movements weak. He looks like he can barely stand. Lucien holds a syringe of mysterious liquid to Max's throat.

"You're going to let me leave," he says.

From behind me the sound of police sirens wafts through the corridor, getting louder.

"Let him go." There's steel in my voice. I'm not negotiating.

"I let him go when I'm gone. Then you may claim him and make your babies."

I know he's lying. He won't let Max go. He takes a step back; I shoot the wall next to him, blowing chunks of concrete onto his feet. In the moment of confusion I've bought myself, I sprint straight at him, betting I can reach him before he can stick Max with whatever he's got in the syringe.

I bet wrong. The needle goes into Max's neck; the plunger goes down. Half a second later, I scream and body-check Lucien away, then shoot him in the chest three times. That's all the attention I give to Lucien.

On the floor Max grasps at his neck. I cradle his head in my arms, paralyzed with fear. His lips move; nothing comes out. He can't breathe. The light in his eyes fades until he's staring at nothing.

Max is dead. I killed him. Oh God he's dead, he's dead, he's dead—

Blur.

I run along a path through a tropical forest. Max runs in front of me, barefoot, wearing only board shorts. I'm barefoot, too, in a bikini. I hear a roar through the trees. We burst from the forest, into a clearing at the edge of a cliff. Water cascades down the side into a crystal blue pool fifty feet below us. My stomach lurches as I consider the drop.

"You can't chicken out now," Max says, panting from our run. He takes my hand. He wears a wedding ring. I have one, too. "Come on," he says. "On three: one, two, THREE!"

We sprint off the side of the cliff, screaming as we fall, hand-in-hand, until the cool water envelopes us.

Val breathed in as she regained consciousness and opened her eyes. Max's warm, hard body lay motionless on top of her. He was still in his trance. She liked his weight on her, like a rock keeping her from floating away. Her arms tightened around him, and she ran her fingers through his fine hair. The feel of him calmed her, counteracted the horrible image of him dying over and over again. She focused on the last part of her vision, holding hands with him as they leapt into the waters of a tropical paradise. It meant there was a future where he lived, with her. She wouldn't let him go again.

Max stirred and made a little gasp as his eyes opened. He pushed himself up to look at Val, reading her face for signs of distress. When he saw none, he relaxed and let his head fall back to the pillow. He laced his fingers through hers and nuzzled her neck.

"I ruined taco night," he mumbled into her skin.

She laughed. "It'll come again next week." Thank God he didn't ask her what she'd seen.

He pulled his head back and touched a spot below her ear. "What's this?"

Shit, the scar. There was no point in lying about it. "Lucien put it there when I was unconscious, probably to administer whatever drug he'd used to wipe my memory."

She felt his whole body stiffen. His eyes boiled with the rage she'd seen at the Mountain Lodge. "That fucking bastard. I'll kill him."

She touched her forehead to his and sighed. "Max, please."

"You expect me to let it go?"

"No, but—"

"Have you?"

No, she hadn't let it go. She never would. But she wouldn't risk Max's life for revenge, now that her visions had shown her what would happen if she tried. "I told the police. They're handling it."

"Lucien's still walking free. I saw him at the art museum."

"That's who you beat up?" Max hadn't brought up the assault during her visits to the psych ward, and she hadn't pushed. The news reports hadn't released the name of Max's "victim," either, but if Lucien was there, it must've been him.

Max exhaled. "Yeah."

She kissed the tip of his nose. "Thanks."

Finally he relaxed, though a deep frown still cut across his face.

"Now that Margaret's dead, the police have no choice but to

focus on finding her killer. The trail will eventually lead them to Lucien."

"They never found my father's killer."

Val flinched. "That was different."

"How?"

"For one thing, Lucien deliberately tortured and killed someone, probably not for the first time. He's got a lab somewhere. And at least a few people know he's involved in the Blue Serpent cult. He's good at covering his tracks, but he's still got tracks for the police to follow."

Max scoffed. "If the police were competent, I'd be in prison right now."

She heard the familiar notes of shame in his voice. He *still* felt guilty for killing his father, after everything that man did to him. She didn't feel guilty about killing Norman Barrister, nor would she feel guilty about killing anyone else who deserved it. Despite what he thought of himself, he had a bigger heart than she did. "I've got...friends on the police force helping me. If they throw Lucien in prison for Margaret's murder, that's justice enough for me."

Max's face softened. He stroked her cheek and searched her eyes with his, warm hazel surrounding brilliant green filling her vision. "I wish you wouldn't be so forgiving."

"It's not about forgiveness. It's about moving on with our lives."

She hugged him and nestled her head in the crux of his neck. If he couldn't forgive himself for his father or for Abby, then he could at least move on with her and build enough happy memories to outnumber the bad ones. There'd be time enough to nail Lucien, after they put each other back together. In fact, the sooner the better.

"Can we go to Fiji?" Val asked. Maybe the pool they'd jumped into in her vision was in Fiji. She could *make* it Fiji.

"Of course," he said, a renewed lightness in his voice. He'd asked her to go to Fiji with him several times when they'd been on the run last year. She'd turned him down each time, preferring instead to face their enemies. "When?"

"Today."

His chest bounced against hers as he chuckled. "I don't own a private jet, so that might be tough. And I need to get my passport from the condo, and Abby told Michael she'd need a week to move her things out, but I can probably coordinate a time to get in sooner—"

"Whatever. As soon as possible."

"Okay." He ran a piece of her hair through his thumb and forefinger. "Can we get married in Fiji?"

He'd said it as if suggesting where they should eat dinner, the question flowing from his lips as a natural consequence of how they felt about each other, no posturing or buildup or pomp and circumstance necessary. As she considered her answer, she did, however, feel his heart quicken. He'd been engaged to someone else just a few days ago—to the wrong woman, which was partly Val's fault. All this time he should've been with her. It was what *they* wanted—the people who called themselves Northwalk—but also what she wanted, and what Max wanted. If she could choose for the pool from her vision to be in Fiji, why not choose to wear the wedding rings, too? She and Max didn't need to have children.

She lifted her head and met his gaze. "I'd love to get married in Fiji."

Max gave her a smile that lit up his whole face, radiating pure joy in a way she hadn't seen him do since the boathouse. He laughed and kissed her, pulling her to him with the enthusiasm of a man who couldn't wait to make love to his future wife. She melted with his touch as he hardened against her, her body a puddle of wetness aching to accept him, her desire for him nearly unbearable. A moan escaped her chest as he slipped inside her again. He moved through her, slow and deliberate, the need for release less acute now that they'd finally had each other after months apart. Through the fog of love that consumed her, she heard Toby bark. Then she noticed the bedroom door.

"Oh shit, stop." She slapped Max's back. "*Stop.*"

He stopped, hot puffs of breath ruffling her hair as he panted. "What?"

"The bedroom door is open."

He looked behind him to see the wide-open door with a view of the top of the stairs. "Huh. Must've been like that the whole time."

She palmed her forehead. "Shit. Stacey probably heard everything. She could have *seen us* if she came up here."

Max's head fell into her chest and he laughed.

"Like she doesn't have enough reasons to be pissed at me. I'm the worst roommate ever."

He laughed harder.

"Just shut the fucking door, will you?"

He curbed his laughter and reluctantly peeled himself off

her, then hopped from the bed and trotted to the door. Watching his naked body move across the room, toned muscles rippling underneath brown skin like Michelangelo come to life, she thought she'd never seen a more beautiful man.

He poked his head into the hallway. "I don't hear anything. I think she's gone." Over his shoulder he added, "I'm going to let Toby out."

Before Val could protest that he shouldn't go down there completely naked, especially with reporters lurking outside, he pulled on his underwear and disappeared out the door. He'd always been comfortable with his body—too comfortable, a more modest person might say—but at least he'd had the sense to cover his erect penis.

God, the things he could do with that cock…She burned for him to be inside her again, and stay there forever. Val could only imagine the orgasms he gave other women. Their prophetic abilities meant they could never completely satisfy each other. Not the way other people did anyway.

A minute later he reappeared and shut the door behind him. "Yup, she's gone. Left Toby a bowl of taco shells, though. Nice of her."

Val would worry about appeasing Stacey later. She stood and met Max at the door's threshold, threw her arms around his neck, and kissed him. He leaned into her; she felt the smile on his lips, the hardness still in his underwear. She snapped the elastic band of his boxers.

"How's your endurance?" she asked.

"Shitty, with you."

Val yanked down his underwear and dropped to her knees.

She kissed the scar a couple of inches above his groin, the spot where Sten shot him. "Tell me when to stop."

Max gasped when she took the full length of him into her mouth. He tasted like she remembered—musky, salty, hot, and something else she guessed was her own taste. Delicious. She glided her lips up and down his shaft, lingering on the tip as she ran her hands between his legs, then around his hard thighs to cup his perfect ass. He stroked her hair, then clutched a fistful as his breath became ragged. His cock throbbed, ready to burst in her mouth. If he came while standing, he'd collapse and likely hurt himself, or hurt her if he fell on top of her. She wondered if he'd risk it. A moment later she got her answer.

"Okay, stop," he said, breathing hard. He laughed. "*Fuck*, Val."

She gave him an impish smile. "That was like eight minutes."

Max mirrored her grin. "Let's see you do better."

He pulled Val to her feet and led her to the bathroom, where he turned on the shower faucet and guided her into the stall. She breathed in the steam that enveloped the room, a match for the thick heat already coursing through her veins, the hot water making the outside of her body as slick as her insides. Max pinned her back against the shower wall and kissed her rougher than usual, his broad shoulders tense, the steel rod pressed against her thigh a testament to the fire she'd stoked, one he barely contained. His hand glided down the path of water that ran from her torso to between her legs, and he slipped his fingers deep inside her. She moaned with each stroke, her whole body moving to his rhythm, as if she were a marionette he delighted in making dance with a mere jerk of his hand. Val bit her lip, then bit his shoulder to keep the end from coming. Her whole body quivered for release, but she wouldn't let him win.

With his hand still inside her, he moved down her body and swept his tongue across her breasts, sucking the firm nipples as he bit them lightly. She dug her nails into his shoulders and whimpered, knowing she probably hurt him but unable to stop herself. The pleasure was so intense she almost cried. When he knelt and replaced his fingers with his tongue, she couldn't hold out any longer.

"Stop stop stop!"

Her body teetering on the precipice of climax, Max stopped. He looked up at her and grinned. It seemed a little evil now, the things that mouth could do.

"Oh my God," she muttered as her chest heaved.

"Six minutes and two seconds."

"It was not! How would you even know?"

"I was counting."

"Bullshit." Not even a math prodigy like Max could keep time in his head. Well, maybe he could. In any case, it hadn't felt like a mere six minutes to her. It had been an eternity, yet also the blink of an eye.

He rose and embraced her. They kissed under the shower head and gathered their strength, two fighters clinching in the middle of a heated bout. When Val felt ready for another round, she wrapped her leg around his waist. In an instance Max grabbed her other leg and hoisted her up. Val slid down onto him as he pushed into her, fanning her flames again. She clutched his wet hair, arms locked around his neck, desperate to withstand his onslaught. *Don't come, don't come...*

His breath burned her ear in time with his thrusts, growing hotter and stronger as his hips picked up speed and his muscles tightened. Then all at once he stopped. He threw up an arm and leaned against the wall, chest heaving into hers. His head collapsed onto her shoulder. She almost begged him to continue, but of course they couldn't here. The shower had too much potential for serious injury if they both passed out, or if he passed out holding her. The only way it worked was if she came first, but he was closer. She'd won this round.

Suddenly giddy, she buried her head in his neck and laughed like a horny teenager on an X-rated Tilt-A-Whirl ride. She loved this game. "Three minutes," she said after she'd caught her breath.

"You just made that up."

She had. "Don't be a sore loser, Max." She giggled. "A sore, blue-balled loser."

He snickered and cut the water. "We'll see about that."

Val yelped when he bear-hugged her legs, scooped her up, and threw her over his shoulder. Both of them still wet and dripping, he marched back to the bedroom and dropped her onto the mattress. He seized her legs and yanked her to the edge of the bed, then slammed into her from where he stood. His eyes were wild and his body hard, thighs and chest clenching and unclenching with each frantic push to be as deep inside her as possible. With every thrust he made her scream. Like a tidal wave he crashed over her, consuming everything in his path, and before she could beg for relief, an orgasm tore her away—

I'm running down a corridor of concrete inlaid with metal doors. As I reach a corner, I slow and raise my gun. My heart pounds against my rib cage. I wheel around the corner and recognize Lucien's back in a white lab coat, scrambling away from me. I almost shoot him before I realize he's dragging someone with him, and that person is Max.

"Stop!" I say.

Lucien spins to face me, holding Max in front of him as a human shield. Max thrashes and tries to fight back, but he's pale and sweaty, his movements weak. He looks like he can barely stand. Lucien holds a gun to Max's head.

"You're going to let me leave," he says.

From behind me the sound of police sirens wafts through the corridor, getting louder.

"Let him go." My voice quavers. I know this won't end well.

"You know, you and he don't technically need to be alive to make your babies. I have your eggs, I have his sperm. That is all that's required. They will forgive me eventually."

My hands are shaking. He has my eggs?

"Let me leave now and I will send him back to you when I'm finished with him."

I know he's lying. He won't let Max go. Even if he's not, it's a deal I can't take. Whatever he plans to do to Max, I'm sure Max would rather be dead. My mind races to think of another option. I can lie, too.

"Fine," I say. I lower my gun and pretend to acquiesce. "Leave him at—"

Lucien shoots me in the chest. I drop to the floor. Blood fills my lungs and I can't breathe. My vision fades. I hear Max screaming—

Blur.

"Get up!" Sten yells in my face as sirens blare all around us. "Goddammit, Shepherd, GET UP!"

I struggle to stand but my legs won't hold my weight. Blood trickles down my forehead and into my eyes. I can't get up.

Sten is frantic. He pulls on my arm but can't drag me far. He's limping. Specs of blood splatter his coat.

"Get up—" Sten's head jerks sideways as a bullet strikes his temple.

Blur.

I'm standing on the balcony of Max's house, the balcony where he threw his father to his death. The sky is overcast, the water is black. All the glass is cracked and trash is strewn everywhere. At my feet I see a weathered newspaper with a headline that reads: "President Barrister Declares War." Before I can check the date or read the article, the brightest light I've ever seen bursts in the sky and mushrooms upward. I hear and feel a rumbling that grows louder, shattering the glass around me, until a shock wave hits and I'm engulfed in flames—

Blur.

"Nah, I don't eat leftovers." Sten tosses the doggie bag of food in the trash next to our opulent hotel bed.

I pop off my shoes. My feet ache. "Then why'd you even ask to have it bagged?"

"Because kids in Africa are starving, Shepherd." He takes off his gun holster and drops it on the dresser. I take mine off and set it next to his, eyeing the old wedding ring I still wear for some reason. A deep, crushing sadness pulses through me before I'm able to suppress it. He's gone.

Poking a spot on my chest, I flinch when I touch a bruise. I prefer physical pain to the pain of memories.

He notices my grimace. "What?"

I strip off my shirt, revealing a fresh patch of black and blue on my rib cage. "One of the bodyguards kicked me."

Sten gathers a handful of ice from a bucket next to the minibar. He holds it out like he's going to give it to me, but instead drops it into a glass, uncaps a tiny bottle of whiskey, and dumps the liquor on top.

"Don't be a baby," he says and takes a sip.

I roll my eyes and turn to walk away. He grabs my arm and yanks me flush against him, his lips a couple of inches from mine. Now I'm hot.

He holds the glass out to me. "Drink this. Booze always helps."

I take the whiskey and gulp it down. His eyes don't leave mine. "Sex helps, too."

"Fuck you, Sten."

"Anytime." He seizes my lips with his, and I wonder if we'll get noise complaints again. The glass drops from my hand and onto the carpet with a dull clink.

Like smoke the vision evaporated, leaving Val's ceiling in its wake. She remembered why she usually tried to concentrate on something specific right before climax; if she didn't, a random jumble of death and mayhem filled the void. A collection of things she didn't want to see—like Max's death, Delilah destroying the world, and a potential future with Sten.

Beside her, Max breathed like he'd just finished a sprint. Sweat and shower water dibbled down his skin, his still-erect penis glistening in the sun's waning light.

"I win," he said.

Chapter Twenty-five

Max always won. They played the game for nearly three days straight, stopping only when they were too exhausted or hungry to continue, or when Toby howled for want of something. Val usually didn't like playing games she couldn't win, but this one was an exception. The control Max wielded over his body was incredible, wrought from decades of managing his ability in a way Val had never needed to. She tried a wide variety of positions to coax him into coming first, but a flick of his wrist, a slide down his shaft, or a touch of his tongue was all it took for her to explode in his arms. It wasn't fair.

She didn't talk about her visions, and he didn't ask. He knew they were generally awful, and instead of inquiring about what she'd seen, he would hold her and stroke her hair if she looked upset, and she loved him more for it. She tried focusing as she'd done with Sten, but she couldn't concentrate on anything but Max and what she felt for him. Their emotional connection was too strong. Could be that was how Sten could work his magic—maybe the *disconnection* was key. Unfortunately, her intimate time with him had knocked loose a slew of possible futures with the dirty cop, none of which she would accept. Not to mention Max's death, or her death, or their stolen child...

I can change the things I see, she had to remind herself.

Val tried to call Stacey half a dozen times during short breaks in their game, but could only get her friend's voice mail. She understood Stacey's annoyance at bringing a third person into the house, but it *was* Val's house. And it was only temporary. Soon Max would move back into his own condo, she'd move in with him, and Stacey would have the whole house to herself. It didn't mean they weren't friends anymore or that Max had somehow replaced her. She had to know that. They could talk it out if Stacey would just return her damn phone calls.

Even if Stacey didn't want to talk about their living arrangement, they needed to talk about what they'd do with the business while Val was in Fiji with Max. If she wanted, Stacey could work cases and keep the full fee while Val was gone. She could even take over the business indefinitely. Frankly, Val's epic fail with the Margaret Monroe case had burned her out. She needed a break from dealing with other people's problems so she could get her own fucked-up life in order. As Max's wife, Val didn't need the money anyway...*wouldn't* need the money. They weren't quite married yet.

As Max's wife. Even when she'd been Robby's fiancée, marriage had always been an idea to her, something other people did for tax reasons or to fulfill obligations. She could never fully picture herself as someone else's wife. Val hadn't thought she was capable of completely giving herself to someone else, to be legally and spiritually bound to another person for life, until she met Max and experienced firsthand the devastation of trying to live without the person she loved most in the world.

After three days of frantic lovemaking, they took an extended break for Max to call Michael and set up a time to retrieve his passport from his condo.

"Abby agreed to this evening," Max said when he got off his cell phone. Clad only in his boxers, he lounged on the couch and tossed his phone on the coffee table. He picked at a pint of ice cream while Toby lay at his feet, then frowned and stared into space for a moment. Val recognized the look—guilt. He made it a lot.

Val plopped down next to him, took the spoon from his hand, and ate a mouthful of fudge ripple. "She could be sleeping with her brother."

He shook his head and paired it with a slight roll of his eyes. "The whole world isn't all incest, rape, and murder, though it seems that way sometimes." He sighed. "I should give her the condo."

"People break up all the time, Max. It's never easy. Sometimes it's straight-up ugly. At least she wasn't hit by a car and left for dead."

By the way he flinched, Val could tell he hadn't considered the possibility that being with him had put Abby in danger. If the people who wanted Max and Val to have a child were willing to kill Val's fiancé to further that goal, there was no reason they wouldn't do the same to Abby. In fact, now that Val thought about it, she was surprised they hadn't killed Max's ex-fiancée already. Maybe they'd decided to play the waiting game instead, betting the bond between Max and Val would eventually pull them back together. If so, they'd bet right.

"And don't just give her your condo," Val said. "That's weird."

"I can always buy another one."

"That's not the point. Money isn't the only way to make people happy. It's not all you have to give."

His eyes softened as he considered her words. The green in them seemed to sparkle, and he smiled. "Did you get psychiatric training just for me?" He kissed her. "How much do you charge by the hour?"

"You can't afford it."

Max pulled her into his lap, dislodging the carton of ice cream onto the ground; a sinful treat for Toby now. She laughed as he leaned down and kissed her, her torso cradled in his arms while her legs kicked the air, and tried not to think of the last time she'd had sex in the living room—with Sten.

Before they could begin another round of their favorite game, someone knocked at the door. They weren't expecting anyone, though reporters still lurked in the area.

Val sighed. "I'd better see who it is." She pushed herself off his lap and walked to the door. When she looked through the peephole, she gasped. It was Jo. *Shit.* She hadn't told Max yet about her last conversation with his half sister. Val glanced at Max; he was shooing Toby away from the ice cream carton, oblivious to the bomb about to be dropped on him. She bit her lip and poked her head out, staying behind the door to hide her flimsy T-shirt and underwear, the only things she wore.

"Hello, Val." Jo spoke with a cordialness missing from their last meeting. Her eyes were wide yet tight at the corners, as if her lids struggled to keep her nervousness from seeping out the sides.

"Hi, Jo."

After a moment where they stared at each other, she said, "So I heard...um, I heard Max was here."

Heard it from the news, no doubt. Damn reporters. "Yeah, he's here."

"Can I talk to him?"

"Uh..." Val looked behind her at Max. He cocked his head trying to see around her, mildly interested in their mystery visitor, likely wondering why Val hadn't sent the person away yet. "Can you wait here for a minute?"

Jo nodded.

Val shut the door and turned to Max. She took a deep breath. "Josephine is here."

He shot up from the couch. "Why?"

"She wants to talk to you."

His eyes narrowed at Val. "Why?"

"I sort of told her you were her brother."

"Val!"

"She came to me and demanded to know why you kept trying to give her money. She thought you were paying her off for killing Dean! What was I supposed to do, let her believe that?"

"It wasn't your choice to make."

"I know, okay? I know. I'm sorry."

He seethed at her for a couple of seconds—though nothing near his anger at the Mountain Lodge, thank God—before his gaze cut to the door and softened. "She wants to talk?"

Val nodded. "If that's what you want, now's your chance."

Max opened his mouth to say something, then stopped, then did it again, then folded his arms and drummed his fingers on his biceps. He looked down at his boxers as if noticing them for the first time. "I have to get dressed." He turned and jogged up the stairs. Val assumed that meant "yes."

She called from the first floor, "Can you throw me down some pants?"

A pair of jeans soared through the air and landed at her feet. She slipped them on and realized they were his—too long and too loose—but they'd do for the short term. She pulled on her sneakers and a light coat, then opened the door again.

"You can come in," she told Jo. "He's getting dressed."

Jo walked into the living room and stood there awkwardly. She scanned the area around her, maybe looking for signs of Robby. Val hadn't changed much since his death. She'd given some of his things away as personal mementos to close friends and family, and Stacey had moved her few belongings in—mostly tie-dyed flair—but the house was by and large the same. Toby trotted over and barked at Jo, his hair raised and bobbed tail stiff in the air.

"Toby, stop it," Max said from the stair's landing. He'd thrown on a clean dress shirt and khaki pants, brushed his hair and probably his teeth, too, Val guessed. Trying to look respectable. Toby met Max at the base of the stairs. Max knelt and scratched the dog's forehead. Neither Max nor Jo said anything, and Val realized neither knew where to begin.

Jo cleared her throat. With shaking hands, she reached into her purse and pulled out a clutch of old papers. "I found these in my father's things last year. Stuff he kept in the back of his closet. They're love letters from someone. I knew it wasn't my mom because it wasn't her handwriting, so I guess"—she swallowed hard—"they must be from your mom."

Max took the letters, his own hands trembling slightly, and flipped through them. "It's my mother's handwriting. She liked to write letters." He looked at Jo. "Do you want coffee or something?"

Jo nodded and sat at the dining room table. Max walked into the kitchen, turned on the coffeemaker, and pulled three mugs from the cabinet.

"You know what, I think I'll pass," Val said. "I need to pick up a few things from the grocery store. I'll be back in a little bit." She walked to Max and whispered in his ear, "Text me if you need me to come back, or stay gone." Despite the audience, Val kissed him. She couldn't help herself. He smelled good. She loved his dirty, marinated-in-sex smell, but his freshened-up scent wasn't too shabby, either.

Val left them alone to have what she guessed would be one of the most awkward conversations of their lives. They were the closest either of them had for family—pretty powerful motivation for learning to get along. She wanted to be there for Max, but connecting with his sister was something he could only do on his own.

It'd been a while since Val made a trip to the grocery store.

Stacey did most of the food shopping, while Val kept their alcohol supply stocked. She poked through the aisles, loading up on junk food Stacey wouldn't approve of, and avoiding the beer. She hadn't had a drink since she and Max reunited, and she wanted to keep it that way until she knew she could control herself again.

As she was weighing which flavor of Hot Pocket that Max might prefer, her cell phone rang—Zach.

"What do you got for me?" she asked. Too late to save Margaret, but maybe he'd recovered a clue to Lucien's whereabouts off the hard drive she'd swiped from the Mountain Lodge.

"How come you never make polite small talk?"

"I'm busy, Zach, and naturally rude. You'd better not be calling just to say hello."

"Well, no, you're weird, that's all. Anyway, I called because I found something off those chunks of hard drive you gave me, but I don't know if it's what you're looking for, and I don't want to waste my time trying to put the thing back together if it's not. Where did you get the hard drive from?"

"A party. Why?"

"Uh, thing is, there's a list of files organized by people's names and, well, one of the names is yours, and another is Maxwell Carressa's, and you two are, like, together now, right? Is this a coincidence, or..."

Shit, Lucien had been tracking them like test subjects. What had he done to her? And what was he *going* to do?

She squeezed her eyes shut and rubbed the bridge of her nose. "What's in the files?" she asked, not really wanting to know.

"I haven't cracked 'em yet. I'm not sure if it's even possible, actually, since the hard drive is in such bad shape. I can try, though, if you want me to."

Val sighed. "Yeah, I do."

"Okay. One other thing—and this is kinda weird, too—the only other name I recognized is the mayor's, Delilah Barrister. Any idea why her name would be on here?"

Her breath caught. Lucien had a file on *Delilah?* No fucking way. He *was* connected to Northwalk—and he might have proof the mayor was, too.

"Crack that file first," Val practically yelled into the phone.

"Sure—if it's possible. The data's all clobbered, though. I'll have to ask a friend of mine who kills it with hardware to try to kludge it back together for me—"

"Whatever it takes. But Zach, don't tell other people about this if at all possible. If you need someone else's help, don't say anything about Mayor Barrister. I mean it. She can't find out. She's dangerous."

"Really? She seemed like a nice lady in her political ads last year—"

"Just promise me, Zach."

"Sure, whatever. I'll be in touch. I've been meaning to beef up my hardware skills, but my mom keeps insisting I go outside and—"

She hung up, trying not to literally squeal with excitement. Could this be the break she needed to finally nail Delilah? If there was any justice in the world, it would be.

With an extra spring in her step, Val paid for the food and stopped at the in-store coffee shop to kill a little more time.

She ordered from the barista, "Grande caramel macchiato, hot, triple-shot, double-caramel, no whip."

The woman smiled. "You got it. That'll be four ninety-five."

The barista eyed her while she dug through her tote for cash.

"You're that chick from the news, aren't you?"

Val looked up. "It depends what news you're talking about."

"The woman who helped Maxwell Carressa prove he was innocent of murder, and then he dumped his fiancée for her."

"That's not exactly how it went down—"

"I knew it! Oh my God, you are so lucky! He is *so hot*. And *so rich*. Are those his pants?"

Val glanced down at her obvious boyfriend jeans. "Um… can I get a blueberry scone?"

"Sure. Three fifty. I heard his new girlfriend lived around here, and he was staying with her, but I didn't realize you were so close. I'm glad he didn't get in too much trouble for beating up that guy in the museum. Whoever it was probably deserved it." The barista held out Val's change.

"Keep it," Val said. She took a seat at a café table and waited for her drink. In her tote, her cell phone chimed. She pulled it out and read a new text message, from "Asshole." *Turn on the news.*

Val cringed. She hadn't heard from Sten since the night he'd tricked her into killing a man. In a drunken haze she'd texted him her plan to deal with Eliot Salier, the last man who'd raped her. After what Sten had made her do, he still owed her. Then they'd be even…if she still cared about getting even. She'd told Max to move on with his life. She should take her own advice. A wiser, less vengeful person would.

Val walked back to the barista. "Can I turn on your TV?"

"Sure!" The barista handed Val the remote. "Just no Fox News, please."

Val clicked on the flat-screen TV suspended in the corner and flipped to the local news. "Holy shit," she muttered when Lucien's face popped into the center.

"—is wanted for questioning in the death of Tacoma resident Margaret Monroe," an anchor's voice narrated. "The police have declined to say if Lucien Christophe is a suspect in Margaret Monroe's murder, but they're asking the local community for any information on Christophe's whereabouts."

Hot damn, the police really *were* looking for Lucien. She didn't know if it was Sten or police competence she had to thank. Maybe justice would be served after all. Today was turning into a pretty good day all around.

Her cell phone chimed again with another text: *But wait, there's more!* She rolled her eyes. Then: *9040 NE 41st Street, Yarrow Point. 1 hour.*

Salier. *Take your own advice and let it go*, Val thought. With Lucien wanted by the police and likely out of the country by now, the Blue Serpent cult and all its rape parties probably left with him. Her new life with Max beckoned. There was no reason to look back. No sensible reason.

Glancing at the TV again, Val felt her lips twisting into a snarl when Delilah appeared behind a podium, flanked by a couple of police officers. "Seattle Mayor Vows to Bring Killer to Justice," the chyron below her read.

I'll get you, you evil bitch—

"Poor guy," the barista said as she put a lid on Val's coffee cup. "He's probably innocent, too. Can you believe it—*another* hot guy accused of a crime he didn't commit?"

Val snatched her coffee and scone off the counter and stomped out before she could say something she'd regret.

When Val returned home, Jo's car was gone. She entered with her shopping bags and found Max sitting alone at the dining room table, tapping his mug.

"You need help?" he asked.

"No, this is all I got, actually. I hope you're not expecting gourmet, because I don't really cook." She put the groceries on the counter. "How did it go?"

"It was...good, I guess. She wanted to know how Dean died, and I told her as much as I could. Then she wanted to know about my mother, and I couldn't..." He rubbed his forehead. "What's having a sister supposed to be like?"

Val sat beside him. "I haven't had one in a long time, but I remember it's equal parts frustrating and amazing."

He smiled. "Yeah, it was something like that."

"When will you see her again?"

"I don't know. We didn't work out a time."

"Do you want to postpone our trip to Fiji?" It pained Val to ask; she *really* wanted to go. But she knew how important family could be. She'd give anything to have her own sister back.

"No." He stood. "Getting married in Fiji is first, before anything else. I booked the tickets while you were out. Our flight leaves this evening."

Val jumped into his arms. They laughed and kissed like

they were already newlyweds. They were really doing this. She couldn't believe it.

He pulled away before things could get too hot between them. "I need to get my passport first."

Val held out her keys. "You can take my car."

"Why don't you drive me there? That way I can drive my own car home and not have to rely on you for rides anymore."

"You don't want to be seen driving my middle-class car, do you?"

"There's that, too. I also want people to guess what I'm overcompensating for."

Val drove Max to his home in Queen Anne, the first time he'd been out of her house since he'd arrived three days ago. He hadn't been to his condo in a week. With his hand on the car door's handle, he looked at the building and frowned.

"Do you want me to go in with you?" Val asked. She remembered the panic attack he had in his father's study, the place where he'd killed Lester. She couldn't imagine what it'd be like for him to wade back into a place where he tried to kill himself.

"No, I'll be fine. I just…I really liked this place. The design, I mean. And the neighbors were quiet."

"Then learn to like it again. Make some happy memories here."

Max grinned at her. "Yeah. I like that plan." He kissed her, opened the door, and got out.

"Should I wait for you?" Val called after him.

"You don't need to. I'm going to pack a few things for the trip, then head back to your house."

"Okay. I'll see you there." She waved good-bye, watched him punch in the code to the front gate, and disappear inside.

For a minute she wrestled with herself to go home. *A wiser, less vengeful person would.*

She entered the Yarrow Point address into her phone's GPS and started the car.

Chapter Twenty-six

The door to his condo creaked open in a way Max didn't recall it doing before. Could be he'd just never noticed, or actively ignored it. Now he thought he should fix it. That, and everything else in the place.

Debris was still strewn about the floor from his rampage. Abby hadn't made an effort to clean it up. And he didn't blame her; it was his mess, after all. Why should she be bothered with it? He noticed some major items missing—end tables, chairs, bookcases displaying knickknacks. Max couldn't remember if any of the things she'd taken had originally been his or not, though he didn't care enough to question her on anything. Abby could have it all if she wanted.

He walked to the bedroom and found it mostly cleared out, as he'd expected. The bedroom had been her favorite space. She'd left the bed sheets, even though she had picked them out. He sat on the bed and ran his hand over the fine blanket fabric. They'd had some good times, he and Abby. He should have loved her. It was illogical that he didn't. Maybe that's why it took him so long to realize it was never going to happen. That a single person could claim your heart and never let go was a foreign concept to him, before Val. Even after Val, his mind couldn't process what his heart told him, so he felt what he thought he should feel.

When he returned from Fiji, he would talk to Abby and tell her the truth—everything he could tell her without putting her or anyone else in danger anyway. Maybe then she'd understand that it really was him and not her, that she'd done nothing wrong. Or maybe she already understood, and hated his lying guts. In any case, he had to try to make things right with her.

Max grabbed a duffel bag from the closet and threw some of his clothes in it. He walked into the bathroom and stopped at the blood splotches on the floor—his own blood, from the cuts on his hands. He should have died, but fate wanted him to live. Now *he* wanted to live. What a difference seven days made.

He tiptoed around the broken glass and crystal, picked up his shower gel and toothpaste, and retrieved some extra razors from the medicine cabinet. Max spotted his empty OxyContin bottle wedged behind the toilet. He picked it up and threw it in the trash—a first step to cleaning up his mess. He'd finish the rest when he returned from Fiji.

Max dumped the toiletries and a few other items in the bag, zipped it up, and trotted back down the stairs. He stopped by the study's bookcase—the only one Abby would let him have on display. She didn't like the look of an entire room of books, even though it was the study, so the bulk of his massive literary collection sat in boxes in the garage. He wedged a half dozen of his favorite books into the duffel's side pockets. In the office desk he rarely used, Max found his passport. Then he heard a footstep on broken glass.

He walked back into the living room. "Abby?"

She wasn't supposed to be back for another hour, but that didn't mean she hadn't returned anyway. Max scanned the entirety of the first floor, including the guest room and patio—nothing.

He called up the stairs. "Abby?"

Nothing. He must have imagined it. Maybe a leftover hallucination from his overdose.

The pain came out of nowhere. It seized his whole body and locked his muscles. His legs gave way and he collapsed to the floor, his lungs frozen so he couldn't scream or breathe.

On the ground, Max opened his eyes and saw Lucien above him, a Taser in the Frenchman's hand. Despite the pain and shock, he was lucid enough to notice Lucien's smooth, healthy face, unblemished by the beating Max delivered only a few days prior. How was that possible?

"Where is Valentine?" Lucien asked in the same manner one might inquire about a good place to get Chinese food.

"*Fuck...you...*" Max choked out.

He forced air into his lungs, building up to a good scream. If the neighbor heard Toby's barking, she was bound to hear his yelling.

Sensing Max's intention, Lucien shocked him again. The

scream caught in his throat as every muscle in his body clenched at once.

"No matter," Lucien said, "You'll do, for now." He pulled a syringe of clear liquid from his coat pocket, took the cap off, and tapped the barrel.

Max begged his legs and arms to move, but blinding pain still gripped him everywhere. All he could do was watch Lucien stick the needle in his neck and push the plunger down. He tried once more to scream as blackness crept over him.

"No plan is perfect, but it helps if your quarry has a critical weakness." He smiled and watched Max lose consciousness. "If I have you, she will come."

Chapter Twenty-seven

Eliot Salier lived in a gray house with charming white trim around the windows and an immaculate lawn dotted with purple rhododendrons in full bloom. Though smaller than Stevenson's McMansion, an unobstructed view of the Cozy Cove waters earned the house its multimillion-dollar price tag. A Porsche and a Lexus were parked in the driveway; behind those, police cars.

Leaving her sedan a couple of blocks away, Val walked up to the house and waded through a small crowd of people held at bay by a beat cop—shocked neighbors, gathered to watch the show. Despite the tawdriness of the spectacle, they couldn't stay away. Eliot Salier's public shaming would provide dinner conversation fodder for years.

In front of Val, two women in cashmere sweaters leaned their heads together. "Unbelievable," one woman said to the other. "I had no idea Eliot was capable of such awful things."

"Disgusting. It's just disgusting," the other replied. "I can't believe he was living right next to us and we never knew."

"Mm-hmm. Do you think he... you know... did it *here?*"

"Probably. In the bedroom."

"Oh my God. Do you think his wife knew?"

The woman scoffed. "They never do. Sad, really."

"Should we un-invite Linda from the country club social next Saturday?"

"Of course. It would be terribly awkward if she was there. Don't want to make anyone feel uncomfortable."

The front door flew open, and the crowd snapped to attention. A lone cop came out first, then a handcuffed man flanked by two officers. Each held an arm and dragged Eliot Salier down the front walkway. Salier shuffled forward, face pale and body stiff as he struggled to hold his head up.

"I didn't do it, you vultures," he spat at the crowd.

"Pervert," the woman in front of Val mumbled under her breath.

"They'll get him in prison," the other woman said. "I hear people convicted of child pornography get it the *worst*."

Salier passed within ten feet of the crowd. "I'm innocent! I didn't—"

His eyes met Val's and he froze. Righteous indignation turned to horror as it dawned on him what crime he was actually being punished for. Killing Salier outright, as had been Sten's original plan, seemed too clean. And even with the video, he'd never be convicted of Val's rape. He was too rich, and Val wasn't innocent enough. But the sexual exploitation of *children* was another matter. If he somehow beat the charge, he'd never get the stink off him. His cushy life was over—a more than fair fate for raping an unconscious woman.

The cops forced Salier forward, but Salier's eyes stayed locked on Val, unable to look away. She felt herself smile, the corners of her lips rising in delicious, primal satisfaction. Like she'd seen Sten do when Mystery Man's life ended as a smear on the asphalt.

She nearly jumped when she heard Sten's voice in her ear. "I have to hand it to you, Shepherd," he said just above a whisper. He'd snuck up next to her like a ninja, and leaned in so only she could hear him speak. "You know how to serve some seriously ice-cold revenge. Didn't know you had it in you."

She didn't, either, until recently. Val took a few steps back, putting some distance between herself and the crowd so they couldn't be overheard. "Why did you make me kill that man at the Four Seasons Hotel?"

"I just wanted you to scare him. His death was an added bonus."

"But why?"

For a moment, Sten said nothing as he watched his fellow officers shove the now-silent Salier into a police cruiser and slam the door. "Know how much a child soldier in Chechnya costs?"

What kind of answer was that? "No idea," she said, ready for one of his usual obnoxious punch lines.

"They cost nothing, other than promises to get them out of Hell. But then they're put into a *different* kind of Hell, so really they're free. You can just pick one up off the street, like a two-for-one coupon for frozen yogurt."

At a loss for words, she could only stare at him in response.

Was he...talking about himself? He'd always been evasive about his past, even when they were dating. The only clue he'd ever given her was that he owed the people trying to control her and Max a debt he could never repay.

"The people that buy these children's lives for nothing—even though they have more money than God—they think their *own* lives are infinitely more precious because they equate money with worth. Like they *deserve* to live more, as if God's granted them divine protection. You proved them wrong."

So he thought she was God's wrath—or Satan's agent. "I've saved people, too," Val said with a frown. She'd wrestled her whole life with the possibility that her ability might be evil, that maybe she somehow caused the terrible things she saw. Over the years she'd convinced herself that wasn't the case, but Sten's insinuation opened up old wounds. "We're even now, got it?"

He looked at her and raised an eyebrow. "It's not about getting even. It's about helping out your partner."

Val's breath caught at the possibility. "We are *not* partners." She wouldn't go down that road, despite what her visions suggested.

Sten moved closer, his gaze flicking between her eyes and her lips. For a crazy second she thought he was going to kiss her. An image slinked into her mind of her and Sten tearing up the world together, setting mansions on fire, putting bullets in the heads of evil people, reveling in their enemy's blood. How *good* it would feel to hurt those who thought they were immune from justice, to leave behind a trail of humiliated Eliot Saliers and Mystery Men hit by buses. Together, they could do it.

After an intolerable few seconds, the corners of his mouth ticked up into a slight, cynical smile. "Tell yourself that for as long as you need to. I'll be waiting."

He walked away to join his cop friends as they vacated the premises, off to deposit Salier into his new, much shittier life.

Bile rose in her throat, spoiling the taste of Max that had lingered there before. So what if she was capable of an all-consuming inferno of wrath, and Sten might be the fuel for that fire? Just because she was capable didn't mean she had to give in to the temptation. Val marched away from the scene, embarrassed to be there. What the hell was she thinking? Why had she come? What was wrong with her?

She drove home in a near panicked state, desperate to be with Max. She needed him. She loved him. He was her light in the darkness.

Chapter Twenty-eight

As if emerging from a fog, the world appeared one piece at a time. First, Max sensed a bright light in his face. Squinting through the glare, he saw walls of plastic sheeting. Abutting those, tables covered in trays of what looked like medical lab equipment. Finally, his bare feet, his bare legs, a hospital gown that came to his mid-thigh, and his wrists encircled in leather straps, binding him to the metal table he lay upon.

Max turned his head and the world spun. He jerked his torso as far to the side as he could go, leaned over the edge of the table, and threw up onto the floor.

"Well, that's a stronger reaction than I expected," Lucien said from somewhere out of Max's line of sight.

Max spit bile from his mouth and flopped his head back on the table. He clenched his eyes shut to stop the spinning. "What...did you...do to me?"

"Not much, yet. Prep work mostly."

Footsteps echoed around the room, moving to Max's right. He risked opening his eyes again and saw the blurry outline of Lucien in a lab coat, doting over a tray of vials and syringes, pausing occasionally to scratch notes on a clipboard.

"When was the last time you achieved sexual climax?" Lucien asked.

"Wh—what?"

"The last time you achieved sexual climax?"

"Why..."

"Based on the gossip news, I'm going to assume it's been within the last twenty-four hours." He wrote on the clipboard. "What are the nature of your prophetic visions?"

"I don't..."

"What do you see? People? Objects? Symbols?"

Max's head swam. He was dreaming. "Numbers..."

"*Interesting.*" A pen scratched on paper. "Now I understand where your fortune must come from. Are your visions stronger when you have intercourse with Valentine Shepherd?"

Mention of Val's name stirred in him a faint lucidity. He strained against the leather straps, but his muscles were jelly. "Why are you asking me this?"

"Because I want to know how we work."

"We?"

"Don't play coy. Northwalk calls us seers—you, myself, and Valentine, and others I've been unable to locate, until they told me about you." He let out an amused *hmph*. "They are very secretive, Northwalk. They only deal directly with seers who have something they want, and even then it's usually through a proxy."

Shit, Lucien *was* like them. Max should have beaten him to death when he'd had the chance.

"Have you sired any children you are aware of?"

"I'll kill you."

"That would be quite a feat in your current state."

Lucien's blurry form walked over to stand at Max's bedside, where his face came into wobbly focus. Max's arms twitched with the desire to wrap his hands around Lucien's neck and squeeze for an eternity. The buckles on his leather straps clanged against the metal table.

"Have you had sexual relations with a seer other than Valentine Shepherd?" Lucien asked.

Max summoned all his strength to escape his bonds, pulling as hard as he could on the leather straps, his whole body bucking against the table.

"This will be easier for you if you answer my questions."

Despite his rage, the thick fog in his head and the weakness in his muscles made his efforts no more than feeble thrashing. He collapsed back on the slab, panting from his effort. "If you touch her again, I will fucking kill you."

Lucien made an exasperated sigh. "They don't like us to know about each other. When one seer interacts with another, it interferes with the Alpha's vision in ways I unfortunately don't understand. Something about too many possibilities. Northwalk won't let me examine her; they think I'm going to kill her and cut her up." He chuckled. "They are correct."

Max should've played along, pretended to sympathize with Lucien, coaxed him into loosening the bonds. But all he could do was glare with useless hatred as tears clouded his vision further. "I'll break every bone in your body...every bone..."

With a slight exasperated roll of his eyes, Lucien walked away, becoming a blur again, then returned with his tray of vials and syringes.

"You know, I've spent over half a century searching for other seers. I have tried conducting experiments on myself in the past, with poor results. You'd think more of us would use the gift for monetary gain, like you with your numbers to predict the stock market, and myself with cures for diseases to sell. Maybe others aren't as enterprising or clever as you and I. Or maybe they're ashamed of their gift. A pity, if that's the case. I've only been able to find and examine one other, and...well, she didn't last long. That lost opportunity was heartbreaking. So when Northwalk told me they needed your sperm and Valentine's eggs to ensure a child would be born of your seeds because you were *seers*, I cannot tell you how ecstatic I was."

Lucien smiled down on Max, a sick, gleeful twist of the Frenchman's lips, like a kid who'd been given the keys to the candy shop. "They told me not to kill you, though they must be very anxious for your progeny if they're willing to take the chance asking for my help. But rest assured, whether or not you die depends entirely on you, and how cooperative you are."

Lucien eyed his vials, chose a pink-hued one with a nod, and placed it in front of him. "It's too bad Valentine sent the police after me. I was on the cusp of creating a new strain of hepatitis in the prostitute population. Now I must abandon all that work I've done. As one of very few men with an intellect to match my own, you must understand the frustration of having your experiments ruined by an unpredictable variable." He picked up a syringe and drew liquid from his chosen vial.

"No," Max said as he watched the fluid fill the barrel. "*No—*"

"Northwalk will eventually forgive me for taking you." Snickering, he added, "I'm keeping half of them alive, after all." He tapped the syringe. A little stream of liquid shot out the needle. "And modern medicine means neither one of you must technically be alive to create a child, only certain parts of you."

Lucien held Max's arm steady and eased the needle under his skin. As Lucien pushed the plunger down, a wave of panic swept Max's anger away. Not panic for himself, but for Val.

"Don't do this to her, please," he said as the pink liquid disappeared from the barrel and into his vein. "I'll cooperate. I'll answer any questions you want. Just leave her alone."

Lucien smiled. "Excellent! I knew you'd come round." He snatched up his clipboard. "Have you sired any children you are aware of?"

Max's heart raced. He was helpless again, just like he'd been under the thumb of his father. "N—no."

"Are your visions stronger when you have intercourse with Valentine Shepherd?"

He turned his head away, bright light burning his eyes. The world began to slew as whatever Lucien had given him started taking effect. "Yes."

"Do feelings of love for her affect your visions?"

He squeezed his eyes shut. Tiny pink beetles scuttled underneath his skin and burrowed through his muscles, moving up the marrow of his bones and into his brain. "Yes."

He tasted smoke. *Please, no.* Heat blistered his face. *Not tonight.* He tried to move away from it but couldn't, his whole body frozen with fear. *Leave me alone.* Lightning cracked outside his bedroom window.

"What do you see, Max?"

His father's voice. *What do you see, Maxwell? Concentrate. Tell me what you see.* He felt wetness slipping down his cheeks—his own tears.

"What do you see?"

Max forced his eyes to open. "Fire," he whispered. "I see fire."

Chapter Twenty-nine

Val paced around the coffee table, Toby at her heels, stabbing her phone with trembling fingers. She dialed Max's number for the eighth time, cursed when she got his voice mail again. He'd been gone for almost three hours. The time had come to panic.

"Fuck."

She should have gone with him into his condo. She should have waited for him outside. She shouldn't have gone to Yarrow Point. She shouldn't have let her lust for vengeance cloud her judgment. She should have been happy with what she had.

"Fuck!"

Val dialed Stacey. Of course it went to voice mail, too. "Stacey, please. Please return my call. I know you're mad at me and I'm sorry. I'm sorry again. I'm sorry forever and all eternity. Max is missing. He went to his place to get some things and he hasn't come back, and I'm really freaking out. I had a vision that Lucien kidnapped him, and I think that's what's happened. I think Lucien has him. If he's doing to Max what he did to Margaret, I—" Her voice choked up. "I need to find him. I can't do it alone. Please call me back."

Val hung up and took a long, trembling breath. She knew how to search for a missing person. Setting aside the fact that this missing person just happened to be the love of her life, the process was still the same. First, visit the place he was last seen. That was easy; she was the last person to see him, entering his condo. He could still be there, maybe having a long talk with Abby. Val might've taken comfort in that, if not for her earlier vision.

She jumped in her car and drove to Max's condo. Val eyed her phone the entire way, praying it would ring and Max's face would pop up on the screen, so she could go home and feel stupid for panicking. It didn't.

She parked in front of his place and walked to the front gate as rain started to fall. A light drizzle dotted the sidewalk a dark gray, not enough to do more than moisten her hair, but the start of something bigger. It hadn't rained since the day they found Margaret's body on the beach, just as Val had seen it. She wouldn't let the same thing happen to Max. She'd either save him, or die trying.

Val found a button on a panel labeled "#3—Carressa/ Westford." She pressed it, and the adjacent intercom buzzed. If she was lucky, Max would answer; less lucky, Abby. Most likely, no one. In the latter case, she'd jump the fence and get in through a window, deal with the police if she got caught—

"Yeah?" a man's voice crackled through the intercom.

For a split second she thought it might be Max, until she realized the voice was too high-pitched. A friend of Abby's maybe.

"Got a package for Abigail Westford," Val said, "Needs to be signed for."

"What is it?" the man asked.

Val rolled her eyes. This idiot definitely wasn't Max. "They don't tell me those things, sir."

A few seconds of silence, then, "Fine, bring it in."

The gate clicked, unlocked. She pushed it open and walked through a manicured courtyard with a wildflower garden and marble fountain in the center. It looked like an apartment complex, though nicer than any she'd ever been to, with doors much farther apart than normal, hinting at the vast space behind them. Val found a sleek gray door with a brass number 3 on the front and knocked.

Footsteps approached, and the door swung open. Standing in the threshold was Ginger. Back from whatever country he'd jet-set off to, so he could support his sister during her painful breakup. Maybe get in a little rape and murder on the side.

Ginger looked at Val, and she looked at him. Confusion dominated his face, then a flash of recognition, then anger. "What the f—"

Val socked him in the face. He screamed and stumbled backward, clutching a broken nose. Before he could escape, she kicked him in the shin and he dropped to the ground. She delivered two more swift kicks to his chest to ensure he stayed down. His arms flailed about his body, to his face, then chest, then leg and back again, unable to settle on which ball of pain he should nurse first.

Val loomed over his pathetic, prone form. "Where is Lucien?"

He swiped at his bloody nose. "Wh— I don't—"

She kicked him in the chest again. He yelped like an injured water buffalo.

"Where is Lucien, you piece of shit?"

"I dunno! I dunno! I swear!"

Val grabbed his arm and twisted it into a lock. He shrieked as his tendons stretched to their limits.

"Wrong answer, fuckface. I know you work for him, so where is his base of operations? Where did he take Margaret?"

"I dunno!"

She was going to have to break his arm. Damn, that would be satisfying.

A thunder of footfalls down the stairs caught Val's attention before she could snap his arm in two. Abby ran into the hallway, stopping short when she saw Val on top of Ginger.

"What are you doing here?" Abby yelled at Val. "What are you doing to my brother?"

"I'm trying to get him to tell me where Max is."

"He's with *you*," Abby spat.

Val let go of Ginger's arm and stood to face Abby, the woman Max loved not long ago—thought he loved anyway. The hurt and anger in her eyes were withering, and Val felt nothing but sympathy for her. Max must not have told her how strong the bond between him and Val really was. Everything in their lives had pulled them together, and objected violently when they were apart. Abby had been an unfortunate casualty in the war between their heads and their hearts.

"He's not with me. Lucien Christophe kidnapped him."

"How do you know that?"

"I saw it."

Abby scoffed. "You watched Lucien kidnap Max?"

"No, I *saw* it. Before it happened."

For a moment Abby looked confused, then the meaning of Val's words dawned on her. A terrible sadness descended over her face, and Val realized Max hadn't told her Val could also see the future. Abby thought she knew him, that Val had stolen Max away from her, but she never had him in the first place.

Movement at Val's feet alerted her to Ginger's attempt to crawl away as the women stared each other down. She kicked him in the butt and he collapsed back to the floor. Abby gasped and threw a hand over her mouth.

"What did Lucien have you doing for him?" Val demanded.

"Nothing!"

She stomped on his hand and left her foot there, grinding his fingers into the hardwood floor. "There are two hundred and six bones in the human body. I will break all of them, one at a time, until you decide to be honest."

"Okay, okay!" Ginger's hand writhed under her heel. He spoke through gritted teeth. "He wanted me to do a bunch of odd jobs."

"A piss-ant like you? Why?"

"I don't know, he just did."

"Like what?"

He swallowed hard. "Give people packages, bring him women, other stuff."

Bring him women. Women like Margaret.

"Since when?"

"Six, seven months ago."

About the time Max and Abby started dating. Lucien didn't care about Ginger—he wanted Max. Why?

"And what did he give you in return?"

He certainly didn't need the money. Ginger hesitated, looked at her, then his sister, then his hand. Val brought her foot down on his fingers again, felt a couple of them snap. Abby and Ginger hollered at the same time.

"Stop it!" Abby said, "He didn't—"

"I have HIV!" Ginger cried at the same time his sister spoke.

Abby fell silent.

"Lucien said he'd cure me. He can! I've seen him do it before! If I helped him, he'd cure me."

Abby's mouth fell open. Her face—already turning paler by the second as the entirety of her ignorance became clear—contorted from despair to horror. She had no idea of the world she lived in, the dark reality under the gilded veneer of her privileged life.

Val checked her hands for blood and heaved a sigh of relief when she saw none. She might've felt sorry for Ginger, if he hadn't helped Lucien rape and murder people in a sick bid to save himself.

"I'll ask you one more time: where did Lucien take Max?"

Ginger shook his head. He still wanted his goddamn cure.

"Harbor Island." Abby spoke just above a whisper. Ginger's gaze cut to hers, his eyes wide. "Daddy put Eugene in charge of one of the Southwest shipping lines; a small one, as a test of responsibility. It docks at Harbor Island and accepts shipment in one of the warehouses. I don't know which one exactly. It's the only place Eugene has access to that Lucien could…could—"

"*What the fuck, Abby?*" Ginger glared at his sister. "After what that asshole and his whore did to you?"

Abby looked down at him, a new steel to her voice despite the tears in her eyes. "He shouldn't die for that. Nobody should've died."

His voice cracked. "*I'll* die. I don't want to be on antiviral drugs for the rest of my goddamn life if there's a cure…"

Abby shook her head and silently sobbed. She wasn't as dumb as her brother; she knew there'd be no cure. Even if one existed, Lucien wouldn't give it to Ginger, not with the police on his back.

Val lifted her foot off Ginger's hand. She dragged him to his feet as he clutched his mangled fingers to his chest. "You're going to drive me to this warehouse. If you don't piss me off, I might let you go after we get there."

He cringed but didn't argue. It was the best deal he could hope for in his situation. Maybe he could clean out his accounts and flee to France before Daddy learned about his extracurricular activities; unlikely, but possible.

"Thank you," Val said to Abby on her way out the door, shoving Ginger along in front of her.

Abby replied with a cold glare. Val was still the woman who'd compelled her fiancé to break her heart after all. But the last few crazy weeks were just a taste of what life with a future-seer would've been like. She'd move on, find a normal, boring guy to settle down with, and be happier for it.

Westford family gatherings from that point on would be a bitch, though.

Chapter Thirty

Stacey poked her head in the front door of Val's house. She paused a moment to ensure she didn't hear any sounds that suggested they might be home, like animated conversation punctuated by excited giggling or fuck noises. Given Val's inability to experience normal orgasms, Stacey couldn't believe how often Val and her boyfriend had sex. Maybe Max got off on her passing out, like some kind of weird fetish. Each time Stacey ventured back to the house to retrieve fresh clothes or entertain the idea of reclaiming her space, she'd been greeted by a symphony of moans and lustful screams—Stacey's very own never-ending porno. Max was giving it to his woman good. How nice for her. Stacey had turned and marched out.

Finally, it seemed the sex-a-thon had ended. Stacey entered the house, keeping an ear out in case she was wrong. The little Jack Russell ran up as she walked into the living room, skidding to a halt five feet in front of her. He bounced on his front legs and barked.

"What is it, boy? Is Max stuck in the well?"

Stacey swore she heard him growl, "Fuck you." She went into the kitchen and sighed at the junk food now packed in the fridge. She pulled out a hot dog and tossed it to the dog. To his credit he sniffed it first, then seemed to decide Max could keep awhile longer in the well and tore into the link. He finished it off, looked at her, and wagged his tail. Typical man—the way to his heart was through his stomach.

Stacey hopped up the stairs, her eyes involuntarily cutting to Val's bedroom door at the top. They'd just *left it open*. After Val blew off taco night, Stacey had gone upstairs to change her clothes, hoping the noises she'd heard on her way up was actually the house settling. But there they were, fucking with the door wide open, his ass in the air, her legs around his waist, moaning as they strained the mattress springs to their limits. She didn't even care if Stacey saw them—or maybe she'd already forgotten her *supposed* best friend existed.

Val's rich boy toy might not be too happy to learn she'd been sexing up the man who'd almost killed him on two separate occasions. Stacey smiled at the fantasy of "accidentally" letting that nugget of information slip at a fancy dinner party in Max's Mercer Island mansion. *Let's invite some common folk. How about my old friend Stacey? She'll provide some local color! Sten who? Let's not talk about Sten. Stacey*... Stacey!

Stacey chuckled, but there was no mirth in it. She sat at the edge of her bed and felt tears coming on. They'd been friends forever. Stacey didn't want to lose Val, though it seemed to her like she'd already lost.

Her phone buzzed in her tote. She glanced at it; Val again.

Stacey let it go to voice mail as she stripped off her clothes to take a shower. It was nice being able to bathe alone and not be pawed like a cat as she tried to wash her hair. Rotating between Michelle, Cindi, and Lucinda's houses over the past few days had her all sexed out. Some alone time would do her good. Then maybe…Francine.

Stacey checked her phone log while she brushed her teeth in front of the bathroom mirror. Wow, four calls from Val within the last two hours. Girlfriend really wanted to talk. Maybe she and Max were on the outs again. Perhaps all that sex they were having didn't equal love after all. Stacey drummed her fingers on the bathroom countertop, then cued up Val's last voice mail, hoping for a heartfelt grovel.

"Stacey, it's me." Val's voice sounded hurried and breathless. "Lucien is on Harbor Island, in the Westford Warehouse Number Four. I've got Ginger with me and I'm heading there now. If you get this in time, meet me there, please. I don't know what to expect but I need someone to keep watch outside while I go in. Please, Stacey." She took in a ragged breath. "I need you."

Stacey stood motionless at the end of the message, staring at herself in the mirror. What the hell had happened in the last few hours? She played the message before last.

"Stacey, please. Please return my call. I know you're mad at me and I'm sorry. I'm sorry again. I'm sorry forever and all eternity. Max is missing. He went to his place to get some things and he hasn't come back, and I'm really freaking out. I had a vision that Lucien kidnapped him, and I think that's what's happened. I think Lucien has him. If he's doing to Max what he did to Margaret, I—I need to find him. I can't do it alone. Please call me back."

Aw crap. Shit was going down, and she'd been too wrapped up in her anger at Val to get the memo until now. Their friendship had been strained the last few months, especially these last few weeks, but they were still a team. Eventually time and chocolate would heal their wounds.

Stacey dropped her toothbrush in the sink, threw on some clothes, and ran down the stairs. Her hand on the front doorknob, she jumped when someone behind her spoke. "Stop."

She spun around and recognized the woman standing in the living room at the same time she recognized the voice. "Kat? What the hell are you doing here?"

Dressed in a black pantsuit with a white corset top pushing up her ample cleavage, Kat cut a perfect mix of sexy and classy—a sort of Mata Hari of the boardroom. Stacey had never seen her like that before. "I'm here to stop you from going to Harbor Island."

"So you *did* know about Lucien Christophe. You bitch."

"I knew *of* him," Kat said, unfazed by Stacey's hostility. "I didn't know what he was up to. They give him a lot of leeway."

"Who're 'they'?"

"My employers."

"The people pulling the strings of fate?"

"Yes."

She folded her arms. "Why are you telling me this?"

"Because I don't want you to rush off to Harbor Island to help Val."

"Why not? It'll upset the order of the universe?"

"No, because you'll die."

Stacey's arms dropped. Kat couldn't be serious. She couldn't mean what Stacey thought she meant. "I can take care of myself," Stacey said, her voice less flippant than a moment ago.

"It doesn't matter. If you try to help her, you'll be caught in the crossfire and die."

Stacey swallowed hard. "How do you know that?"

"The Alpha told me."

"Who?"

"Cassandra, the Alpha. She sees all, every future. She's slowly going insane and talks in riddles a lot, as all Alphas eventually do, but she seemed pretty clear on this. If you go to Val, you will die."

Stacey stared at Kat, her mouth hung open. Was Kat lying? What an incredibly bizarre lie, if that's what it was. But everything Stacey knew about Kat was built upon lies layered like Russian nesting dolls.

"Why should I believe anything you say? All you've ever done is blow smoke up my ass."

Kat took a step forward, the grace of her namesake in even that small motion. She held up her hands in a conciliatory gesture. "What I did was for the greater good," Kat said. "Why has Val been lying to you?"

A trick question, and Stacey knew it. Still, she was curious. She rose to the bait. "What do you mean by that?"

"You died once before."

Stacey's breath left her lungs.

"You died in a boating accident almost ten years ago. The Alpha is absolutely sure about this. Val changed your future."

Stacey gawked. It wasn't true. It couldn't be true. Val would've told her...wouldn't she? According to Val, she'd changed people's futures before; it was rare, and hard, but she could do it. She'd failed with Margaret, but had she succeeded once before with Stacey? Had Stacey been *dead* for years, defying the universe and walking the world a metaphysical zombie?

"One possible future takes you to Val and your death, again. The other possible future takes you to me."

Stacey felt numb. How could Val keep this from her? She supposed she should be glad to be alive, but the fact that her "friend" made a literal life-or-death decision for Stacey without telling her felt like a betrayal at the deepest level. How was she supposed to come to terms with that decision if she hadn't even been allowed to make it? Was the world *different* now with her in it? Was she supposed to be dead?

Swallowing back a lump in her throat, she snapped, "Why do you care if I die again?"

Kat moved closer to Stacey until the two were a mere foot apart. Her ice blue eyes surveyed Stacey's dark brown ones, Sphinx-like composure tempered by an emotion Stacey swore looked a lot like affection.

"Because I care for you," she said. Kat ran a finger across Stacey's jawline. A thrill shot through Stacey like nothing she'd experienced since...well, since the last time she'd made love to Kat.

But Kat was a liar. So was Val. Everybody lied.

"What do you *really* want from me, Kat—or whatever your real name is?"

"It's Claire, but I always thought that was boring." Kat left her hand on Stacey's face, caressing Stacey's cheek in slow circles. Stacey didn't remove it. "What I really want is for you to come with me now."

"Where would we go?"

"The Cayman Islands first. After that I don't know. Depends where our orders take us."

"You want me to work with you. For those people who told you to blow up the car at the Pacific Science Center last year."

The corners of Kat's lips twitched. "Gotta pay the bills somehow."

So that was Kat's endgame—to recruit her. These goddamn people were obsessed with Max and Val—something about the Alpha, something about their future child. Made sense to poach someone close to them. That was the root of Kat's continued interest in Stacey, not love. But so what? Val had her *man*. She'd soon be jetting off with him to wonderful, exotic locations to have oodles of orgasm-less sex. Stacey would be left behind, squatting in Val's empty house, propping up Val's business, caretaking Val's old life until it eventually atrophied and died.

I'm already dead.

"And what do I get out of this?" Stacey asked, the hostility in her voice subdued by curiosity.

"Adventure. A reason to live. Me."

Kat kissed her then, soft lips against soft lips, tongue against tongue. It wasn't unlike the sensation of licking dark chocolate mousse off a spoon. To hear Kat explain it, she was Stacey's payment, a commodity to be traded for other useful things.

A resource. And what was Stacey to Val anymore? She was tired of investing in a one-sided relationship. At least Kat was honest about what she could give Stacey—her playful fingers, skimming Stacey's breast, said it all. Stacey considered what she had to lose, and decided it was nothing.

I'm already dead.

Their lips parted and hovered an inch apart. Stacey ran a hand through Kat's lustrous blond hair and looked into her Arctic eyes, thawed just a little. *Mine, all mine.*

"All right, baby, let's go," Stacey said.

Kat smiled. "Do you need to pack a bag?"

"No. No baggage. Pun intended."

Chapter Thirty-one

Fallout shelters are really not necessary for short nuclear wars if you survived the initial blast you'd be at higher risk of cancer and birthing children with defects but you could immediately resettle as long as you avoided ground zero and don't drink the water and mind the cannibals and prime numbers—"

Max's eyes popped open. Pockmarked ceiling tiles filled his vision. Who was talking? He'd been talking. Babbling. What about? He had no idea. His eyes darted back and forth, taking in his surroundings. A dark space, not very big, silhouettes of metal shelving against the walls. A storage room. He still lay on the metal table, still in a hospital gown, after—what? What had happened to him? What did Lucien do? He remembered fire, then pain. Then drugs, so many drugs, an endless stream of rainbow serums pin-pricking his arms and neck. He'd been on the moon, then under the sea, then flying in the clouds, then the size of the Chrysler Building to the size of an ant, down and up the rabbit hole over and over again.

All those memories were indistinct smears against the walls of his skull. But one he remembered vividly. At some point he'd felt intense pleasure like he'd never known before. It'd seized him head to toe, as if his body were a giant brass bell given a single strong rap, waves of ecstasy flowing through him until they dissipated with a quiet moan. What had that been? It was almost like...almost like what he guessed a normal orgasm would feel like. What regular people experienced at the climax of lovemaking. No, he'd imagined it. But had he? Had Lucien found a way to turn his ability off. How? *How?* He had to know.

Max tried to sit up. Though his muscles were weak, it was the leather straps still around his wrists that kept him down. *Technically, I can live without knowing,* he admonished himself. *I won't live if I don't escape.*

He pulled on the restraints and felt the left one give more than the right. Focusing on the left arm, Max twisted his wrist and pulled as hard as he could. The leather strap dug into his flesh, ripping his skin in its fight to hold on to him. Still weak from the drugs, he paused to gulp down air, then pulled with all his might again, and again, and again. Teeth clenched and a growl rising in his throat, he yanked viciously a final time and his hand popped free.

Panting, he clutched his mangled hand to his chest. After gathering his meager strength, he reached to his right side and fumbled with the strap. Half a minute later, his numb, trembling fingers worked the leather out of the buckle and both hands were free.

Max rolled off the metal table and fell on his hands and knees onto a linoleum floor. He wasn't nauseous anymore, but his muscles were still jelly. His whole body begged for him to lie down and sleep again; his desperation forced him to stay awake and fight. Across the room he recognized a pile of rumpled clothes. Naked except for his flimsy hospital gown, he crawled over the cold ground toward it. He reached the pile and teased out a shirt and jeans. In the dim light he couldn't tell if the clothes were his or not, but when he pulled them on, they fit enough to be serviceable. No shoes in the pile, though.

He walked his hands up the wall and pushed with his legs until he stood. Slouched against the wall, he put one foot in front of the other until the smooth surface yielded to a flush door. He grasped the handle and pushed down—

Flames engulfed the door. The inferno burned so hot that chunks of wood sloughed to the ground and dissolved into ashes upon impact. Max jerked backward, stumbled, and fell. Throwing his hands up to protect himself from the flames, he blinked—and the flames were gone. The door stood before him unblemished, the room dark and silent.

He was seeing glimpses of the future again; in this instance, probably the destruction wrought by the nuclear blast Val had witnessed repeatedly in her visions. Max was lucid enough to realize that much. Lucien had been tinkering with Max's ability. Whatever the Frenchman had pumped into Max not only made him so weak he could barely stand, but it still had a hold on his cognitive brain. He couldn't wait for it to wear off. If he didn't escape now, Lucien would kill him—*eventually* kill him, after more torture.

"Nothing strange I see is actually happening now," he whispered to himself. He repeated the words in his head as he heaved himself to his feet, shuffled to the door, and turned the handle.

Light blinded him for a moment. He'd only opened the door a crack, but the difference between the storage room and whatever lay outside was stark. When his eyes adjusted, he saw a bare hallway with scuffed plaster walls. He pushed the door open farther, wincing when the hinge squeaked. To his right, the hallway dead-ended at a door half ajar, light pouring forth as proof of an occupant. To the left, craning his head around the storage room door, were stairs leading down.

Lucien's words, spoken in French, echoed down the hallway through the open door. They bounced off the walls like ricocheting gunfire. "Results of Serum B on subject thirteen show great promise."

Heart thumping hard, Max slipped into the hallway and eased the storage room door closed behind him, the slight click of the latch a crash to his ears.

"Cortisol and adrenal levels abnormally high, but that's to be expected. Enlarging and shrinking of the amygdala appeared to have no effect on the subject's prophetic visions."

Max raced toward the stairs; unfortunately for him, his "race" wasn't much faster than a crawl. His legs felt slogged down in knee-high mud, and he had to lean against the wall to stay standing. His breath rasped like sandpaper on wood. He tried to quiet his gasps, but he was too desperate for air.

"However, Serum B was able to shut down the lateral orbitofrontal cortex while stimulating the hypogastric and pudendal nerves, as well as suppress some function of the cerebellum which I'm as yet unable to discern."

The floor began to crumble beneath Max's feet. A yawning chasm unzipped down the hall, swallowing the linoleum and ancient wooden floorboards in its path. Max pressed his back against the wall and grasped for handholds that weren't there. He clenched his eyes shut as the roar of falling debris grew louder. *It's not real, it's not real—*

"This 'witch's brew' combination triggered a euphoric response accompanied by the subject's ejaculation while he maintained a nontrivial level of consciousness. Very promising."

Max took a blind step forward. His foot landed on solid ground. Opening his eyes, he saw the hallway as it was now—old, cracked, and scuffed, but intact.

"Still too many unknowns to definitively declare success, not without running many more trials. I shall attempt to replicate these results on subject fourteen, if I'm able to procure her in a timely manner. Unfortunately, my present situation forces me to temporarily put my work on hold as I must move my equipment and subjects to another location."

Finally, Max reached the stairs. Gripping the handrail with white knuckles, he descended one step at a time. Lucien's voice faded into a menacing drone behind him, words like a swarm of wasps with poison-dripping stingers at Max's back. On the final step his legs gave way and he slammed face-first into a concrete floor. He pushed himself up on shaking arms, tasting blood in his mouth from a split lip. A huge room sprawled in front of him with rows of pallets stacked on top of each other nearly to the ceiling. Some kind of warehouse. The lights flickered, and he heard quick footsteps. From around a corner maybe a hundred feet away, five silhouettes emerged, crying as they ran for their lives. Max blinked and they faded to smoke. A glimpse of something to come. Something soon.

He struggled to stand on legs made of rubber, sweating despite a chill that gripped him to the core. The wasp droning behind him stopped. He was nearly out of time. Max shambled forward, as close to a run as he could muster, toward where the silhouettes had appeared. Eyes scanning for an exit, he turned the corner and saw five large metal shipping containers embedded in a row of pallets. Past the containers the corridor ended at one of the building's outer edges. If he followed the wall, it would eventually lead him to a door to the outside. All he had to do was get there.

As he shuffled past the containers, he heard it. Crying. Max stopped. Had he imagined it? Hallucinated it? He heard it again, coming from the red container on the end. Lucien would soon find Max missing and scour the warehouse, claim back the prize he'd worked too hard to leave without. But Max couldn't escape if it meant leaving other people behind to suffer like he'd suffered, like Margaret had suffered.

Keenly aware of every second he stayed exposed, he approached the container, certain now of someone crying within its metal walls. He pushed up on the latch's long handle as his body begged him to sit down, rest, maybe take a quick nap. After what felt like a Herculean effort, the bar holding the door closed shifted up, and the latch released. Max used what was left of his strength to swing the metal door open.

The smell hit him first—bleach, so strong he nearly gagged. A woman lay on a metal table, clad in a hospital gown, as Max had been. She lifted her head and squinted at the bright light, eyes red and wet from crying.

"Help me," she begged when she recognized Max wasn't Lucien. She jerked her arms and legs against the straps holding her down. "*Help me!*"

Max hurried to her and fiddled with the straps, his lame left hand hindering his ability to manipulate the buckle with any skill.

"Hurry, hurry, oh God," she said, saucer-sized eyes darting back and forth between Max and the door.

Wrinkles overtook her young face, not from age but wear. Her skin sallowed, her teeth yellowing as her eyes sank into her face. Then her body went still and a police officer draped a sheet over her body, a needle still in her arm—

"*Wake up!*" she shrieked at him.

Max jumped and blinked at the woman, her face still young, smooth, and terrified. Another hallucination of the future. Bad times ahead for the poor girl.

He loosened her strap enough so she could yank her hand out the rest of the way. She tore into her other hand's strap. With frenetic speed she undid all her remaining restraints and leapt off the table, sprinting out of the container in a near panic. Obviously whatever drugs Lucien gave her hadn't resulted in the terrible weakness afflicting Max.

"Wait!" Max called after her. He slouched against the metal wall, his legs trembling with the effort to stay on his feet. "The other containers... You have to open them. There could be more people inside. I can't do it myself."

She stopped and spun in a strange circle for a moment, as if physically warring with herself over whether to run for it or spare a few precious seconds saving others.

"Please," he said, "I'll give you money, lots of money."

She stopped and looked at him, seemed to recognize who he was, that he was serious. The appeal of a windfall overrode her survival instincts—*so much for using something other than my money to solve problems*—and she ran to the shipping containers and unlatched all the doors in a fraction of the time it'd taken him. Max dragged himself to the next closest container and unbuckled the straps of an Asian man with hollowed cheeks and pallid skin. He looked like he'd been there awhile.

"Thank you, thank you," he said over and over as Max worked his wrists and ankles free. He slid off the table and stumbled a step; weak, though not as weak as Max. "Mark!" he called as he pushed past.

Back in the corridor, the soon-to-be-rich woman had been joined by the Asian man and three more people, another man and two women, all in matching hospital gowns. The two men embraced each other in a tight, heartfelt hug.

Lilies decorated the archway of the gazebo where the two men, both in tuxes, held hands and gazed into each other's eyes as a modest crowd looked on.

Mark's voice trembled as he spoke. "Jin, you were my reason for living when I thought I couldn't go on anymore. I heard your voice on the other side of that metal wall, and I knew everything would be all right. Not only did you save my life then, you save it every day now. I can't wait to spend the rest of my life with you. I love you."

Mark slipped a ring on Jin's finger. With tears in their eyes, they kissed. The crowd cheered—

"What are you doing?" Jin pulled on Max's arm. "Stop clapping and come on!"

The gazebo was gone, replaced by the warehouse. He shook his head. Back to reality. *Keep it together, Max.*

"This way!" a woman yelled to the group, as if she knew a quicker way out than following the wall. They rushed ahead, in the same direction the silhouettes had gone. Max tried to keep up, but his legs refused to move faster than a slow walk. Jin glanced behind him, noticed Max trailing, and doubled back.

"Hurry—"

Jin's face erupted in terror as Max felt an arm like steel clamp around his neck and jerk him backward.

Lucien. Shit.

A gunshot right next to Max's ear nearly deafened him. A pallet a foot away from Jin exploded where a bullet struck the side. Jin cried out and ducked. For half a second his eyes held Max's, wanting to help, knowing he couldn't. He turned and sprinted out of sight.

"*Merde,*" Lucien said.

Max struggled against Lucien's hold, but it was useless. He could barely stand, let alone fight.

"Look what you have done!" Lucien said through clenched teeth. "All of my work, ruined! No time to clean up properly. We must leave *now*."

Lucien dragged Max down the corridor, toward some kind of egress route, away from freedom, away from Val, to live out the rest of his life as a lab rat.

Chapter Thirty-two

Westford Warehouse Number 4 sat two blocks away from Harbor Island's busy piers, packed among a row of similar-looking bland buildings with no windows. Heavy rain battered the windshield of Val's car where she sat parked half a block away. Through smears of water she could make out the faint glow of light under a heavy rolling door in the front.

She looked at Ginger in her passenger seat, arms and legs bound by duct tape. "Who's in there besides Lucien?"

"How the fuck should I know?"

"You should know because you *own the building*, idiot."

"I don't go in there."

"Oh that's right, I forgot—you're an incompetent man-child leeching off Daddy's money, so why would you bother to learn any aspect of a job you're supposed to be responsible for?"

He gritted his teeth and fumed in his seat, but said nothing. Probably didn't want to get punched in the face again.

She had to admit her antagonism of him was a little juvenile, but damn if it didn't feel good. Val itched to go in with guns blazing, a course of action she knew Max wouldn't approve of. He'd want her to think it through, come up with a plan that involved stealth or subterfuge or cunning. Or better yet, call the police.

Val called the police.

"Seattle Police Department. How may I direct your call?"

"I've got information on the whereabouts of Lucien Christophe."

"Hold, please." After thirty seconds a different man's voice came on the line. "This is Detective Belden."

"I know where Lucien Christophe is."

"Okay." He sounded oddly disinterested. "Who am I speaking to?"

"I'd like to remain anonymous."

"Uh-huh. And where do you think Christophe is?"

"I don't *think*, I *know*. He's at the Westford Warehouse Number Four, on Harbor Island. He's keeping people prisoner here. It's where he kept Margaret Monroe before he murdered her."

"Uh-huh."

Dammit, she sounded like a loon. Detective Belden's bored responses suggested he agreed.

"Can you just come, please? At least send someone to check it out. Someone with a gun."

"We will head out there as soon as possible, ma'am."

"When will that be?"

"As soon as possible."

"Why not now?"

Detective Belden sighed. "Because you're the fourth person to call *within the last hour* with a tip on Christophe. It's in the queue."

"Like how Margaret Monroe's disappearance was in your missing persons queue?"

A couple of seconds of chilly silence followed. "We take every tip seriously, ma'am, which is why it takes time to investigate them all. We will be at the"—he paused, probably to look at his slapdash notes—"Westford Warehouse Number Four as soon as possible. Thank you for the information. Is there anything else you'd like to report?"

Val mashed the disconnect icon on her phone. Goddamn police. Cringing a little, she called Sten. She wanted to stay as far away from him as possible, but she was quickly running out of options. She'd never be rid of him at this rate.

The line rang and rang. It clicked over to his voice mail.

"If you're a hot chick, leave a message. If you're the boyfriend of a hot chick, wrong number." *Beep.*

"For the record, that's one of the most obnoxious voice mail greetings I've ever heard. And I'm at the Westford Warehouse Number Four on Harbor Island. It's where Lucien is hiding, and where he's been taking people to perform sick experiments on them. He's got Max, and I need…Listen, I'll give you whatever you want, or…*be* whatever you want, okay? *Anything.* Just please…Please—Forget it." She hung up and shook her head. "Fuck."

Stacey wasn't coming. No one was coming. It was up to her, and her alone, to get Max out of that building alive. To hell with her visions. To hell with fate. To hell with everyone and everything that stood in her way. Valentine Shepherd was an avenging angel, and the time for retribution was now.

From the passenger seat Ginger sneered. "Out of friends?"

Val considered punching him again, but had a better idea. She returned his sneer. "Nah. I've got you."

The smile wiped off his face.

Five minutes later, Val stood in the rain next to the driver's side door with a football-sized rock in her arms. She'd moved the car into an adjacent dark lot, its headlights turned off and pointing at the building about fifty feet from the rolling door. Ginger eyed the rock with wide eyes. He made muffled grunts of disapproval through the duct tape Val had slapped over his mouth. With the parking brake on, Val slipped the car into drive. Then she wedged the rock onto the accelerator. The engine revved, straining against the brake like a wild horse tethered to a post. Ginger's eyes somehow got wider, his grunts more frantic as he shook his head at her.

She'd put a seatbelt around him. He'd probably live.

"Ride the lightning, Eugene."

Eugene: "*Nnnnn nnnnn!*"

Val reached in and popped the brake. The tires skidded in place for a second before the car bucked forward. She watched it pick up speed, the driver's side door dangling open as it went, until it crashed into the building at maybe thirty miles an hour. Her good old car kept trying to go, its wheels spinning against the slick pavement, the horn stuck on and blaring. Poor thing. She wasn't sure how she'd explain this to her insurance company. She'd think of a feasible lie later.

Val swiped water off her face, drew her gun, and raced to the other side of the building, careful to dodge big puddles and stay in the shadows. From around the corner, she saw the rolling door slide up. Light poured forth into inky wet blackness, the silhouettes of two people cut into the glow. They took cautious steps outside, toward the crashed car, hands on their hips—on their guns. Security forces. A simple warehouse would make due with a lock and an alarm system. These boys must've been hired by Lucien as his private muscle, probably a smaller contingent of the same guys at the Mountain Lodge event. If Lucien really was keeping kidnap victims in the warehouse, he wouldn't want a bunch of possible witnesses hanging around. That only two guards had emerged, and not an army, was a good sign. She hoped.

Staying light on her toes and holding her breath, Val snuck toward the open door as the two men moved away from her. They threw open the passenger side door as Val reached the lip of the building's bright hole. Ginger's muffled shrieks poured out. He'd lived. Really, he'd just die slower. Congrats to him.

"Well, he's obviously not the one shooting," Val heard one of the men say to the other, no idea what they referred to.

"I told you it came from *inside* the warehouse, not out here."

"Then what the hell is this..."

She leaned her head into the light and peaked around the corner. A plastic table covered in snacks and magazines stood a few feet away, flanked by a couple of metal folding chairs. Beyond those, short stacks of palletized goods, then tall stacks of palletized goods, formed neat rows through the belly of the warehouse. But in her visions of Lucien dragging Max away, she'd been in a concrete corridor with metal doors—

"Hey!"

Val snapped her head toward the guards. She met their eyes. *Shit.* They saw her gun, then raised theirs.

"Put it down!"

She wasn't about to give up now. Val lunged forward, into the building's mouth. Gunshots rang out, whizzing through the air a few inches behind her. She reached a short stack of pallets and skidded to a halt behind it, breathing hard.

She pushed wet hair out of her face. "Do you know who you're working for?" she yelled behind her. It was possible they didn't, if they went through a middleman. "You're protecting Lucien Christophe, wanted by the police for murder. You wanna go down with him?"

She heard feet shuffling toward both sides of her, boxing her in.

"Put the gun down, come out, and we'll talk."

Val wasn't sure if they'd shot at her with the intention of hitting her or only as a warning. Either way, they weren't on her side. Her gaze cast about the warehouse for any clues to where Max could be. A concrete corridor with metal doors—

Movement on Val's left caught her eye. They'd almost flanked her. She let loose a bullet ten feet above one of the guards, then spun and did the same thing to her right. They retreated behind her, though she knew they wouldn't stay back for more than a few seconds. She needed to move.

Val sprinted to the next stack of pallets. Two more bullets cut through the air, only missing their target because the men had been in the act of backing up when she ran. She heard their careful footsteps approaching again.

Then she saw the sign on the far wall with an arrow pointing to the right: "Cold Storage." A concrete corridor with metal doors that opened into freezers. That's where Max was.

It was too far from her pallet to the next. They'd shoot her for sure. She was trapped.

I have no choice, I have to try. Just run. Just—

Wait—did she hear screaming and weeping sounds, coming from in front of her? A group of five people in hospital gowns burst into view from behind one of the tall pallet stacks. Panicked and huddled together, they ran toward the open door Val had come through. When they saw the guards, they slowed and erupted into a cacophony of frantic shouts, yelling on top of one another.

"Don't shoot!"

"Help us!"

"I'm not going back! You'll have to kill me first!"

When the shouting wasn't met with a volley of gunfire, Val chanced a look around the corner and saw the guards gawking at the group, their guns still out but pointed at the ground, unsure what to do. They weren't homicidal henchmen after all, just a couple of guys trying to do their job. Beyond the guards, through the open door, flashing lights approached. Police cruisers, at least three of them. The guards glanced behind them as sirens became audible.

"Aw, hell," one of the guards said. "Screw this." He holstered his gun. The group in hospital gowns rushed past them and out the door, eager to embrace the police.

The cavalry had arrived. They'd want to talk to her, take her statement, eat up time she didn't have. Lucien had an escape route, an emergency exit plan he'd set up for just this kind of contingency, one that led through cold storage. If she didn't go there now, she'd never see Max again.

Ignoring the growing circus behind her, she raced deeper into the warehouse.

Chapter Thirty-three

Val found the door marked "Cold Storage" and threw it open. A long concrete corridor with inlaid metal doors stretched out in front of her, exactly as it had been in her vision. She took off down it, running toward her future. Running toward Max's death.

I can't kill him. I will not kill him. Fuck you, fate.

She reached a corner, slowed, and raised her gun. Her heart pounded against her rib cage.

I can change the future.

She wheeled around the corner and recognized Lucien's back in a white lab coat, scrambling away from her. Though Lucien's body blocked her view, she knew he was forcing Max forward in a chokehold.

"Stop!" Val yelled.

Lucien spun to face her, holding Max in front of him as a human shield. Max thrashed and tried to fight back, but his face was pale and sweaty, his movements weak. He looked like he could barely stand. Lucien held a gun to Max's head.

"You're going to let me leave," he said.

From behind her the sound of police sirens wafted through the corridor, getting louder.

She eyed him down the barrel of her gun, training the sights back and forth between Max and Lucien's head; an eighth of an inch difference, from her vantage point. "No, I'm not."

"You and he don't technically need to be alive—"

"Shut up, Lucien. You're so full of shit I can smell it on your breath from over here. Let him go and I'll let you live."

Lucien laughed, a hint of hysteria in his voice. Though he held Max prisoner, he was the one who was trapped, and he knew it. He jammed the barrel of his gun into Max's temple. "What happens now, hmm? You've seen it, yes? Do I kill him, or you? Maybe both? How do you stop me?"

Val's jaw tightened. He saw it and grinned.

"You *don't* stop me, do you?"

Emboldened by her hesitation, he took a step back. Max still covered him too completely for her to get a clean shot. Her gun sights stayed on them.

"You want him to live? Let's make a deal—I'll trade him for you."

Val fought to keep her face from giving away her shock. Why was her ability to change things so goddamn important? Wasn't knowing the future enough for these people?

"No!" Max choked out.

Lucien tightened his grip on Max's throat, and Val felt her own throat constrict. Angry-looking puncture marks covered his arms. Blood dribbled from a cut on his lip. The pain he must have been in, the suffering he'd endured...Max would *not* die here.

What if she *did* trade places with him? She was in a lot better shape than he was at the moment. She could escape. If not immediately, then eventually. She could endure whatever Lucien did to her in the meantime, bide her time until she knew Max was safe, then save herself.

Val lowered her gun a couple of inches. Max's thrashing increased. How would it work? If she lowered her gun completely, Lucien would just shoot her and leave. Maybe she could walk to him, go with him to whatever escape vehicle waited for him on the other side of cold storage, then lower her gun after Max got a safe distance away.

"If you come with me, I will let him go. Simple. See, I'm not unreasonable. I'm not heartless. I erased your memory and blessed you with a life free of shame. I did that. For you. I can erase all your memories when we're done."

She almost laughed as cold rage rushed up her neck, prickling the skin along her spine. A life free of shame—not anger; shame. The same shame that killed her sister, silenced millions of people every day, and let evil fuckers like Lucien walk free. A shame society had fashioned to be her shackles. And he thought because of what *he* did, that *she* should be ashamed? Her gun inched up again.

"Don't throw away your life and your gift chasing me."

A life free of *shame*.

"You have nothing to gain, *nothing*—"

Val pulled the trigger. A bullet exploded out of her gun and whizzed toward them. Lucien and Max stumbled backward and fell. Neither man moved.

Max is dead. I killed him.

In a horrified daze, Val ran to them. Blood splattered the floor where they'd been standing. A couple of feet from Lucien, Max lay on the ground, splotches of crimson staining his T-shirt. Why did she get so angry? Why did she break her promise not to risk Max's life? Why did she think she could fight fate, when Margaret Monroe was bloody proof that she couldn't? A scream tried to claw its way out of her throat.

Oh God he's dead, he's dead, he's dead—

Max stirred. His eyes flickered and opened. He pushed himself up on shaky arms. "Val," he breathed.

The scream fell back into her throat. She dropped to her knees and crushed Max to her chest, burying her face in his neck as he did the same to her.

"Max." She let out a single sob into his skin. Her whole body trembled as she clung to her rock in the storm, warm and alive in her arms.

Lucien groaned. In a flash Val's gun was in the air again, pointed at Lucien's writhing form. He rolled onto his back and sat up, clutching his shoulder. Blood leaked into his white coat through a bullet hole underneath his fingers. She scanned the floor and found Lucien's pistol where he'd dropped it next to Max. Val pulled the gun closer to her, farther out of the Frenchman's reach.

"Damn, that hurts," he said. He looked up and saw Val's gun pointed at him. "Going to kill me, are you? You shouldn't. I have so much to offer the world. Cures for terrible diseases that plague mankind. Cancer, multiple sclerosis, Alzheimer's..." He licked his lips as his eyes flicked between her and her gun. "I can enhance your ability...or take it away, if that's what you'd like. What do you want, hmm? What would it take?"

Her finger itched against the trigger. "What I want," she said, "is for you to be dragged into a court of law, admit what you've done to the world, then rot in jail for the rest of your fucking life."

He spit out a bitter laugh, winced at the pain it caused his shoulder. "Aren't you a dreamer."

Lucien raised his head and focused on something behind Val. She twisted around and saw Sten strolling down the corridor toward them, arms swinging lazily at his sides. Max tensed in her arms, then grabbed Lucien's pistol where it lay at his side and pointed it at Sten.

"*No!*" Val jerked his arm to the side just as he pulled the trigger. A bullet ricocheted off the wall two feet from Sten. Sten glanced at the new concrete divot, more annoyed than scared. If he'd ever experienced real fear, she'd never seen it.

Max's trembling hand fell back to the floor as if he'd used all the strength he had left just holding up the gun. He looked at her with burning eyes: Why did she stop him? Val shook her head. She didn't totally understand it herself. She couldn't let Max die. She couldn't let Sten die, either.

Max's grip tightened on Val's back as Sten approached. If Max's eyes could light fires, Sten would've been a pile of smoking ash. Val tightened her hold on Max as well. She had no idea what Sten would do.

He stopped in front of Max and Val, and put his hands on his hips. His face remained deceptively passive as he surveyed the situation with quick eyes.

"Finally," Lucien said to Sten. "You must be Northwalk's inside man. About time you got off your ass and helped get me out of here."

Sten looked at Lucien and cocked his head at what, Val recognized, was a dangerous angle. "Just got the order to get off my ass today, actually. You must be this Lucien person I've heard so much about." He cocked an eyebrow at Lucien's prone figure. "You people never stop asking for things. There's only so much of me to go around."

Lucien struggled to his feet, still clutching his shoulder. He crooked a thumb down the corridor. "Help me to the back. There's a ventilation tunnel that leads out. I've got a car and supplies there." He cocked his head toward Max and Val. "Bring them, too."

Sten didn't move.

Lucien made a disgusted scoff. "If you must arrest me for show, then fine. First let me stop by my lab and heal this wound. I don't want it to leave a scar."

Sten unholstered his gun.

Oh shit. Maybe she should've let Max shoot him after all.

"It won't just heal automatically?"

"Of course not. I need—"

Val gasped when Sten shot Lucien three times in the chest. Lucien fell onto his back, four holes now blooming crimson through his lab coat. Sten stalked past Max and Val, and as Lucien gaped in horror, blood oozing out of his mouth, put a final bullet between his eyes.

He turned to face Max and Val. She wondered if he planned to shoot them as well. Hell, he would've done it already if he intended to do it at all. He looked at Max, and the two men stared at each other for several long seconds. Last time they met, Sten had shot Max in the gut. Now Sten had ostensibly done Max a favor. Also, Sten and Val shared a recent…history. She swallowed hard at the thought of Sten blurting it out in front of Max. God, not now.

Sten holstered his gun and walked to Max. "Come on, get up." He grabbed Max's arm and hefted him to his feet. Val braced Max from the other side, his arm around her shoulders. Looked like Sten was their ally, or her *partner*—the thought made her shudder—at least for the moment.

Max twisted in Sten's grasp. "Let go of me, asshole."

Sten let go. Max collapsed back to the floor, nearly taking Val with him.

"You want her to drag you all the way out of here by herself? Be my guest. Not very chivalrous of you, though."

"*Sten*," Val said. "Max, just let him help."

"Why? He tried to kill you! He tried to kill me!"

"He's not trying to kill us right now." She looked into Sten's heavy, dark eyes, then at Lucien's bloody body a few feet away. Feeling a cool draft through her damp clothes, she shivered. Tears welled in her eyes. "Let's just get out of here, Max, please. Let's go home."

Max saw her wet eyes, and the defiance in his demeanor relented. He lifted his arm up to her, let her brace his weight on her shoulders again. Though his jaw remained tight, he didn't resist when Sten braced his other arm. They lifted him up until he could stand.

"Good thing you're not as fat as you look," Sten said.

Max's jaw got somehow tighter. "Good thing you're not as psychotic as you look."

Val looked away and cringed. *My two lovers. Fantastic.*

Together they took baby steps out of cold storage, back through the labyrinthine warehouse, and finally outside, to freedom. A fleet of cop cars, ambulances, and fire trucks choked the hole Val had come through. Red and blue light flooded the darkness, glinting off puddles of rainwater pooled around cracks in the pavement. Each of Lucien's former captives had an army of paramedics and police officers tending to them. Ginger, bloodied and bedraggled, complained from the inside of a cop car. Lucien's guards answered questions off to the side, eyes downcast and wrists handcuffed behind their backs. Though the rain had stopped, the air still felt wet, fresh. Sweet. No one had noticed the trio emerge through the chaos.

Sten led them to the back of an open ambulance, then sat Max down on the back bumper. Max hunched over, breathing hard despite having been carried most of the way.

Max left a smear of dirt where he wiped sweat from his brow. "Why are you helping us now?" He narrowed his eyes at Sten. "What do you want?"

Sten gave Max a slow blink as if he'd asked the stupidest question in the history of the world. Then he looked at Val.

For the briefest of moments she saw in his eyes the same rare emotion he'd shown in her house weeks ago—sadness. *I owe a debt I can never pay back.* She knew what he wanted—her partnership to take down Northwalk and be free of them, when the right time came. He'd killed her rapists for her, as well as the man who'd orchestrated it, probably incurring the wrath of his powerful handlers. She owed him a debt that could only be settled with blood—Northwalk's blood, same as him. Now their fates were truly bound. Maybe that'd been the plan all along.

As quickly as it had come, the sadness was gone, suppressed. He smiled at them, the lazy curve of his lips like a snake bathing in the sun. "Be seeing you." He walked away and was swallowed by the circus of swirling bodies.

Max let out a long, exhausted sigh, and his head collapsed onto Val's shoulder. He buried his face in her hair, his body slack against hers and shaking. Or was she shaking? They both were. She closed her eyes and leaned into him, the world fading to a drone, his heat combining with hers to make a furnace against the cold.

"Let's go," he whispered.

"Yes."

"We've got a couple more over here!"

Val opened her tired eyes to a mob of medics descending on them. She shrugged off an EMT who tried to take her blood pressure. "I'm fine, really."

A barrage of questions followed: *Who are you? What are you doing here? How did you get here? How do you feel? Are you hurt? Did someone try to hurt you?*

Max stayed leaning against Val, half asleep already, unresponsive to anyone else. A medic grabbed his limp arm to take vital signs while others prepped a gurney.

Then they were recognized: *Holy shit, that's Maxwell Carressa. And that's his new girlfriend.*

Fiancée, actually.

"Let's go," he whispered again.

Chapter Thirty-four

They were married on a beach in Fiji. Max wore an untucked light blue dress shirt that rippled in the soft ocean breeze, khaki pants, no tie, and no shoes. Val wore a white summer dress not much more substantial than a nightgown, a white frangipani flower in her hair and a small bouquet in her hands. A local celebrant officiated, said something about eternal love and commitment, but Val missed most of it. She was lost in the turquoise blue of the ocean and the emerald green of Max's eyes. Together, in sickness and in health. Together, through good times and bad.

He slipped a ruby solitaire ring on her finger with trembling hands. She did the same to him with a plain gold band. He cupped her hands in his and kissed them. Tears were sliding down her cheeks by the time the celebrant finally declared them husband and wife. Max swept her up in his arms, carried her waist-deep into the ocean, and kissed her as the warm water lapped their skin.

* * *

They ran along a path through a tropical forest along the Navua River. Max ran in front of her, barefoot, wearing only board shorts. She was barefoot, too, in a bikini. Val heard a roar through the trees. They burst from the forest into a clearing at the edge of a cliff. Water cascaded down the side into a crystal blue pool fifty feet below them. Her stomach lurched as she considered the drop.

"You can't chicken out now," Max said, panting from their run. He took her hand. Light broken through the canopy glinted off his wedding ring.

This was one of her favorite recurring visions, one of the rare pleasant ones. And now it would be a memory.

"Come on," he said. "On three: one, two, THREE!"

They sprinted off the side of the cliff, screaming as they fell, hand-in-hand, until the cool water enveloped them. Val broke the surface and gasped, taking in a lungful of air, her heart racing with the current. Max's head popped up a second later. He laughed, then swam to her. In the turquoise water of a tropical paradise, she wrapped her arms around his neck and kissed him.

"I love you," she whispered against his lips. "I love you."

* * *

The air-conditioning on their little boat had broken down again. Since they'd started sailing around the Fiji Islands in a thirty-foot-long yacht she wasn't sure if Max had rented or bought, they'd already fixed it once on the island of Vanua Levu. But it'd started whining again the day before, and now spat only warm ocean air into their cabin. She didn't know how long it would take them to get back to an island with a boat repair shop—she didn't even know how long they'd been sailing; a few weeks at least. Maybe they wouldn't bother fixing it again. A dip in the ocean was enough to cool them off in the day. At night, a myriad of possibilities presented themselves.

Max slid an ice cube over Val's heel, across her bare calf, and into the crux of her knee. Her skin prickled in the wake of the cube's path.

"Cooled down yet?" he asked.

From where she lay on her stomach atop the bed, she glanced over her shoulder. A single dim lamp bathed his sun-kissed skin in sepia, hair mussed with salt water, bedroom eyes turned a dark brown. "The opposite, actually. Keep going, though."

She closed her eyes and felt the cube pass over her backside, then down the valley into the small of her back. It made a lazy zigzagging path up the slope of her spine, between her shoulder blades, and up to the nape of her neck.

"When I was with Lucien, I...felt something," he said.

Val opened her eyes and looked at him again. He hadn't talked about his time as Lucien's captive since he gave his statement to the police. In fact, neither of them had mentioned Lucien or the last couple of terrible months in more than passing, instead relishing their newfound happiness as they ignored the rest of the world. She wondered if his broaching of the subject meant he was considering a return to reality.

"What did you feel?"

"It was..." He squeezed his lips together, then nudged her. She flipped over onto her back. He picked up another ice cube from the bucket and pressed it to her ankle. "It was something I've never felt before. Like an explosion of light in my gut." He snaked the cube up her leg, to the inside of her thigh. "A sun flare through my entire body." The ice slid across her belly, then between her legs. Her back arched when it touched her wet insides. Despite the cold, she felt heat building in her. "What does that sound like to you?"

Hot, cool, excited, dreamy, and dizzy, Val exhaled. So many sensations at once made her light-headed. She reached for him and played with the fine hair at the nape of his neck. "Sounds like a hallucination."

"I thought so, too, but when I was trying to escape, I heard him say into a tape recorder, 'Serum B triggered a euphoric response accompanied by the subject's ejaculation while he maintained a nontrivial level of consciousness.' I'm paraphrasing." The ice cube moved up, slow and lazy across her rib cage, then up the mountain of her soft breast and over the hard outcrop of her nipple. "He offered to turn your ability off."

"He was lying."

"What if he wasn't?" Water tricked down Val's breast, and Max licked it off. She let out a soft moan as her dizziness increased. "Technology sufficiently advanced is indistinguishable from magic. We saw him do stranger things."

"I don't know what we saw."

"What do you think the police did with all his notes?"

"In a just world, gave them to the National Institutes of Health. In *our* world, Sten probably gave them to Northwalk."

Max stood and gently lowered himself on top of her. His skin slick with a fine sheen of sweat, his hardness pressed against her middle, he ran a thumb over her lower lip. "But wouldn't you like to know what other people feel? What normal people feel? *Be* normal?"

She threaded her hands through his hair. His chest rose and fell with hers, in time with the waves that lapped their boat. "Where would that leave us?"

His head fell and he kissed her neck, his full weight settled atop her. She closed her eyes and imagined a world where they'd been normal, awkward kids, grown into normal, boring adults, never knowing great pain, and never knowing each other. It was duller, gray, incomplete. Val's eyelids drifted open, the dim orange of their cabin a warm blur, air thick with musk and sex. A pocket of pure love floating across the ocean. He pushed into her, and as the flare grew in slow steady strokes, his breath hot against her lips, chest sliding against hers, she knew whatever he'd felt would never be as good as this.

***

Val shot up from bed. Overcome with nausea, she ran to the toilet and threw up. After a couple of heaves her stomach calmed, but she stayed hunched over the bowl, clutching her belly, until she was sure the worst of it had passed.

"You okay?" Max asked behind her, his voice still sleepy. She heard him get up, then felt his hand on her back.

Val wiped her mouth and tried to recall what she'd eaten the night before, now amorphous chunks floating in the toilet. Noodles, canned peaches…unlikely to cause food poisoning. Maybe the motion of the boat…

"I'm—"

Faint light through a porthole told her it was early morning. Morning sickness. When was the last time she had her period? Over a month ago. She felt the blood leave her face.

"I'm p—pregnant."

"*What?*" His voice didn't sound sleepy anymore.

She tried to think as nausea still roiled through her. "I think I'm pregnant."

Max sat on the floor with her and leaned back against the wall. His eyes wandered to his feet. "Whose is it?"

Val laughed. "It's *yours*, Max."

His gaze cut back to hers, eyebrows raised. "How?"

Whatever really happened during her rape, Lucien had ensured she stayed STD and pregnancy-free. Since then, she'd only been with Sten and Max. She'd always used protection with Sten, whenever they'd done anything capable of making a baby anyway; never with Max. It hadn't been necessary, since he couldn't have children. Or so they thought.

"When you were shot in the stomach last year and went into surgery, they could have reversed your vasectomy at the same time."

"That's…that's crazy."

"Yeah, but our world is fucking crazy."

He chewed his thumb. "Abby never got pregnant."

Val shrugged. "Maybe she's infertile for some other random

reason, I don't know." She took a swig from a bottle of water on the sink, then sat across from him. "Of course it's yours. There's no way Northwalk would go to all this trouble if it wasn't yours."

"But they dispatched Lucien to steal your eggs and my sperm. Why would they do that if they'd already ensured I could get you pregnant the old-fashioned way?"

"Probably as a fail-safe. Maybe"—Val drank more water as she thought—"maybe their ability to manipulate the future has limits. Maybe they're not all-powerful, even with their Alpha."

Maybe they can be hurt. Maybe Sten and I can kill them all.

His eyes found the floor again, and she could see the gears of his mind working furiously. After a moment he looked up. "What are you going to do?"

Val hugged her legs to her chest and shook her head. She didn't know. She'd envisioned a future where they grew old together, just the two of them. Even though she'd never seen it, she still thought it was possible. She thought she'd changed their future. She hadn't.

"Keep it," Max said.

Keep it? "I thought you didn't want children."

"That was before I had a family—a real one. You're my family now. Josephine's my family. And Michael. And Toby, I guess. Turns out it's not so bad. In fact, I think I like it. Kids round it out. Hell, at that point we'd almost be *normal*." His eyes lit up at the possibility. He'd always dreamed of being a regular person with a regular life, and this was his chance.

Val pulled at her hair. "But not only will we be constantly

looking over our own shoulders, we'll have to watch out for our child as well. I don't think I can live like that."

"*We* can." He held his hand out to her.

This was why they'd broken up before. He'd wanted to fight for their future; she couldn't. Now he wanted to fight again, and her first instinct was to run, to end it. But she'd been wrong before, and the result had been an agony for them both.

Val took his hand and gripped it tight. His eyes filled with a warm glow that spread across his face, and he smiled. She imagined the warmth traveling through his hand, into her, fusing them together as two bonfires meeting to become one blaze.

"Okay," she said. This time, they would fight together.

Epilogue

Val stood in front of the Northwalk conspiracy diagram on the wall of her office—or *crazy wall*, as Sten called it. Hopefully Max wouldn't mind her transporting it to his study. He could even help her with it, maybe tease out connections she hadn't seen before, if he was willing—which he probably wouldn't be. Despite returning to reality and making plans for their future with gusto, he didn't want to talk about the evil organization stalking them and planning to one day steal their children, changing the subject whenever she brought it up. He preferred to revel in their newfound happiness while ignoring the coming danger, and she obliged him for the time being. He'd been miserable almost his entire life; eventually he'd have to face the threat with her, but for now he had every right to enjoy being a husband and expectant father.

With her finger, she traced the string that went from the top of the wall—Northwalk—to the single pin below her and Max—their child. She picked another pin from her desk drawer and stuck it next to the original pin. Twins. The corners of her lips ticked up. *My babies.* Not only was she having a kid she hadn't expected, she was having *two* of them at once. And already she loved them. She hadn't expected that feeling so soon, either. By her obstetrician's guess, her pregnancy wasn't more than four months along, but already she felt tired and distended all the time. She had to put up with this for five more months? And it would only get worse? At least now, with her future children already claiming a massive spot in her heart, she was sure it would be worth it.

Eyeing the dozens of strings, pictures, newspaper clippings, article printouts, and handwritten notes, her gaze kept coming back to those two pins. Though Northwalk was all the way on the opposite side of the mess, they were still too close for comfort. She couldn't take on the organization in her current state, but she could still follow them, plan her next move, and be ready to strike when the opportunity came. She could certainly work on bringing down Delilah, starting with whatever info Zach gleaned from the pieces of Lucien's hard drive.

Walking to the kitchen, Val plopped down in a chair at her kitchen table. She flipped through the nearly two months of mail stacked on the table. Stacey hadn't kept up with it since Val had been gone, because her friend had taken off to travel the world—so said Stacey's note anyway. Val had followed up with a phone call to make sure Stacey was really alive and somewhere she wanted to be. Stacey confirmed she was fine, though she refused to entertain the idea of coming home anytime soon, or talking through the rift between them. She needed time, and there was nothing Val could do about it. If

Val had been a better friend, maybe this wouldn't have happened. Hopefully, she'd have an opportunity to make things right.

On to the future. While Max and a contingent of hired help cleaned up his condo, she was supposed to begin cataloging which items in her house she wanted to toss and which she'd move into her new husband's place. Before reviewing the conspiracy diagram, she'd gotten as far as picking up her undelivered mail from the post office and dumping it on the kitchen table. Now she needed to rest.

From the stack of mostly junk mail, she pulled out a manila envelope with an odd bulge in the middle. No return address. A slow drip of dread began in the back of her mind. Max had warned her they might start getting mail from crazy people, now that they were a local celebrity "power couple." He'd received it sporadically all his adult life, courtesy of his high-profile millionaire bachelor status. Now that he was officially off the market, all those spurned, delusional men and women could begin directing their wrath at her. Maybe this piece of mail was just the first.

She'd dealt with worse. *Bring it on, loonies.* Val ripped the top of the envelope open and jiggled the bulge out. A big, silver ring shaped like a skull and crossbones clinked onto the tabletop. The slow drip of dread turned into a deluge. It was Zach's ring.

Val yanked her phone from her pocket and called Zach's number. She'd talked to him only a couple of weeks ago, reminding him to keep everything he found on Lucien's computer to himself, while quietly getting her hopes up that maybe, finally, she'd have something to nail Delilah with. She was so close…

A woman answered his cell.

"Hi, I'm looking for Zach?" No one besides the teenage hacker had ever answered before. Maybe he'd changed his number, or got a girlfriend.

"He's not here anymore," the woman said, a deep sadness in her voice.

"Where did he go?" It couldn't be. "Who is this?"

"I'm his mother, and he's not here because he's passed on."

Oh God no. "But…but I talked to him just recently."

"He"—Zach's mom paused to take a ragged breath—"he took his own life eleven days ago. He's always been troubled, and…I'm sorry. He's gone."

Val's mouth went dry. "I'm so sorry for your loss," she choked out, not knowing what else to say.

"Thank you. Good-bye." Zach's mom hung up.

Val sat frozen, the phone still pressed against her ear. There was absolutely no way Zach would kill himself, no matter what his mother said about his state of mind. Dropping her cell, she stared at the ring as if it were the bony finger of death pointing at her. *You did this*, it whispered.

There was something else inside the envelope. Swallowing hard, she pulled it out with trembling fingers. It was a plain white piece of paper with two words written on it: *Nice try.*

Val slapped a hand over her mouth. She knew Delilah was capable of manipulating people into killing for her, but to murder a *kid?* Poor Zach. She shouldn't have gotten him into this. Now his blood was on her hands.

She wrapped her arms around her belly. She'd be damned if that evil woman, or Northwalk, or anyone else got anywhere near her babies. Protecting her family had to be her number one priority now—which meant staying away from Delilah and Northwalk.

With tears in her eyes, she crumpled up the letter, walked back to her conspiracy wall, and started pulling pieces of it off and throwing them in the trash. "You win," she said. "For now."

Please see the next page for a preview of *Reckoning*, the next book in the Valentine Shepherd series!

Chapter One

Five years later

Valentine Shepherd sat cross-legged on her son's bed, gritting her teeth as she watched Simon dig through a pile of brightly colored books. The kids' room sported an abundance of short bookcases, but still they had too many books to fit, the excess strewn across the floor as miniature mountains of knowledge. Like father, like son.

"Just pick one, Simon."

He kept rooting. Val took a deep breath and tried to control her annoyance. It was already an hour past the twins' usual bedtime, as they'd insisted on "helping" her bake a batch of gingersnaps for the holiday cookie exchange between her group of playdate moms the following day. As she juggled cookie trays, they had decided to have a raw egg fight in the living room. She'd ordered them upstairs, then cleaned up the slimy mess. Toby, their Jack Russell terrier, helped by licking egg yolks off the walls. Then he puked them up on the carpet. At that point, she'd smelled the cookies burning.

"*Just pick one, Simon.*"

After a minute he snatched up a book he liked, sprinted back to Val, and dropped it into her lap.

Val read the cover. "*The Night Before Christmas*. Appropriate enough."

Simon launched himself onto the bed and snuggled up to his mother. He beamed at her, beautiful hazel eyes with starbursts of emerald green at their centers radiating the pure love of a devoted four-year-old. Val's irritation ebbed, her love for her children an aloe that always soothed her most frayed nerves. She ruffled his blond hair and kissed his head.

"Lydia, come on," Val called out.

A moment later her daughter wandered into the room, head down and eyes glued to a tablet computer.

"Turn that off. It's time for a story, then bed."

Lydia looked up and pushed black hair out of her big gray eyes. "But Mommy," she whined. She turned the tablet toward Val. Flashing stars danced across the screen; some kind of numbers game. "I almost have the high score."

"That's great, honey. Turn it off."

Lydia's delicate pink lips curled into a pout, then she pressed the power button until the screen went black. She dropped it on top of a book pile and curled up next to Val, opposite her brother.

"Okay." God, finally. "The Night Before Christmas, here we go…" Val flipped to the first page. "'Twas the night before Christmas and all through the house—"

"How does Santa get down the chimney?" Simon asked.

"It's a trade secret."

"Santa's not real," Lydia told Simon in her usual serious tone.

"Lydia!" Val frowned at her daughter.

Simon's lips trembled and he looked at his mother with big doe eyes.

"Of course Santa's real," she said to Simon. "In a way. He lives in our hearts." She smiled at her son, and his wounded innocence turned to confusion. It was good enough. "Okay, so where were we..." She cleared her throat and tried to read with the practiced animation Max was so good at when he did this. Her exhaustion made it a hard sell. "'Twas the night before Christmas, and all through the house, not a creature was stirring, not even—"

"When's Daddy coming home?" Lydia asked.

"In two days."

Simon: "Where is he?"

"Fort Lauderdale. That's in Florida, America's flaccid wang." Val cracked a smile. They wouldn't know what that meant for several years. There was no shame in enjoying a dirty inside joke with herself. Reminded her she technically still belonged to the adult world, despite being consumed by the daily grind of four-year-old affairs. She took her small pleasures wherever she could get them.

Lydia and Simon peered around their mother and at each other. Their eyes widened and misted over with a glaze Val recognized, the one that sent a cold chill racing up her spine.

Simon said, "Daddy was in Florida—"

"But he's not there now," Lydia finished.

Val swallowed hard. She wished they wouldn't do this. More than wished—she *prayed to God* they wouldn't do this. She'd hoped the twins had escaped the curse that afflicted her and Max, but since their verbal skills had exploded over the last six months it was becoming clearer by the day they hadn't. They knew things they shouldn't, and they didn't need to be in a trance to see it, like Max and Val—they were *Alphas*, like Cassandra, the woman in white she'd only seen in her visions. Other parents expressed amazement at how *advanced* Lydia and Simon were, sometimes through teeth clenched together in jealousy at their own child's implied inferiority. But what made them special made them vulnerable. *They* would be coming for her children. Maybe someday soon. Sten Ander, her sometimes-enemy/sometimes-ally, had told her they called themselves Northwalk. They owned Cassandra, and they wanted Simon and Lydia as well. She would burn down the world before she let her children be stolen from her.

Val began again, her throat suddenly dry and sapped of the meager enthusiasm she'd worked to channel a minute ago. "'Twas the night before Christmas, and all through the house—"

"Daddy reads it better," Simon said.

"Well, Daddy's not here, so do you want me to read the story or not?"

Simon nodded, resigned to his fate of a subpar book reading. A long sigh escaped Val's chest. She flipped through the book and cringed at the walls of text. *Ten pages of this?* She didn't remember the poem being so long.

"'Twas the night before Christmas and all through the house, not a creature was stirring, not even a mouse...Except Santa was there! He spread gifts everywhere for all the good little boys and girls, and when he left he said, 'Merry Christmas to all, and to all a good night!'" Val snapped the book shut.

Lydia frowned. "That's not what it said."

"That's the abridged version. And since when do you know how to read?"

"I've always known how to read."

"Jesus Christ," Val muttered to herself. To Lydia: "Don't tell anyone else that." She clapped her hands. "Time for bed. Chop, chop."

Lydia scrambled off Simon's bed and slipped into her own, kitty-cornered to Simon's in the same room. Val tucked them in with hugs and kisses.

"I love you, my beautiful babies," she said as she held Simon's tiny body against hers, then Lydia's. "Love, love, *love* you."

"We love you, too, Mommy," Simon said as Val walked to the doorway. "And Nana."

She froze. "Who?"

"Nana," Lydia answered. "She's the best grandma ever."

They didn't have a Nana...Well, technically they did, but she might as well be dead. Val hadn't seen or heard from her mother in almost thirty years—until recently, that was. To choose not to have contact with your own children for decades, even after one of them took her own life...she was certainly *not* the best Nana ever. The kids must be referring to someone else. Maybe one of their friend's grandmothers. That must be it.

Val flipped off the light, a constellation of blue stars from a nightlight making slow circles across the ceiling as she shut the door. It was nothing. She didn't want to see her mother again, anyway. She couldn't even remember what the woman looked like. All she could recall was red hair like Val's—probably gray now—and the acrid odor of the menthol cigarettes her mother liked to smoke. And her mom's eyes, a paler blue like Val's sister, that crinkled at the edges every time she laughed. And her mom's voice, shrill and frantic as she screamed about the injustice of the Gulf War. And she remembered the feel of cold hardwood on her knees as she knelt at the foot of her bed, praying for her mother to return. What kind of person abandons their own children? How could she—

Val leaned against the hallway's wall and blinked back tears. She was working herself up over nothing. Who knew what the twins really saw? They didn't know themselves half the time—a blessing for their poor four-year-old minds. Her own children would grow up with a loving mother and father, and that was all that mattered.

Nana wasn't real. Her mother was dead to her. Or might as well have been.

Val pushed herself off the wall, took a deep breath, and fought the urge to walk straight to her bedroom and read *the letter*, again. No, she wouldn't let it distract her. She had more important things to do, good-mother things. Instead she made her nightly round through the condo: first the kitchen, then the indoor pool and surrounding patio, then the living room, the study, the den, each bathroom, and ending at the guest room—checking all the guns she'd hidden out of the children's reach but within her own. For when *they* came. They'd had a crazy-conspiracy dry spell since the twins had been born, but it couldn't last forever. With all the effort Max and Val's tormentors had put into bringing the two of them together, it was only a matter of time until they resurfaced to resume their torture. This time, she'd be prepared.

Rounds completed, she considered watching some TV, maybe the Real Housewives of Something, to numb her mind up. But if she stumbled on a news report about Delilah Barrister, Seattle's ex-mayor and Washington State's newest Congresswoman, she might punch the television. It'd taken a massive amount of willpower to resist going after the woman who'd murdered Val's fiancé and manipulated Val into killing her husband—the late, terrible Norman Barrister—in order to fuel her political ambitions and assist Northwalk in forcing Val and Max together to create their special children. But Val had left her alone. Delilah had proven she was capable of killing anyone to get what she wanted—the fate of poor Zach, the teenage hacker who'd helped Val almost nail Delilah and had "committed suicide" for his trouble—still gave her nightmares. She wouldn't put her family in danger of a similar situation, even if it meant backing off her enemy—for now. Delilah would get hers someday. Val fucking swore it.

Yep, no TV tonight. She went to the laundry room and collected warm clothes from the dryer, carried the load to her bedroom, and dumped it on the mattress. She stared at the pile for a moment. Goddamn laundry. There were many techniques a person could use to fold a four-year-old's underwear, though she'd been told by another stay-at-home-mom only one was correct. She'd love to get a second opinion from someone else, a real friend maybe, but the last one she had took off after Val imploded a few years ago. She hadn't connected with any of the other rich, stuck-up moms in her kid's play group, and they weren't interested in connecting with her. She and Max were tabloid fodder with a salacious history, after all, though they'd kept a fairly low profile since the Lucien Christophe nightmare. Maybe she should put out a personal ad: *Looking for a no-frills, down-to-earth, big-hearted bestie with a bohemian streak who likes to watch bad movies, solve mysteries, and can keep a secret.* Yeah, right. There was no replacing Stacey.

If she didn't fold the clothes now they'd wrinkle, and she'd get disapproving looks from the other mothers in her kids' playgroup. What a tragedy. Her hands balled into and out of fists. Dammit. Of all the ways she could be torturing herself at that moment, she could think of at least one better than laundry. Turning her back on the pile, she made a beeline to her nightstand, yanked open its drawer, and took out a worn envelope.

Val stared hard at the letter gripped between her fingers, an unassuming piece of mail holding only one piece of paper and sliced open along the top. It was just a rectangle of white with her address scrawled on the front in loopy cursive, ordinary to anyone but Val. What normal person sent personal letters via snail mail these days? Her eyes traced the path of those handwritten letters and cut between her name in the center and the sender's in the corner—Danielle Shepherd.

She'd read the short letter dozens of times.

Sorry I haven't kept in touch, it's a long story, I'd love to tell you all about it, can I come visit?

Could her long-lost mother come visit? Was she serious? Silence for over thirty years and now she wanted to reconnect? Did Danielle's sudden interest in Val's life have something to do with her new, rich husband? Or the conspiracy that surrounded their lives, lurking out of sight, haunting her dreams and her visions, waiting for the right moment to close in on them? Be nice if she could ask Stacey what she thought. Val would never let a stranger into their home, because that's what Danielle was...but the twins had seen her, knew her—

Val froze when she realized someone was standing right behind her.

Acknowledgments

Thank you to everyone who made this book possible! That list includes: my husband, Chris, as all the sex scenes in this book are based on our love life (just kidding…or am I? Since he'll never read this, he can't get mad!); my mom, Sandy, for standing up in the "notable events" part of her weekly office meeting to tell her coworkers that her daughter wrote a risqué romance novel and they should read it; my stepdad, Tim, for his unwavering support since the day he married my mother, even during those rough teenage years; my valley-girl West Coast sister, Nicole, for moving across the country to provide my daughters with some fabulous female influence as I hang out in the desert for six months; my gruff Bostonian East Coast father-in-law, David, for letting my sister live with him, Odd Couple–style; my best friend, Kendall, for buying my books and swearing she's going to read them any day now, they're at the top of her TBR pile!; my agent, Carrie, for responding to my e-mails in a timely manner, always being positive, and having a cute bunny icon as her profile pic that I always get excited to see in my in-box; my editor, Madeleine, for gracefully telling me things I don't want to hear; my boss, Chad, for talking up my books and encouraging people to read them, even though they're not, shall we say, safe for work; my old pugs, Zeus and Roxy, for letting me stroke them, Dr. Evil–style, as I pondered narrative arcs; and finally, my daughters, Clementine and Violet, for being the wildest, loudest, most perfect little balls of energy any mother could hope for.

About the Author

Shana Figueroa is a published author who specializes in romance and humor, with occasional sojourns into horror, sci-fi, and literary fiction.

She lives in Massachusetts with her husband, two young daughters, and two old pugs. She enjoys reading, writing (obviously), martial arts, video games, and SCIENCE—it's poetry in motion! By day, she serves her country in the U.S. Air Force as an aerospace engineer. By night, she hunkers down in a corner and cranks out the crazy stories lurking in her head.

She took Toni Morrison's advice and started writing the books she wanted to read. Hopefully you'll want to read them, too!

Learn more at:
ShanaFigueroa.com
Twitter @Shana_Figueroa
Facebook.com/Shana.Figueroa.9

www.ingramcontent.com/pod-product-compliance
Ingram Content Group UK Ltd.
Pitfield, Milton Keynes, MK11 3LW, UK
UKHW040135180625
459803UK00001B/90